A VISION
of LOCUSTS

Nothing devours like revenge

S L RUSSELL

instant
apostle

First published in Great Britain in 2017

Instant Apostle

The Barn
1 Watford House Lane
Watford
Herts
WD17 1BJ

British Library Cataloguing-in-Publication Data

A catalogue record for this book is available from the British Library

This book and all other Instant Apostle books are available from Instant Apostle:

Website: www.instantapostle.com

E-mail: info@instantapostle.com

ISBN 978-1-909728-71-4

Printed in Great Britain

Contents

November 1980

His hands clenched, gripping the rusty railings, his slippered feet poised on the low wall. He heard his heart battering the insides of his ears. Then another sound: a siren was wailing, coming closer, then another, and he could see a whirling blue light. It was time to hide. He slithered down, dusting his hands down the side of his ratty old dressing gown, and scuttled silently into the bushes that lined the perimeter of the school. He squatted, watching, smelling the acrid smoke, seeing with a lurch of glee the tongues of orange destruction leaping and curling into the night air. Now people were gathering, moving up to the school gates a few yards to his left, talking in rumbling undertones, looking up, mouths open, eyes wide. He heard someone say, 'Thank God no one's inside.' Then someone else said, 'How can it have started?' And he grinned to himself, wondering if they'd find that little broken window, or the remains of the stolen firework, or if the fire would destroy everything, and he hoped that it would be just a pile of smouldering ash like one of Bill's bonfires, and then he'd never have to go to school ever again.

People were being moved away from the gates. Two fire engines had screamed to a halt, their engines thundering, and firemen were piling out. They looked like aliens in their yellow helmets. There was a lot of shouting. He saw Mr Clegg, the caretaker, unlocking the gates, and then the engines were roaring into the school yard. They were unravelling the hoses, yelling to each other. More people were appearing out of the night, moving up to the railings. He heard a woman say, 'It's just the mobile classroom, isn't it? Maybe they'll be able to save the main building.' Someone else said, 'Who called the fire brigade?' But no one seemed to know.

Now the hoses were playing water high over the fire, and the glorious chaos of roaring and crackling orange and red and yellow was being reduced, bit by bit, to sullen black. It was time to get home, before anyone noticed he wasn't in his bed. Mum was at work, and Bill was at the pub with his mates. His sisters were supposed to be looking after him, but they wouldn't know if he was there or not. They didn't know anything.

He slipped out from the bushes, eyes darting left and right. No one was looking his way. Crouching, he crept round the outside of the gawking crowd, into the darkness of the lane that led up to the school approach. He was taking a deep breath, ready to dart up the lane away from the school and towards home, when he felt a heavy hand come down on his shoulder, nearly making him puke with shock.

'What the blazes are you doing out, you little sneak?' hissed the voice that came with the hand, and a waft of beery fumes made his nostrils wrinkle. *Bill. His brother, who acted like he was his dad. But he didn't have a dad, not any more. Just Bill.* He wriggled, but that hand was heavy and strong. 'You wait till Mum hears about this. You'll be for it.'

He twisted in that relentless grip. 'I was just looking, OK?' he whined. 'I couldn't sleep. I saw the flames from my window. Came to see what it was. Don't tell Mum, Bill. She don't need to know.'

Bill turned back to look at the dying fire, his hand still gripping the boy's shoulder. 'Your school, isn't it, our Paul? Your classroom, even.' His lip curled. 'I suppose you think you'll be let off school, don't you? Well, you might be, while they clear up the mess. Then you'll have to go in with the other kids. Maybe in with the little ones. The babies.'

Paul writhed. 'I won't! I won't go!'

'Maybe you'll have to,' Bill said grimly. 'Poor little kids, is all I can say. Now – home. I'll think about whether to tell Mum.' He pushed the boy roughly ahead of him.

'I'll be good, Bill. I will, I promise, from now on. I'll help you with the chores and stuff.'

'Well, we'll see. Get along.'

December 2005

It was probably, while it lasted, one of the most frightening moments of Julie Hasan's life. She thought of herself as a level-headed woman, not easily thrown off-balance; but the sight of her daughter staring at the wall, blind to everything but what was going on in her head, deaf to her mother's urgent calls, chilled Julie to her core.

Abbie, in her navy blue and white school uniform, her long black hair tied back but escaping, as it always did, in tendrils round her face, came down to breakfast that unremarkable morning, slid into a chair at the kitchen table and poured cereal into a bowl. Then it happened. She had the spoon in her hand, but simply froze as if a spell had turned her to stone. Her eyes were staring, her mouth slightly open.

'Mum,' her brother said with his usual pithy style, 'Abbie's gone loopy.'

Julie dropped two slices of bread into the toaster, barely glancing at her children. There were other things on her mind. 'Abbie, wake up, eat your breakfast.'

A moment later, Daniel's voice contained an edge of panic. 'Mum, I'm not kidding.'

Julie turned. Abbie had not moved. 'Abbie. Abbie, what's the matter?'

'I elbowed her,' Daniel said helpfully, 'but she never moved. What's up with her?'

Julie crossed the kitchen, shook Abbie by the shoulder. 'Abbie! Can you hear me?' She looked at her son, who sat watching, a spoon half way to his mouth, which hung open. 'What happened, Dan?'

The boy shrugged. 'I dunno. She put some cereal in her bowl. Then she just … stopped.' He frowned. 'What's going on?'

Julie shook Abbie again. The girl swayed in her seat and mumbled something incoherent. Julie bit her lip. 'Dan, is your dad still in the house?'

The boy shoved his chair back. 'I don't know. I'll go and see.' He ran out of the room, banging the kitchen door, yelling. 'Dad!'

Julie pulled up a chair beside her daughter, trying to face her. She passed a hand in front of Abbie's eyes. Nothing. She shook her again, less gently. 'Abbie!' The silence in the room seemed huge, uncanny, and Julie felt sweat spring out on her forehead. 'Abbie, for pity's sake!' But the girl's unseeing eyes were fixed on the kitchen wall, and whatever she was seeing was invisible to the outside world. *Lord, help, something's very wrong with my child.* Panic rose in her chest as once again she flapped a hand in front of Abbie's face. To her immense relief the girl blinked languidly, coughed, shook her head from side to side. She looked at her mother. 'Mum. Hey.' Her voice was slow and slurred, like someone coming out of a deep sleep.

'Abbie, what happened?'

'What?'

'Where were you?'

The girl's brow furrowed. 'Where …? Oh. Somewhere, oh yeah, it was … it was … Mum, it was …' Suddenly she seemed to choke, and her eyes welled with tears. 'Oh, Mum! It was that earthquake, you know, where Daddy used to live. When he was a boy.' She clutched her mother's arm, hard enough to hurt. 'Mum, it was horrible.'

Daniel erupted, breathless, back into the room. 'The van's gone, Mum.' He looked his sister. 'Oh. Hiya, Abs. You're back.' He saw the tears. 'What's up?'

Abbie shook her head, unable to speak.

'Dan, put the kettle on,' Julie said. 'Finish your breakfast, then brush your teeth and get off to school, or you'll be late.'

12

'What about Abbie?'

'If she's up to it I'll take her in later. Go on now. Make your sister a cup of tea. And one for me while you're at it.'

Ten minutes later, with Daniel reluctantly gone and two cups of tea steaming on the table, Julie said, 'Abbie, are you going to tell me what happened?' It came out more sternly than she meant, and Abbie's eyes welled up again. Julie put her arm round the girl's shoulders. 'Just tell me, sweetheart.'

'I don't really know, Mum,' Abbie said, her voice breaking. 'I just saw horrible things. Buildings falling down. Bridges collapsing. I heard things too, only not clearly, kind of muffled. The sounds of the bricks and stuff falling, clouds of dust, and … and people, Mum, people crying out. Children. Babies crying. Underneath the buildings, in the rubble.' She moaned, held her head in her hands, as tears ran down her face. 'People running about, shouting, panicking. It was so frightening.'

'Did you hear me calling you?'

'No. All I could hear was the rumble and crash of the buildings, and the people crying.'

Julie thought. 'Abbie, love, has anything like this ever happened before?'

Abbie raised her tear-streaked face to her mother's. She swallowed. 'Yes. A few times. Since I was little. Not like this.'

'You never said.'

'I thought it happened to everybody.'

Julie's eyebrows shot up. 'You thought everybody could see things, hear things, that aren't there? I don't think so, darling.'

'Oh, great,' Abbie muttered. 'Another way Abbie Hasan is weird.'

'What? Says who?'

'Says everyone,' Abbie said defiantly.

'Weird how? There's nothing wrong with you, Abbie.'

'You don't know, Mum. I'm too tall. I'm a beanpole. I have no friends. Nobody likes me. And I have a moustache.'

'Oh, Abbie.' Julie gave her daughter an awkward sideways hug. 'You're tall and slim. You're beautiful and clever. Yes, it's a real shame Lucy had to leave, and I know it's hard to make new friends. But you will. One day the beanpole will be the envy of all the dumpy girls, the girl all the boys are queuing up for. And you don't have a moustache.' She held her daughter's face in her hands. 'Red baggy eyes, yes. But no unwanted hair.'

Abbie managed a tearful smile. 'I'm going to be late for school.'

'Don't worry. Drink your tea, and I'll drive you. I'll explain to the school if necessary.'

'Don't say why, Mum,' Abbie said anxiously.

'No, I'll think of something.' Julie frowned as a thought struck her. 'Abbie, why now? What have you heard about the earthquake?'

Abbie wrapped her hands round the mug of tea. 'Well, I saw stuff on TV, back when it happened, but I didn't think too much about it. Only after that, well, I know Dad's been anxious, trying to find out about his family there, hasn't he?' She glanced at her mother. 'And then, last night, I woke up, and it was really late, and I heard you and Dad talking, quite loudly, and I heard Dad crying. It made me so sad. Dad doesn't cry. Something bad must have happened. But you wouldn't tell me, would you?'

Julie sighed. 'My darling, you're only twelve.'

'Nearly thirteen,' Abbie interrupted.

'Yes, I'm not likely to forget. Nearly thirteen. Parents like to defend their children, you know, from some of life's harder realities. Until they're older and more able to cope. Perhaps that's wrong. Would you like me to ask your dad to talk to you about his family back in India? Perhaps if he told you a few things you wouldn't worry so much.'

Abbie nodded. 'Yes. But maybe he doesn't want to. Maybe it makes him too sad.'

'Sad things don't go away by being ignored,' Julie said gently. 'I think he will be OK with telling you things. There's one person who doesn't think you're weird, honey. Your father. He thinks you're pretty special. As do I.'

Abbie smiled, and her strange green eyes lit up. 'I think I'd better get to school, Mum. There's a science test.'

'Can't miss that, can we?'

That afternoon Julie pushed her seat back from her desk and rubbed her eyes. On the screen in front of her were the business accounts, and she'd been working on them for so many hours that the figures were dancing up and down. She sighed and glanced at the clock on the wall. A quarter to four. Dan would be at his friend Ryan's, and she hadn't heard from Abbie's school, so presumably Abbie had got through her day unscathed and would now be on her way home on the bus. She stood up, rubbing her back, and then the phone rang and she padded through to the kitchen in her socked feet and plucked the handset off the wall.

'Julie? It's Maggie.'

'Oh, hi.'

'Is everything OK?' Maggie asked cautiously.

Julie frowned. 'Why do you ask?'

'Well, your Dan's been saying some strange things today.'

'What, in your classroom?'

'Yes, something about Abbie behaving very oddly.'

Julie took a deep breath. 'Yes, at breakfast. Staring at the wall. Deaf to me calling her. Blind to the real world. Several minutes before she came out of it, and it felt longer. Said it had happened before, only this time she was seeing the earthquake, graphic images.'

'Oh, Julie!'

'I know. I'm her mother – how come I didn't know she'd had these episodes?'

'Why would you, if you'd never observed one and she never said?' Maggie reasoned. 'Any idea what might have brought it on?'

'Yes, that's another thing. Last night, we – Tariq and I – were arguing. Obviously woke Abbie up. Maybe we were louder than we meant. Riq got very upset.'

'About the situation in Kashmir? Still no news, then?'

'Not a thing. He's tried everything he can think of – the Kashmiri community in London; his Uncle Nasir, who was very frosty; even the Red Cross. No news. And he hasn't heard from his sister – that's the killer.' She paused, thinking. 'You know what, it may be that Uncle Nasir actually does know something. But Tariq's the enemy now, and he won't tell him. I do wonder.'

'That would be pretty vindictive,' Maggie said. 'But it's all speculation.'

'It's all we've got,' Julie said. 'That and going round in circles.'

'Mm. Meanwhile, Tariq's in a state,' Maggie mused. 'And Abbie's close to her dad. If he is upset it will be difficult for her. Oh dear. Poor Tariq.'

There was a silence, then Julie said abruptly, 'I know I'm not supposed to feel like this, but I wish he'd just write them off. They rejected him, didn't they? And now he wants to go there, Maggie – in January, as soon as Abbie's birthday's been and gone, he wants to travel to Jammu, in winter, with money we haven't got, to search for people who don't want to know him. How does that make sense?' Her voice rose to an indignant squeak.

'I know it doesn't seem to,' Maggie said quietly. 'But they're still his family, and I imagine he has grieved for them all these years, even if he's never said anything. And there's so much guilt there, which makes it all the harder for him to bear if he thinks he's lost them all for ever.'

Julie groaned. 'I know. Don't think I don't feel for him, Maggie. It carves me up to see him so distraught. But it all seems so pointless. I just pray every day that the postman will bring a

Christmas card from Aleesa. That'd go a long way to calming him down.'

'Have you told him about Abbie's funny turn?'

'No, he'd already left for work when it happened, and he's not back yet. What should I do, Maggie? You've had so much experience of kids.'

There was a silence again, and Julie registered her friend's reaction and mentally kicked herself.

'I suppose,' Maggie said bleakly. 'Just not my own.'

'It's not too late, Maggie. Think of those childless women in the Bible – Sarah, Hannah, Elizabeth. They'd given up, and they were much older than you. But God had other ideas, didn't he? Wasn't Sarah about ninety or something, when she had Isaac?'

'At least those ladies had willing husbands, presumably,' Maggie said sourly. 'But let's not rehash all that now. You need to think about Abbie. I would have thought you'd need to take her to the doctor, at the very least. Just to check her out. Talk to Tariq when he gets in.'

'Yes, of course I will.' She paused. 'Are you all right, Maggie?'

She heard her friend sigh. 'Yes, hanging in there. Had a bit of a long, fraught day at school. The children are high as kites with Christmas round the corner.'

'I hope Dan's not playing up.'

'No.' Maggie's tone softened. 'He's a good little lad, your Dan. You're very blessed, you know, Julie. With your children.'

'I do know,' Julie said. 'And I keep praying you'll have that blessing too. God is good. And nothing is impossible.'

'Thanks. Well, keep me posted about Abbie, won't you? And give Tariq my love.'

Tariq phoned to say he had to visit someone to take measurements and it wasn't worth coming home first. The way things were he couldn't afford to turn down potential jobs. 'Put my dinner in the microwave, love, will you,' he said. 'I should be back by eight.' He was obviously in a hurry, phoning her on his mobile with a breaking signal, and she didn't mention Abbie.

As it happened he didn't get home till 8.15, dusted with plaster, weary, but hopeful that the visit might produce work. Finally, when his plate was cleared and he'd run out of his day's news, he lifted his eyes to where Julie sat opposite, chin in hand. 'How was your day?' he asked. 'Kids OK?'

'Well, perhaps not.'

Tariq was instantly alert. 'What?'

Julie described what had happened at breakfast. 'She went to school as normal, not even late, because I took her. The bus would have gone. And she came home apparently fine, didn't mention anything about this morning, had her tea and went off to do her homework.'

'Where is she now?' Tariq got up, pushing his chair back.

'In the shower. Sit down a minute, Riq, we need to think this through.' She waited till he subsided. 'I'll get some coffee on. Do you want some?'

'Please.'

Julie put the kettle on. She turned to face him, leaning back against the kitchen counter, arms folded. 'What do you think we should do? Maggie says we should take her to the doctor.'

Tariq snorted. 'He's pretty useless, you know that. He won't know what to do, not with something as unusual as this.'

'But he would have to refer her, wouldn't he?' She poured hot water into a cafetiere. 'Have you heard of anything like this before?' Tariq was silent, staring at the table. 'Riq?'

When he looked up at her, his face was sombre. 'I never told you,' he said. 'I didn't think it was important. It happened to me, something like it, when I was young. Nothing like Abbie's experience, from what you tell me. Just brief flashes, chaotic images. No meaning. And I didn't hear anything – it was just pictures.'

Julie stared at him. 'Did your parents know?'

He shifted in his seat. 'I mentioned it. But I never made much of it – because of my sister.'

Julie frowned. 'What? Which one?'

'The oldest one. The one I never met. The one they never spoke about.'

'Riq, you're going to have to spell this out. You're doing my head in. Let me just pour this coffee.'

A moment later she set a steaming mug in front of him and sat down. 'OK, from the top, please,' she said. 'As far as I know you have three sisters – Farida, Mahasin, Aleesa. How come you never mentioned another one? For Heaven's sake, Riq – I've known you more than fifteen years and suddenly you spring another sister on me!'

Tariq stretched over the table and took her hand. 'I'm sorry, love. But I never knew her, and I know hardly anything about her. Just bits of gossip and family rumour from Aleesa.'

'Well, go on.' Julie took a sip of her coffee.

'She was the oldest, their firstborn. Called Zaynab. All I know is she died when she was eighteen. From what Aleesa said there was some mystery about her death. But there was a six-year gap between Zaynab and Farida, the next sister down, so by the time I was born, Zaynab'd been dead for two years, and Aleesa only remembers her vaguely. She was just a little kid. But she said Zaynab was a bit strange. No use asking the other two – they'd obviously been told to say nothing. Well and truly under my father's thumb, even after they got married and left home.'

'Strange how?'

'Sweetheart, I have no idea. Aleesa wondered if the poor girl was mentally ill, maybe even committed suicide – hence the family silence. But I don't know.'

Julie thought. 'But you didn't make much of your – what? Visions? – to your parents in case they thought you were going the same way?'

Tariq grimaced. 'I don't think I really analysed it that much. I just instinctively avoided rocking the family boat. Especially as far as my father was concerned.'

'And you think there might be some connection – with Abbie?'

Tariq shrugged. 'Look, it's all speculation. Maybe Zaynab had an ordinary disease. Maybe they just blotted her out because they couldn't cope with their grief. You know something of what my family was like. Very buttoned up.' He looked at her, saw the worry in her face and spoke gently. 'Darling, I'm not crazy. I grew out of it. Abbie's certainly not crazy, and I don't think she's sick. Sure, take her to the doctor, get her checked out. Of course that's what we should do. But we mustn't give her the idea we think she's weird.'

Julie sighed. 'She already thinks so. But that's a teenage thing too. Whatever, this has happened because she heard us yelling at each other. I said you'd go and talk to her, maybe tell her a bit about your background, set her mind at rest. Better not mention poor Zaynab, though.'

'As if I would. I'll tell her it's just some sensitivity thing she's got from her dad's peculiar genes. Nothing to fret about.'

'Go on, then. She's probably out of the shower by now.'

Tariq finished his coffee and got to his feet, wincing as his back protested. He crossed to where Julie sat, nursing her empty coffee cup, squeezed her shoulder and kissed the top of her head. 'Don't worry too much, love. She's got your genes as well.'

'Ha! Poor kid. What a mixture.'

Tariq tapped on Abbie's bedroom door. 'Hey, Abbie, you decent?'

'Yeah, Dad, come in.'

He squeezed round the door, which was partly blocked by a damp towel. 'It's pretty dark in here. How can you see to do your homework?'

'I finished it.' Abbie was perched on a pink fluffy stool, her long hair hanging wet round her shoulders. 'You all right, Dad? You worked late.'

'Yeah, I'm OK. What about you, though? You gave your mum a fright this morning.' He perched on the edge of her rumpled bed.

'I never meant to.' She picked up the towel and wrapped it round her head, trapping her hair. For a moment her face registered anxiety. 'D'you think it means anything, Dad? What happened?'

'Probably not, sweetie. I never told you this, but something similar used to happen to me when I was growing up. I just grew out of it, and maybe you will too.'

'You really think so?' Abbie bit her lip. 'I think Mum thinks I'm crazy.'

'Of course she doesn't, silly. But mums worry. It's their fate.' He grinned.

'Don't dads worry as well?'

'Yes, but about different things.'

'Such as?'

He frowned, pretending deep thought. 'Like whether their clever daughter is going to throw her prospects away on some spotty boy with a stupid haircut.'

Abbie pulled the towel off her head and threw it at her father. 'Dad, I suppose you think you're funny. Just chuck me over my hairbrush, can you?'

She took it from him and started the laborious process of untangling her hair. 'So what's Mum going to do?'

'Take you to see the doctor. We can't ignore it, Abs. Even if it's nothing, we have to check it out. You have to see that.'

'I suppose.' Abbie scowled. 'Dr Palmer won't do anything, you know.'

'I know, but he might refer you to someone who knows about these things.'

'What things? Screwed-up brains?'

'There's no evidence your brains aren't perfectly OK,' Tariq said. 'You look as if you're having a battle with that thatch. D'you want some help?'

'Yes, please.'

Abbie crossed the room and sat beside her father, handed him the brush and leaned against his shoulder, suddenly sleepy and looking much younger than her years. Patiently he started to tease out the tangles.

'So what did you see when you saw things?' she asked.

'Nothing much. Nothing like you. But I think that was my fault, wasn't it? I'm sorry, kiddo. Mum and I woke you up.'

She turned to look at him. 'I was worried, Dad. I don't like thinking you're sad.' She hesitated. 'Do you mind if I ask you about your mum and dad and your family? Why you don't see them? Why Dan and I don't even know them? I mean, do they even know we exist?'

'I think you have every right to know,' Tariq said quietly, still gently parting tangles. 'And I don't know if they know anything about my life. Maybe not. My sister Aleesa – she's the youngest of my sisters, and my favourite – she kept in touch from time to time, so she knows about you and Dan and Mum. But she won't have told anyone else, because she wasn't supposed to talk to me.'

'Why not? Did you do something terrible?'

'According to them I did.'

'What was it? Did you kill someone?'

'Abbie! Of course I didn't. You watch too much TV. Can you see me as a murderer?'

Abbie grinned. 'I guess not. So what was it?'

'I came to London to study. A good Muslim boy from a very strict family. And I converted.'

'What?'

'I became a Christian.'

'I didn't know that was a bad thing to be.'

'It's the best thing to be. But your Grandpa Rashid wouldn't agree. He thought I was a traitor.'

'That's terrible, Dad.' She thought, her brow furrowed. 'Was he a cruel father?'

'No, but he had very high expectations. I was the only son. Converting was probably the worst thing I could do to him.'

'Have you ever been back?'

'Yes. Hold on. I think you're tangle-free. We need to start applying the hairdryer.'

Abbie turned to face him. 'I can do that in a minute. It won't take too long now. But we can't talk with that making a racket, and I need to know what happened.'

Tariq lounged back against the wall, his hands behind his head. 'I went back after my second year at university. I wasn't supposed to waste money on air fares, and it's a long way to India. But I thought I should tell my family what was going on, face to face. By that time I'd met your mum too. So I had two things to tell them that they'd absolutely hate. I knew they'd be terribly upset. But it was worse than that. My father told me not to come back, unless I came back a good Muslim. And he said they'd accept your mum as my wife, but only if she converted. *That* was never going to happen.' He fell silent.

'Oh, Daddy. You poor thing. How awful.'

'Well.' Tariq sat up and plumped up Abbie's pillow. 'I've got you guys now. Things could be a lot worse. And, young lady, you need to get your hair dry and go to bed, or you'll be a puffy-eyed wreck and your mum will blame me.'

'Dad,' Abbie said thoughtfully, 'if I said I wanted to be another religion, what would you do?'

'Wow, Abs, that's some question.' He sucked in his breath. 'I'd be appalled. I'd try to talk you out of it. But you would always be my child, no matter what.' He scowled. 'I hope you aren't thinking anything like that.'

Abbie shook her head. 'I don't really know what I believe, actually. I can't say what I am for sure. But I wouldn't want not to be your daughter. So I'm glad you're kinder than Grandpa Rashid.'

'Riq?' Julie's voice was muffled by the pillow. 'You awake?'

'Mm.'

She turned to face him, though she could see little in the darkness, and, despite being almost asleep, he wrapped his free arm round her and pulled her close.

'I've decided what to do.'

'Right.'

'I'll make an appointment for the beginning of the holidays. Abbie won't want to miss school, and they break up next week anyway. But I'm going to talk to John as well. Maybe tomorrow.'

'OK,' Tariq said cautiously. 'Why's that?' He blinked, coming suddenly awake. 'What are you getting at? You don't think what happened is somehow ... I don't know, spiritual?' He shuddered.

Julie wriggled into a more comfortable position. 'Well, I don't think Abbie is possessed,' she said caustically. 'No, but John's known her since she was a toddler. He knows us, our situation. He might have some insight. And at least he can pray. He's our pastor. He needs to know.'

'OK.'

Tariq sunk back into sleep, but Julie lay awake. She thought about their promising daughter, their light-hearted, energetic son, their children's mixed and muddled heritage, and what might flow from it. Sometimes she feared for them, wondering about the impact of the decisions that she and Tariq had made. She shook her head. What else could they have done?

She remembered with painful clarity the shattered boy on her doorstep that night sixteen years before, his handsome face haggard with weariness, misery and shock. She hadn't expected him home for at least two weeks. It had taken him most of the vacation, labouring on building sites when he should have been preparing for the following academic year, to raise the air fare. She'd said goodbye at the airport, trying to seem upbeat for his sake, and gone back to her flat, empty now of all her flatmates, resigned to lonely study without him. Then, barely five days later, he was back – exhausted, shaken, almost speechless. He'd drunk several glasses of water, mumbled something incoherent about explaining later, and collapsed onto her bed where he'd slept for twenty-four hours. Knowing little of his family and his cultural background, she'd had no real idea what to expect from his journey back to his homeland, but she could not fail to see that things had gone disastrously. Even so, when at last he'd dragged himself out of bed and into the shower then come to sit at her kitchen table, she was not prepared for the story he was to tell her.

At first, he said, his family were pleased to see him – amazed, dubious about the waste of time and money, but pleased, especially his mother, Jamila. She'd wanted to gather all his sisters, brothers-in-law, nephews and nieces to celebrate the return of the favoured son. But Tariq himself had said no, first he must tell them what he had come to say. He'd gathered his courage and tried to speak quietly and reasonably and explain how he'd come to where he was, a committed disciple of Jesus Christ. He'd got no further. Rashid, gasping with horror, then icy with contemptuous rage, had cut him off. Jamila, seeing at once the enormity of the family rift, had wailed and pleaded until her furious husband had sent her out of the room. Then he turned on his treacherous son. They had sent him to London at considerable expense. They had trusted he would return, qualified, to serve his native land. Such had been their hope and his avowed intention. Now he had betrayed their trust in the worst possible way, throwing away faith and heritage. Rashid ground to a halt, speechless with incomprehension, disappointment and shattered pride.

'Go,' he said to Tariq. 'I will send for you when I have had time to think.'

Tariq ran from the room, away from his father's glare, and found his mother weeping in the back sitting-room. He threw his arms around her, in tears himself. When they had both calmed down she said, 'Go to your sister Aleesa. Her husband is away on business. I'll phone her and tell her you're coming. Just stay there till your father sends for you. Take a taxi, go now. If he finds you are still here he will be angry with me.' She'd pushed him away. 'Oh, Tariq,' she whispered, mopping her face. 'What have you done?'

'*Ammi*,' he'd said. 'There's more. I am engaged to be married.'

'What?' she shrieked. 'And your fiancée? She is a Christian too? Was it she who has led you away?'

Tariq shook his head. 'No, it was not she. It was Jesus who led me away. But yes, she is a Christian too. And I am going to marry her, as soon as we have our degrees.'

'I can't bear to hear any more,' Jamila moaned, covering her face. 'Go away, son. You are breaking my heart.'

He'd spent two days with his sister, who tried to encourage him. 'You, out of all of us, have got to live your own life,' she said. 'You escaped. I'd like to, but look at me, married, two little children. My husband is doing well in business, the family think he's a great chap, and he's not unkind, but … well, little brother, you know how it is. Anyway, what can I do? I can't desert my kids.' She handed him a glass of tea. 'It's a choice, you know,' she said thoughtfully. 'Father won't back down. It'll kill him, but he won't give. You'll lose your family. Or you'll lose your faith and your fiancée. Sorry, but you knew that really, didn't you?'

He took a deep breath, sighed, and nodded.

Rashid hadn't called for Tariq. He simply telephoned his youngest daughter's house and coldly laid out his ultimatum. Perhaps if Tariq had waited, sought advice, left it to his mother, something might have been salvaged. But he was not Rashid's son for nothing, and in angry pride he'd left Aleesa's house and camped out at the airport until he could secure a return flight.

'I have to go before your husband returns,' he said. 'The last thing I want to do is make trouble for you.'

He'd barely seen his little niece and nephew, and he didn't see his other sisters or their families at all. He'd slept on a bench at the airport and lived on water and snacks, making his meagre funds stretch as best he could, waiting only to get away. Six hours before his altered flight, his mother had found him. How she'd managed to leave the house without her husband's knowledge he never found out. She'd come with his aunt, her sister, and Aleesa, and she sat beside him on the bench and pleaded with him to reconsider. 'Your father isn't such a terrible man,' she said. 'Give him time.'

'He'll never relent,' Tariq said sadly. 'He'd rather have no son at all than an apostate. You know that, *Ammi*. I'm sorry, I am truly, to give you such grief. But I can't, I won't, give up my faith, and I'm going to marry Julie. I hope you'll forgive me one day.' He turned to Aleesa. 'Please,' he said earnestly, 'if you can, without trouble, let me know how you all are once in a while. I know it's hard – it's hard for me too. I knew I would be causing a lot of uproar, but I have to do what I believe I am called to do, what is right. You understand, I know. But you are still my family. I want to know how you are. Please don't cut me off altogether.'

Aleesa gripped his hand. 'I'll try,' she said quietly. Then she led her weeping mother and aunt away.

Sixteen years on, in the silence of her dark bedroom, Julie remembered how he had told her what had happened, his voice faltering and choking, his normally perfect English accent lapsing into Indian vowels, sometimes breaking altogether into weeping. His sorrow cut her to her heart, and she could barely hold back her indignation at his father's treatment of him. Yes, she could understand his horror, but to reject your own child seemed to her a negation of love, a wiping out of the family ties he claimed to stand for. And seeing Tariq return, bowed with weariness, grimy, with several days' stubble, and hollowed out by grief, changed something within her, awakened a protectiveness which she had not truly felt before.

Julie and Tariq had resolved to defer sex until after finals and after the wedding. But the powerful emotions kindled by Tariq's disastrous journey to Jammu proved stronger than either of them could withstand. When term began and Julie's flatmates returned,

Tariq had to move back into his one rather barren little room; but long before the next vacation, Julie discovered she was pregnant.

They consulted nobody. This was their problem, theirs alone. Life must be radically altered, plans ditched, new ones adopted, disappointment faced, and they did so with a resolution that was, perhaps, only possible to youth. Both resigned from their university courses. Tariq found work with the builder who had employed him over the vacation, and Julie took on a course in bookkeeping. For the moment they coexisted awkwardly in Tariq's inhospitable cell, until eventually a bigger, better flat was found that they could just afford. In November they married, a modest ceremony attended only by a few friends. Julie's grandmother in Yorkshire, her only close relative, was too old and frail to make the journey, but sent them a present of money, most of which Julie invested. Some of it went on baby things, frugally sourced from second-hand shops.

But then, over Christmas, Julie suffered bleeding and cramping pain. The baby was lost, and Julie spent the beginning of the new year in hospital.

That bleak and barren time, when their hopes had all fallen to pieces, might have broken them, but when she looked back, as she did now in the small hours of another December night, Julie thought it may have been the making of their fragile household. Certainly her new husband, young as he was, looked after her with endless loving patience, even when worn to the bones by a long day of labouring. When the worst of the faith-shaking anger and grieving was over, Julie saw with convincing clarity that among all the calamities she had made a sterling choice. She resolved then that they would come back up, make the best of things, create, God willing, a solid family and a worthwhile life, and it would be based on what she now recognised as a God-given love.

Tariq worked in the day to keep them afloat, learning every possible skill and supplementing what he picked up by evening study. Julie took exams and started keeping books for other people's businesses. After a few years they moved to Halstead, to a house which they could never have afforded in London. Tariq started his own building business, which, after a rocky start, flourished as his reputation for honest work spread, and Julie did all the resulting paperwork. By this time they had Abbie, who was three, and Julie was pregnant with Daniel.

The beginning that could have been catastrophic was fading. From time to time, and reliably on his birthday and at Christmas, Tariq would have news from Aleesa, sometimes late, sometimes tantalisingly brief. In Jammu the elderly thought about retirement, became frail or forgetful, and there were one or two deaths; the young grew tall and achieved or went off the rails; businesses waxed and waned. These dribbles of news were just enough contact to keep Tariq from a longing that could not be assuaged. He said little to Julie, and his children, friends and neighbours, with some exceptions, barely knew of his former life. But now, with graphic images of the earthquake on the news, the silence from Jammu which followed, and Abbie's frightening response, that history, ancient and buried, had risen with fearful power and thrown a brick through their window.

The next day, Friday, Julie walked down to the vicarage after the children had gone to school and Tariq to work. She'd phoned to see if it was convenient – or, if she was honest, if the coast was clear. John Westwood's wife, Hilary, a fine Christian lady in many respects, could be formidable in defence of her husband's peace and privacy, and Julie was not feeling strong enough to face her. But when she phoned it was John who answered, and Hilary, happily, had gone out.

It was a dreary day, spitting with rain from low, grey cloud. Julie tugged off her boots in the vicarage porch. The Westwood children had long since left home, their small dog was rubbed down every time she ventured out, and they could afford to have light-coloured carpets.

'Come through to the kitchen,' John said. 'I'll get some coffee brewing.'

'I hope I'm not interrupting anything desperately important,' Julie said, following him along the hall. She noted with an inward smile that Hilary had made few inroads into her husband's determined lack of style: his bushy white hair needed a trim, and he wore his favourite baggy green cardigan.

'No, I'm glad of a chance to chat.' Once they were settled he said, 'So, still no news from Kashmir? What a terrible disaster that was. So many lives lost. And even for the survivors, lives shattered.'

'No, no news.' Julie sighed. 'The thing is, Tariq's family have, or at least had, a place up near Srinagar. He has no way of telling if any of them were there when the earthquake struck. If they were, they'd have been nearer to the epicentre. Normally, in October, Rashid would have been back in Jammu for the new term, lecturing at the college. But he must have retired years ago. Tariq says his mother would have wanted to be at her home in the capital for the autumn, because the flowers and shrubs would be out in her garden in full glory. But really he's just going round in circles. And in the circumstances, Aleesa's silence seems ominous, doesn't it? She'd know he'd be anxious. Wouldn't she make all the more effort to get news to him?'

John shook his head. 'It's all speculation. Has it occurred to you that it may not be the earthquake that's causing the lack of news?'

Julie frowned. 'What do you mean?'

'Horrible as it may be to contemplate,' John said gently, 'might it not be that something has happened to Aleesa herself? She was the only source of news, wasn't she?'

Julie sighed. 'You're right, of course. It could be anything. Perhaps Aleesa is ill, or even dead.' She shuddered. 'I don't think that has occurred to Tariq. I hope it hasn't.' She took a sip of her coffee, and looked up. 'But actually it's not him I wanted to talk to you about, John.' She glanced anxiously at the clock. 'When is Hilary due back? I don't want to mess up your day.'

'She won't be back for a while yet,' John said with a complicit smile. 'And if she did come back early we would decamp to my study, which for now at least is sacrosanct. Tell me what's on your mind.'

'It's Abbie,' Julie said. 'Something quite worrying happened yesterday morning.' She described Abbie's strange absence at the breakfast table, her blindness and deafness to the real world, and the vivid vision she had seen and heard of devastating destruction. 'It was our fault,' Julie said. 'We had a bit of a ... disagreement the night before, pretty late. Tariq was very upset. We obviously woke Abbie. She's a sensitive kid.'

John thought for several moments, his lips pursed, his pale blue eyes unfocused. 'Well, I don't really know what to say,' he said. 'I'm no expert in altered mental states. Has this happened before?'

Julie nodded. 'So she says, but this was the first I knew of it. And Tariq says he experienced something similar when he was young, though nothing so, I don't know, so organised, so coherent, so terrifyingly real as Abbie's vision.'

'Odd,' John said. 'It almost seems like something in the genes. Are you thinking of getting her checked over medically?'

'Yes. Just as soon as they break up for the holidays. Abbie won't like it, but we can't just let it pass.'

'No, of course not.' John finished his coffee. 'Abbie is, as you say, a sensitive child. And there've been a few pressures on her recently, I think.'

Julie smiled. 'Apart from the march of rampant hormones? Yes, she's been quite lonely, ever since her friend Lucy moved away. And, though she'd never admit it, I suspect she might be getting a bit of verbal bullying at school. Just because she's different.'

'Abbie's differences are all good, it seems to me,' John said.

'She doesn't quite see it that way,' Julie said wryly. 'But John, could there be some, I don't know, spiritual element to this? I'm not sure what I mean, but I feel uneasy. Suppose they don't find anything physical or neurological to account for it? What then?'

John shook his head. 'I really don't know, Julie. I will pray for Abbie, of course, as well as for Tariq, for all of you. I don't know what else we can do. Would Abbie come and have a chat with me herself, do you suppose?'

'I very much doubt it,' Julie said. 'Yes, I know she's known you since she was little, but teenagers suffer from terminal embarrassment, don't they? She might even think you were going to quiz her about her lack of attendance at church just lately.'

'I wouldn't dream of mentioning it,' John said with a smile. 'Young people of her age need a long rein in spiritual matters, I find.'

Julie got up. 'John, I won't take up any more of your time. But yes, please do remember us in your prayers. It's a tough time for Tariq, but he's a grown man. Abbie's just a child, and not a very happy one at the moment.'

John got up too and followed Julie to the front door. He watched as she pulled her boots back on. 'I will pray. You must too, Julie. And please keep me informed, won't you? She's a special lass, your Abbie. And if she's being bullied, perhaps you need to talk to David Calladine.'

Julie made a face. 'Call me a coward, John,' she said, 'but if I talk to David, and David talks to Abbie, I'll be in massive trouble. She may not be quite thirteen, but she can already pack a punch.'

'Well,' John said, smiling, 'it's one of the joys of parenthood, isn't it? Running the gauntlet of irate adolescents. I can remember a few instances of making myself extremely unpopular when my own were growing up. I thank the Lord that time is over. Grandchildren tend to blame us far less, I've found.'

Julie stood on one leg, her boot in her hand. 'It seems such a long time while you're living it. A bit like when they're toddlers, giving you grief in the supermarket. And then it's over, so quickly in retrospect.' She stuffed her foot into the boot. 'Thank you, John. We'll see you on Sunday. Well, some of us will.'

Hilary Westwood was used to her husband's nocturnal ramblings, but that night she half-emerged foggily from sleep to find him sitting on the edge of the bed, in his rumpled pyjamas, Bible in hand, muttering. '"When there are prophets among you, I reveal myself to them in visions and speak to them in dreams."'

'What's that?'

'Numbers 12, verse 6,' John said. 'God to Miriam and Aaron.' He turned round to look at her, his glasses perched so far down his nose that they sat sideways. 'Is it possible, do you think, that we might have a twelve-year-old prophet among us?'

Hilary frowned, her eyes still barely focusing. 'What are you talking about?'

'Never mind, my love,' John said gently. 'I'm just rabbiting. Go back to sleep.'

March 2010

Maggie Calladine, dressed in her worst old jeans and one of David's discarded jumpers, knelt on the cold concrete floor of the garage, surrounded by the accumulated junk of the years. She was supposed to be looking for things they no longer needed, but which might be sold at the boot fair that some of David's staff were organising on the first Saturday as the Easter holidays started, trying to raise money for the school funds. David's deputy, newly promoted, wanted to extend the gym changing rooms and add a wing to the school library, and had somehow galvanised her younger colleagues, as well as some of the pupils and their parents, to embark on a many-pronged fund-raising campaign. Walburn High was a sprawling ugly jumble of buildings from several eras, and had the neglected look of a place that had never enjoyed the benefit of a proper architectural plan.

Maggie sighed, and rubbed a dusty hand across her forehead, leaving a streak of dirt. *Just shows it's not the state of the classrooms that determines a school's performance. It's David's doing that's brought that place up to where it is. He's turned it round in the eight years he's been Head, I know that, and you know what, I'm proud of what he's done. He really cares about his kids. If only he cared half as much about me. About us, about the kids we don't have.*

She scrambled to her feet, wincing as her back protested, and wandered round the bits of the floor that weren't littered with the contents of numerous collapsing boxes. She'd agreed to rummage, out of a long habit of, she felt, largely disregarded helpfulness, while David was searching for similar items in the loft. Listlessly she kicked some of the things around, trying to find something that might be useful. There was a camping gas unit, but the plastic was cracked, so that wouldn't do. It made her think of the camping trips she and David had embarked on, years ago, when camping had been all they could afford while they were shelling out enormous mortgage repayments and trying to run a car that was always breaking down. It had been fun in a Spartan kind of way – but perhaps better in the telling and the remembering than in the original experience. Now, financially, they were better off; but they hadn't taken a holiday for three years – at least, not together, just the two of them. *What on earth would we talk about? All that's gone, dried up. Is it my fault? I don't know any more.*

Squatting, she upended one last cardboard box, and that was when she found it: a raggy, squashy toy rabbit with half an ear missing, something she'd doted on as a small child, refused to be parted from, even to let her mother wash it when it had turned greasy and grey from handling. She didn't remember having kept it – why had she? Now, standing in her chilly garage on a rain-spattered Sunday, with evening darkening the one window, she stared at the poor neglected thing in her hand, unprepared for the great wave of anguish that came welling up, making her knees sag and her fists clench as the wave hit her throat and poured out of her eyes. She huddled over her find as if it was a lost treasure, and howled.

Sobbing till her chest ached and her throat was raw, spilling out grief that she had kept down for so long, at first she didn't hear David, in his soft-soled shoes, coming in the open door that linked the garage to the house, in his arms a box of things he'd found. Then he must have seen and heard her, because he exclaimed something, who knew what? What was his tone, even – disgust? All she could recall later was the silence as he stood there, and then the sound of him throwing the box down, and turning back into the house.

The crying fit passed, and through tear-bleared eyes she gazed at the rabbit, seeing there her own childhood, her parents, the modest house she grew up in, her grandfather, and she thought about the children she, it seemed, would never have. *Is it my fault that our lives are so miserable? Should I just write it off, this crazy fruitless yearning, and try to be cheerful? But I can't, I can't stop this ache. I think I'm incurable. I can't even pray. But I must, I must try.*

She straightened up, the rabbit dangling from her hand, pushed her hair out of her eyes. *Father, help me with this. I am out of ideas. Out of strength. I don't know how to go on.*

Julie put the phone down slowly, and wandered back into the kitchen. Tariq, sitting at the kitchen table, a broken clock in pieces in front of him, looked up and saw her expression.

'Maggie?'

Julie nodded. 'I'll just make some tea, shall I?' She filled the kettle at the sink and plugged it in. 'Riq, I'm worried. Really worried.'

'You've been worried about Maggie for years, love. What's different today?'

Julie shook her head. 'Not just today. The last few weeks. She sounds flat, as if all the feeling's been knocked out of her. But today, just now, was the worst I've heard her.' She put teabags into cups and waited for the kettle to boil, silent in her thoughts. The kettle clicked off, and she poured water into the cups. 'I'm serious, Riq. I think she might actually be suicidal.'

'What? How can she be like that?' Tariq said. 'She's a Samaritan, she helps sad people all the time. And anyway, don't they have some kind of support system? Can't some of her pals help her?'

Julie drizzled milk into the cups and put them on the table, one in front of Tariq. He grunted his thanks. 'Normally, yes, of course,' she said. 'But that's just it. She told me a few minutes ago that she's resigned from the Samaritans. Well, she's written a resignation letter. And she's even talking about resigning from her job.'

Tariq took a sip of tea and winced at its heat. 'Maggie loves her job.'

'Riq, it adds up, don't you see that? Isn't she putting her affairs in order, saying goodbye?'

'I don't know, love,' Tariq said helplessly. 'It all seems so … melodramatic, out of proportion.'

Julie ran a hand through her cropped fair hair. 'Only from the outside.' She thought for a moment, then looked up and held his gaze. 'Do you remember,' she said quietly, 'what it was like for us, when we lost our first baby?'

He nodded. 'Of course I do.'

'We were lucky,' Julie said. 'We held on together, we got through it, and we went on to have Abbie and Dan. But I've never forgotten that time, how it felt, like it was the end of everything. Maggie doesn't have even that. It's a perfectly normal thing, you know, for women to want kids. Not all women, but I'd say probably most just assume that they will, one day. It's not just normal, Riq, it's kind of, I don't know, part of our basic biology, a physical thing. And Maggie's spent years waiting and hoping, with nothing happening. It must wear out your soul. And it's not as if she knows definitely that she can't. They had those tests, didn't they, back in the days when David cooperated.' She grimaced. 'Nothing wrong with either of them that they could find. Maybe, if it had been found to be totally impossible, she could have somehow got on with her life. But it's that tiny thread of hope that makes it so hard. Not to mention David's attitude.'

Tariq said nothing, staring down at the bits of clock on the table. It seemed to him he had heard all these things before. He looked up at Julie and smiled tentatively.

'Do *you* understand it?' Julie said. 'Speaking as a bloke, can you figure out why David is so, well … so *unkind?* He isn't normally, not to anyone else, is he? I can't believe you would handle it the way he does.'

Tariq stretched across the table and took Julie's hand, stroking her fingers with his thumb. 'Thanks for the vote of confidence,' he said, smiling crookedly, 'but I don't know what I'd do. Like you said, we were lucky. And I have no idea what makes David behave as he does. Maybe he just can't cope with Maggie being so depressed. Kind of a self-preservation thing.'

'That makes him a selfish coward, in my book,' Julie said, her eyes narrowed. 'From what I can gather, they barely talk. No wonder she feels so alone.'

The phone rang again, and Julie heaved herself up with a sigh and padded into the hall. Moments later she was back, brows creased in puzzlement. 'That was very odd,' she muttered. She looked at Tariq. 'Maggie again. Only now she's unnaturally bright, saying she's sorry she bent my ear, it's not so bad really, it was just a passing moment, to take no notice of her (as if I could do that), and of course she's going to tear up the resignation letter.' She picked up her mug and stared at its contents as if they contained arcane wisdom. 'I don't know what's going on. But I can tell you I don't like it.' For a long moment she was silent, then she said, 'I used to be able to tell Maggie things, ask her advice, especially about the kids. I haven't done that in a long time. Even though she works with children every day, even though she has stacks of experience, it's the one thing I know will hurt her.'

Tariq took a swallow of tea and put his mug down, wiping his mouth with the back of his hand. 'Why do you need advice about the kids?'

Julie shrugged. 'You know, just things that came up, over the years.' She paused, looking away from his eyes. 'And how Abbie's been. Is, I should say. It's no use saying it isn't so, Riq. We used to be close, didn't we, Abbie and me? I looked forward to her growing up, so we could be more like friends. But it hasn't happened. She's always pleasant and civil, but there's a barrier there never was before. I don't think she's ever really forgiven me.'

'You didn't do anything wrong,' Tariq said softly. 'You, we, did what any reasonable parent would have done. It would have been neglect if we hadn't.'

Julie rested her head in her hands. 'I know all that,' she said, her voice muffled. 'But it was what it did to her.' She looked up, and Tariq was dismayed to see tears in her eyes. 'The other day,' Julie said, 'I asked her whether she's ever had those vision things since then – since we finished with the psychologist. She gave me a hard stare, and said "No". Just like that. And went back very deliberately to reading her book. I got the message: basically she was saying, "If I have, I'm not going to tell *you*." I'm her mother, Riq. It hurts.'

Tariq finished his tea in one gulp, pushed his chair back and stood up. 'She's a teenager. They can be very, I don't know, self-righteous.' He moved towards the door. 'She knows it's not really your fault, love. She may even be looking for a way to mend fences. She's not got so many mates that she can do without her mum, eh?' He smiled and patted Julie's shoulder as he passed. 'Look, I'm supposed to be taking her out for some driving practice in a minute. She talked me into it. I know you need the car to pick up Dan from football – we'll take the van. She won't think much of it, but it's that or nothing. I'll talk to her. OK?'

'Pull in here a minute, Abbie, can you? I need a break from all this drama.'

Abbie gave him a withering glance. 'My driving's not that bad, Dad.' She slowed and pulled off the road, braking with a jolt as the van's front wheel dropped bone-jarringly into a muddy rut. 'Oops.'

'You're doing all right,' Tariq said. 'You just need plenty of practice. I just wanted to stop here and look at the view. Think I'll get out for a minute, get some fresh air. There's a bench over there.'

'Oh. OK.'

They sat side by side in easy silence for a while. The cloud had broken, revealing a weak spring sun. The rough surface of the weathered bench was slightly damp from the afternoon's drizzle.

'It's nice and peaceful out here,' Abbie said. 'Good for driving. Not too many other cars on the road.'

'Mm,' Tariq said, flexing his shoulders. 'Bit of a different story in the middle of Walburn on a Saturday.'

Abbie shuddered. 'I think I'll leave that till I've got a bit more experience. And not in the works van, if I can help it. I like to have windows to look out of.'

Tariq smiled. 'You get used to it.'

'So, Dad, how long d'you think it'll take me to pass my test?'

'Steady on, girl! You've only had three lessons.'

'Four. And I've got one on Wednesday, right after school.'

'Well, I don't know, Abs. Depends how much practice you get. You could ask your mum to take you out.'

'Hm, maybe. I don't think Mum would be as patient as you.'

'Sure she would. Well, perhaps not quite.' He grinned.

After a pause, Abbie said, 'Dad, I've been thinking.'

'Sounds ominous.'

'No, I'm serious. Last night I couldn't sleep, right? So I decided to tidy up my wardrobe.' She caught her father's expression. 'Yeah, OK, don't faint. Anyway, I found this old box at the back, under all my shoes and junk, and inside it were all these exercise books. My journal, d'you remember? When I was thirteen, what that psychologist said I should keep. And being the good little girl that I was, I did keep it, on and off, for over a year. It brought it all back to me, that time when I went through all that stuff.' She paused for a moment, staring at the landscape before them, as if waiting for her thoughts to settle. She glanced at her father and sighed. 'And yeah, Mum went through it all with me. I do know that, Dad. And I know I haven't really been fair to Mum. But it *was* awful, especially for a thirteen-year-old who already thought she was weird.'

Tariq said quietly, 'You weren't weird then, and you aren't weird now.'

'Says you. But you're my dad.'

'Yes, says I,' Tariq said firmly. 'OK, so you do something, or something happens to you, that isn't usual. It's a bit of a mystery. But there's nothing wrong with you. We know that, because all

41

those tests proved it. So you had to have one of those scans, whatever they're called. And we knew you didn't have a brain tumour – thank God. So you had to wear that thing on your head all one weekend. So we know you don't have epilepsy.'

Abbie smiled. 'Do you remember, I refused to leave the house all the time I had to wear that thing?'

Tariq nodded. 'And you say that all those visits to the psychologist were a waste of time and money, but they were just another way of knowing you were, are, perfectly normal.'

'I don't know about "normal," Dad,' Abbie murmured. 'That might be going a bit too far. But I didn't want to keep going to that smarmy woman, because of all the money being spent on me.' She turned to him, scowling. 'I thought it would have been better spent sending you to India to find your family.'

Tariq grunted. 'Well, sweetheart, that's another story.'

'I know, you don't really want to talk about them,' Abbie said, 'just like I'm not too happy talking about that time. Except to you.' She grinned suddenly. 'I was such a little diva, Dad. Did Mum tell you when I yelled at the psychologist and ran out of the room?'

'She mentioned it.'

'I threw the door open and charged out into the corridor – I was going to lurk in the toilet for a while, just to annoy them, to make my point – and I crashed into this poor guy who was just walking along with a pile of folders. Everything went flying. I spent the next five minutes apologising and helping him pick them up. I could hardly look at him, I was so embarrassed. Which made me even more bad-tempered. I remember I gave Mum such a hard time in the car on the way home.'

'That was the last time you went, wasn't it? The money ran out, I seem to remember.'

Abbie nodded. 'I don't think I would have gone back anyway. And it *was* really expensive, I know. I feel bad about that.'

'Well, you shouldn't,' Tariq said. 'It was our decision to go private, when we found out we'd have to wait five months for an appointment otherwise. And I don't regret it.'

Abbie chuckled. 'Yes, I remember Mum picking up the post that day and the look on her face when she found out we were going to have to wait that long! Didn't she rant!'

'Not surprising, really. I think you would have had the urgent stuff done sooner, but there was a great long waiting list for the talk sessions.'

'Which definitely *were* a waste of time,' Abbie said sourly. 'Anyway, we can't undo it.' She stretched. 'Incidentally, Dad, do you think Mum's come round to the idea of me having driving lessons yet?'

Tariq smiled. 'I reckon so. I told her that if you were using the car to take your mates for a night out, at least you wouldn't be able to drink. She hadn't thought of that.'

'Ha! Nice one.' Abbie bit her lip. 'Now all I need is some mates to go out with.' Tariq said nothing. 'I mean, there are *some* OK people at school now. Since they took on some sixth form students from that other school. I wouldn't exactly call them mates, though.'

'Maybe you don't really encourage anyone to be friendly,' Tariq said gently.

'No wonder, after what that little weasel did to me. Zara Chesterfield – sounds quite posh, doesn't it?' Abbie spat the name out as if it were a mouthful of poison. 'But turns out she was an absolute snake.' She stood up suddenly, her fists clenched. 'Do you remember, Dad? How she pretended to be such a nice girl, and I was so lonely after Lucy left and so desperate for a friend that I let her come round the weekend I was wearing that helmet thing with all the electrodes, feeling like a total alien, and she must have taken a photo because the next day it was all over the school.' She let out a long breath. 'And then, *of course*, all the little dears were sniggering and calling me names and it went on for ever.'

'She's not still at your school, is she?' Tariq asked. 'Didn't she leave at the end of that term?'

'Yes,' Abbie said. 'Just as well, because I might have bashed her brains out with a hockey stick.'

Tariq heaved himself up off the bench and put his arm round her shoulders. 'And your mum and I would be visiting you in some secure facility,' he said. 'So I'm glad you held off. Time to go back? It's getting a bit dark and cold.'

'OK.' She swung the keys from her fingers as they ambled back to the car. 'I know I've built a kind of cocoon round myself the last few years,' she said slowly. 'But it's hard when someone does that to you, especially when you're that age and you've been through some bad stuff. How do you know who to trust, Dad?' She looked up at him, her eyes wide.

Tariq shrugged. 'It comes down to instinct and judgement, I suppose. We can all make mistakes about people, though. And for sure there are some real wrong 'uns out there.'

They got into the car, and Abbie carefully reversed and started to drive back the way they had come, down the hill, as dusk masked the trees that bordered the road. 'Dad, I've been meaning to ask you: how is Mr Westwood?'

'John? Very poorly, I'm afraid.' Tariq shook his head. 'Poor man. I haven't seen him for a few weeks – Hilary guards him like a fierce dog. Your mum and Maggie Calladine have been to see him, though, and apparently he's lost a lot of weight. But he's cheerful and positive. I don't know how he manages that.'

Abbie rounded a corner into their road, signalled and parked. They got out and Abbie walked round the car with a critical eye. 'Hm, not my best bit of parking. You might have to put the van on the drive later. I'm scared of hitting the wall.'

'Coward.'

'Yep. So who's taking services?'

'We are. All of us, in turn. And sometimes we have a visiting clergyman to take Communion.'

44

Abbie stared. 'Are you telling me *you've* preached a sermon?'

'Not exactly. I thought that was a bit beyond me. Are you planning to stand around on the drive much longer? Only I'm getting cold.'

Abbie, still in her own thoughts, pushed open the back door. 'How long's he got, do you think? Poor Mr Westwood. He was always nice to me.'

'He's always nice to everyone,' Tariq said soberly. 'I don't know, Abs. Months, maybe. I think he's starting a new course of treatment next week; maybe that'll keep him going a bit longer.' A thought struck him. 'Why don't you go and see him, next time your mum goes? It would do him good to see a fresh face.'

'You think?' Abbie said dubiously.

'*And* it would please your mum,' Tariq persisted. 'Think of that. First step to mending fences.'

'I'll think about it,' Abbie said. She paused at the foot of the stairs. 'You know what, Dad? I might start keeping that journal again.' She grinned. 'Just in case anything actually happens round here. Anyway, time for a little homework, I think. Thanks for taking me driving.'

June 1989

Bill White stared at his younger brother with something very like loathing. The boy was lounging up against the kitchen counter, his arms folded across his chest, one ankle crossed over the other. His thick blond hair fell over his forehead, and once in a while he uncrossed his arms to flick it back in a gesture that Bill found annoyingly affected. But then, most of what Paul did annoyed him, and that was on a good day. The boy's handsome features were marred only by a crop of spots on his chin, and the sulky, mutinous, uncooperative look that was always there when faced with his brother.

'You said I could have the car,' he said. His voice had broken deep, in manly contrast to his slim body.

'You can have the car,' Bill said. 'But you can have it when you've listened to what I have to say. And since I have the keys –' he held the car keys up, jangling them – 'you'd better listen well. Or I just might change my mind. With me so far?'

Paul grunted, but his eyes flashed and his brows contracted.

'Good,' Bill said. 'I'm going to spell it out. I'm not going to go over it all again, all that's happened recently, but it does make me wonder, Paul, when you're supposed to be a bright lad, how you could have been stupid enough to get expelled a year before your A levels. That beats all. Why can't you think once in a while?'

'I told you,' Paul said with sarcastic emphasis, 'it was that new teacher grassed me up. Little Melanie didn't mind, she liked me, it was only him making her feel bad and going crying to her dad that wrecked everything.' Paul scuffed the floor with one jabbing toe.

'For a start, you don't know it was him. You just assume it.'

'I saw him, didn't I? Talking to the Head and looking at me. Big grin on his face.'

'For all you know he could have been talking about the blasted weather!' Bill said with mounting impatience. 'And as to poor Melanie, I shouldn't have to remind you that she's only *fourteen*. Even if your intentions were pure, which is the unlikeliest thing I've heard this year, that makes her vulnerable. You utter fool, Paul.'

'I never touched her,' Paul muttered.

'So you say,' Bill said grimly. 'But you stalked her, and sent her all sorts of dodgy messages. How long till you *did* go a bit further? All that hassling, Paul, it amounted to bullying in the end, whatever you say. You're lucky to have got off as lightly as you did.'

Paul scowled. 'I told you, it was just a joke, I was only mucking about, I thought the silly little fool understood. Whatever. I thought we weren't rehashing all that. Get to the point, can't you?'

'Do you want the car or don't you?' Bill roared, lunging forward with his fists clenched at his sides.

Paul flinched and held up his hands. 'OK, OK. I'm listening.'

Bill took a deep breath and stepped back. When he spoke his voice was cold, his control back in place. 'Right, here's the deal. I've looked after you since Mum died. I didn't especially want to, it cramped my style, but there wasn't anyone else, and I didn't want to see my own flesh and blood in care. I feel differently now; I'm giving you fair warning. You've been nothing but trouble, a constant headache. When I think of some of the things you've done, it beggars belief. Anyway, you're seventeen. Not too far off being an adult in the eyes of the law. Once you're eighteen I'll gladly wash my hands of you. You'll be on your own. But it would be bad for you and uncharitable on my part if you left school without proper qualifications, when you're more than capable of getting them, if you'd only do some work. So this is the deal: you can carry on living here and do your A levels by correspondence. I'll pay for the course – but you have to buckle down. Any slacking and the deal's off – I'll put your belongings on the front lawn and get the locks changed. Don't think I won't.'

He fixed his brother with a baleful stare, but Paul said nothing. His eyes were narrow, his lips a thin line.

'This time next year I'm getting married,' Bill said. 'You know Lisa – well, she said yes. And she'll be moving in here, with her little boy, Robbie. Lisa's not at all happy living in the same house with you. You give her the creeps, apparently. Not to mention she's probably heard talk. Anyway, she certainly won't subject her four-year-old son to your interesting ways. And Lisa and I might have children of our own one day.'

'Oh yes,' Paul said in an exaggerated drawl, 'we can't have nasty Uncle Paul round the sweet little darlings, can we?' He shot Bill a venomous look. 'What have I ever done to Robbie? Or any child?'

'I hope I never find out,' Bill said. 'But at the very least, your influence is hardly going to be benign, is it? So, once your A levels are over, you leave. Mum's money will come to you when you're eighteen, and you can do what you like with it. If you've got any sense you'll apply to university or train for a job. Or you could always buy a fast car and wrap yourself round a tree. But you won't be my problem any longer.'

There was silence for a moment. Paul stared at the floor, then he looked up, his expression all truculent defiance. 'You done? Only my friends are waiting.'

'You have to agree to my terms.'

'Sure I agree.'

'Remember – keep your nose clean or you're out, a lot earlier than eighteen. I've had enough. If you can't think of other people, think about yourself – you're good at that.'

'You made your point, big bro. Now can I have the keys?'

Bill handed them over reluctantly to the outstretched hand. 'Come home quietly. Don't drink, don't get pulled over, and don't crash the car.'

Paul waved the car keys in front of his brother's face, smiling gleefully. 'As if I'd do such terrible, wicked things,' he said with a childish lisp. 'Anyway, I'm a much better driver than you.' He spun on one leg and capered out of the room, and his whoops of laughter rang in Bill's ears long after he'd disappeared.

March 2010

On Monday morning Maggie was still on Julie's mind. She had
plenty of work to do for the business, especially with the tax year
coming to an end. With the house quiet, Tariq off to a site meeting
and the children at school, she should have been at her desk long
since. Instead, she stacked the dishwasher slowly, then opened the
freezer door with a view to seeing what shopping was needed, but
found herself staring at the freezer shelves in a state of distraction,
chewing her bottom lip, her thoughts chaotic.

*Bother, bother. I can't settle, not like this. I'm going to have to find out, one
way or another.*

She closed the freezer door and walked briskly into the hall,
pulled a coat from its peg and stuffed her socked feet into a pair of
Abbie's boots that had been left in front of the door. She pocketed
a house key and went out into the crisp morning. The sun was
shining, melting off an early frost, and there was a clean smell in the
air, as if the trees were breathing benignly. Halstead had been a
village once; now it was a rather remote suburb of Walburn, but on
the far side there were fields beginning to show a blush of green,
and hidden birds were chattering in the trees.

She turned left, in the direction of the country and away from
the sprouting developments that connected Halstead with the city.
She didn't much like them, but they represented work for Tariq so
she had to accept them. Her direction took her down the road
where she lived and left into a narrower lane, where there stood a
row of Victorian cottages, one of which was the Calladines'. David
and Maggie had extended over the years, with off-road
hardstanding for two cars and a sunny conservatory at the back,
and their house was freshly painted and well-maintained. Of the

other three, two were in their original state but tidy and cared for, but the end one, next to the Calladines', was empty, the lower windows boarded, the patch of garden at the front rampant with bramble and goosegrass, the path stained and cracked. An estate agent's board, weathered and warped, lay at a drunken angle behind the overgrown hedge. Julie noted that there were no cars in the Calladines' drive, but her attention was taken by a scruffy green saloon parked outside the abandoned cottage. There was nobody about that she could see, but on the back seat of the green car a large yellow dog sat, its tongue lolling, its brown eyes mournful.

Julie whistled under her breath. Could someone finally have bought the old place? Was someone – the estate agent, perhaps? – taking responsibility for the grounds? There was a long garden at the back, Julie knew, like Maggie's, and it was a jungle of weeds and rubbish. David and Maggie often complained about the eyesore on the far side of the fence. The old lady who had lived there, Mrs Wilson, had died the previous summer, and nobody seemed to know what was going to happen to the property. There was plenty of speculation – some legal wrangle, perhaps – but the estate agent was not forthcoming and the cottage remained an ugly, neglected blot.

Julie turned and retraced her steps, back up her own road and into the centre of Halstead, where there was still an oval of trimmed green, overshadowed at one end by a giant oak. On one side was the local pub, the Stag's Head, on the other the church, St Mary Magdalene, where the Calladines and the Hasans, among others, worshipped. Between, down a narrow lane, was the primary school, also called St Mary Magdalene, where Maggie had taught the Year Fives for several years. Abbie and Daniel, in their time, had been taught by Maggie.

Julie crossed the green and walked soft-footed down the lane to the school. She hardly came here now, since her children had moved on to Walburn High; but the green chain-link fence and the strip of mown grass between the fence and the classrooms were as she remembered them.

She peered through the fence. At this time of day assembly would be over and morning lessons underway. An adult figure was moving round in one of the classrooms, bending over children as they worked, and Julie, with a wash of relief, recognised Maggie's navy-blue cardigan and dark, curly hair. Then Maggie stood upright, facing the window, and saw her friend at the fence. Her face broke out into a smile, and she gave a little wave.

Julie smiled and waved back, and made an exaggerated gesture as if holding a phone to her ear. *I'll call you later.* Maggie nodded vigorously. With another wave Julie went on down the lane, past the school, into the strip of woodland bordering a farm field. *A bit of fresh air, then back to work.* She raised her face to the sky, feeling the sun's still feeble warmth on her cheeks, and she closed her eyes momentarily, breathing in the scents of damp leaves and turned earth. *She's in school, not at the bottom of the river. She hasn't resigned. She's smiling. Perhaps she really is OK. Thank You, Lord.*

Julie left it till 5.30 before she rang Maggie, reasoning that she'd be home by then, even if she had a meeting after school, but would probably not have started preparing the evening meal. David almost always stayed at his school for hours, and with no children to cater for, they often ate late. But when she rang she got only the answerphone. She sighed, a little puzzled, left a message and went back to scrubbing vegetables.

Twenty minutes later Maggie rang back. 'Sorry, hon,' she said, a little breathlessly. 'I was next door.'

Julie frowned. 'What, at the Prestons'?'

'No, the other side,' Maggie said. 'Good news, Julie my love – finally, after all this time, someone's bought Mrs Wilson's place.'

'And you've been hobnobbing with the neighbours already?'

'I wouldn't say *hobnobbing* exactly,' Maggie said with a touch of acidity. 'He called round and asked for advice. And it's "neighbour" in the singular. A most charming young chap, as it happens. With a dog.'

'Ah, yes, I saw the dog,' Julie said. 'Battered old green car?'

'That's the one. When did you see the car – and the dog?'

'Oh, I just passed that way this morning,' Julie said casually. 'But I didn't see your new neighbour. When you say "young", how young's that?'

'Oh, well, perhaps not so very young, maybe only a year or two younger than us. But he's very lively, very personable, and he has all sorts of plans for the cottage.'

'It needs someone with a bit of oomph,' Julie murmured.

'Which brings me,' Maggie rattled on, her voice rising excitedly, 'to where our new neighbour might have a beneficial effect on the Hasan household.'

'Really?' Julie said. 'Hold on, I think something's burning. Back in a tick.' A moment later she picked up the phone again. 'OK, disaster averted. So how's he going to be of help to us? He doesn't know us.'

'Because, my love, he has a neglected old house to renovate, and he asked me if I knew any local builders.'

'And you said …?'

Maggie's tone was triumphant. 'I said, "You know what, there's a splendid chap pretty much on your doorstep. Honest and reliable. The one and only Tariq Hasan." So tell Tariq to expect a phone call soon.'

'Wow. Well, work is always welcome. I'll tell Riq when he gets in. Thanks for the plug. Where's your new neighbour from?'

'Oh, I'm not sure, not from round here, I don't think. He said he's inherited some money recently, and he was looking for somewhere peaceful – to write a novel he's been planning.'

'So does he work – other than writing?'

'He didn't mention that. But I have to say he seems very nice, very sociable and friendly, easy to chat to, and keen to get involved in the community. When he found out I teach at the school, he offered to come in and help, hear the younger children read, that sort of thing. I said he'd have to get a CRB check for that – you can't be too careful these days, can you? Even if he already had one, the Head would insist on a new one being done. So he laughed and said, "What a palaver!" or some such, and said maybe there was some other way he could help me with my school work.'

'Quite a paragon! Does he have a name, this novelist?'

'He's called William Chambers. Known as Will. And the dog's Molly.'

I said to Dad I might keep this journal again, but I meant it as a bit of a joke. I read those old exercise books full of my scribbles from four years ago, dutiful little girl that I was (not any more.) I wrote down any seeings I had – nothing much at all, all short flashes of nonsense, really – and I put stuff in about school, all my loathing for that creep of a non-friend Zara, and how I wished she'd fall in a hole etc etc. All kiddie stuff in my neat handwriting. Sometimes I think, Was this really me?

Anyway, it was a joke to start with. I never thought I'd keep it for more than a week, what with all the schoolwork I've got and exams looming. But now somehow I think I'm going to need to keep a record. Otherwise I'll start mistrusting my own thoughts, write it all off as a mistake, or something I imagined – and I know it isn't. Right now I couldn't be more certain of anything.

But I'd better start at the beginning. Before I knew what I know now. When Mum decided to invite our oh-so-fascinating new neighbour to dinner.

'I've been thinking,' Julie said to her assembled family at the dinner table. Tariq raised an eyebrow; the children barely looked up. 'We should invite Will round. Do the neighbourly thing. He's been here quite a few weeks now.'

'Invite him to what?' Daniel said in his rough breaking voice, casting a threatening look at his sister who was smirking.

'Dinner. A dinner party,' Julie said. 'Get David and Maggie to come too.'

'Do we have to come?' Daniel said dubiously. 'I mean, Mum, what am I going to talk to him about? Don't these sort of things go on for ever, with people doing a lot of boring talking? Can't I just have my dinner early and stay in my room?'

'Oh, Dan!' Julie said. 'Really! Don't you ever want to do grown-up things?'

'No.'

Julie turned to her daughter. 'What do you think, Abbie? You could help me do the meal.'

'I suppose.'

Tariq put down his knife and fork. 'How about this,' he said before Julie could say another word. 'It's a nice idea, love, and we should all help. Dan, you could clean the place up a bit, get rid of your rubbish from the hallway, tidy up the lounge. Abbie, you could make that dessert you did the other Sunday. Or peel the vegetables. You could both make polite conversation for a while, and disappear after the pudding. It wouldn't do you any harm. You'd get a special meal out of it, at least. And maybe you could have one glass of wine.'

'Make that two,' Abbie said. 'I'm nearly old enough to drink, anyway.'

'I don't even like wine,' Daniel said.

Abbie looked at her mother, who seemed to be on the point of erupting.

'OK, Mum, we'll do it.' She glanced at her brother. 'Shut your mouth, Dan. You look like a fish.' She turned back to her parents. 'But there are conditions. Absolutely no embarrassing remarks about us. In fact, no remarks at all. We'll be dining with our Headmaster, don't forget. That's quite awkward enough.' She saw Tariq try not to smile. 'And we scarper graciously after dessert. I don't mind helping, as long as it's not a school night. I don't even mind doing some of the washing-up. It's a big sacrifice, so it'll mean about 2 million brownie points. Each.'

Later, in her pyjamas, she lounged on the end of Daniel's rumpled bed.

'Why did you have to drop us in it like that?' Dan said. 'You gave in without a fight! And got me into it as well.'

'Look at it this way,' Abbie said. 'Mum seems dead set on it. She and Mrs Calladine obviously think this guy's some kind of wonder-boy. Not to mention he's giving Dad work. It would only cause trouble if we dug our heels in, and this way we'll be in credit. Anyway, it won't kill us, will it? Mum does loads of stuff for us. With any luck we'll be the nicest kids in the world for a while. You have to give a bit sometimes – like an investment.'

Daniel groaned. 'But eating a whole meal with Mr Calladine! How many courses is that?'

'Probably three. We won't be required for coffee, I guess.'

'This is going to be *really* embarrassing,' Daniel said gloomily. 'Mr Calladine used to be OK. Way back when. But now he hardly even notices us. Unless he wants to moan about something, like wearing football boots in the corridors.'

Abbie stretched. 'He was friendlier before we actually went to his school. You can't expect him to be matey any more.'

Daniel made a face. 'As if I want him to be matey,' he growled.

'Yeah, I know,' Abbie said. 'But I remember that camping holiday we all went on together – don't you?'

'Maybe,' Daniel grunted. 'But I was only about seven. I sort of remember kicking a ball around in the rain, with Mr Calladine and Dad. He seemed all right then. Mr C, I mean. I fell over in the mud, and he gave me some chocolate he had in his pocket.' He paused, remembering. 'It was a bit melty.'

'He probably still is all right, under that crusty exterior,' Abbie said thoughtfully. 'Maybe he'll be a bit more human in a, you know, social situation.'

Daniel shrugged. 'But what about Mrs Calladine? Once Mum and her get stuck into the wine she might start remembering all the hilarious things we did when we were nine.'

'Hm. You have a point there, little bro.' Abbie thought for a moment. 'I'll talk to Mum about that, while she's in a good mood. Maybe we aren't so friendly as we used to be, but Mum and Mrs Calladine still are, big-time. Maybe Mum can warn her to be discreet. Anyway, they'll all be far more interested in this Will character to be bothering much with us.'

Daniel picked up a soft ball and threw it at the wall. It landed with a thud in a pile of his dirty washing. 'Have you met him? Will Whatsisface?'

'I've seen him driving around. He looked like he wanted to stop and chat, but I just stared into the distance and pretended I didn't know who he was.'

'His car's a heap of rusty rubbish,' Dan said dismissively.

'But he's got a nice dog.'

Will arrived promptly at seven o'clock. The Hasan home was unnaturally neat and gleaming, not a speck of dust visible, no discarded shoes as a trip hazard, cushions plumped up, and family members scrubbed and decently clothed. Tariq introduced Abbie and Daniel, who murmured politely. Daniel sat on the very edge of the sofa, a fixed smile on his face. Abbie sidled into the kitchen, shut the door and made herself available. Ten minutes later, taking in a tray of exotic-looking nibbles, she was astonished to find her father and brother chatting freely to their guest and laughing. She caught her brother's eye as she handed round bowls of nuts, and he shrugged. 'Mr Chambers used to play for one of the big clubs,' he said.

Will helped himself from Abbie's proffered bowls. 'Call me Will, please, Dan. You make me feel old with all this Mr stuff.'

'So you were a footballer ... Will,' Abbie said. 'Do you play now?'

'No, unfortunately I was in a car accident when I was nineteen,' Will said. 'Messed up my right ankle. I just kick around a bit now.

Maybe I'll come and watch you one day, Dan. Your dad says you're pretty good.' Abbie saw her brother blush, and she shook her head.

The Calladines arrived, each carrying a bottle. Soon Maggie took over Abbie's role in the kitchen, and Abbie was obliged to sit in the lounge with the guests. Tariq poured drinks for everyone, and the conversation grew more relaxed. Then Maggie Calladine emerged from the kitchen, fanning herself with her hand. 'Your mum needs you, Abbie.' Abbie nodded and escaped to the kitchen. From the open door she saw Maggie take a brimming glass from Tariq, and heard her say loudly, 'So, Will, how's the work coming along on the house?' Her face was flushed, and she sounded unusually excited.

'Abbie, love, can you get the starters out of the fridge while I drain these veg?' Julie said. 'Then put them on the table. And ask your dad to open the white wine that's in the fridge too. Two bottles.'

'Right.'

So far, so good. The meal was really nice. Mum had made a big effort, and everyone was eating and drinking and chatting. The adults were mellow. Dan and I kept quiet as much as we could. What were they all talking about? I hardly know. Will did a lot of talking and laughing, and Mum and Mrs Calladine were laughing along with him, obviously charmed. Dad just smiled and quietly played host. And Mr Calladine looked, I don't know, thoughtful. He's not a big smiler at the best of times, at least not in school. It was just as we were eating dessert (my recipe, a triumph if I say so myself) that things started to get interesting.

'That was delicious, Abbie. Your work, I gather?' Will said, laying down his spoon.

'It's quite simple – ' Abbie said, but Will was already turning away, saying something to Julie, who threw back her head and laughed. She got up from the table, wiping her eyes with her napkin. 'Abbie, Dan, help me clear away, will you, please?' They pushed their chairs back, hurried into the kitchen and took trays down from the shelf. Daniel, sensing that freedom was near, went round the table at speed, gathering dirty dishes. Afterwards, thinking about that moment, Abbie didn't know why she paused in the doorway. Perhaps it was something in David Calladine's tone as he remarked, 'Tell me, er ... Will, do you have a brother, perhaps? You remind me of someone I used to know.'

Will turned to David, his brown eyes moist and kindly. 'A brother? No, no brother.' He sighed, his face suddenly sad. 'I had a sister once. Rachel.' He fumbled in his jacket pocket. 'Here we are together.' He passed round a small black and white photograph of two children, a boy about four years old and a bigger girl.

'What happened to Rachel, Will?' Julie asked quietly.

'She died when she was sixteen,' Will said. 'Some horrible tropical disease. My parents never got over it.'

'I'm so sorry,' Julie murmured. 'How terribly sad.'

There was a solemn pause, then Will looked up at David, one eyebrow raised. 'So who do I remind you of, David?'

David waved a hand. 'Oh, it was years ago. I hardly knew the lad. I was a rookie teacher, in my probationary year. He was a bit of a bad lot, got expelled for some misdemeanour. I didn't really know much about it at the time. But the resemblance is only passing, anyway. He was blond, as I recall.'

Will chuckled. 'And I've always been quite dark, like Rachel. Anyway, I don't think I could be your bad lad, David. I grew up abroad mostly. Dad was a diplomat, so I went to international schools all over the world. We were in Pakistan when we lost Rachel.'

I realise it was then I began to have uncomfortable feelings about Will Chambers: kind of waves of coldness, a prickling up my arms. There was something about him that didn't seem quite right. I thought about it later, after they'd all gone home, and somehow all the stuff about playing for an English football team and a career cut short at nineteen by a car accident, and then that story about going to school abroad – how did that fit? I'd looked at his photograph too, when the others did, and I know he's a man and the boy in the photo was very young, but there was no resemblance at all. When everyone had left, all a bit merry and full of thank you and goodbye and what-a-lovely-evening, with Will clapping Dad on the shoulder and saying, all matey, 'See you in the morning, Tariq! Bright and early!' I lay on my bed and the thought came to me – out of nowhere, it seemed – that he was totally fake, and everything he'd said was a pretty parcel of lies.

The only trouble was, I couldn't fathom why.

The seeing didn't happen straight away. I shrugged off my misgivings, went to school and forgot about Will Chambers. He was nothing to do with me, whatever he was or pretended to be. And apart from schoolwork, which was getting pretty intense, I was just a bit distracted by a boy in Dan's football team, and my year, who came to our school last September from Ketley College. Dan, smirking and laughing at my expense, said this guy Olly'd asked for my number. I can say to these pages, since no one but me will ever read them, he is rather good-looking and has a very cheeky smile. I'm in no hurry, though – he can wait. Chances are he'll turn out like every other male. Not that I'm any expert.

I was sitting at my desk, laptop open, page blank, history textbook at my elbow, when out of the empty ether it struck – the longest, brightest, scariest seeing ever, before or since. Easily as bad as the earthquake four years ago which gave me so much grief.

How to describe it? Well, the hideous bug came first – about three inches long, yellowy-brown, with long spotty wings and massive skinny legs arching up above the body, plus huge insect eyes and twitchy antennae. And the eyes were looking right at me. As soon as I saw it I felt sick. I don't like bugs at the best of times, and this one looked fierce and wicked. Then it was like a camera panning back and back, and the thing disappeared, but immediately the sky went dark and there was an ominous humming, and I saw that it wasn't a black cloud but a huge swarm, miles long and wide, moving about in the wind but going on and on and on.

Then like a snap it stopped. Blank. But it wasn't over. There appeared a scene that seemed to unroll, ever so slowly: somewhere round the fuzzy edges there was green which I understood to be forests and fields, but in the middle was utter devastation: bare dark earth, not a blade of grass anywhere, and black leafless stumps of trees. It was like pictures I'd seen of the battlefields of the First World War. No life, no growth. A vision of death. A vision of hell.

And then it was gone. A spell of blankness, and I could see and hear again, normal sights and sounds: my bedroom, my desk lamp, my books. The washing machine chugging away in the kitchen. A car door slamming in the street. Everything was normal. Except it wasn't. I put my hand to my face, and found tears on my cheeks.

I took a tissue and wiped my eyes. My breathing came back to being regular, and my brain kicked in. I recognised the bug as a locust, because of the swarm and the stripped fields. (You don't go to church all your childhood without having some notion about that plague in old Egypt and Moses and Aaron and Pharaoh.) But I didn't know much about them so I looked them up on the internet. That gave me some references, and I found the Bible I got as a Sunday school prize when I was ten and tracked down the bits about locusts – not just the plague in Egypt, though that was pretty dramatic.

> So Moses raised his stick, and the LORD caused a wind from the east to blow on the land all that day and all that night. By morning it had brought the locusts. They came in swarms and settled over the whole country. It was the largest swarm of locusts that had ever been seen or that ever would be seen again. They covered the ground until it was black with them; they ate everything that the hail had left, including all the fruit on the trees. Not a green thing was left on any tree or plant in all the land of Egypt.

That was the story in Exodus that I remembered from when I was at Sunday school. Now, imagining the scene, it made me shiver. 'Not a green thing was left.'

But there was more. In Joel, chapter two.

> The great army of locusts advances like darkness spreading over the mountains ... Like fire they eat up the plants. In front of them the land is like the Garden of Eden, but behind them it is a barren desert. Nothing escapes them. They look like horses; they run like

62

war-horses. As they leap on the tops of the mountains, they rattle like chariots; they crackle like dry grass on fire ... They swarm through defenses, and nothing can stop them. They rush against the city; they run over the walls; they climb up the houses and go in through the windows like thieves.

By now I was wishing Joel hadn't had such a way with words. The thought of these creatures climbing walls and flying around your house was horrifying. I wasn't feeling too good by this point, but I had to keep on. This is what I found in Revelation.

The locusts looked like horses ready for battle; on their heads they had what seemed to be crowns of gold, and their faces were like human faces. Their hair was like women's hair, their teeth were like lions' teeth. Their chests were covered with what looked like iron breastplates, and the sound made by their wings was like the noise of many horse-drawn chariots rushing into battle.

Enough. I shut the Bible with a shudder and put it back on the shelf. I didn't really get the locusts looking like people or lions or wearing armour, but I could understand them being used as a horrifying symbol of unstoppable destruction. I did a bit of research on the internet, and I found accounts by travellers in parts of Africa which echoed the biblical stories. The horrible things are still active now! People still dread them more than anything, more than fire, because they destroy all the food and the people starve.

I went back to my blank page, but somehow I didn't feel like starting my history essay. Luckily I had a day or two before it was due in, plus a couple of free periods. I like to keep a bit ahead, especially now, because soon it'll be the Easter holidays and I'll be thinking about revision. I got up in a bit of a daze and went and lay down on my bed. The house was quiet; obviously the washing machine had finished its cycle. Only Mum and I were in the house, and Mum was in the office wrestling with the business accounts, or the VAT returns, or whatever. There must be some deadline coming up. Mum keeps all that side of things in order – it's pretty much double Dutch to me.

I thought it had to mean something, because it was so vivid, and so, I don't know, complete, almost like a message. Only one thing that I could think of was out of the ordinary in my life, and that was Will Chambers. The seeing was scary enough, but that thought made me go cold. What did it mean? And what should I do?

I must have been lying there for quite a while, because the next thing I knew was Mum's voice calling up the stairs. 'Abbie? You still alive up there? I've made some tea.'

So I went down and confirmed that I was still breathing and had a cuppa with Mum, who's still working on the accounts and looks worn out, and it was nice and friendly, just like old times. And then Dad and Dan came in and I went back upstairs to contemplate my history essay, but that's all I did: contemplate. Because now I was doubly conflicted: I didn't, and don't, want to talk about my seeings ever again, but if this is something different, should I warn Mum about our new neighbour? On the other hand, what has he done? Not a thing. Also, ever since Mum and I went together to see Mr Westwood, we've been getting along much better, and I don't want to mess that up. So I decided to wait and see. But that didn't stop a nasty little worry niggling away at the back of my brain.

Mr Westwood was occupying my thoughts as well. I hadn't really wanted to go and see him, not that I don't like him, because I do: he's a kind old gentleman who doesn't ask stupid questions or patronise you, but I was a bit afraid of what he would be like. I hear Mum and Dad and Mrs Calladine talking in quiet voices and looking sad and worried and I understand because he is very ill and they all love him. I was afraid he'd look like a skeleton or something. Cowardly, I know. Not to mention Mrs Westwood is a terror, though Mum says she has a heart of gold, whatever that means. No, I just went along because Dad thought it would make Mum happy. She probably thinks I am a typical selfish adolescent wrapped up in my own affairs and uncaring about anyone else. Maybe there's a bit of truth in that.

So I was apprehensive, to say the least. But it was OK. Mrs W let us in a bit grudgingly, but after a while she relented and made a cup of tea. (Actually she asked if I would prefer lemon squash! What am I, five years old?) Mr Westwood was sitting in an armchair in their conservatory. The heating was on full pelt because he felt the cold, and I had to peel off a few layers. He had a tartan rug over his knees as well. He seemed really pleased to see us, held on to Mum's hands, and looked at me with his pale blue eyes and a big smile. He looked a lot thinner and his hair was completely white and a bit patchy, but otherwise he seemed OK. He said he was on a new course of drugs and the medics were hopeful it might prolong his life for a while, but he didn't seem a bit bothered about dying. I suppose if you really believe in Heaven, dying might not be quite so bad. I don't think I could be quite so – what's the word? – stoical about dying, whatever I believed in. But then Mr Westwood is quite old.

Anyway, he asked me a few questions about my life and what I thought about various things, nothing about religion or Heaven or death, I'm happy to say, and in the end I was glad I went, because he really did seem pleased to see me. I guess he remembers dear little Abbie when she was a cute kid. Why would he have any interest in me otherwise?

The next day after seeing the locusts it was Sunday. Dad said I should come along to church, because they had a visiting speaker. Both Mum and Dad try to get me to go back once in a while, but just as an invitation: I don't have to go any more, and I guess they think if they made me go it would be counterproductive. They're right about that. I told Dad I hadn't finished my schoolwork, which was true enough, but he'd asked so nicely that in a moment of rashness I said I'd go along with them at Easter. Anyway, that Sunday Dan was playing football somewhere, as usual, so I was left to my own devices. I made some notes a bit half-heartedly, earned some brownie points by peeling the potatoes, then I decided to go out for a walk. I had a bit of a headache, the locusts thing was worrying me, and I thought a bit of fresh air might help. Do I sound middle-aged or what?

I wandered around for a while in the little belt of woodland down the end of the road where the Calladines live. I passed the cottage where Dad was working for Will Chambers, and saw sacks of cement and stuff down the side entrance. The front garden had been cleared quite roughly – there were still stalks of brambles and nettles sticking up and the grass was yellow. Down in the woods it was quiet, just the wind making the branches sway around, and there were primroses out in little clumps, and everything smelled earthy. I was thinking about getting back when I heard a sharp yelp, like an animal in trouble. I thought it might be a fox, but then I came round a big tree trunk and about twenty feet away there was our new neighbour, and he was bending over his dog, holding her by the collar, twisting it, and she's backing off, whining and trying to get away. He was saying something to her and his tone was angry. Then I saw him quite clearly pinch her ear with his free hand and heard her yelp again.

I can't stand people being mean to animals. No one is forced to have a pet, but if they have one they should be kind to it. I didn't really think whether I should – I just yelled, 'Hey!' He released the dog's lead and straightened up as I came level with him.

'Oh, hello, Abbie,' he said, smiling as if nothing had happened.

'What were you doing to her?' I demanded.

'What?' he frowned, looking puzzled. 'Nothing at all.'

'I heard her yelp. I saw you pinch her,' I said.

He actually laughed. 'No, no, you're mistaken. I wouldn't hurt my Molly, would I, girl?' And he bent and ruffled her head, and she cringed a bit but still wagged her tail. 'She had a thistle stuck in her fur, that's all.'

I didn't believe him. I knew what I'd seen. But there wasn't much I could say. After that, seeing me frowning and silent, he just said, 'Well, we'd better be off. Nice seeing you, Abbie.' And he went back up towards the lane, whistling. Whistling! As if we'd just had a pleasant neighbourly chat, and I hadn't seen him abusing his dog.

I walked slowly home, feeling sick. Dan and I have wanted our own dog for ages, and I'm sure we'd know how to treat one. If we don't persuade Mum and Dad soon it'll be too late for me – in a year and a half I might be at university. And Will Chambers was making me feel more and more uncomfortable, but there was still not much I could do about it. I wasn't even sure if my instincts were right.

Something happened the next day, though, that added to my feeling that there was something about him that stank.

I was standing at the bus stop. I'd missed the bus I usually get to school, because I couldn't find a clean white shirt. I had to iron one at the last minute, and it made me late. Dan and all the other kids had caught the bus OK, but I was on my own at the stop, waiting for the next one. To my horror a battered green saloon pulled up at the kerb with a squeal of brakes, and Will Chambers wound down the window and called out to me. 'Morning, Abbie! Lovely morning.'

I muttered something in reply and looked down at the pavement – anywhere but at him. But he wasn't going anywhere, it seemed. 'Missed the bus?' he said. 'I'm going into Walburn – I'll give you a lift if you like.'

There was Molly sitting on the back seat, wagging her feathery tail. My stomach churned. But there was no way I was getting into any car with him. 'No, thank you,' I said in my frostiest voice. 'I'm waiting for a friend.'

He seemed unperturbed by my obvious hostility. 'Sure?' he asked. 'You don't want to be late.'

'No, thank you. I prefer to wait.' And I rudely turned my back on him.

There was a pause. Then he muttered, 'Suit yourself.' He crunched the gears and roared away. At that moment, very briefly but unmistakably, I saw it again: the huge creepy insect with its twitching antennae. When it was gone, I found I was shaking. But any doubts I may have had up till then had completely disappeared.

All the way to school on the chugging bus I thought about what I should do. More and more I thought, I have to tell someone what I've seen. Perhaps I can do it casually, without mentioning the locusts. But there are some things I need to find out first, and I need to tread carefully. The trouble with being young is so often nobody takes you seriously.

April 2010

Soft-footed, Abbie came down the stairs, pausing every few steps to listen, holding her noisy breath. The thought came to her that she was like a thief in her own house; her anxiety about Will Chambers had robbed her of her easy life. But then, remembering the yelping dog and the vision of the swarm, anger rose up in her, and with it resolve, that if he were bent on some kind of destruction she would oppose him.

She heard her parents talking in the kitchen. Tariq, working close to home, had come in for a coffee break. Normally she wouldn't have thought of eavesdropping: why bother, when parental conversation was so boring? But words she caught, Julie's words, Tariq's grunts of agreement, held her there, listening. The kitchen door was ajar, and they weren't whispering.

'He seems like quite an asset, doesn't he?' Julie said. 'Will, I mean. D'you think this renovation might go on a while?'

'Hm. I don't know,' Tariq answered after a pause. 'There's a lot to do, and he's got plenty of plans. He keeps changing his mind, though. I seem to spend a lot of time persuading him to do the sensible thing. He goes off at tangents.'

'Is he always there, then?'

'Most of the time. I wish he'd leave me be, let me get on with the work.'

'So isn't he working on his novel? He told Maggie it was coming on in leaps and bounds.'

'Who knows? I've not seen him working. He's got the little bedroom at the back kitted out with a table and chair and there's a laptop there, but I've not seen him use it.'

'Perhaps you being there's a distraction and he works at night,' Julie said.

'Maybe. The only time I get any peace is when he takes the dog out. Oh, yes, and when he's round at Maggie's, or chatting to her over the fence.'

'Maggie said he's been talking to her about all sorts of deep things,' Julie said. 'Apparently he was raised Catholic, but hasn't been to church for years. He was asking her about John, and the situation here, even said he might come along one Sunday. Told her he's searching for some meaning in his life.'

'Just up Maggie's street, then,' Tariq said, obviously munching on a biscuit.

'What?'

'Maggie being a Samaritan.'

'She wouldn't tell him that, would she?' Julie said. Abbie could hear her moving around the kitchen, opening and shutting cupboard doors. 'Anyway, she said he's thinking about joining the bell-ringers. Says he's got experience.'

'Oh, right.'

'*And* he's volunteered to mow the churchyard. That's what I mean about him being an asset.'

Abbie heard her father get up, stretch and groan. 'If he carries through with all these things, I'll agree with you, love. But as I say, he's a man full of plans.'

'Sounds like you don't trust him, Riq.'

'No, I just don't know him very well. Anyway, I'd better get back to work. I'll see you at lunchtime.' Abbie cringed back against the wall, prepared for flight. But then she saw her father pause in the doorway, his back to her. 'Is Maggie all right? She seems OK, but not so long ago you were convinced she was at the end of her rope.'

'I never told you, did I? Sorry, darling, things just got away from me a bit. Blame it on the business accounts.' Abbie heard her mother chuckle, as if this was some kind of private joke she shared with Tariq. 'I had quite a chat with Maggie the day after those puzzling phone calls. The same day I noticed Will's car in the lane. Maggie said she felt like she'd got to the bottom of a very dark pit, for sure. But then she prayed and thought, and decided it was up to her to make things better. If she waited for David to change, she'd die waiting. David's a good chap, but he's very peculiar.'

Abbie saw Tariq scratch his head. 'Probably true of all men, according to you. The peculiar bit, I mean.'

Julie snorted. 'Definitely. Anyway, she's making a big effort to be more cheerful, supportive and wifely. Ugh. Maybe she's softening him up, ready for another assault about this baby thing.'

'If it isn't working, what can he do?'

'Be willing to discuss it. Be open to the possibility of IVF, maybe, or even adoption, before it's too late. Maggie's thirty-nine this year – time's not on her side.'

'Oh, I see.'

'Anyway, for now, things have settled down. And Will being next door is providing a distraction, at least. She seems to enjoy his company.'

'That's true,' Tariq said. 'He's often round there.'

'It's the school holidays, isn't it?' Julie reasoned. 'So Maggie's at home more. I doubt you'll have seen anything of David, though. He'll be at school, catching up with things, even in the holidays. Sometimes I think Maggie's on a loser with him – whatever her brave resolutions, he isn't reciprocating, it seems to me. What a foolish man. I'm sure he loves Maggie, somewhere in that well-hidden heart of his, but he's very hard work.'

'On that cheery note,' Tariq said, 'I must get back to work.'

Abbie heard her mother sigh. 'So must I. I said I'd get it done by Easter, and tomorrow is Good Friday.'

Abbie saw her father step further into the kitchen, out of her line of sight. His voice came to her slightly muffled. 'So it is. A few days off. Nice.' Then he turned back to the door, and Abbie bolted silently back up the stairs.

A few moments later she saw her father walk down the front path, and leaned out of her bedroom window. 'Dad!'

Tariq turned, shading his eyes. 'Oh, you're up, then.' He grinned.

'I've been up ages, actually. Working, just like you. I was wondering, any chance of a bit of driving practice later?'

'I'll see. If I finish at Will's in good time I'll take you out for half an hour before dinner.' He paused, and thought. 'Your mum's really busy, though, so see if you can give her a hand sometime, OK?'

'Hang the washing out, chop the carrots, that sort of thing?'

'Yep.'

'No problem. I'll see if I can get Dan out of bed too.'

'Good girl.' And he was gone with a wave of his hand.

Abbie slid into the driver's seat. 'Feels weird, driving a proper car.'

'What's not proper about my trusty van?' Tariq sounded pained.

'Bumpy, clattery, stiff gears, violent brake ...'

'Just drive.'

She pulled out onto the road and signalled right. 'Where shall we go?'

'Out of Halstead towards Walburn, left at the crossroads, right at the Hare and Hounds, into that housing estate and we'll practise a three-point turn.'

'Right.'

Twenty minutes later, after several rocky starts and stalling embarrassingly in the middle of the road with other cars waiting to pass, Abbie finally executed a reasonable manoeuvre.

'Can we stop for a few minutes?' she said. 'My nerves are frayed.'

'*Your* nerves? What about my nerves?' Tariq said. 'They're in tatters.'

'I know, Dad,' Abbie said soothingly. She parked rather abruptly at the kerb. 'You're an absolute saint to come out driving with me. Brave too.'

'I am. Phew.' He leaned back in the seat.

'I was thinking, Dad – something I wanted to ask you.'

'If it's money, I don't have any.'

'No, nothing like that. At least, I don't want any. I was wondering how a builder gets paid.'

'How do you mean?'

She turned to face him. 'Well, do you get cash upfront? Or after the job's done? You have to buy materials, don't you? Suppose the client changes his mind – you'd end up with a load of stuff you couldn't use.'

Tariq squinted at her and pursed his lips. 'A lot depends on the size of the job. You give the customer an estimate, and they agree to it. If there's any chance of it changing, you have to consult them, of course. For example, if something comes up neither of you has thought of, or if they want something extra. If you were building a house, say, you'd get a payment before work began, to cover the initial purchase of materials, and for your labour. Then there'd be one or two more payments which you'd decide on beforehand, and the final account once the job was finished and the customer said he's satisfied.'

'What about smaller jobs?'

'You'd still have upfront money, but maybe just that and the final account.'

'Is that how you've arranged things with Will Chambers?'

Tariq sighed. 'Well, funny you should mention him, because he keeps having new ideas and changing his mind. In a case like that I make sure he knows how much more it's going to cost, and I always write it down. He just shrugs and says "OK" to everything, like he's a millionaire. Maybe he is. All I know is he's paid up for the start of work. He gave me a nice fat envelope full of notes, your mum counted it and put it in the bank. That's the businesslike way, the safe way.'

'Can't trust anyone these days, Dad.'

'Are you taking the mickey?'

Abbie grinned. 'As if.'

Tariq looked at his watch. 'We'd better make tracks. Shall I drive home?'

'OK.'

They changed seats and Tariq pulled smoothly away. 'See? That's how it's done.' Abbie pulled a face. 'Funny, though,' he said thoughtfully, 'he's a strange one, Will, a bit erratic and disorganised. Seems to have a lot of money just lying around.' He turned onto the main road, changed gear and accelerated away. 'Oh well, as long as he pays me it's not my problem.'

Abbie lay on her bed, her eyes closed. Apart from her desk lamp, the room was in darkness. Ostensibly she was doing exam revision. She could hear the sound of the television from the lounge, and the occasional burst of masculine laughter. On another day she might have joined them, but not today: her thoughts were too insistent and chaotic.

Now what do I do? OK, I have a bad feeling about this guy Will Chambers. But who's going to believe something so feeble? What's my evidence? Yes, I saw him being mean to his dog. But he'll deny it, like he did to me. OK, so I had a really clear seeing I think was about him, and that's harder to account for. But if I can avoid talking about it, I will. And who would I tell? Dad would listen but he wouldn't do anything. He thinks my thing is like his, small insignificant flashes that you grow out of. He'd just go and tell Mum, anyway. I know I was angry with Mum for putting me through all that, after I saw the earthquake. But if I am being fair, she had to do what she did. If I was a parent, I guess I'd have done the same. But then, because she found out I didn't have anything physically wrong with me, she kind of discounts it. Or perhaps she doesn't, but I don't tell her I still have the seeings, so how can she know? If I tell her my thoughts about Will Chambers, she'll want more reasons than I've got. If I tell her about the locusts, will that add weight? Or convince her I'm nuts/sick? I think I have to tell someone, but who, what and when? I don't want this problem – I want to hand it to someone else. But is there anyone who won't laugh or rationalise or just ignore? What the heck do I do?

Easter Sunday

Abbie sat half way down the nave on the pulpit side, sandwiched between her father and brother. Julie was on the other side of Daniel. Abbie looked surreptitiously round the church as it filled up. Her family had arrived early as always: she never knew why. There were people she'd never seen before, just because it was Easter, she supposed, but also people she knew, most of them elderly. Mrs Cocksedge who lived opposite had just come in with her friend, another widow, Mrs Lyons. They were often together, on the bus, drinking tea in each other's houses, sitting together in church: old-school Anglicans, liked things done the way they should be, critical of visiting preachers, simply because they weren't John Westwood. Abbie watched them get settled in their seat, caught Mrs Cocksedge's eye and smiled. The old lady smiled back, and Abbie almost knew what she was saying as she nudged her friend and whispered. *So nice to see all the Hasans in church, isn't it, dear? My, how those children have grown! Such a lovely family, such devout parents. Etc.*

Abbie turned and faced the front, smiling to herself. She saw Julie looking at her, frowning. *Oh, dear. Am I misbehaving already? Those dear old ladies are funny, though. I bet they're giving us the once-over, checking out Dan's incipient moustache. I suppose, from his point of view, that's one advantage of being half-Indian. All his little fourteen-year-old mates are still as smooth as babies. It's no advantage for a half-Indian girl, though. That's the one good thing that came out of that grim episode when I had to see the shrinks and have all those bizarre tests: I managed to persuade Mum to let me get rid of mine, permanently. Can you imagine? If I ever got to kiss Olly Bradshaw, with a prickly upper lip! No, I shouldn't really snigger in church. And it probably won't ever happen.*

The old ladies still talk about Dad as well. 'Did you know, my dear, he was born and raised a Muslim?' Honestly! Dad's been a Christian for twenty years! And to the best of my knowledge he's never wavered, even though it cost him his family. He likes to make it very clear, though, that him being converted wasn't Mum's doing. I suppose it would look pretty feeble, and not very convincing, changing your religion because you fancied someone. He always says he met Jesus before he met Mum. Thinking about what Dad had to give up for God, I hope God appreciates it. Anyway, that's Dad's path, not mine. I have to follow my own way, if I ever find out what it is.

She felt Dan nudge her, and looked up and round. The Calladines were making their way up the nave, into the pew opposite and a few rows down, and between them, sporting a collar and tie and respectable jacket, was Will Chambers. David was as expressionless as ever, but Maggie was flushed and breathless. She was handing Will a service sheet and a hymn book, and as he took them from her with a word of thanks he glanced up and saw Abbie staring. The smile that spread across his handsome face was knowing, triumphant and complicit all at once. Abbie turned abruptly again to face the front, her heart lurching, and she caught a glance that passed between Julie and Tariq, a look that spoke of delight and satisfaction. Abbie groaned inwardly. *Oh, parents. Sometimes you are so naïve. Maybe it's something to do with being Christians and always having to think the best of everyone.*

All through the service she was uncomfortably aware of him, not far behind her, his eyes on her back. She could almost feel them burning her skin, and once or twice she squirmed. She could hear him too, singing far too loudly. His voice was sweet-toned but slightly off-key, and it clanged in her ears like a discordant bell. *Pipe down, can't you, you show-off. You know perfectly well how sick you make me, and you're enjoying every minute. Not to mention all this adulation – is that the word? – just because you're someone different who might swell this tiny congregation, and who isn't a hundred years old. I remember how they all fussed over that young family who turned up last summer. They came for a few weeks, and then vanished. Can't say I blame them.*

76

At last it was over, and they all trooped out into the churchyard, speckled through the trees with weak spring sunshine. The visiting preacher was shaking hands heartily with everyone, *even though he doesn't know us from Adam,* and people were greeting each other, and Abbie had to recognise their genuine joy because their Lord was risen. *Oh, boy. What am I to make of all this stuff?*

Julie and Tariq went to speak to Will and the Calladines, and with a stiff little smile in their direction Abbie grabbed her brother by the elbow and sidled past the knots of people, down the church path and out of the gate.

'Shouldn't we wait?' Daniel said, frowning.

'OK, but out here by the wall, where we won't be clobbered by sweet old ladies.'

'Or where you won't have to talk to Will Chambers,' Daniel said, his voice gruff. He cleared his throat. 'You don't like him much, do you?'

Abbie looked at her brother, her eyebrows raised. 'That's very perceptive of you, bro. What makes you think I don't like him?'

'Maybe the faces you pull when he's around,' Daniel said.

'I do not!' Abbie punched his arm. 'Just because you think he's so very wonderful with his football tales.'

Daniel looked at his feet, scuffing the ground with the toes of his trainers. 'Well, actually,' he said slowly, looking up at his sister through long, dark lashes, 'I think he might have been exaggerating a bit there.'

'Go on, tell me.'

'Don't say anything to Mum or Dad, though, will you?' Daniel said, suddenly anxious.

'Not a word.'

'I asked him a few innocent questions, when you were in the kitchen, about the club he was supposed to have played for, and he was kind of vague, but when I went on asking he came out with a name of some team I'd never heard of, so I looked it up, and I don't think it exists.'

Abbie nodded. 'Why am I not surprised?'

'Maybe he was just trying to impress his new neighbours,' Dan said. 'Probably nothing to get excited about.'

'I thought you were the excited one,' Abbie said sourly. 'Especially when he said he'd come and watch you play.'

'Whoa, do me a favour, Abs. I'm not that stupid. He can come if he likes, I don't care. I don't need any new mates, not if they're almost as old as Mum and Dad.'

'Is he?'

'I heard Mrs Calladine tell Mum. He's thirty-eight, she said.'

'Old as the hills, then, bro.'

'What was it Mum used to say? "Old enough to know better, young enough not to care." Was that it?'

'Ha, yeah, something like that.' Her voice sharpened. 'Enough about him, Dan. They're saying goodbye. Maybe we can go home. I don't know about you, but I'm starving.'

Then momentarily, like a cloud passing across a summer sky, her vision darkened, and the cloud became the swarm, heaving, swaying, blotting out the sun. She felt Dan pinch her arm, and she gasped as her vision cleared. She looked up, and there was Julie right in front of her with Will Chambers. Tariq and the Calladines were close behind, chatting and laughing and taking no notice, but Julie was staring at Abbie as if she had sprouted an extra head.

'Abbie? Mr Chambers was speaking to you.'

'Oh, sorry,' Abbie said, hearing her own voice shrill and false. 'Wool-gathering, I'm afraid.' She forced herself to look pleasant. 'What were you saying, Mr Chambers?'

'Will, please! Really, it was nothing important.' He smiled at her, and then there seemed to flash in his dark eyes something like recognition, and the smile took on a knowing slyness that made Abbie's stomach shrivel. *He knows. But how can he know? He saw something, saw I was not here for a moment. Is that possible? Somehow anything could be possible with this man.*

The moment passed, and as they all came through the gate, Will turned and waved his hand expansively around the churchyard. 'Once it dries up, I'll get this cut and tidy,' he said loudly. 'Maggie kindly said she'd lend me her mower.'

Abbie saw the remaining group of worshippers turn and smile, but noted a look of surprise on David Calladine's face. He said nothing, and in a few minutes the Hasans were at their own front gate and everybody was saying goodbye.

It took another two days before Abbie felt brave enough to approach her mother. Tariq had taken the van to a job the other side of Walburn, on his way dropping Daniel off to meet some friends in the shopping centre.

Abbie stared at her cluttered books and folders with something like desperation. *How am I supposed to concentrate? I have to get this over with, whatever the result. I have a horrible feeling it's going to get messy.*

She made two cups of coffee and put her head round the office door. 'Mum? I thought you could use a break.' She put a mug down carefully on a corner of the desk. 'How are you getting on?'

Julie leaned back in her chair and rubbed her eyes. 'Almost there. It shouldn't have taken this long, but I made a mistake.' She took a sip of coffee. 'Thanks, love. This is welcome.'

Abbie perched on the edge of a small stool next to the desk. 'I guess it's easy to slip up among all those numbers,' she said. 'Even with something you've done loads of times.'

Julie nodded. She looked weary: her eyes were heavy. 'You doing OK?' she asked absently, still studying her computer screen.

'Not really,' Abbie said. She took a deep breath. 'Mum, there's something I need to talk to you about. Please don't yell at me. Please just hear me out, OK?'

Julie looked at her, frowning. 'Why, what have you done?'

'I haven't done anything. But I'm worried.' She paused, looking at her mother. 'It's Will Chambers. I think there's something, I don't know, not right about him.'

Julie's frown darkened. 'You hardly know him, I'd have thought. Has he said or done something to give you this rather wild opinion?'

'Apart from abusing his dog, I guess not.'

'What? What are you talking about?' Julie jerked her head up, spilling coffee on the desk.

'It was last Sunday,' Abbie blurted. 'I was in the woods, down at the end of the lane. I saw him pinch her ear, really hard, and she yelped. I challenged him, and he said he was pulling a thistle out of her fur. But I know what I saw. Mum, I swear, there's something dodgy about him. When he came to dinner, all those stories he told us, they just don't add up.'

'Hang on! All this, on the basis of something you *might* have seen him do to his dog, and a bit of social exaggeration?' Julie said. 'Really, Abbie, it's not what I would call evidence.' Abbie said nothing. 'As far as I can see, Will Chambers is an ordinary, pleasant new neighbour. Work for your father, which is always welcome. Someone who's willing to get involved in the community, help Maggie out with school stuff, ring bells, mow the grass. You heard him. For Heaven's sake, Abbie. Curb your imagination. What you're telling me is fantasy, not reality. If you want to know what reality is, it's right here. Getting these numbers straight so the business prospers, so you and Dan can have the things you want. In your case, it's doing your best in your exams so you can have some kind of career. Not all this nonsense.'

Abbie swallowed. 'I didn't want to have to tell you this,' she said, her voice small. 'After he came here for the meal, I had a seeing. What you would call a vision, I guess. Like the one of the earthquake four years ago. Only this was different. It was like a message. And I've had more little flashes of the same thing and every time it was in connection with him. Mum, it was horrible.' Her voice rose in desperation. 'I saw a big winged insect with huge eyes and waving antennae, and a massive swarm that ate everything up until the green fields were a desert of black stumps. It was just like the plague of locusts in the Bible.'

Julie stared at her. When she spoke her voice was harsh. 'You told me, not so long ago, that you didn't have these ... these visions any more.'

Abbie felt herself choke with rising tears. 'I know. I lied, and I'm sorry. But don't you see why I didn't want to talk about it ever again? That was a really bad time for me. I felt like a freak. I still do, quite often.' Tears were running down her face, and she stretched out her hand to her mother, but saw her stony face and let it fall. 'Mum, look, I know I was horrible to you. I know you did what any parent would have done in the circumstances. I just hated it, that's all – the seeings themselves, the sense of being weird, all those tests, that awful helmet with the electrodes, people at school laughing at me behind my back, that sneaky treacherous little rat Zara Chesterfield, all of it. And what I said to you then wasn't so much of a lie, anyway. I've had hardly any episodes since then, none of them so, I don't know, *organised, significant*. Until now.'

Julie said nothing for a long moment, but her face was haggard. She let out a long breath. 'You're saying that these visions have come back because of Will Chambers? Someone we barely know? Someone who's done nothing to harm anyone, that we know of?'

'Locusts are destroyers. People's lives are wrecked because of them.'

'I know what locusts do,' Julie said impatiently. 'But this all sounds to me like a bad case of overdramatisation. And frankly I don't have time for your fantastical tales. I have far too much to do. *Real* stuff, not fantasy. Perhaps that's what you should be concentrating on as well.'

'I didn't want to tell you any of this,' Abbie whispered. 'Any more than I wanted to have the seeings in the first place. I want to be normal. But I had to tell you. I really, really hope I'm wrong. But if I'm not, at least I tried to warn you.'

Julie sighed. 'Do you want to get checked out again?'

Abbie shook her head violently. 'That's the last thing I want. I only told you about the locusts to try and convince you my fears are for real. I don't seem to have done a very good job, have I? Perhaps I should let you get on with your version of reality.'

She slid off the stool and left the room. Julie sat with her back to her daughter, her head in her hands. Abbie felt tears rise again, and closed the door.

Lying on her bed, the curtains closed, Abbie heard the front door shut and the car start up and roar away. Where her mother had gone, she had no idea. She got up, went to the bathroom and washed her face. Downstairs, she ran a glass of water and took painkillers: her head was throbbing. She realised she'd had very little breakfast, so she made herself a sandwich. She sat at the kitchen counter as she ate, hearing the small sounds of the house all around her: the lazy ticking of the kitchen clock, the hum of the fridge, her own ragged breathing. She closed her eyes. Distantly, birds were chattering in the garden – nesting, probably, busy with their instinct-driven lives. It was spring, so you built a nest and found a mate and laid eggs, hoping no predator would find them, that they would have a chance to hatch and fledge and fly. A life full of hazards, but simple, determined by the need to survive. How much more complicated to be human, with all its social and cultural expectations. Abbie sighed and took her plate to the sink. *I wouldn't mind trying a bird's life, maybe for a day. Though I'd probably get picked off by something big and fierce.*

She trudged back up to her bedroom, listlessly opened her folder and tried to revise. Around mid-afternoon she heard the car return, the door slam, her mother's key in the lock. She tensed. *I wish Dad and Dan were home. I feel I've opened a door I can't shut, and nasty things are pouring out of it.*

Then she heard footsteps on the stairs and a quiet knock on her door. She got up and opened it. 'Mum.'

'Can I come in?'

'Of course.'

Julie took a step or two into the room, and turned to her daughter, her face anguished. 'Oh, Abs. What a mess.' She opened her arms and hugged Abbie tightly. Then she took her hand and sat beside her on the edge of the bed. 'I'm sorry, sweetie, I wasn't very nice earlier. You took me by surprise.'

'I know, Mum. I dropped it on you from a great height.'

Julie heaved a sigh. 'Thing is, that episode with you and the medics, after the earthquake, was a tough time for me as well. And your dad. We were terribly worried, and he felt guilty into the bargain.'

Abbie's head came up. 'It wasn't his fault.'

'I know. But he blamed himself, not only for letting you see how distressed he was, but also for some kind of genetic blip. Maybe he was thinking of your aunt Zaynab.'

Abbie frowned. 'Who?'

Julie smiled faintly. 'I didn't know of her existence either till four years ago. He never even knew her – she died before he was born. And it could have been just something normal – tragic, of course, but easily explained in the ordinary way of things: she was ill, or had an accident, and died. But because his family either knew nothing or refused to mention it, your dad got the notion that there was something odd about her. When you had your vision he began to make connections that may have been completely wrong.' She paused, and thought for a moment. 'That's one of the awful things about your father's situation – there's so much he can't ever find out. He doesn't say much, does he? But it's there. Always.'

'Poor Dad. And I woke it up again.'

Julie squeezed Abbie's hand. 'No way your fault. But there it is. It's something we're aware of, something that worries us. The average parents want their kids to be safe, to be doing all right. Threats to their well-being knock them off-balance. They say things that aren't helpful.'

'It's OK, Mum.'

Julie got up with a quiet groan, flexing her shoulders. 'Did you have any lunch?'

'A sandwich. Tasted like sawdust.'

'I'll make us some tea. Come down in five minutes.'

'OK. But Mum – what about him? Will Chambers?'

'I don't know, Abbie. I can't honestly judge someone on what you've told me – it seems unfair. I believe you, of course – I believe you believe, if you get me. But I can't sit in condemnation of a man I barely know.'

Abbie looked up at her mother, pleading in her eyes. 'Can you just, I don't know, keep a watch on things? I don't think I can do it on my own.'

Julie nodded. 'You'll have to accept I bring my own prejudices, though. Like giving people the benefit of the doubt.'

'Yeah, OK.'

Dinner was unusually quiet. Tariq and Daniel, sensing something had happened in their absence, kept their own counsel. They talked about their day, but there was none of the normal fooling around, and once they had all eaten and the dishes were disposed of, both Abbie and Daniel escaped to their own rooms.

Just before nine o'clock there was a tap on Abbie's door and Tariq's head appeared. 'You decent?'

Abbie looked up from her open book. 'Well, if I wasn't, it would be too late.' She grinned. 'But seeing as I am not dancing round the room naked, come in.'

'No, come outside with me. There's something I want you to see. Be quick.'

'Will I need shoes?'

'Yes, the grass is damp.'

Abbie tugged on a pair of shoes that she had carelessly discarded by her bedroom door. Tariq took her hand and pulled her after him down the stairs. She could hear the sound of the TV from the lounge and harsh music from Dan's room. Tariq put his finger to his lips as he opened the back door.

It was almost dark. When her eyes adjusted, Abbie could see darker clouds building up above the silhouettes of the trees at the end of the garden, but there was just enough light to see by.

'Where are we going?' she whispered.

'Shh. Look. On the overhead wire.'

She focused. 'I can't see anything. Oh – yes, I can. What is it?'

Tariq's voice was hoarse. 'It's an owl. A barn owl, I think. He'll know we're here. Wait, see if he flies.'

A moment later the bird lifted off, its great rounded wings rising and falling silently, its shape momentarily etched against the darkening sky as it disappeared among the trees.

'Isn't that a beautiful sight?' Tariq breathed.

'It's so quiet. I didn't hear any flapping or fluttering.'

'They fly in almost total silence,' Tariq said. 'No wonder they're such successful hunters. That and their huge eyes. Watch out, voles.'

'Wow.' Abbie wrapped her arms round her body. 'Can we go inside now, Dad? It's getting chilly.'

'Sure. I just wanted you to see him. Owls are amazing, aren't they? I'm hoping he's thinking of nesting round here.'

'Wouldn't that be *she*?'

They went back inside the kitchen.

'Maybe,' Tariq said. He smiled, and his eyes crinkled. 'But both parents help to raise the babies, like us.'

'D'you want a cup of coffee now I've stopped work?'

'Mm, yes, please.'

'I'll make one for Mum and Dan while I'm at it.' She filled the kettle and plugged it in. 'I was thinking about birds earlier today, oddly. Listening to them making a racket in the garden. I thought how much simpler it would be to be one.'

Tariq shook his head. 'Dangerous, too. But it's a privilege to be human, Abs.'

'Is it?'

'Of course it is. With all its ups and downs and trials, we have choices, the ability to think outside our circumstances, to make things different.' He paused, thinking. 'Well, at least, some of us do. Of course, some poor souls are too busy trying to survive for any of that, a bit like animals and birds. But it shouldn't be so.'

Abbie lined up four mugs and put a spoonful of instant coffee in each. The kettle clicked off and she poured water into the mugs. Tariq took some milk from the fridge and handed it to her.

'I'll take these to your mum and Dan,' he said, picking up two mugs after she had added milk. 'Don't go away.'

When he came back he slid into the seat opposite her at the kitchen table. 'Your mum was telling me about what you and she were talking about earlier.'

'Oh. Well, I suppose that was inevitable.'

'What?'

'Do you and Mum always tell each other everything?'

Tariq made a face. 'Pretty much. Not necessarily the boring details, like how many cups of tea I've had all day or how long the lights took to change at the crossroads. But important things, yeah. If it concerns you and your brother, of course. We're just like Mr and Mrs Owl.'

'Ha, ha. Voles for breakfast tomorrow, then? So would you ever consider keeping a secret from her?'

Tariq shrugged. 'Only if you'd bought her a birthday present and wanted it to be a surprise, or something like that. Otherwise, probably not. Why? Have you got a secret you want kept?'

'No. Just asking theoretically. I thought you'd probably say that anyway. You're lucky, Dad – do you know that?'

'Blessed beyond measure, love. Thankful every day.'

Abbie fell silent for a moment, drinking her coffee, staring unseeing at the table. Tariq also said nothing, watching her covertly, seeing her expressions change, waiting.

'So, Dad,' Abbie said, looking up at him, 'tell me what you really think about these, you know, these visions I get. Especially just lately. The locusts.' She shuddered.

'I don't know, Abs,' Tariq said slowly. 'I just don't know. Your mum mentioned my sister, didn't she? Zaynab, the one I never knew. I wish I could find out what became of her. Maybe it's got nothing to do with what happens to you. Maybe she got run over. Maybe she had cancer. Maybe she took her own life. I have no idea. But maybe she saw things too, things that weren't there. Maybe it's something in our family.' He sighed. 'When all that kicked off, four years ago, we were really worried you had something major wrong. Like a brain tumour. What a terrible thought. Makes me shiver even now to think about it.' He sipped his coffee. 'But that wasn't the first thing your mum thought of. Obviously she was going to make an appointment with the GP soon as she could. But the first thing she did was go and see John Westwood.'

Abbie frowned. 'Really? I never knew that.'

'Well, it wasn't as if he could really throw any light on it. He'd never come across it before, not in his own experience. Plenty of examples in the Bible, though.'

Abbie's eyes widened. 'What! You're kidding me, Dad, for goodness' sake! You'll be telling me next I'm some kind of wailing prophet. Please!'

'I don't think you're anything, except super-clever, of course. But it gave John Westwood something to think about. Maybe you never noticed this, but he's always taken an interest in you. Unobtrusively, discreetly. He's asked the occasional question over the years.'

'Has he?' Abbie muttered. 'So nice to be the freak.'

'Not a freak,' Tariq said gently. 'Perhaps a bit different, that's all.'

'I don't want to be different,' Abbie said bleakly. 'Not in that way. Different as in stunningly beautiful, now that would be OK. Or even super-clever, which I'm not. You're just biased.'

'Yes I am,' Tariq said. 'And yes, you are. Beautiful *and* clever. As I've told you before, many times.'

'Well, I get whatever it is from you and Mum, and neither of you were exactly stupid,' Abbie said. 'I know, Dad, you didn't take your degrees. And I know why.'

Tariq raised his eyebrows. 'Oh, you do, do you?'

'It's a shame things were so backward in those days,' Abbie said with some heat. 'These days, if you were students and you had a baby you could put it in a crèche and carry on with your studies.'

'Neither of us regrets it,' Tariq said softly. 'Things have worked out OK.'

'Even though you needn't have given it all up?'

'Even so. We still have everything that's important to us. Of course we were devastated at the time, and still are sad, to have lost that little one. A girl, did you know? Which is probably why it was extra special that you turned out to be a girl. But we have everything to be thankful for.'

'Maybe one day I'll have that too, Dad. That certainty. What do you think?'

'I hope so. I pray so.'

Abbie took a deep breath. 'I'd better get on. Perhaps fit in another hour before my brain shuts down. Anyway, isn't it time for the news?'

Tariq glanced at the clock. 'So it is.' He leaned over and ruffled her hair. 'Don't work too late, kiddo.'

Abbie dutifully put in another hour, as she'd promised herself. With her thoughts whirling around so chaotically it wasn't the most profitable hour she'd ever spent. Finally she gave up, got undressed and slithered barefoot to the bathroom, showered quickly and brushed her teeth. Back in her bedroom she put on her pyjamas and brushed her hair, then ran lightly down the stairs and put her head round the door of the lounge. Tariq was sprawled full-length, his head in Julie's lap, his socked feet on the arm of the sofa.

Abbie's nose wrinkled. 'Dad, your socks are disgusting. Remind me to get you some new ones for your birthday. Without holes. I'm going to bed now. Can you turn the TV down a bit?'

'I'll turn it off,' Julie said, and flicked the remote. 'All right, sweetheart?'

'Yeah. Night, Mum, Dad.'

Well, now, that was interesting. I knew all that stuff, most of it, anyway. Not about Dad having another sister, though. That was a surprise. Still, doesn't hurt to revisit things once in a while. And I didn't know Mum went to see Mr Westwood just after I saw the earthquake. Now I kind of understand why he was pleased to see me the other day, when I went with Mum. He probably thinks I've got prophetic tendencies! What a joke. Pathetic, more like. I might look it up tomorrow. About prophecy. Just out of interest. The thing is, he might have been someone I could talk to. Someone who thinks I am interesting rather than odd, even if he's mistaken. He might have been an ally. If trouble is coming, and I guess it might be, he might have helped me, given me some advice.

If only he weren't dying.

Hours later, when the house was asleep and the street quiet, when nothing moved except the foxes that looked for food in dustbins and prowled round chicken coops, a sudden clatter woke Abbie from a restless sleep. She sat up and peered groggily at her bedside alarm: five o'clock, and still dark. She got out of bed, shivering, and closed her window. Climbing back under the warm covers she tried and failed to recapture sleep, her mind casting back and forth across the events of the past days. A frightening thought came to her, that when she saw in Will Chambers' eyes that look of recognition at the church gate, it was perhaps not recognition of Abbie's odd gift but of Abbie herself. Was that possible? How could he possibly know her? But then, how could he have known what had just passed through her mind? She'd thought she knew without a doubt what she had seen in his face – but could it just have been her imagination? Was she letting go of reality, as Julie had accused? What was reality, anyway?

These were cold thoughts for five o'clock on a chilly spring morning when all the world around was lost to consciousness and she alone lay wakeful; but colder still was the tiny flicker in her memory that *she* had seen *him* somewhere before too. But where, and when? Was she losing her mind? Was she still asleep and dreaming? What was going on?

May 2010

Around mid-morning Abbie stretched and groaned. She was stiff from sitting hunched over her notes. She got up, walked slowly downstairs and into the kitchen, flexing her shoulders. Sunlight was streaming in through the window, and the birds were making their usual polyphony. *I know it's probably all, 'Hey, you, get off my patch! But it does sound more like 'Hey, it's great to be alive.' What's that called? Anthropomorphism, that's it.*

She made a cup of coffee and rummaged around for a biscuit, but the tin was empty. She thought for a moment, then ran back upstairs, stuffed her feet into the first pair of shoes she found lying around and, on an afterthought, brushed her hair and tied it back. She pulled her purse from her school bag and inspected its meagre contents. Returning to the kitchen with the purse in her pocket she put her coffee mug into the microwave, took the back door key and left the house, locking the door behind her. She had the house to herself: Tariq was working on the job the other side of town, Daniel was at school, and Julie was shopping. *Maybe she'll buy some biscuits. I can only afford boring ones.*

She walked briskly up the road, breathing in the cool, fresh air, hoping it would clear her head. She crossed the green by the footpath, and angled left to the tiny shop. As she came out a few minutes later, a packet of biscuits in her hand, she met Mrs Cocksedge on her way in.

'Good morning, dear! How are you?'

'Fine thanks, Mrs Cocksedge. You?'

'I can't grumble. Well, not too much.' She smiled. 'No school today?'

'No. I have a study day. It's exam time – I have one tomorrow afternoon. And more next week.'

'Oh, I see. Well, best of luck! I'm sure you'll do well.'

'Thanks.'

Abbie waited politely for Mrs Cocksedge to say goodbye and go into the shop, but the old lady seemed inclined to chat.

'Lovely to see you and your brother in church at Easter, dear! And so nice, wasn't it, to see a new person there? A neighbour of the Calladines', so I hear. Oh, and isn't your father helping to renovate the cottage? It certainly needed it. Such a shame about poor Mrs Wilson. I'm thankful I can still be in my own home, but maybe there'll come a day...

'Yes, and that young man – Mr Chambers, isn't it? –' she rattled on, 'did you know, he's been in church every Sunday since! Sings so beautifully, too. Perhaps he was a choirboy once.'

'I'm afraid I've no idea,' Abbie murmured. But Mrs Cocksedge seemed hardly to hear.

'I don't know if you noticed the churchyard as you came over, dear. He's given it its first cut. Looks so neat now. They say he's a writer, so I supposed he has plenty of time in the day. You've met him, I suppose?'

'Yes,' Abbie said, her voice neutral.

'I hear he's even going to join the bell-ringers!' Mrs Cocksedge smiled, her eyes wide. 'Sounds quite an asset for our little congregation, don't you think?' Abbie smiled back weakly. 'Well, this won't do, will it? You have your exam to study for, and I need some groceries. Lovely to chat to you, dear. Hope to see you in church again soon.' And she was gone with an airy wave.

Abbie stood irresolute for a few moments, then on an impulse, instead of going straight home, turned in the direction of the church. She paused at the wall, her eyes roaming over Will Chambers' handiwork. *So perhaps he's not all empty promises. On the other hand, perhaps he's just softening everyone up. But for what?*

What is it about that man? Is Mrs Cocksedge actually right? Is it me that's losing it? I don't know, and I don't know who to ask. There isn't anyone, is there?

Maggie put her head round the Hasans' kitchen door to find Julie pulling wet washing out of the washing machine and into a laundry basket.

'Morning! I seem to have disturbed a scene of tranquil domesticity.'

Julie grunted. 'I don't know about tranquil. I was going to hang this lot out, but it seems to be raining.'

'It's just a passing shower, I reckon,' Maggie said. 'Get the kettle on, make me a cup of coffee, and I'll help you hang it out when the rain stops.'

'Done,' Julie said. 'Have a chair. Make yourself at home.' She filled the kettle and switched it on. 'So, what's the latest?'

Maggie wriggled in her seat, finding a more comfortable position. 'Actually, that's what I've come to tell you.'

'Not gossip, I hope,' Julie said, pretending to be stern.

'Not exactly,' Maggie said. 'More … news, I'd say. I'll have mine black today, please. Got any decent biscuits?'

'Sorry, not even a crumb. The children have demolished them. Why black? You don't usually.'

'Oh, I don't know. Sometimes the idea of milk makes me queasy.'

Julie made two cups of coffee, slid one across the table to Maggie and sat down opposite her. 'So, spill all, O mine of information.'

Maggie took a sip. 'Ouch, that's hot.' She looked round the room. 'You all on your own?'

'Mm. Abbie's out driving with her father. Her first time in town.'

'What, braving Walburn on a Saturday? That's daring for a wannabe driver.'

'I think that was the point,' Julie said. 'So far she's just driven the country lanes, so not much of a challenge. Anyway, there was an incentive: she needs some new shoes, so I said she should go and get them herself.'

'And no doubt Dan's at football?'

'You guessed.'

'Better than spraying graffiti on the bus shelter, I suppose.'

'He might be doing that as well for all I know.'

'Nonsense,' Maggie said firmly. 'Not our Daniel.'

'Anyway,' Julie said, putting her mug down, 'you were going to tell me something.'

'So I was.' Maggie took a gulp of her coffee. 'I've been getting to know our new friend and neighbour a bit better. Well, actually, quite a lot better.' She ignored Julie's raised eyebrows. 'You remember I told you he said he wanted to come and join the bell-ringers? Said he had some experience from years ago, when he was a teenager? So along he came with me yesterday evening, and everybody was very welcoming, as you'd expect. But I have to say he was a complete disaster. He had no clue whatsoever. Which wouldn't have been a problem if he'd come as a beginner, so Hugh and everyone else knew what to expect. But because he'd said he knew what he was doing, and he obviously didn't, it was quite embarrassing. Well, *I* was embarrassed, because I was the one that took him.'

Julie frowned. 'So what happened?'

'Well, Hugh was very patient at first. More than I would have expected of Hugh, to be honest. He can be quite tetchy when the ringers mess things up. But he was quite gentle. Tried to put Will right, showed him what to do. Unfortunately Will couldn't handle that at all. Heaven knows how he would have reacted if Hugh had bawled him out, like he's done to me a few times! Will lost his temper, shouted at Hugh very rudely. That's when it got really embarrassing. I was cringing, I can tell you. I hardly knew where to put my face. Everyone was standing round with their mouths open. And then Will stormed out and banged the door behind him.'

'Bizarre.'

Maggie pulled a face. 'It was.'

'So what did you do?'

'I just apologised. Not that it was really my fault, because I couldn't have known what he'd be like, but I felt responsible.'

'And then?' Julie prompted.

'Well, we just got on with the practice as usual. But the atmosphere was a bit strained.'

'I imagine it was.'

'But that wasn't the end,' Maggie said, her face growing more serious. 'When I got home, Will was sitting on my doorstep.'

Julie looked at her friend in astonishment. 'Really?'

Maggie nodded slowly. 'He looked utterly miserable, like a bad little boy.'

'This is extraordinary. All over a dodgy bell practice.'

'It was more than that, though. As I found out. What could I do? I invited him in, said I'd make him a fortifying cuppa.'

'Was David there?'

Maggie grimaced. 'Of course not. He was, still is, at a Head Teacher's conference, one of those regional things. Decided to stay over. He won't be home till this evening. Anyway, in came Will and sat at my kitchen table, and out poured this story.'

'With you, of course, in Samaritan mode, oozing empathy.'

Maggie shrugged. 'I suppose it's second nature after all these years.'

'Hm. So what did he tell you?'

'He actually waited for me to come home so he could apologise. Said he felt really stupid for losing it like that. Apparently dear old Hugh reminded him of someone who'd been mean to him as a lad, and he reacted badly, but he felt he had let himself, and me, down and how could he face people in church now, etc. So I told him not to be silly, he could pop round to the Prestons' in the morning and make his peace with Hugh, and it would all blow over. That was that. But then he started telling me about his life, and I have to say he's had a tough time. I felt really sorry for him.'

'Do you want another cup?' Julie got up from the table. 'I'm sure I do.'

'I'm not holding you up, am I?' Maggie said.

'Only from sorting this washing,' Julie said. 'And that can wait.'

'Did you get your accounts done?'

'Yes, thankfully. Go on, I can listen while I make coffee.'

'He was born the only child of a single mum, apparently, in some horrible place I've never heard of, in Scotland, I think. His mother was a nineteen-year-old waitress.'

'Hang on, he told us his father was a diplomat, and that he grew up in various exotic places overseas.'

Maggie nodded. 'That family adopted him when he was four, he said. His mother couldn't cope. Gave him away.'

'What? You're not serious!'

'That's what he told me. He wonders whether his adoptive father was actually his real father, that he was the result of a passing fling. He said his adoptive mother was always cold with him, and maybe that was the reason. Anyway, he didn't feel very accepted or loved growing up – felt his mother didn't want him, and his father was never around, so he rather went off the rails.'

'Poor thing.'

'Yes, he had every material asset and a decent education, but no real family life.'

'What about the sister? Rachel?'

'Ah, well, she was the golden girl. The parents' only child together. So her death was a disaster, of course. Will said he always felt his mother must have wished it had been him that died, not Rachel.'

'Horrible. No wonder he's a bit of a mess.'

'Mm. But some time later he really did get ill, almost died, he said. It wasn't then, when he was still a boy living at home, it was later. He hinted that it might have been something tropical, caught while his father was posted somewhere in Asia, and that it recurred. Maybe the same nasty thing that did for his sister. He was a bit vague about it, and I didn't like to press him with too many questions. It's why, he says, he can't work.'

'He seems healthy enough now. Managed to mow the churchyard without collapsing.'

'Yes, but apparently he never knows when this illness is going to strike. So holding down a job is a problem.'

Julie sat down again and handed Maggie another mug of coffee. 'He says he can't work, but he doesn't seem to be short of money, does he? Riq says there's always money lying around the cottage.'

Maggie shook her head. 'I don't know. Being a well-brought-up Englishwoman I was far too polite to quiz him about his finances. Frightfully bad taste.'

'So, when did he go off the rails? Before or after the illness?'

'Before. Got mixed up with some very strange people. Sounds like some kind of cult.'

'Wow. That's grim. But not surprising, in the circumstances, I guess, if he felt rejected by his adoptive family. But how did he get out of that? From what I've read people get almost brainwashed, don't they?'

'Well, he'd been raised a Catholic, and it was some old priest that rescued him. Father Jerome. Became a spiritual father-figure as far as I can gather, and Will found faith for himself and managed to turn his life around. But of course all this happening messed up his education and his chances of employment, even if he hadn't become ill. Until quite recently, he said, he was employed in an old people's home, just part-time.'

'As what?'

'A carer of sorts. He doesn't really have any qualifications. Not that he's stupid, not at all. And looking after old people in a place like that doesn't really need much in the way of formal qualifications, does it? You have to get checked out, of course – I know that. You need to be quite a special kind of person to do it, in my opinion. And he does seem to be naturally kind and sensitive.'

'Which brings us to why he's wound up in Halstead, doing up an old wreck of a cottage.'

'Well, it seems he got very close to an old lady in the home. I would have thought that sort of close personal relationship would be frowned upon in a place like that – wouldn't they think it was overdependency? Or at least cause trouble and resentment among the other clients as well as the staff? Who knows? Whatever the case, she died and left him quite a substantial sum of money. Enough for him to leave work, and buy Mrs Wilson's old place, and a junk heap of a car. And, I hope, enough left over to pay Tariq for his work on the house.'

'Why here, I wonder?' Julie murmured.

Maggie shrugged. 'Maybe there aren't too many cheap old places on the market. I don't know. But he's here, and he obviously needs a bit of peace, and friends who understand and accept him. He's known tough times, and OK, some of it was his own doing, but which of us can say we were never responsible for our own troubles?'

'True enough,' Julie said. She smiled at her friend over the rim of her coffee cup. 'I hope he appreciated you spending all that time and sympathy on him.'

'Oh, yes,' Maggie said modestly. 'He was very grateful. Said I was a wonderful listener and hoped we'd be good friends. He even asked me a bit about my own life – he seemed genuinely interested.'

Julie stretched. 'Why not? You're an interesting person.' She looked up, out of the kitchen window. 'Hey, I believe you were right. The sun's out. Worth hanging this washing out, do you think?'

'Sure. I'll help you.' Maggie pushed her chair back and stood up. Julie took the basket and Maggie followed her into the garden.

'Better keep to the path,' Julie said. 'The grass is wet, and your shoes look flimsy.'

Sharing the pegs they hung the washing on the line. Maggie looked at her watch. 'Where did the time go? It's almost twelve. I suppose I should go home.'

'Incidentally,' Julie said, picking up the empty laundry basket, 'if I'm not being too nosy, and tell me to butt out if you like, are you and David OK? You did have a bit of a funny moment not so long ago.'

Maggie turned to her, shading her eyes against the sunlight. She sighed. 'Well, you know I told you I had a big think. Decided I was going to try and do better. To pray more. To attempt to understand things from David's point of view. And it worked, at least for then. Things went more smoothly. He seemed happier. Actually started to talk to me a bit more, which was nice. So I guess we're OK. No more than that, not joined at the hip and more or less telepathic like you guys, but OK.'

Julie laughed. 'Come off it, Maggie, Riq and I aren't telepathic!'

'Practically! Don't tell me you don't talk to one another all the time.'

'Your logic is dodgy, darling,' Julie said, putting her free arm round her friend's shoulders as they walked back down the path. 'If we were telepathic we wouldn't need to talk at all.'

'You know what I mean,' Maggie said.

'I suppose so. And I know I'm hugely blessed. I don't know how it happened, really, except that for once I had enough sense to pick a good one and hang on to him. But David is a good person too, and no one is perfect.'

'I shall depart with that wise truism ringing in my ears,' Maggie said. 'Maybe I will cook something tasty, welcome the old man back. All very wifely and supportive.'

'See you tomorrow?'

'Of course. Bye, dear. Thanks for the coffee.'

David Calladine ground to a halt in his drive at 11.15 that evening. His left eye was twitching, his head throbbing dully, and his stomach felt sour from the greasy meal he'd eaten at a roadside restaurant. He rubbed his hands over his face, feeling his stubble rasp, and yawned. He got out of the car, leaned into the back seat and picked up his bulging briefcase.

As he locked the car he looked up at the house. Everything seemed to be in darkness. Guiltily he felt a twinge of relief: if Maggie was asleep he wouldn't have to talk to her, not this evening. He would have a night's sleep before he had to tell her what he knew would be unwelcome news.

He opened the front door quietly and put the briefcase down. Then he saw a faint light from the kitchen. He frowned, kicked off his shoes and crept down the hall. The door was slightly ajar, and he pushed it open.

Maggie was sitting at the kitchen table, a small lamp beside her casting a pool of light in the darkness. Her head was bent over a book, and as she looked up he saw she had been reading her Bible. The kitchen was immaculate, but there was one dirty plate and some cutlery on the table at Maggie's elbow.

'Oh. You're back, then.' Maggie's tone seemed to David almost studiedly neutral. His stomach churned: was this Maggie in restrained mode, ready to erupt?

'Yes, sorry I'm so late – '

'I cooked dinner.' Maggie indicated her plate.

'I ate on the way. It was pretty horrible.' David smiled ruefully but Maggie's face was set.

'I thought the conference ended at five.'

'Yes, it did. But there's always the informal chats afterwards, and that's when a lot of the important news gets circulated, and when you have the opportunity to collar people. I'd had enough, as it happened – I was intending to come home straight away. But that chap from Ketley – perhaps you remember him: Andrew Marks – he waylaid me, practically at the door. And I'm glad he did, because he told me something I needed to know.' When she didn't respond, he said, as gently as he could, 'Thank you for cooking. I could eat it tomorrow.'

'I don't think so,' Maggie said, her voice grating. 'I binned it.'

'Oh!'

'You might have phoned, let me know you would be late.'

'Yes, I should have. I'm sorry.'

After a silence that seemed to stretch painfully out, Maggie said, 'So what was this important thing Andrew Marks had to tell you?'

'It's late. It can keep till tomorrow.'

'No, I want to know now.' He could sense her efforts at restraint crumbling, hearing the beginnings of fear and anger in her voice, and he felt himself flinch.

'Well, it's only more or less a rumour at the moment. But these things are usually right. What's harder to anticipate is the timing. Ofsted – coming our way. And almost certainly before the end of this term.'

Maggie looked at him for a long moment, then she swore. It startled him: she'd been brought up in a family that used foul language with careless freedom, but Maggie herself – perhaps as a reaction – almost never did, and in her mouth it sounded harsh and alien, as no doubt she had intended.

David felt his knees protesting and slid into a chair. He forced himself to continue. 'You know as well as I do what that means. You've been through it, more than once. But not as Head, of course – that does make a difference.' He smiled humourlessly. 'I'll be at school a lot.'

'Will I notice?' Maggie said bitterly. 'You might as well live there.'

'No, wait,' David said, his voice rising, 'I've been trying to be at home more, do stuff around the house. Don't say I haven't.'

'It was nice while it lasted, I suppose,' Maggie said, her lip curled. 'But I always knew you'd default. And now you have a nice excuse.'

'I'd hardly say there was anything "nice" about an Ofsted inspection,' David protested.

'Unless it means keeping away from me!' Maggie flashed.

David pushed his chair back with a sudden scrape and stood up. 'I'm much too tired to have this conversation now.'

'You just proved my point. Anything but speak to me.'

'I have been speaking to you.'

'I'm talking about important things, things that matter to us, to me, not just to you.'

'And what does matter to "us", in your opinion?' In his anger David felt his defences click into place: the cold tone, the refusal – perhaps the inability – to compromise, the withdrawal of all but his physical presence, and often not even that. Now he took a weapon he knew would cut deep. 'I suppose you're referring to this whole baby thing.'

Maggie looked up at him, her eyes hollow. 'No,' she said slowly. 'I've come to the sad conclusion that only matters to me. You've given up. And it's your right – you don't have to care about it, not for yourself. It would be nice, though, if you cared because I do. But perhaps all that's gone.'

'You're quite wrong. But now is not the time. We're both tired, fraught. There's pressure ahead, things I absolutely have to do, for my school, for my staff and pupils. It's my job.'

'And we all know that comes first.' Maggie heaved herself to her feet. 'I do wonder where I figure in the pecking order of your priorities. A long way down. Perhaps I don't appear on it at all.'

'That isn't true. It's nonsense,' David muttered.

'Is it? Well, perhaps you believe that. But in my book it's what you do that counts. Solid, concrete evidence. There's not much of that about.' She put her plate in the sink, pushed past him to the door, then paused, and turned. 'You know what, David? I admire you. You're good at your job, dedicated, and I'm sure well-liked and respected. You've turned that school around, the kids do well, the staff stay for years, the parents are happy. That's quite an achievement, and I applaud it. I know it hasn't been easy. But somewhere along that rocky road you've lost something. Something

I'd call important, but apparently you've lost sight of it altogether. You're an excellent Head Teacher, for sure. Unfortunately, you are a lousy husband.'

On Sunday morning Julie turned just as she was about to go into church and saw David striding up the path behind her, head down, arms held stiffly by his sides. She nudged Tariq. 'David,' she murmured. 'But no Maggie. She said she'd be here.' Louder, she said, 'Morning, David!'

David's head jerked up, and Julie noted his shadowed eyes and tight mouth. He cleared his throat. 'Oh, yes, morning Julie, morning Tariq.'

'Maggie and Will not with you?'

'Maggie is unwell. Migraine. I can't speak for Will.'

'Oh, that's rough. Poor old thing. I didn't know she suffered from migraines. Shall I pop round and see her after church?'

'I wish you would. Unfortunately, I have to go into school straight after the service.'

Julie was startled. 'On Sunday?'

'Possiblity – no, probability – of Ofsted.' David's face was grim. 'Oh.'

'Sorry, will you excuse me?' David said. 'I need to check the safe before the service begins.'

'Of course,' Julie muttered, and stood aside. David hurried past them with a strained smile. Julie looked at Tariq, frowning, and shook her head in perplexity. 'What's got into him?' she said quietly.

'Ofsted?' Tariq suggested.

'It's more than that. I'll call and see Maggie before lunch. You and the children can do the vegetables.'

'Sure. Now hadn't we better go in?'

Maggie sat on the garden swing, soaking up the morning sunshine. The garden was edged with high trees, and she felt secluded, which was what she wanted. Her ribs ached from crying, and she was wearing sunglasses as a defence against both the sun and the world – not that she expected anyone to be about to see her red, swollen eyes. She clutched a sodden tissue in her hand. Gently she rocked the swing, feeling the rhythm soothe her bones, as if some loving unseen hand was rocking her cradle. *Oh, Lord, what a mess. Things were getting a bit better. Not enough for my liking, of course. We are so fragile, David and I, these days. I wonder if we were ever robust. I guess we were, in the beginning, when hope was high. Anyway, I've blown it now. I don't know if we can retrieve anything, not this time. He seems only to want superficial things, and I want something else altogether. Something he can't, or won't, supply.* She sighed, and felt a tear trickle down her cheek. Listlessly she wiped it away. Then her head jerked up as she heard a sound from the direction of the house. Someone was calling her, quite softly. 'Maggie? Are you there?'

She gasped, and swallowed. 'I'm in the garden.' Her voice sounded strangled in her own ears. She smoothed her hair down and turned slightly as Will appeared round the side of the house.

'Hello,' he said. 'Aren't you going to church today?'

'Mm, no, I'm not feeling too well,' Maggie said, trying to brighten her voice. 'But don't let me stop you.' She made a show of looking at her watch. 'You'd better hurry if you're going. You're already rather late, aren't you?' She was sitting awkwardly, half-sideways, so he couldn't see her face. But instead of taking off to church he came further into the garden, and without hesitation sat beside her on the swing and took her unresisting hand, tissue and all.

'My dear Maggie, whatever is the matter?' His voice was so full of tender compassion that she felt fresh tears well up.

'No, no, nothing at all, I have a headache, nothing serious.' Her voice choked, and she gulped, trying to stem the flow of her weeping.

'You don't fool me for a minute,' Will said quietly. 'Why don't you come indoors, and I'll make you a cup of tea.'

'I thought you were going to church,' Maggie said feebly.

'I was, even if I only got there in time for the sermon, but you are far more important.' He stood up and pulled her to her feet.

'All right.' She let him lead her back into the kitchen. 'How did you know I wasn't already in church?'

'I was looking out of the window,' Will said, smiling. 'I saw David stride off on his own. Wondered if you were OK.'

A few minutes later he passed her a mug as she sat at the kitchen table.

'Thanks. We could sit in comfort if you like.'

'This is quite comfortable enough for me,' Will said. 'Especially if you compare it to my building site next door.'

Maggie took a sip. 'How's the work going?'

'Fine. But I don't want to talk about that, not now. I want to know why you are so upset. I don't like to see you like this.'

Maggie smiled sadly. 'Unfortunately, just lately I am all too often like this.'

He leaned back against the sink, his arms loosely folded across his chest, and considered her, his face sombre. 'Only just lately?'

'On and off over the last few years, I suppose. But worse recently.'

'Do you think I am being too nosy? I only want to help.'

Maggie shook her head. 'I know, and I'm thankful. You're missing church because of me. Really, I guess there's not much anyone can do or say. It's something we, David and I, have to sort out between ourselves, if we can. But I of all people shouldn't underestimate the benefits of a listening ear.'

Will frowned in puzzlement. 'Why's that? Have you been in therapy or something?'

Maggie managed a faint smile. 'No, not that. Why don't you come and sit down? Don't you want any tea?'

Will sat in the chair opposite her. 'I only just had breakfast – got up late. So?'

'I'm not really supposed to tell you this, but I'm a Samaritan.' She laughed bitterly. 'Supposed to help people who are up against

105

it, suicidal people sometimes. Look at me – I can't resolve my own problems. What use am I?'

'Probably more use than someone who's never had anything go wrong,' Will said seriously. 'Now I understand why you are so good at listening.' He reached over the table and took her limp hand in both of his. 'I don't know, though,' he said, 'if you're any good at sharing your own troubles.' He looked straight into her eyes. 'I hope you think of me as a friend. At least, a friend in the making. I'd like to help if I can, but not to pry. And I understand about sensitive things, and confidentiality.'

Maggie laughed shakily. 'You sound like a Samaritan yourself.'

'I think it would be a wonderful thing to be,' Will said. 'I have great admiration for what you do. As it happens,' he added diffidently, 'I've had cause to phone them in the past.'

'You have?'

'Yes. You know something of my trials. Those strangers on the end of a phone saved my life once, no exaggeration.'

Maggie nodded slowly. 'That bad?'

'Look, tell me to shove off if you like, I won't be offended, and you don't owe me any kind of explanation. If, as you hinted, this is a marriage problem, I don't have too much experience. But it wouldn't hurt to offload.'

'You're very kind. But aren't other people's problems a bore?'

'You ask me that?' Will said. 'Do *you* think they are? When you go down to your centre, wherever it is, and pick up the phone?'

'No, of course not. But ...' She took a deep breath and drank a gulp of tea. 'We were OK for a long while, David and I. Working hard all the time, of course, as teachers do. But lots in common, and we had fun times as well, times with friends, holidays. When Julie and Tariq came to Halstead we became good friends too, especially Julie and me, and that was great. We did things together – board games at Christmas, weekends camping, that sort of thing.' She thought for a moment. 'It's just gone downhill the last few years, when I've felt my time was running out.' She looked up. 'I work with kids, David does too. But you'll note we don't have any of our own. That's not a decision we made; children were something we wanted, or at least I assume he did too, but it never happened. Years ago we went through some tests, and they didn't find anything obviously amiss with either of us.' She looked away from Will, and a slight blush stained her cheeks. 'And it's not as if we didn't try. Even now, even recently when things have been difficult, that's been OKish. But I'm getting a bit personal here – don't want to embarrass you. Frankly, Will, it's eaten me up. Become a bit of an obsession, however hard I try. I'm thirty-nine, David's forty-five. And he's just shoved it aside, or at least that's what it seems like. Won't even talk about it, except to say there's no point in talking. Julie's understanding, of course, but she has two lovely children already. She's right, she says it's not too late, to keep praying, cites those Bible ladies who had babies when they were barren or ancient or whatever. But sometimes I just feel hopeless, and totally isolated. And now David thinks Ofsted is coming, so he's going to be super-busy and stressed, and it'll mean one more excuse to distance himself from his miserable old bag of a wife.'

Will was silent for a while, almost absent-mindedly stroking her hand. Maggie found she didn't mind; it was rhythmic and soothing. Then he looked up at her, and shook his head. 'Oh, Maggie. It's so sad. You must think sometimes about the children who are abused and neglected, or living somewhere where they are starving or in danger or forced to do horrible work, and here's you, with a nice home and a loving heart, and you have no one to care for. How does that seem right?' He bit his lip. 'I can understand a little bit, maybe. I'm sure it's not quite the same for a man, but I don't suppose I'll ever be a dad either, even supposing I met the right woman. I had mumps as a teenager. Messes up the vital bits.'

'Not necessarily, Will,' Maggie said. 'As I understand it, mumps only makes a boy sterile in very rare cases.'

'Well, who knows? I haven't been very lucky in love, that's for sure.' He scowled. 'But I do know that if I had a wife like you, I'd treat her better.'

Maggie smiled slightly. 'I'm sure you'd be a model husband, but don't paint David black. He's a good person at heart, and it's not easy for him either.'

'But it's such a dreary cliché,' Will said with sudden vehemence, 'the man who buries himself in work because that's all he can cope with, leaving his wife to carry all the burdens.'

Maggie pulled her hand away from his and stretched, flexing her shoulders. 'I know,' she said quietly, 'but I have to remind myself that I have many blessings, and other people have worse problems.'

'Does that help? Really?'

Maggie shook her head and smiled. 'Not much, no.' She stood up. 'I mustn't keep you, Will. You've been very kind, but you must have a lot to do. That novel of yours ... How's it going?'

Will stood up too, leaning his hands on the table. 'It's a bit difficult, as it happens. I've set up my computer in the little bedroom at the back, but the building work is very noisy and distracting. I'm thinking of asking Tariq to take a break for a couple of weeks, so I can make a bit of progress in peace.'

'Well, he has other jobs on the go, that I know.'

'Maybe that's what I'll do, then.' Will turned towards the door. 'He's an interesting chap, Tariq. An Indian Christian.'

'He wasn't always,' Maggie said. 'Although there are Christians in India, of course. He was born and raised Muslim, but converted when he came to England as a student.'

'Really?' Will's eyebrows raised enquiringly.

'But that's his story, not mine,' Maggie said. 'If you want to know about that, you'll have to ask him.'

'Fair enough, Mrs Ever-so-discreet,' Will said with a smile. 'Now I'd better go. The service will be over soon, and I wouldn't want David to get the wrong idea.'

'Oh, well, as to that, he's gone straight into school. Can't let the grass grow with Ofsted looming.'

Will shook his head. 'Look, Maggie, don't suffer alone. I'm only next door.'

'Thank you, Will. I appreciate it.'

There came a tap on the door, it opened suddenly, and Julie's head appeared. 'Hi, Maggie, it's only me – oh! Hello, Will, sorry, I didn't know you were here. I just came over to see if everything was all right. David said you had a migraine, Maggie.'

'I did, Julie, thanks, but it's going. Will came to collect me for church and stayed to succour the ailing.'

'Oh, right. Well, if you're really OK, I'll go and relieve Riq. He's peeling potatoes. Come round later if you want, Maggie. I'm not doing anything much. We could sit in the garden and enjoy this lovely bit of sunshine.'

'Thanks, dear, maybe I'll do that. And thank you, Will. You're both very kind.'

On Monday Tariq came home white from plaster dust. 'I'll need to shower before I do anything else,' he said to Julie, who was preparing dinner.

'Certainly before you come anywhere near me,' Julie said, smiling. 'You look very peculiar, I have to say.'

Tariq fished in the back pocket of his jeans. 'But before I do that, I have something for you.' He handed her a fat, crumpled brown envelope. 'Interim payment from Will. I haven't counted it – I'll leave that to you.'

'Right. But why today?'

'Oh, he said he wants to call a halt for a couple of weeks. Needs to get on with the famous novel, he says, without me crashing about, dropping lengths of timber and singing.'

'Understandable. Your singing has to be heard to be believed.'

'That good, eh?' He chuckled, then sobered. 'I had quite an interesting talk with him today, actually. He seemed in the mood for chat – even made me a cup of coffee. He was quizzing me about my youth, what it was like to start off as a Muslim, and then what happened when I came to England.'

'I wonder how he knew.'

'Apparently Maggie mentioned it. Just that, nothing more.'

'Did you tell him?'

'Some. He said I was lucky.'

'In what way?' Julie tipped dirty water into the sink.

'He said in some places he's lived, a boy like me, abandoning the faith of his ancestors, wouldn't just have got thrown out of the family. In some places they murder converts.'

Julie shuddered. 'Dear God, what a world.'

'But we knew that, didn't we? Anyway, I told him about the earthquake, which he remembered, and he asked me if I would like him to have a word with some of his old diplomatic contacts, or rather his father's, to see if he could find out anything. No promises, but he could try.'

Julie looked and him, and sighed. 'Are you hopeful?'

'After all this time? Not really. But I suppose it's worth a shot. And it's kind of him to offer.'

'Is his dad still alive?'

'Yes, in a home now, he said, but still with his wits about him, so he'll probably start with him.'

'Well, you never know. But don't get your hopes up, will you? I don't want a repeat of that awful time. I hated seeing you like that.'

'I wasn't crazy about it myself.'

'Riq, go and have your shower, or you'll still be warbling and splashing when I'm dishing up.'

'OK.' He paused at the door. 'How did Abbie's exam go?'

'All right, I think. But you can ask her yourself.'

The man who called himself Will Chambers looked around his temporary domicile and saw that it really wouldn't do – not for what he had in mind.

He started with the bathroom, collecting up a number of incriminating items and stowing them in an old school sports bag which he stuffed into an empty cupboard. He gave the whole area a thorough clean. Then he moved on to the bedroom, looking at it with a critical eye. It was barely more than a squat, just a mattress on the floor. Good enough for camping out, but that was all. He would have to buy a proper bed. He frowned: despite the cash left lying carelessly around to give a certain impression to his builder, funds were running low. But it was a necessary investment. He would go into town today and arrange it. And he would need to be discreet – no great lorries turning up outside. Perhaps he could buy something you could put together yourself, and bring it home flatpacked in the boot of the car. Meanwhile he would clean up here as well, and give the kitchen a going-over so that it wasn't too unpleasant, all the while maintaining the image of a house being renovated, and in a state of picturesque disarray. He laughed quietly to himself. Things were going satisfactorily, but he had to keep on top. There was a timescale to be considered, but there were matters that couldn't be rushed. It was a tricky business.

He made himself a cup of coffee and sat on an upturned bucket in the living-room, stripped down to bare boards and covered in dust sheets. *I have to be careful. I shouldn't have offered to help with the kids in Maggie's school, for a start. Forgot about the CRB check thing. Not that there's anything illegal on there, because I've always been careful not to get caught. But it would have shown up my real name, and that's definitely not a good idea. Luckily I managed to retrieve that one, and I don't think Maggie suspected anything. But then I nearly made a hash of that business with the bells. Stupid to lie unnecessarily, and even stupider to lose my temper. I patched it up the next day, of course, charmed old Penny Preston, but Hugh, I thought, despite his acceptance of my apology and general bluff civility, was still a bit sceptical. I have to remind myself that even stupid people aren't necessarily completely stupid. If only he hadn't reminded me so much of Bill! Bill and his domineering. Still, that whole episode paid off pretty well, didn't it? Getting in there with Maggie. What a coup, and sooner than I thought. It's going to be a* bore going through with the whole charade, but sweet if it all goes according to plan. To see his face, to see light dawn, to see him realise you can't shaft me and get away with it. Not even now, when you might think I would have forgotten. Oh, no, sunshine. I never forget.

He gnawed at his thumbnail. It would be better if I could think of something more elegant, though. Something that didn't involve quite such a charm offensive on my part. Maggie may be miserable, but she's what people think of as an honourable person, as well as a Christian. It won't be easy. And I might feel sick at prostituting myself. But I have to remember: it will be worth it. Watch out, Calladines, a shambles is coming. Wreckage and ruin, fire and destruction. He grinned, then scowled. If only I could think of something to frighten that knowing little snoop, Abbie Hasan. She's got her weird green eye on me, and it isn't friendly. Yes, I've got dear old Tariq in my sights, but that's just a sideline, a bit of fun while I'm waiting. He's not entirely fooled, I know, but even so, he's thinking about that little bit of hope I'm giving him, and when it all crashes he'll be disappointed and his loving daughter will be very angry. So much the better. What can she do, anyway? What's really niggling me is I'm sure I've seen her somewhere before. If only I could remember where. It might give me a weapon. Knowledge is power, the best there is.

I mustn't let hate get the better of me. Not yet. I have to stay cool. The Hasans aren't the real deal, even though I'd like to take them down too – complacent, got everything they want, stupid happy people. No: maybe stupid isn't the right word – maybe what they are is naïve. Trusting. Giving everyone the benefit of the doubt. Forgiving the sinner. Ha! This sinner is beyond forgiving, even if he wanted it. Which he doesn't.

He stood up and stretched, rubbing the back of his neck. Meanwhile I have to keep up my little campaign. Dear Mrs Lyons needs her hedge cutting. Far too big a job for an old lady and far too expensive for a pensioner with limited means. Her son does it once in a while, but he lives in London and May is here and nature is getting a little too rampant. 'So that nice young man Will said he'd do it for me, dear, isn't that kind?'

Oh, Mrs Lyons, if you but knew what that nice young man really thinks of you.

June 2010

It's a while since I wrote anything in this journal. Life suddenly got very busy. First, of course, there were exams. I can be forgiven for being a bit preoccupied. They went OK, as far as I can tell. Now it's just a case of waiting till August to see if anyone likes what I wrote. After all the work I did I'm inclined to forget school for a little while, especially as we now have a few days off before we have to get started again on the A2 work. At least I might be able to drop a subject in September.

I have to admit, though, the second big distraction has been a certain Olly Bradshaw. It all started that afternoon when I was stuck in the gym, on a sweltering day, with sixty other suffering students, ploughing through a two-hour paper. He had an exam too that afternoon, but he finished a bit sooner. I just looked up for a moment, and there he was, out of the invigilator's line of sight, gazing through the long window straight at me and pulling a stupid face. I gave him a stern look, but he wasn't fooled. He made a show of tapping his watch, holding up two hands' worth of fingers, and winking broadly. Sure enough, when I staggered out of the exam a little while later he was lounging at the corner of the building, wearing a pair of flashy sunglasses and chewing on a blade of grass.

To dredge up a cliché, the rest is history. I've come to the conclusion that the old Abbie Hasan was a boring little swot with no life. Not that I'm going to get slack with school stuff, even if the teachers would let me – but there has to be room for a little fun.

Unfortunately, though, what it meant was I took my eye off the ball for a time. And while I've been a bit busy, getting to know Olly's little ways, things seem to be getting out of control.

First of all, I found out that Will Chambers had offered to see if he could find out anything about my Kashmir family via his diplomatic contacts. Oh, really? I never believed in those, right from the outset. I don't think my dad is gullible exactly, but he thinks well of everyone, and the thing is he wants to believe – he'll clutch at straws. That Chambers guy is a sadist – why's he gunning for my father, who's never done him any harm? It made my blood boil when I heard about it, and I feel almost murderous rage even now. Then he told my dad to stop work for a while so he could write his novel. He's no more writing a novel than I am. He's fake, top to bottom, but I'm the only one who seems to see it, and I still have no real evidence. Or at least, I didn't have – till yesterday, but I still don't know if anyone will believe me, or see him as he really is.

We had one more day of freedom before the academic treadmill caught up with us, ie we had to go back to school, and no more skiving. Olly and I decided to go into town – not Walburn, where half the sixth form would be hanging around, just waiting to get their claws into us and spread gossip round the school, but a bit further afield, to Moxhurst. The shopping centre's better there as well. We took the bus and rode on the top deck, and Olly was his usual daft self. I wore a nice lemon-yellow top and white jeans, and I suppose it's one advantage of being half-Indian: I never have to worry about my tan, or my legs being horribly white at the beginning of the summer, like fish on a slab. Olly seemed to like how I looked anyway, judging by the expression he sometimes wears, like a hovering raptor. I said this to him once, and he howled with laughter. But he didn't deny it.

We'd worn ourselves out round the shops, and neither of us could afford to buy anything much. It was lunchtime, so we decided to get a sandwich and a cold drink, sit outside one of the cafés and watch the world go by. Luckily we were by the shop window, partly hidden by other tables, all of which were crowded. Because I saw them, and they didn't see me: Will Chambers and Maggie Calladine. They weren't holding hands, or even touching at all, but they were walking very close together, and he was bending down and whispering in her ear, and she was looking up at him, because she's quite a short lady, and maybe I'm no expert but I'd say her expression was one of total adoration: kind of simpering and unfocused. (If I ever find I'm looking at Olly like that, I'll shoot myself.) I must have looked gobsmacked, because Olly frowned and asked me what was the matter, but I shushed him and carried on watching them. They looked at our café but it probably wasn't quite posh enough for them, and I hid my face behind a menu till they passed. Olly, meanwhile, was making all sorts of bizarre, baffled faces. Eventually they went into a café on the other side of the mall, and sat at a table in the window. I got Olly to swap seats with me so I could watch them, and lend me his flashy shades in case they saw me. But there was little chance of that. It was quite obvious to anyone with any wits at all that they weren't noticing anybody except each other. Or at least, she was fixed on him. Once in a while he looked up and swept the area with his eyes. Odd, that: you'd think that if those two were having some kind of secret meeting she'd be the one with more to lose. But maybe she's past caring, and frankly who can wonder at it, when she's married to Mr Calladine? He makes a stick of wood look exciting. And with, as we are told, Ofsted arriving at the beginning of next week, he'll be even less fun to be with.

The worst of it was, I had another seeing right then and there, in the shopping centre. Not locusts this time, but a great bird like an eagle, wings wide open as if in flight, and screeching from an open beak so I could see its red throat. The next thing I knew Olly was pinching my arm, and looking very worried.

'What's going on?' he hissed.

I tried to shrug it off. 'What?'

'Where were you?'

'Here, of course.'

'Don't give me that. Something happened.' He sounded quite stern, and I found I rather liked the new, manly Olly.

I realised I was going to have to tell him. But not there. We finished our drinks and left, and while we were waiting for the bus home, and on the bus, I told him the whole story. I hadn't wanted to; I thought it might put him off if he thought I was some kind of nutter. But I should have known better – he's doing psychology as one of his A levels and when he talks about people with abnormal psyches he positively lights up.

So I told him about the earthquake, and the seeing I had then, and what happened afterwards with the psychiatrist and the psychologist, and all the tests I had to have, and he never said a word. Then, and this was even harder, I told him about Will Chambers and my concerns about him, and while I was *explaining to him it seemed to me that my evidence was good, not flimsy like when I tried to tell Mum. He listened with absolute attention, never interrupted once, so I know he was taking me seriously. And when I finally came to a halt, to my utter astonishment, there on the top deck of the bus, right at the back, he took my face in his hands and kissed me! I was astonished. 'Abbie,' he said, 'you are a marvel. If this wasn't our stop, I think I'd get down on my knees and beg you to marry me.'*

Of course, at that I whacked him with my handbag and told him to stop being a fool.

'I don't want to go home just yet,' Abbie said as they watched the bus trundle into the distance.

'Me neither,' Olly said, unusually serious. 'Let's take a little stroll in the woods.'

Abbie's eyes narrowed. 'You sound like the big bad wolf, with me as little Red Riding Hood.'

'I'll try and behave. Anyway, I want to talk about this wicked neighbour of yours.'

They walked slowly down the street, empty in the sunshine, and he took her hand and swung it. They found an alley between the houses that led out onto farmland, and after tramping round its rough edge, found a shady bank to lounge on just inside the narrow belt of trees, looking out onto a field of corn, ripening to yellow.

'My jeans will get grass stains,' Abbie complained.

'You could take them off,' Olly suggested innocently, then caught her look. 'OK, bad idea, sit on my jacket.'

'Olly, seriously, do you think they are having an affair? Will Chambers and Maggie Calladine?' She turned to him, suddenly anxious. 'You mustn't say anything about this to anyone. You won't, will you? It's not that Mr C's our Head, it's because they are really good friends of my parents'. I don't want to cause trouble.'

'I won't say a word,' Olly said softly. 'But trouble there already is, wouldn't you say? As to whether they're having an affair, I'm not exactly an expert, since I am only seventeen and have never been married … But I'd say it was as obvious as that nice little mole you have on your cheekbone.' He reached out and brushed it with his forefinger. 'In fact – and of course I only base this on the trashy TV programmes I watch – I'd bet all the money I don't have that they've already done the deed. Many times.'

'It makes me sick.'

'What, marital infidelity or the mere thought of sex?'

'Be serious, will you,' Abbie said miserably. 'This isn't a joke. I'm going to have to tell my mother, and she probably won't believe me.'

'Why do you have to tell her? Is it really your business?'

'You don't understand. Mrs Calladine is a nice person, my mum's best friend. She was my teacher in Year Five. We've known each other for ever. She can't realise what a snake Will Chambers is. If I don't say anything and it all goes horribly wrong, I'll feel really bad.'

'And if you tell your mum, what'll happen then?'

Abbie shook her head. 'I don't know. But this is an adult problem, and I want it off my hands.'

'You know what,' Olly said thoughtfully, taking her hand and studying her palm as if all wisdom resided there, 'next January in your case, and next April in mine, *we* will be adults. Officially.'

'Yeah, officially. It might take a bit longer to be a proper one, to really feel that you are one.'

He lay back on the grassy bank and looked up at her. 'Maybe you never do.'

'Maybe. But my mum is more of one than I am. And right now I'd rather be a kid who knew nothing. I never thought I'd ever say *that*.'

'I'm quite pleased you aren't a kid. I think you are very nice just the way you are.' He rolled his eyes suggestively, then saw her stern look and tried, unsuccessfully, to resume an air of innocence. 'I'll tell you something, though, my lovely Abbie: that man, Will whoever he is, dyes his hair.'

'What?'

Olly nodded knowingly. 'Sure as eggs is eggs.'

'How do you know? I didn't see any roots.'

'I know, because I have been known to, hm, how shall I put this, improve on nature myself.'

'What, you dye your hair?' She looked at his blond head in amazement.

He grinned broadly. 'Not any more. But when I was fourteen I went a sort of dark gold – I thought it would turn me into a sex god overnight. So I'm acquainted with the look. If I'm not very much mistaken, and of course I rarely am, that dark brown mane came out of a very expensive bottle.'

'Wow,' Abbie said thoughtfully. 'Why, do you suppose?'

Olly shrugged. 'Could be anything. Maybe he's going prematurely grey. Maybe he just likes the look. Maybe he's terribly vain.'

'Or maybe he's pretending to be somebody he's not,' Abbie said.

'Well,' Olly said, 'from all that you've told me, he sounds like a bit of a psycho. Not that I would ever use such a term in an exam paper.'

'Isn't that really bad?' Abbie said anxiously.

'It's not great, but don't go thinking he'll be running amok with an axe round your streets. He's probably quite nasty, but not necessarily a murderer. Or even at all violent.'

'Some relief that is.'

'You can borrow one of my psychology books if you like. Lots of info in there.'

'Maybe I will.' They were silent for a moment, Abby chewing her lip distractedly, Olly watching her through half-shut eyes. Finally she sighed. 'I think I'd better get home. This needs thinking about.'

Olly heaved himself up onto his elbows. 'You're going to tell your mum, then?'

'I guess I have to. Wish me luck.'

'Yeah.' His face was serious. 'Let me know what happens.'

'I'll message you.'

Maggie got home from school after five that afternoon. Late as she was, she had no expectation of seeing David till well into the evening. If previous evenings were anything to go by, he would come home looking stressed and distracted, eat a meal she had prepared, talk about nothing but the impending inspection – if he talked at all – take a shower and disappear into his study, where he would remain for hours, on his computer or on the phone. Ofsted had finally announced their imminent arrival and he had just a few days left to complete his preparations.

Once, not long ago, this behaviour would have angered and distressed her, whatever allowances she might have made for the exigencies of inspections. Now, she didn't care. Everything was different, and the difference was Will.

The June sun was still warm, and she lay stretched out on a sun-lounger on the decking that overlooked her lawn – a lawn in need of a mow, she noticed with a sight frown. Then the frown vanished, and she smiled to herself, picked up a glass of chilled wine from the low table next to her, and let her thoughts go where they pleased.

It didn't seem possible that just a few weeks ago she had been such a sodden, dishevelled, miserable mess at the end of her tolerance. Not long after that heart-to-heart with Will, when he had been so kind, he had appeared at the fence one morning, looking boyishly pleased with himself. 'I knew you wouldn't be at work,' he said, 'because I can hear children about. It must be half-term.'

Maggie was pulling weeds out of a flowery border. 'It is,' she said, straightening up and pushing her hair off her hot forehead. 'And I'm catching up with some jobs.'

'If you have a minute,' Will said, 'I wondered if you'd like to come and see how the alterations are going in the house. Tariq's not working at the moment, so it's an ideal time.'

'I'd love to,' Maggie said. 'Only I'm a bit grubby.'

'That doesn't matter,' Will said. His eyes seemed particularly bright. 'Come round. I'll even get the kettle on.'

She wiped her soil-streaked hands down the side of her jeans and followed him round the side of the house. His step was full of spring and bounce, and she smiled at his retreating back. He ushered her in through the open front door.

For the next half hour he showed her round the ground floor, full of energy and enthusiasm, and she followed him, nodding her head as she listened to his plans which seemed at times to cancel each other out. She wondered how Tariq coped with so many sudden changes; but Tariq was a patient man.

'This wall is coming down,' Will said, waving his arm. 'It's just a partition, so when it's out of the way the room will be not only bigger, but brighter, because it will have light from the window, do you see? I'm hoping we can make the window bigger as well.' He took her out of the room that was shrouded in dust sheets and white with plaster and into the tiny scullery. 'I don't mind this being small,' Will said. 'Kitchens should be compact, don't you agree? Easy to use, with everything to hand. Lots to do in here.' He threw open the back door, which squealed in protest. 'I've been hacking in the garden.' He proudly showed her heaps of brambles and ivy drying in the sun. 'I'll have to burn this lot. But not when your washing is on the line, I promise.' He smiled down into her eyes, and something twisted inside her, as if a forgotten key had turned in an old, rusty lock.

'Would you like to see upstairs? We haven't done much up there – I've just tried to make it more or less habitable for the time being.'

'Lead the way.'

She followed him up the narrow staircase that wound round to a sloping landing. 'We're going to have to sort these floorboards out,' Will said cheerfully. 'Mind how you go. I wouldn't want you to trip.'

He indicated a small room at the end of the short corridor. 'Bathroom,' he said. 'Small, antiquated, but scrubbed within an inch of its life, and the plumbing works, after a fashion, so quite safe for a lady to use, should she need to, and adequate for a solitary bachelor for now.' He opened another door at the back of the house. It was almost completely bare, but for a table, a chair and a laptop with a trailing cable.

'So this is where the great work is being written,' Maggie murmured. 'How's it going?'

'Better, now that I have a bit more peace,' Will said.

'Can you tell me what it's about, or is that a closely guarded secret?' Maggie asked.

Will laughed. 'Well, I don't normally answer that question, but since it's you ...' He sobered, sighing. 'There's quite a lot of autobiography in there,' he said, 'even though it's fiction, of course. I'm finding it quite, what's the word, cathartic, yes, drawing on my own experiences.' His shoulders seemed to slump. 'Sometimes rather tawdry ones, I'm afraid,' he muttered.

'Are those difficult bits to write?' Maggie asked gently.

Will nodded, and his hair flopped onto his forehead, making him look much younger. 'Mm, yes, they are.' Then his mood changed again, and he beamed. 'One last room,' he said. 'My bedroom. It's going to be a nice room when it's done.'

He pushed open the last door, at the front of the house, standing aside to let Maggie enter.

'It's nice now,' Maggie said, surprised. 'You've done great things already.'

'Just a couple of cheap curtains,' Will said modestly. 'And somewhere to sleep other than the floor.' He paused, letting her take in the reality of the bed with its bold, striped linen. 'Pity about the ghastly flock wallpaper, isn't it?' He shook his head. 'Who in their right mind could have chosen such a hideous shade of green?'

'Maybe it was going cheap,' Maggie said. She turned, finding herself closer to him than she had expected, close enough to smell his particular scent, masculine and fresh. He didn't move for a moment, and she found, to her slight dismay, that she liked being close to him. She smiled to herself. *Bad girl, Maggie.* Aloud she said, 'Did you say something about putting the kettle on?'

Will made her a cup of coffee that May morning, and even produced a plate of biscuits, bought in her honour. 'I don't eat much in the way of sweet things myself,' he'd said. 'But I thought you might like them.'

Maggie was touched. 'Thank you.' Then she added, 'That's probably why you haven't run to fat.' She ran her eyes over his lean torso and flat stomach. 'Not like some of us, I'm afraid.'

'You aren't the least bit fat!' Will protested. 'You are just right – rounded and huggable.' For a moment he looked worried. 'Sorry – perhaps I am being a bit too personal.'

Maggie shook her head, smiling. 'I can hardly be offended at a description like that. How nice to be thought of as huggable.'

Lying in the sun weeks later, remembering, she thought that moment was probably when, perhaps not specially noticed at the time, something had changed in the air between them, as if an unspoken agreement had been reached: 'If not today, then soon.'

She knew, intellectually, that it was wrong; she was a Christian and adultery was forbidden: the seventh commandment. She couldn't argue with something so plain and clear, and she didn't try. She was a married woman, cheating on her husband. *A husband that doesn't care. Who doesn't see me or hear me, let alone love me. A husband who neglects and sidelines me, and would probably not notice if I wasn't there, as long as meals and clean shirts turned up on time. And that was true before Ofsted reared its picky little head.*

She shifted on the sun-lounger, twirling the glass in her hand, and her thoughts turned all too willingly away from David and towards Will, like a sunflower opening its face to the sun. *It's not even just sex. Though that is nice, it's no better than with David. Just more frequent! Probably, if I'm honest, not as good as with David, though I'd never let Will suspect that. Men are so sensitive, and he's probably more so than most. I'll let him think he is Don Juan reincarnated. It's just lovely to be close to someone, to be appreciated and, frankly, adored. Not something I'm used to.*

But, oh boy, am I enjoying getting used to it! I wonder what happened to my conscience? I really don't know. Because I ought to feel guilty, and I suppose I sort of do, but the happiness overwhelms any negative thoughts, and when I'm with Will he fills me up – mind, body, senses, imagination, the whole shooting match.

I don't even want to think about the future. Now is quite delicious enough. That's what I want – a lifetime of todays. He's always on about how we'll run away together – he's such a child! I said to him, laughing at him, 'But you live here now, you're having the house renovated, I live and work here, where do you think we're going to run away to?' And he just turned over, and took my face in his hands, and said solemnly, 'We'll find a way.' I just cannot resist that man when he looks at me with those soft brown eyes and talks such nonsense.

When Julie came back from the bathroom she found Tariq sitting on the edge of the bed, still damp from his shower and dressed only in a towel. His head was bent, his arms resting on his knees.

'You all right, love?'

He grunted and lifted his head. 'Shattered. Aching. I'm getting too old for this job.'

'What else are you going to do?'

He shrugged. 'No idea.'

She sat beside him. 'Want a back rub?' She gently massaged his shoulders and spine, and he stretched and flexed his muscles. 'Any better?'

'Mm.'

'You were very quiet this evening. Is everything OK?'

He looked up, and she saw with a pang his bloodshot eyes. 'I didn't want to talk much in front of the kids,' he said. 'It's harder to talk in the evenings these days now they're older. They never seem to go to bed!' He smiled, then his smile faded and the worried look returned. 'I went back to work at Will's today. That's how we left it, that I'd go back after a fortnight. I could have done without it after all the heavy work over Walburn way, but I don't like to let a customer down if they're expecting me. And he behaved really oddly. When he opened the door he looked at me as if he'd never seen me before. Then he said quite rudely, "What are you doing back here?" I thought he was joking, so I just said something like, "What, haven't you got the kettle on yet?" And he went off on a great rant, got really shirty, swore at me, the works.'

Julie frowned. 'So what did you do? Don't tell me, you slugged him with a handy piece of four-by-two.'

'Very funny. I backed off, reminded him as politely as I could manage that this was the day we'd prearranged for me to come back. And he changed, like someone had cast a spell. All apologetic, said I'd caught him at a bad moment, he'd forgotten the date, and so on. Talk about laying on the charm! Anyway, I got on with the work and he went upstairs and I guess got on with his, and I even heard him singing! Later on he came down, offered me coffee, still all sweetness and light, very chatty, said he'd hit a snag in his plot which had kept him up late into the night, but now he'd resolved it and all was going well.' He took a deep breath. 'And then, drinking coffee, just by way of casual conversation, I asked him if he'd had any success with trying to find news of my family in Kashmir via his father's diplomatic contacts.'

'And?'

'Well, it was very strange. He looked at me blankly, as if I'd just spoken to him in Urdu.'

'Do you actually speak Urdu?'

Tariq smiled faintly. 'Well, I did once.' He shook his head. 'For a moment there I doubted myself. Had he actually offered to do some research? Because by his expression you'd think I'd asked him something, I don't know, totally outlandish. Then obviously he remembered, because he started looking really annoyed, and said no, he hadn't had time – very huffily. And after that he took his coffee upstairs. It was like he was angry because I'd caught him out in something. That man can change faster than I can blink.'

Julie nodded. 'He is a strange one, for sure.' She hesitated. 'Actually, I heard something today that puzzled me a bit.'

Tariq looked at her. 'What?'

'Shouldn't you dry your hair? It's getting late.'

'In a minute. Tell me what you heard first.'

'Well, I bumped into Mrs Lyons.' When he looked blank she said, 'You know, the lady who sometimes comes to church with Mrs Cocksedge.'

'Oh, yeah.'

'She was all of a flap because she'd misplaced some money. She was saving up for the holiday the Seniors' Club are going on in September. The holiday itself is all paid for, she said, but she was squirrelling away a few pounds here and there for spending money, and she had it, guess what, in an old tea caddy on her kitchen shelf.'

'Who would have known it was there?'

'That's just it. Only she does – so she said. And she could have sworn there was £100 in there, but when she went to add some she counted it and found only seventy. I don't know, I guess anyone can be mistaken, and she's over eighty so she's allowed to be a bit forgetful. But – '

'But what?'

'Well, she … she kind of lowered her voice and went all solemn, and said she didn't want to seem to be accusing anyone, but Will has been doing some garden work for her and he's the only one who's been in her house apart from Mrs Cocksedge and she'd trust *her* with her life. So I said maybe you made a mistake and she shook her head, looked quite bewildered, said she was *so sure* there was £100 in there. And it wasn't so much the money, £30 isn't after all a king's ransom, it was the worry – was she going crazy? Or had someone robbed her? And the thing is too, there's not a lot she can say or do.'

'Hm. Apart from keep her money somewhere safer, like the bank.'

'Yes, I know, but that means trailing into town to put it in and take it out. And I remember how my grandma used to keep pots of money, a few coins here and there, for the coal, or the insurance, that kind of thing.' She paused. 'It seems an awful thing to even think it, but could Will have stolen it?'

'How do I know? He seems to have plenty of money. Leaves it lying around the house.' He got up. 'I'm going to get a dry towel.'

When he came back Julie was still sitting on the edge of the bed. 'I feel a bit concerned sometimes,' she said slowly. 'Was Abbie actually right, that Will is dodgy? We know so little about him. And I said I'd keep my eyes open, and I haven't really. We've been so busy lately, and there's all the worry with John.'

Tariq rubbed his hair vigorously. 'When are they moving him to the hospice?'

'Soon. Maybe tomorrow. Poor man. I don't suppose he's got long, but he keeps unbelievably cheerful.'

Tariq thought for a moment. 'Abbie hasn't mentioned Will recently, has she? Not to me, anyway.'

'Nor me. She may be wary of saying anything. I was a bit sceptical the last time. But also she's had a few distractions the last few weeks.'

'Oh, yeah, the exams. She seems to think they went OK, as far as I can tell.'

Julie looked up at him and smiled. 'Not just exams. There's a boy on the scene.'

Tariq's eyebrows shot up. 'What? How come I didn't hear about this?'

Julie chuckled. 'She's been keeping the whole thing very quiet. I only know the little I do know because I wormed it out of Dan, who really didn't want to tell me. The lad's called Olly, he's in Abbie's year, came over from Ketley College last September, and Dan knows him because they play football together. We might even have seen him without knowing it, when we've gone to pick Dan up. Anyway, I imagine some of the mysterious outings she's been on just lately have been with him.'

'Doesn't she tell you where she's going?'

'Oh, yes, kind of, she shouts out from the door, "Just going out for a while, Mum, I've got my phone." She's seventeen, Riq. You've got to trust them, let them grow up.'

Tariq scowled. 'But what do we know about this boy?'

Julie took off her dressing gown, hung it on the back of the door and got into bed. 'Do give over, darling. You've got a look on your face that says. "How dare you mess around with my daughter, you swine!" He's just a boy. She'll be OK.'

'Hm.'

'Are you dry yet? It's getting late and I want to go to sleep.'

Tariq threw the towel on the floor with an expansive gesture. 'Here I am, Your Highness, at your service as always.'

Julie sniggered. 'Watch it, I just might take you up on that.' She leaned over and switched off the light.

Will lay on his bed, the covers kicked off. The thin curtains offered little protection; it was hot in his bedroom and sleep was elusive. On the other hand, the night's silence gave him the chance to think, to review, to plan. *I shouldn't have taken that money. Not that my conscience is troubling me.* He laughed quietly. *Isn't that a bit of a pious myth, anyway – conscience? Poor Mrs Lyons, fancy stealing from a dear old lady. Well, it could be seen as payment for my hedge-cutting, even though I said I'd do it for free, noble chap that I am. The trouble is, funds are getting perilously low, and I said I'd take Maggie out to dinner. Why did I do that? I don't want to sit in a restaurant for several hours being charming to Maggie. I don't really need charm any more, it's done its work and I can have her when I like. Except that I don't want her. There's the irony. But I have to keep her sweet for a little while longer, unfortunately for me. Maggie is a demanding, clinging, irritating bore – but she may need to be my bank, sooner than I thought.*

I suppose it was all right for a week or two. Good for my ego. But now, for crying out loud! She's so grateful, ugh! So needy. So guilty! Guilty, really? If she really felt so guilty would she always be wheedling me into bed? And why are women so loud and unrestrained? It makes me feel sick, but I still have to perform like an actor. I'll be glad when I can get out of here, get shot of her. She makes me queasy with her soft rolls of fat.

I'm going to have to up the ante. Revenge on a man by seducing his wife is rubbish revenge if the man has no idea what's happening. I need something more elegant. He thought, his brow creased in concentration. *What does that man value, more than he values his wife? Of course – he values his reputation. I have to think of a way.*

For a few minutes he dozed. Then his eyes flew open, bright and blue. *Yes, and there's another thing. That sneaky little know-all, Abbie Hasan. If I could take her down I would. I made a mess of that thing with Tariq; could have played it better. I have to pick up the pace – strike and disappear. But there's still work to be done. And every time I see her – Abbie – even in the distance, I think of that moment by the church gate. She saw something – what was it? She knows something, but how can she? Or does she have an idea she's seen me before too? I wish I could remember. It was something about those eyes of hers.*

In the early hours of the morning he woke, not to hot sluggish half-consciousness but to full clarity. He had a mental picture of a pair of green eyes, looking at him not with suspicion and hostility but in apologetic embarrassment. And he remembered, sat up in bed and laughed aloud, punching the air. *Yes! Yes, yes, yes! Now I know. Now I remember. She was younger, of course – gawkier, less assured. She came flying out of the psych's room like a tornado, not looking where she was going, smack into me, and those delicious confidential folders went all over the corridor! She looked up at me, all stricken with humiliation, and there were tears in those eyes. Oh, yes. So that was you, Miss Hasan, when you were a tormented little girl. I remember: it wasn't long after that that they rumbled me and kicked me out. 'Falsifying my CV.' How disgraceful. It was fun while it lasted, but I don't recall reading any of her notes on the quiet – I'd have remembered that. Pity. But if she was there seeing the shrinks she must have had a problem, a nice juicy mental problem. Probably still has, although she doesn't show it. Oh, surely I can use that? I must think. There has to be a way to use her to bring Calladine's world crashing down.*

A sweet, neat solution. That's what I need. Primed and ready, like a bomb, while I'm off and away.

I'll go without Maggie if I can. But it's no matter. If I need her for now, for my little cash flow problem, I can ditch her later. It's a nuisance, like a biting, buzzing fly – but flies can be swatted and squashed. Sometimes you have to make small sacrifices to reap big rewards. He grinned. *I could write a book. One of those 'How to' guides, like the ones you see in libraries and doctors' surgeries and DIY shops. Only mine would be, 'How to be a total rat: with examples.'* In the silence of his pre-dawn bedroom, he laughed aloud.

June 2010

Julie woke to a light tapping on her bedroom door. She pushed herself up onto one elbow and frowned. Was she hearing things? She looked at the glowing numbers on the bedside clock: 4.15. Tariq was a gently snoring sheet-tangled sprawl beside her; otherwise all was quiet. Then the tap came again, and an intense whisper: *'Mum.'*

She couldn't tell which child it was, but she hissed back, 'Hold on a minute.' She got out of bed, pulled her dressing gown down from the hook and stuffed her arms into the sleeves. She opened the door.

Abbie was hovering on the landing. 'Mum, I'm really sorry to wake you, but there's something – '

Julie closed her bedroom door behind her. She took in her daughter's anxious face. 'Put a jumper on, and come downstairs,' she said, her voice low. 'I don't want to wake your dad.'

Moments later Abbie joined her in the kitchen. Julie already had the kettle on.

'What's the matter, Abbie?'

'I wouldn't wake you, Mum, you know I wouldn't, but I had a … I don't know what it was, maybe some kind of dream, nightmare more like, and then I woke up and I was thinking about it and I had a seeing as well.'

'Are you sure you weren't still asleep?'

Abbie shook her head. 'Positive.' She slid into a seat at the table. 'Thing is, I can't really remember much about the dream, except it was scary … I think I was running over the fields in my PJs and something was after me and I could feel its breath and hear it snorting and snuffling. And I wouldn't have woken you up just for that. I'm not five any more, calling for Mummy when I've had a nightmare.' She smiled faintly. 'It was the seeing that clinched it.'

'Do you want some tea?'

'Yes, please.'

Julie waited for the kettle to boil. 'Go on, I'm listening.'

'It was so clear, Mum,' Abbie said slowly. 'A huge brown hooded cobra. Like in that picture book Dad used to show us when we were little. *Animals of India*, or some title like that. Hood fully extended, mouth open, long pointed fangs poised to strike. Very, very frightening.' Julie waited, watching Abbie's haunted face. Abbie looked up, and her expression spoke of pleading: to be believed, Julie understood, to be taken seriously. 'Mum,' Abbie said, her voice soft but urgent, 'it was him. I know it. Will Chambers. *He's the snake.*'

Julie poured boiling water into two mugs and stirred. She took milk from the fridge. 'Tell me why you think so.' After a moment she pulled the teabags out, added milk and passed a mug to Abbie.

'Not just because of the locusts. It's been happening again. My seeings.'

Julie sat down, her tea steaming in front of her. 'When was this? Where were you?'

'Just the other day. At the shopping centre in Moxhurst.'

'What were you doing there?' Although she thought she knew.

'Don't worry about that now,' Abbie said. 'I was there. And I saw Will Chambers, and I had another seeing. A huge bird of prey, an eagle maybe, wings spread, sharp beak open. It just seems when I see him I have a seeing, of something menacing and destructive.'

'But Abbie – '

'You're going to say we don't know anything concrete,' Abbie said, her voice rising. 'But we do. Mum, *now we do.*'

'Why?'

'I know you'll be upset,' Abbie said. Her voice shook. 'But you have to know. I can't cope with this on my own. He was with Mrs Calladine.'

'What? How do you mean, "with" Maggie?' Julie's brain felt sluggish, barely able to process this new and unwelcome information.

'With her as in more than very friendly,' Abbie said. 'In a café. I watched them. Talking very intensely. And she was looking at him ... honestly, Mum, no other way to put it, with total adoration.'

'I don't understand. Why wasn't Maggie at work?'

'Well, it was lunchtime. Maybe she'd scarpered during the break.'

Julie took a deep breath and shook her head, frowning.

'Please, Mum, tell me this time you believe me.'

Julie took a gulp of her tea and spluttered. 'Ugh, too hot.' She put the mug down and sighed. 'I do believe you, that's just it. Not that I want to, but I've been thinking about what you said and everything that's happened – little things but ... maybe we *have* been too trusting. Innocent as doves, but not wise as serpents.'

'What?'

'No matter. I said I'd keep my eyes open, didn't I? I haven't, and I should have. I don't know – I've just been so busy, so preoccupied. What with work, and John ... I should have clocked that Maggie hasn't been around much just lately. If I'd really thought about it I might have realised: with David so eaten up with Ofsted I'd have expected her to be round here more, or at least on the phone, having a good moan. But I've hardly seen her. And it adds up, I suppose. She put a good face on it, but she wasn't happy, and Ofsted would have made it worse ... that feeling of being neglected. Unloved.' She saw Abbie watching her, as if following her thoughts. 'Which would make her very vulnerable to someone so good-looking and charming. Someone who cared, or said he did. Oh, Maggie.' She closed her eyes and shook her head. 'My poor friend.'

'What will you do?' Abbie said after a pause.

'I'll try and talk to her. See what's actually going on.' She reached over the table and took Abbie's hand. 'But you did the right thing telling me, sweetheart.'

To her dismay Abbie started to cry, her eyes welling up, tears dripping down her cheeks. 'Thank goodness.'

'Abs, I'm sorry.' Julie gripped her daughter's hand more tightly. 'I should have believed you sooner. You shouldn't have had to bear this on your own.' She fished in her pocket and handed Abbie a tissue.

Abbie wiped her eyes, blew her nose loudly and managed a shaky smile. 'Not quite alone, actually.'

Julie leaned back in her chair and folded her arms. 'Yes, so I hear,' she said, trying to look very fierce. 'When was I going to hear about this young man of yours?'

'Who told you?'

'Your brother. Very reluctantly and with no details.'

Abbie shook her head. 'I should have known. You can wind Dan *and* Dad round your little finger.'

'Dan, sometimes. Your dad, only in trivial matters. He may look soft and obliging, and so he is. But if he's made his mind up, and he disagrees, no charm on my part will shift him.'

'Yeah, I guess that's true.'

'So – what about this guy?'

Abbie grinned. 'Olly Bradshaw. Age seventeen. Birthday in April. Lives in Walburn, Mum, Dad, little sister. Studying politics, sociology and psychology. I'm probably a case study to him. Blond, blue eyes, stupid sense of humour.'

'You like him, I see.'

'Yeah, he's OK. More to him than meets the eye, I suspect. Has occasional flashes of maturity.'

'Wow. *That* good!' Julie chuckled. 'Well, I won't press you any more. Just, Abs – ' Abbie raised her eyebrows. 'Be a bit sensible, OK? Not like your mother.'

'I don't think you did too badly, Mum, did you?' Abbie smiled. 'But no, I'll be good.' She got up, pushing her chair back, and moved toward the door. 'Good*ish*, anyway.'

'Cheeky,' Julie growled. 'Now, back to bed for both of us, I think. It's a good job your exams are over.'

Abbie shook her head. 'I think what's going on with Mrs Calladine and – and that man is more important that my AS levels. Night, Mum. Thanks for not being cross.' She left the room quietly, but a moment later she put her head back round the kitchen door. 'I forgot,' she whispered. 'Has Dad said anything about Molly? No one seems to be worried about her.'

'Who?'

'The dog, Mum.'

'Oh. Right. Well, as far as I know they put the dog in the shed while your dad's working. To keep her safe.' She saw Abbie frown. 'With the door open, and water, but tied up.' She smiled. 'Oh, Abbie. Trust you to worry about the dog.'

'I do worry,' Abbie said seriously. 'She's just a helpless dog. And I think he's a very bad man.'

Julie hesitated at her kitchen door, chewing her bottom lip. Should she phone Maggie to check if it was OK to call? But then Maggie might say, don't come, it's not convenient. On the other hand, if she, Julie, were simply to drop in, as she always had in the past, it might be embarrassing, if Will was there. It would be embarrassing too for Julie, after Abbie's disclosure, if David was there. She sighed crossly and left the house with sudden determination, as if she was afraid that if she wavered any longer she would change her mind. It was a fine summer day, the birds were merry and the leaves rustling in the light wind, showing undersides of white and gold as they turned. On any other day, walking past fields swaying with ripening wheat, Julie would have taken time to look and rejoice in beauty and bounty. Today her mind was darkened with the prospect of the unwelcome task she had set herself – a task of duty and friendship, as she saw it, but heavy and fearsome. It seemed she was about to beard an ogre in its den, not visit her long-known and beloved friend.

She walked soft-footed down her street and into Maggie's lane, finding herself actually creeping and barely breathing. *For goodness' sake, Julie.* She arrived at the Calladines' gate, and glanced over at Will's cottage. To her relief the battered green car was not there, but both Maggie's and David's cars were in their drive. Just lately she knew David had often been into school at weekends, but now, with Ofsted over, perhaps he was allowing himself some respite. She hesitated again. If David was here, should she be disturbing them? It had never been a question that had ever needed to bother her before. David was a friend too, after all.

She steeled herself and walked down to the Calladines' back door, her feet heavy and her stomach churning. She tapped nervously. No reply. She tapped again, a little harder, and heard Maggie's voice. 'Come in, whoever you are!' Julie put her head round the door. The kitchen was immaculate and deserted. She stepped inside and shut the door behind her, and then saw Maggie through the open door of the conservatory, lying full-length on a brightly striped sun-lounger.

As Julie approached Maggie turned her head. 'Oh! Hello, stranger.' Her voice was friendly enough, but something in her expression gave Julie pause – a wariness, even a hardness. To her eyes Maggie looked somehow different: shinier, plumper, sleeker, like a basking cat. Her dark curly hair was longer, shining with copper highlights, and her cheeks were slightly flushed.

'You're the stranger,' Julie said lightly as she approached. 'Haven't seen you in a while. Been busy?'

Maggie didn't reply for a moment, then she said, 'Oh – as ever. How about you?'

'Likewise.'

'Do you want some coffee?' Maggie hardly stirred, and Julie felt that the offer was not really meant. 'No, thanks. I had some not long ago. Just thought I'd pop round, see how you were.'

'Well, I'm fine, as you see.'

'David's at home, is he?' Julie asked. She sat down gingerly on a small stool.

'Yes, Ofsted's behind him, but he's still closeted in his study. Paperwork, I suppose.'

There was a silence. Maggie watched Julie, and Julie looked away.

'Maggie – '

'Seems to me you've come with something to say,' Maggie said coolly. 'Why don't you just say it?'

Julie opened her mouth to speak, but nothing came out. She felt her heart pounding. 'You're so … so different.'

Maggie's bright black eyes narrowed. 'Am I? Different how?'

'I can't explain. You look so well, but somehow you don't seem to be yourself.'

'Perhaps,' Maggie said softly, 'I am more myself than you have ever seen me. Perhaps you don't recognise me when I am not wretched.'

'I'm glad you aren't wretched, but – ' Julie faltered, feeling sick.

Maggie gazed intently at her friend. 'Say what you have come to say,' she said.

Julie gulped. 'Maggie, are you – are you having an affair with Will Chambers?'

Maggie sighed, and to Julie's dismay she smiled – a secretive, inward smile that spoke of neither joy nor humour but satisfaction and triumph. 'Well, that's very direct! But since you ask, and I don't really care who knows, yes, I am.'

'Oh, Maggie – !'

'And,' Maggie ploughed on as if Julie had not spoken, 'I don't regret it for one moment. It's nice, you know, for once, to be cared for, appreciated, listened to, yes, adored.'

'But what about David?' Julie whispered. 'Surely he doesn't know?'

'Of course he doesn't!' Maggie snapped. 'Don't you realise, he wouldn't notice if I danced down the High Street naked and singing! You, you're so cocooned, Julie. In your own sweet, safe little world. I've been trying to tell you for a long time how he barely sees and hears me. But it seems you haven't been hearing either.'

Julie felt her eyes fill with tears. 'I have heard you!' she wailed. 'And I know David has been terribly neglectful, especially lately. But Maggie, is this an answer? How will this help?'

'Well, that's a stupid question. Of course it helps. It helps *me*. And I've finally found the gumption to help myself for once.'

'But Maggie, it's *wrong*. It's the seventh commandment. Don't you believe that any more?'

Maggie's nose wrinkled and she waved her hand, if to dispel an unpleasant smell. 'Oh, please, spare me your moralising! How would you know what I've been through, you with your devoted husband and charming children!'

Julie gaped. 'I've never heard you speak like this before,' she said. 'As if you hated us. Maggie, please. We've been friends for years. That's why I came today, as a friend, because I care about you.'

'If you really cared, you would be pleased for me,' Maggie said flatly. 'You'd be pleased that I'm happy.'

'Of course I want you to be happy,' Julie said in despair. 'But not like this. This is awful, Maggie.'

Maggie shook her head, her lip slightly curling. 'No, it's not. It's absolutely marvellous.'

Julie winced. It seemed Maggie intended to make her friend feel uncomfortable.

'Maybe it is marvellous now,' Julie battled on. 'But it can't last that way. What do you think's going to happen? You stand to lose everything – your husband, your home, your reputation, the respect of people who know you – your whole life.'

'I won't care,' Maggie said, looking at Julie disdainfully, as if she were a complete idiot. 'Because I won't be *in* this life any more.'

'You're going to leave?' Julie cried out. 'With him? Oh, Maggie, I beg you, please don't!'

Maggie frowned. 'Why shouldn't I?'

'Because you don't know him. You don't know what he's like.'

Maggie's eyebrows raised. 'I think I know him rather better than you do.'

Julie fell silent and stared at the ground. She took a deep breath and looked up at her friend, horrified by the closed-in look on her face, as if she were a castle with drawbridge up and battlements bristling with soldiers. 'I have to tell you what Abbie saw.'

'Abbie? What's she got to do with anything? She's just a child.'

'It's Abbie who saw you and Will together, and told me.'

'Oh, did she, indeed.' Maggie's tone was unnervingly hostile. 'So?'

'You know she has these visions, "seeings" she calls them.'

'She still has them?'

'Once in a while. But she had one just after we first met Will, after he came to ours for dinner. A vision of locusts, stripping fields bare. She's had others, of a bird of prey and a cobra, very frightening visions, all in connection with him. She's convinced he is bad, Maggie. That he means you harm.'

Maggie snorted. 'What total rubbish! I can't believe what I'm hearing! You say you want me to be happy, but when I find someone who really cares for me you'd rather listen to the self-important claims of a deluded, puffed-up, hysterical adolescent!'

Julie leapt to her feet, her fists clenched. 'How can you say that about a girl you've known since she was a toddler – my daughter! I hate to have to say this, Maggie, but you're the one who is deluded! I hope you don't fall too hard, that's all. But when you do, don't expect me to pick up the pieces – not when you can talk about my Abbie like that!'

Maggie stared at the ceiling, unblinking. 'Nobody likes the truth, do they,' she said as if to herself. 'I think you'd better leave now, Julie.'

'Oh, I'm going. Goodbye, Maggie. I wish you well, though I strongly doubt any good can come of this ... this shameful shambles.' She choked on her words, turned and stumbled from the room, but not before she saw the strangely knowing little smile on Maggie's face.

On Monday morning the atmosphere in the Hasan household was unusually strained. Abbie sat at the kitchen table, munching on cereal, her eyes apparently on her book, but not seeing the words. Dan, always preferring to avoid any emotional scene, had long since eaten and gone back upstairs, ostensibly to sort out his school bag. Julie was doing something at the sink, her silence almost palpable. Tariq got up with a sigh, put his bowl on the work surface, and gave Julie's shoulder a squeeze. 'I'll be off to work now, love.'

'Yeah, OK.'

When he had gone Julie pottered around the kitchen for a while, opening and closing cupboards, staring at their contents distractedly, biting her lip and frowning.

'You all right, Mum?' Abbie said tentatively.

'Not really.'

'You still thinking about Mrs Calladine?'

Julie frowned. 'It's not something you can easily dismiss, is it?'

'I guess not.'

Julie groaned. 'I wish I could dismiss it, believe me. I'm sorry, Abbie, it's not your fault. I just can't get over how she's willing to throw everything away. *Everything.* Her marriage, her job, even us, her friends. For what? Some illusion.' She looked at Abbie, and her face spoke of anger and hurt. 'I mean, even if he was by some chance a decent bloke who really loved her – '

'Not much chance of that, I'd say,' Abbie murmured.

'But even then, it would be so crazy!' Julie ploughed on. 'How well can she know him? He's only been here, what? Three months?'

Abbie opened her mouth to speak, then she stopped and turned towards the open window. 'That sounds like Dad's van. I'd know that chugging old engine anywhere.'

A moment later Tariq came into the kitchen. His wife and daughter stared at him.

'There's no one there,' he said, shaking his head. 'At Will's. The place is all locked up. No car.'

'Was he expecting you?' Julie said sharply.

'Well, I thought so. I was supposed to be putting that partition in … But that's not all.' He sat down next to Abbie and looked up at Julie, a puzzled frown creasing his forehead. 'While I was there a car drew up. A young bloke got out, said good morning, and started putting up a For Sale sign. I said to him, you sure you've got the right address? And he looked at his paperwork, and said the address, and it was right. I think Will has gone. He's put the cottage back on the market. Not only that, but he was supposed to be going to the bank this morning, so he told me. He owes me almost seven hundred quid.'

Julie gasped and sank into a chair opposite. 'Oh, no! Now what?'

Tariq shook his head and said nothing. Then he seemed to notice Abbie. 'Hey, won't you have missed the bus?'

Abbie looked at the clock. 'Oh … bother. Can someone drive me? Please? Sorry, I was a bit distracted. We didn't even notice Dan leave, did we?'

'He must have gone out the front,' Julie said. 'He quite often forgets to say goodbye.'

Tariq heaved himself to his feet. 'You can drive yourself,' he said to Abbie. 'If you're thinking of putting in for your test during the school holidays you need lots of practice.' He turned to Julie. 'We'll talk about this when I get back, OK, sweetheart? Don't worry, we'll figure something out.' He paused, his hand on the door handle. 'What a mess. To be taken for a fool like this. I can't believe it.'

'I'll get my bag, Dad,' Abbie said. 'And clean my teeth. Two minutes.'

She had only just crossed the kitchen and stepped into the hall when there was a loud banging on the front door. She opened it. On the doorstep, dressed for work, stood David Calladine, his face grim and set.

'Hello, Abbie,' he said. He spoke quietly, but as any pupil knew, there were tones of his voice that meant you were in deep trouble, and Abbie gaped, speechless. 'Is your mother in?'

'Y-yes,' Abbie stuttered. 'She's in the kitchen. And my dad. Come through.'

He followed her down the hallway, walking fast, almost treading on her heels. She pushed open the kitchen door. 'Mum, it's Mr Ca – '

David elbowed past her, and she saw he had something in his hand. 'Do you know anything about this?' he said to Julie, ignoring Tariq, who had been half out of the door but now came quietly back into the kitchen.

'What?' Julie said, bewildered. 'What are you talking about, David?'

David laid the sheet of paper on the table and smoothed it out with exaggerated care. When he spoke, his voice shook with barely controlled fury. He looked at Julie, his expression dark; he seemed to have forgotten that Tariq and Abbie were even there. 'This is a letter,' David said, his voice grating. 'From Maggie. My wife. Telling me she has left me, to run off with that Will Chambers. His place is locked up, his car is gone, there is a For Sale sign outside the cottage. She is gone too, as is her car, some of her clothes and her handbag with credit cards and money, I dare say. She must have gone very early, while I was still upstairs.' He paused, breathing heavily. 'Did you know about this?'

'Of course I didn't, David – ' Julie stopped, biting her lip.

'Perhaps you knew something,' David said harshly. He raised his hand, and Tariq moved towards the table. But David simply ran his hand through his hair. 'You were at our house on Saturday. You spoke with her. Did you know what was going on?'

'Only then, David. Not before, I promise you. I asked her if she was having an affair with him, and she admitted it. I was appalled.'

'So you didn't encourage her?'

'What? Why would I do that? Of course I didn't! I don't know how you could think that of me, not for a moment. For Heaven's sake, David!'

David stared at her for a long moment. 'What do I know?' he said bitterly. 'You two were always thick as thieves.'

Julie's voice rose indignantly. 'I tried to argue with her, to try to make her see sense. I can't believe you would think I was conspiring.'

'Whatever,' David said, waving his hand impatiently. 'So you don't know where she might have gone?'

'No, I don't. I am angry with her too. It's not just you she has rejected. So it's a bit much you thinking I am involved in some way.'

David did not reply. He stuffed the letter into his pocket and turned back to the door. 'Well, if Chambers has really left, perhaps someone could do something about his wretched dog. It's howling fit to wake the dead.' He left the room, and a moment later the front door closed with a crash.

Tariq and Julie stared at each other for a moment in stupefied silence. Then Julie burst into tears and Tariq crossed the room in two long strides and pulled her close. 'Darling, don't get upset,' he said into her hair. 'It's a mess, I know. But we have to keep calm if we're going to be of any use.'

'Dad, Mum,' Abbie said urgently. 'Sorry, but right now you're missing the point. Seems to me that snake has gone and abandoned Molly. We have to go and get her out. She might have been in there for days!'

'Right,' Tariq said grimly. 'But she'll be OK for a few more minutes. I'm going to make your mum a cup of tea.'

Julie wiped her face with her hands. 'No, Riq, Abbie's right. I saw Maggie two days ago, and then there was no sign of Will or the dog. We have to go and find out. You'd better get your axe from the shed.'

'But –'

'Look,' Julie said, 'destroying a shed door is no big deal if he's really left her to starve or die of thirst. The door can be replaced. The dog can't.'

Tariq nodded. 'You two go on ahead, find out exactly where she is – could be in the shed or in the house. I'll get some tools.'

Julie kicked off her slippers and stuffed her feet into a pair of old trainers she kept by the back door, for gardening or hanging out washing. Abbie was already haring up the drive and into the street. Julie locked the door and followed. By the time she arrived at Will's cottage, Abbie was already hovering anxiously outside the garden shed.

'Mum, she's in here. I can hear her panting. Poor dog! She must be dehydrated. I've been talking to her, so at least she's stopped howling.' She looked out into the lane. 'Where's Dad got to?'

Moments later Tariq arrived, holding a pair of sturdy bolt-cutters. 'No need for breaking down doors,' he said. 'We don't want to hurt the dog, do we? I remembered he bought a padlock and chain for the shed. Stand by in case it tries to escape.'

'*She*, Dad,' Abbie said. 'Molly's a she.'

'Whatever.' Tariq positioned the cutters and with a loud snap severed the chain. He pulled the shed door open.

'Oh, Molly! What has that evil man done to you?' Abbie was on her knees, her arms round the dog's neck. Molly's legs were shaky, but she managed a wag of her feathery tail.

'Dear Lord, what a stink,' Julie said, wrinkling her nose.

'Not surprising, is it?' Abbie said indignantly.

'There's an outside tap,' Tariq said. 'He might have left the water connected. If he has, you can get a drink for her straight away. That's what she needs most right now. Hang on, there's a bit of rope here – you can use it as a temporary lead.' He tied the rope to the dog's collar. Abbie took the rope and the empty drinking bowl that was upended just inside the door, and walked slowly with the dog to the back of the cottage, talking softly to her. 'Dad, there's no water,' she called after a moment.

'OK, stay put,' Julie said. 'I'll go up to the Prestons' and borrow a bottle of water. Back in a tick.'

Abbie sat with her back to the wall of the cottage, her arm around Molly, and Tariq looked around the shed that had been Molly's prison, shaking his head. 'Well, I guess it's not my problem,' he muttered.

Ten minutes later Julie returned at a run, breathless and holding out a fruit juice bottle full of water. She poured it into Molly's bowl. 'There you go, old girl.'

The dog drank without taking breath until the brimming bowl was empty. Then she looked up at Abbie and Julie, her tongue lolling.

'She needs a bath,' Julie said.

Abbie scrambled to her feet. 'I'll take her home.'

Julie shook her head and took the rope from her daughter's hand. 'What you'll do, sweetie pie,' she said firmly, 'is go to school. In the van. You can drive, or Dad can drive you, as you please. Get your bag and go, and you might just be in time for registration if you don't hang about.'

'Mum!' Abbie protested.

Julie said nothing, just stared with eyebrows raised.

'OK,' Abbie capitulated, 'but you won't give her away, will you? Or take her to the rescue centre, or anything?' She turned pleading eyes on her father, then looked back at Julie. 'Dan and I've wanted a dog for years. And Molly is such a nice dog. And she's had a horrible time.'

Julie gave Abbie a hug. 'I'm going to give her a bath,' she said. 'Make her smell a bit better. Dad can buy some dog food on his way home. She'll be here when you get back. Yes, we'll keep the poor creature for now. Till we see how the land lies, at least.'

An hour later Tariq came home.

'Did you get her there in time?' Julie asked.

'Just. By breaking a few speed limits. Not that Abbie was bothered if she'd got there at lunchtime. All she cared about was the dog. Anyway, I bought some food, and a bowl.' He eyed Molly, still damp from her bath and curled up in a corner of the kitchen. 'She's quite a nice-looking dog really,' he said. 'What do you think she is?'

Julie put food into the bowl and put it down in front of Molly. The dog heaved herself up and began to eat. 'I think she might be some kind of retriever cross,' she said. 'She's quite hairy, and the right colour. Anyway, she's safe now.' She looked at Tariq. 'What are you going to do? Presumably you'd expected to work at Will's.'

Tariq shrugged. 'I hadn't really thought. I suppose I could go and get some supplies for the Walburn job.'

'Could you stay here for a while? Keep an eye on the dog? Thing is, when I went up to the Prestons' for the water, I saw that David's car was still in the drive. He might have gone by now, but he might not, and if he's there I'll see if he'll talk to me.'

Tariq frowned. 'I'd have thought he's the last person you'd want to talk to right now. Aren't you angry with him?'

'You know what, I'm furious with both of them,' Julie said. 'But I also understand, kind of. And David wasn't really himself this morning. He's just seen his life crashing down. We can't abandon him.'

'I guess we can't. But what about Maggie?'

'What about her? We can't do anything about Maggie, can we? We don't know where she is.' Her tone hardened. 'And I know David's been a complete fool, but he's a man, and sometimes men don't see what's under their noses.'

'Huh. Thanks,' Tariq said.

'Not you, love, you're a shining exception. No, Maggie's made her bed, and maybe she needs to lie in it.'

'That's a bit unforgiving, isn't it?'

'Yes, I suppose. But I feel she's just trodden on our friendship as if it meant nothing at all.'

Tariq sighed. 'Well, when Abbie wasn't going on about the dog, she said she thought Maggie was, is, in danger.'

'Moral or physical?'

'She didn't say. You can ask her this evening.'

'I'll go and see David now. I'll probably be back in five minutes with a flea in my ear.'

Julie tapped on the Calladines' back door. Just two days ago she had stood here, feeling just as anxious. Now she knew how right she had been to feel anxiety. David's car was still in the drive, but there was no response to her knock. She gently pushed open the back door, remembering at the last minute to mutter a prayer. *Lord, help. Don't let me put my foot in it. Give me the right words, please.*

David was sitting at the kitchen table, his head bowed. He had taken off his suit jacket and pulled his tie loose.

'David.'

He looked up, and Julie's stomach seemed to contract. David's face was flushed, his eyes swollen, and Julie noticed then what was in his hand as it rested on the table: a ragged, grubby, child's toy rabbit. Julie bit her lip. 'Oh, David.'

'Hello, Julie.' David's voice was rough. 'I'm so sorry – '

Julie crossed the room, sat down opposite him and took his hand. 'It's OK, David. I understand, I'm not offended. I hope you believe I had absolutely nothing to do with Maggie going. I tried to dissuade her. I'm her friend: I wouldn't want her to do anything so stupid.'

'You think it was stupid?' David said heavily. 'According to her she plans to be a lot happier with him. And maybe she's right.' He leaned back, releasing his hand from Julie's, and took Maggie's note from the pocket of his jacket which he had slung on the back of his chair. He put it on the table in front of Julie. 'You should read what she says.'

Julie shook her head. 'No, I'd rather not. It's private, between you and her. I do know, though,' she added hesitantly, 'from what she's said to me over the past few months, on and off, that she felt very isolated. Lonely. Convinced you didn't care.'

'She says I have driven her away. And I suppose I have. It's my fault, I understand that. All the pressures I can cite in my defence are just not enough. I've let everything get away from me. The worst of it is – ' his voice cracked and broke, and Julie saw the effort he had to make to master himself. 'The worst of it is, I *knew*. But I did nothing.'

'Why didn't you?' Julie whispered.

'Because I didn't know what to do, I felt so useless, I'd failed to give her what she most wanted, hadn't I? I even made a stupid joke of it, well, sort of a joke, I said what Elkanah said to grieving Hannah, you remember? In 1 Samuel. "Hannah, why are you crying? ... Don't I mean more to you than ten sons?" How can I have done that, Julie? I've brought all of this on myself.' A tear ran down his cheek, and he wiped it away with an impatient hand. 'I deserve all of it. I am a coward. Couldn't even face my own wife's sadness. It wore me down, do you understand? Chipped away at my confidence, my sense of being someone worthy. Oh, I don't know.'

Julie heaved a deep sigh. 'Well, it's tough, I guess, living with something you believe simply can't be fixed. But yes, speaking as a woman, you should at least have gone on talking to her. She knows it's not your fault you haven't got children – she's not so foolish.'

'I ran away from her,' David said dully. 'And now she's run away from me. I suppose there's some poetic justice in that.'

The phone rang shrilly in the hall. David flinched. 'Could you get that, please, Julie? It might be my school. I'll go in later, but I need to take a bit of time.'

'Sure.' Julie went into the hall and picked up the receiver. She listened for a moment. 'No, but Mr Calladine is here. I'll get him.' She came back into the kitchen. 'David, it's not your school, it's Maggie's. Wondering what's happened to her. You need to talk to them.'

David grimaced. 'What am I going to tell them? "Oh, sorry, Mrs Calladine has absconded with the chap next door?" I can't do it.'

Julie thought. 'You have to say something. Look, David, just in case we can retrieve something from this awful mess, tell them you're very sorry, you've been up all night with Maggie, she's got a nasty bout of food poisoning, must have been the prawns she ate, and you haven't had a moment to ring them but you'll keep them informed. I know it isn't true, but we have to say something.'

David shook his head. 'I don't know about that creep Chambers writing a novel,' he muttered. 'You've missed your vocation.'

'Ha, not likely. You could even ring your school and tell them the same story.'

David got to his feet, pushing his chair back. He paused in the doorway. 'Yes, maybe I'll do that. Look, Julie – thank you. For not taking umbrage. For being a good friend. I appreciate it. I'll talk to Maggie's school, get myself cleaned up and go to work. Get some stability back into my life for a moment.' He went into the hall, then stopped. 'Did you find the dog?'

'Yes – in the shed, no food or water. She's with us now, fed, watered, bathed and safe.'

'That's good.'

'I'll head off home now, David. I don't know what you want to do next, but don't forget where we are, will you? If you need to talk things over, or even if you only fancy a cup of coffee or a glass of wine, just come.'

He nodded gravely and gave her a little salute. 'Yes. Of course.'

I just wish I knew what to do. It's been a week now, almost, and things have gone very quiet. I feel this sense that something should be done, and it's urgent, but when I mentioned it to Mum she said very sternly, 'Don't interfere.' I'm sure it's on her mind all the time – I mean, Mrs Calladine is Mum's best friend, and it's like she's lost her. That must be awful, but Mum won't talk about it. And Dad's no use either. If he thinks Mum needs defending he'll go all manly and protective and switch his brain off. That's how it seems to me, anyway. It's really frustrating. It's like where Mum's concerned he can't let reason rule. As for Mr Calladine, there's no way I can talk to him. If I see him in school he gives me a painful little smile and all I want to do is run and hide.

It's not that I want to interfere. I really, really don't. It's quite embarrassing and cringe-making even thinking about the problems a bunch of middle-aged people have got themselves into, people that you'd think would have their lives sorted by now. Anyway, what do I know? This whole situation makes me feel young and ignorant and helpless. But the more I think about it, and the longer this silence goes on, the more convinced I am that she, Mrs Calladine, that is, is in danger. I have this really heavy oppressive feeling that Will Chambers hasn't finished with any of us. It's like, I don't know, like any minute now the sky will turn black, and the swarm will come roaring back – do locusts make a noise? – and everything green will be gone for ever.

My exams are over, it's nearly the end of term, other people are thinking about the summer and where they're going for their holidays, and I want to be thinking about taking my driving test so Olly and I can go where we want and be free and have some fun before we have to get back to the grindstone. But this thing is hanging over me and I can't blank it out. I have this awful feeling that if no one does anything, something truly awful will happen. I've even been avoiding Olly because I'm afraid if I talk about it he'll get fed up with me being so moody, and maybe he'll want to be with someone else, someone who's more chilled and carefree, someone he can have a laugh with.

It's horrible, I hate it, and the worst thing, what I've been trying to avoid admitting even to myself, is that if the adults won't do anything I might have to do something myself. But what?

It's like – what do people call it? Yes – 'The elephant in the room', that's it. Where everybody knows something, it's on all their minds, but it's the last thing they'll admit. They all go on pretending everything is normal, and have

conversations about stupid trivial things, anything but face the truth. It makes
me want to scream. Maybe I will. Maybe I'll climb to the top of the church
tower and yell, 'WAKE UP!'

On Sunday morning Abbie woke to the sound of Molly whining.
She stretched and yawned and turned over resolutely, but sleep
deserted her. She groaned quietly, swung her legs out of bed and
sat up, running her fingers through her tangled hair. She put on a
bathrobe and ambled downstairs.

Molly greeted her with a lick and a wag of her tail and Abbie
bent and stroked her smooth, warm head. 'What's all the fuss about,
then?' she said. 'I'm sure you've been walked and fed.' She glanced
up at the clock. 'It's almost eleven. Let's see: Olly and Dan will be
kicking a ball, Mum and Dad will be in church. So were you just a
bit lonely? Thought you'd wake me up, is that it? It hasn't taken you
long to be queen bee, has it?' She thought for a moment. 'Tell you
what, Molly, let me have a quick shower and get dressed, maybe
have a bit of toast, and we'll go out for a little walk, OK? No more
whining, though.' The dog licked her hand again as if in answer,
and flopped down on the kitchen floor with a patient sigh.

Half an hour later, girl and dog emerged from the house into
the hazy sunshine and up the street towards the green. They walked
slowly across the grass, pausing every few steps for Molly to
investigate fascinating scents left by cats and foxes and other dogs.

'Come on, dog,' Abbie said, exasperated. 'I'd quite like to get to
the shop before it shuts. I know you don't care, but I want some
chocolate.' She tugged on the lead and Molly reluctantly followed
at her own lackadaisical pace.

As she turned towards the shop, Abbie could hear the sound of
singing from the church. It was a fine morning and someone had
opened the windows; the sound of a hymn floated across the green,
and something about the sound gave Abbie an unexpected pang, as
if all the world was somewhere that meant something to them, and

only she remained outside and alone. But then the dog grunted and lay down heavily, looking up at her with her tongue lolling.

'You've got a cheek, hound,' Abbie said. 'I have to stand around waiting while you sniff every blade of grass and every tree trunk, but if I stop to look at something, or just to think, you complain. Come on, I'm going to tie you up outside the shop for a few minutes. You'd better behave.'

Abbie heard nothing from the dog while she was in the shop making her modest purchase, and when she came out there were three small children clustered round Molly, patting her awkwardly and treading on her tail. Two women were talking beside them, taking little notice of the children, but when Abbie started untying Molly's lead they turned and one of them said brightly, 'I hope you don't mind. My kids love dogs.'

Abbie murmured, 'Sure, it's OK.' But as she walked away, with the children calling out goodbye to the dog after her, she muttered crossly, 'It's a good job you're so easy-going, Molly. That woman just let her kids pet a strange dog and didn't even watch them. Supposing you'd snapped at one of them? I suppose that would have been my fault.'

She crossed back over the green with Molly sauntering in her wake. There was silence now from the church, and no sound except the murmuring of sleepy pigeons and the fading high-pitched voices of the children. Abbie paused, fished in her pocket, unwrapped her chocolate and started munching. 'Sorry, old thing,' she said. 'You can't have any. Chocolate will give you bellyache. You can have a dog biscuit when we get home.'

Arriving at edge of the green she heard the growl of a car engine and became aware of a black saloon slowly circling. Narrowing her eyes against the sunlight she watched it pass the church, then the shop, and then come round full circle and roll past her as she stood at the kerb. She was about to cross the road when the car reversed, drew level with her and braked. She frowned, momentarily faintly alarmed.

A man climbed out of the car and closed the door, flexing stiff shoulders. He smiled tentatively. He said, 'Excuse me, young lady. Sorry to bother you. I wonder if you can help me. You seem to be the only one about.'

Abbie nodded warily. 'If I can.' He was a middle-aged man, older, she thought, than her parents, his light brown hair going grey round the edges. He wore a checked shirt and blue cotton trousers and, she noted with an inner smirk, sandals with plaid socks. He was little taller than she was, built square with a bit of a pot belly straining above the waistband of his trousers. He wore steel-rimmed glasses; as he stood facing her he took them off and rubbed his eyes. It made him look vulnerable, and Abbie had the feeling he was all right, that she didn't have to prepare for flight, that he was probably not about to kidnap her. Besides, Molly was standing beside her, quite unconcerned.

The man said, 'I'm hoping I've come to the right place. This is Halstead, right?'

'Yes, it is.'

'Oh, good. Thank you. I wasn't sure I'd taken the right turning off the dual carriageway. You live here?'

'Yes,' Abbie said guardedly. Perhaps he was a kidnapper after all.

'Only I'm looking for someone,' the man said. 'This is a small place, so I wonder if you know him. Name of Paul White.'

Abbie shook her head. 'No, sorry, I don't know anyone of that name. But there are some new houses here, down along the road to Walburn. I don't know everyone.'

The man sighed and looked up and down the road as if he expected the person he sought to appear. Then he shook his head. 'I've been trying to track him down. Like a bloodhound.' He looked at Molly and smiled. 'I've traced him to here – but now what? All I know is he's probably bought a house here recently. Probably something very small, or some derelict cottage, because he wouldn't have been able to afford anything else.'

It was as if someone had taken a cold knife and slid it into Abbie's heart. She felt sweat bloom on her upper lip, and she wiped it away with a jerk of her sleeve. 'I only know of one person who's done that round here,' she said. 'But it wasn't any Paul White. He said his name was Will Chambers.'

Despite the feeling of dread rising up from the pit of her stomach, she was unprepared for the man's reaction.

'What? Will Chambers, you say?' He gave a bark of mirthless laughter. 'Well, that's typical!'

Abbie frowned. 'What do you mean?' she whispered. Her voice seemed to have disappeared.

The man said, 'Hold on.' He went back to his car, opened the passenger door and emerged with a bag. He rummaged in it, and found a battered notebook. 'It's in here somewhere.' Flicking the pages he exclaimed, 'Yes, here it is. Is this him?' He held out a photograph to Abbie, and she took it gingerly.

She saw a rather fuzzy shot of a young man, perhaps younger than twenty, slim and wiry, wearing a white shirt half-hanging out of dark trousers. His fair hair flopped over his forehead, and he was smiling: despite the differences in appearance, an eerily familiar smile.

Abbie looked up at the man and swallowed. Her mouth seemed suddenly dry. 'It looks like him, yes,' she said. 'But the man I know is older. And he has dark brown hair.'

The man standing before her nodded. He took the photo back from her hand and studied it for a moment, his expression unreadable. 'This is an old photo,' he said. 'It's all I have. Taken almost twenty years ago. Even so … ' He slapped his forehead lightly. 'Oh, but I'm forgetting myself, asking you all these questions, a perfect stranger. I'm so sorry. My name's Bill White. Actually,' he said with an apologetic smile, 'my name isn't really Bill – I just got called that to distinguish me from my father. He was John and I was called after him. But I've always been known as Bill. Chambers was my mother's name before she married.' He gave a bitter laugh. 'Just typical of Paul to call himself that. His idea of a nasty little joke.'

'You've lost me a bit,' Abbie said. 'Why are you looking for him? And who is he to you?'

'I'm sorry,' Bill White said again. 'I'm confusing you. Why I'm looking for him is a bit of a long story. But Paul's my brother. My not-at-all-loved-and-lost younger brother. I was hoping he'd gone out of my life for ever.' He made a face. 'Seems that was not to be.'

Something like hope flared in Abbie at that moment. She bent over the fidgeting dog, quieting her, and looked up. 'You know what, Mr White,' she said slowly, 'it may be that we can help each other.'

Bill White frowned. 'Really? So you think you know my brother?'

Abbie nodded. 'It may sound rude, but unfortunately, yes.'

Bill said, 'Is there somewhere we could go to chat? Rather than standing out here in public? I could drive you.'

Abbie's eyes narrowed. 'I'm not getting into any strange man's car,' she said. 'My parents will be home from church very soon. The church is just over there.' She waved her hand. 'When they come out, you can come to our house and I'll make you a cup of coffee.'

Bill White smiled, transforming his face. 'I'm glad you're cautious,' he said. 'I have a daughter about your age – Laura. I can't count how many times I've told her to be careful. You hear such things.' He shuddered.

'We're in the open,' Abbie pointed out. 'And I could tell my dog to bite you.'

Bill White laughed aloud. 'That dog's no more ferocious than I am,' he said. 'Look – what's your name?'

'Abbie. Abbie Hasan.'

'Look, Abbie, I'm no threat to you or anyone. It's a beautiful Sunday morning, I don't get a lot of free time, and right now I'd be happy doing anything other than looking for my miscreant brother. But I think I have to. So if you can help, I'd be very grateful.'

Abbie nodded. 'Fair enough.' She looked past his shoulder. 'Seems the service is over. People are coming out. There's my dad. I'll give him a wave – maybe he won't stop for the usual after-church chat. Actually,' she added, 'if he sees me talking to a strange man he'll probably start running. Like your Laura, stranger-danger's been dinned into me for years. Normally I'd probably be beating a very hasty retreat. But it seems to me the circumstances are anything but normal.'

Moments later Tariq arrived, followed by Julie, both panting a little from fast walking, and they ranged themselves on either side of Abbie.

'Mum, Dad, this is Mr White.'

'Please,' Bill White said. 'Call me Bill.'

Tariq frowned, but his voice was pleasant. 'Can we help you, Mr White?'

'Bill is looking for his brother,' Abbie said. 'Someone we know as Will Chambers.'

Tariq's eyebrows shot up. 'Oh!'

'Bill,' Julie cut in. 'Come down to our house, if you have time. There's a lot we'd like to know.'

'Gladly,' Bill said. 'And there's just as much you can tell me, I imagine. I'll follow you in my car.'

Moments later he was sitting at the kitchen table. Julie filled the kettle and Abbie gave Molly the promised biscuit.

'Coffee OK, Bill?' Julie said.

'Yes, thanks. Milk, no sugar.'

Tariq sat down opposite Bill White. 'How sure are we that Will Chambers really is your brother, Mr White? Bill.'

Bill sighed. 'Unfortunately I don't think there's much doubt about that. Abbie here seemed to recognise him from this photo, even though it's twenty years old.' He pulled the photo out of his pocket and laid it on the table. Tariq looked at it and his eyes widened.

'He's blond in the picture,' Abbie said. 'But when Olly and I saw him in the shopping centre Olly reckoned he'd been dyeing his hair.'

Bill gave a sour laugh. 'That would be very much Paul's style.' He glanced up at Julie as she put a cup of coffee in front of him. 'Thank you. That's his real name – Paul White. I guess he called himself William because of me. He's always resented me. And as I told Abbie, Chambers was our mother's maiden name. He's always liked dressing up, disguises, that sort of thing. Fooling people. Makes him feel clever.' He sipped his coffee, set it down and took a deep breath. 'You should know, my brother has always been trouble. Endless, off-the-scale trouble. I can't believe he'd have reformed. He hasn't got it in him.'

Abbie sat on a kitchen chair, her coffee cup in her hand. 'No, he hasn't reformed,' she said slowly, watching the bubbles swirl in her mug. 'In a way that helps, because sometimes I doubted myself, even though everything I saw made me certain he's what my dad would call a wrong 'un.' She looked up at Bill, and his expression was sombre. 'He's been around here for a few months, doing up an old cottage. But now he's put it back on the market – there's a For Sale sign up. So he's not here now. Nobody knows where he is. Which is a problem, because a nice, God-fearing, decent woman has run off with him. A nice, decent, God-fearing *married* woman.'

Bill groaned and shook his head. 'Why am I not surprised?' he muttered. 'Perhaps I'd better tell you how I fetched up here.' He took a gulp of his coffee. 'Where to begin?' He shrugged. 'I could start at the beginning. But I haven't got all day, and I guess neither have you.' He cleared his throat. 'Bear in mind I hadn't seen Paul for a very long time, hardly at all, ever since I chucked him out as soon as he'd taken his A levels. Twenty years, give or take. I'd had enough. But that's another story – I'll fill you in if there's time.

'Around the beginning of the year, it was, we had a series of peculiar phone calls at home. Silences, laughter, even singing. At first they'd come late at night, and it was usually me that intercepted them. Whoever it was never actually spoke. But then they'd come as we were all having breakfast. Those would be the silent ones, or the just-audible breathing. I thought it was probably Paul – it was the sort of creepy thing he would do – but I didn't want to think about it. I tried to put it, and him, out of my mind. I have good reason, believe me, to want nothing to do with him.' He pressed his lips together. 'But then Lisa, my wife, told me that our daughter, Laura, had picked up the phone when he called. She's only sixteen, and she was scared. Oh boy, was Lisa angry. Angry with *me*, it seemed almost, just for having a brother like Paul. Fair enough, she's concerned for Laura, and she knows quite a bit about what Paul's like. It was because I was getting married that I kicked Paul out of the house in the first place – or, no, that wasn't the only reason, but she wouldn't have moved in with me if Paul had still been there. She had a little son from her first marriage, four years old at the time, and she didn't trust Paul as far as she could throw him. Wise woman.

'Well, of course, that little lad's a grown man now and has a flat and a job and a nice girlfriend, but a few years on we had Laura, so Lisa feels defensive, as you would expect of the good mum she is. Anyway, you can imagine, life at home was a bit strained. Not that there was much I could do. It went on, on and off, for several weeks. We were talking about going ex-directory when Paul rang and this time I took the call. Nice as pie, he was – if you didn't know it was all false. He can turn on the charm like a tap – that's how he manages to deceive people, I suppose. Maybe that's why this lady you know has fallen for it. For him.'

'I don't think that's the only reason,' Julie said. 'But go on with your story. We're all ears.'

'Well, Paul pretended to be contrite. "Sorry, Bill, I didn't mean to worry you. Your daughter sounds like such a nice girl. You must be very proud." Etc. I told Paul I didn't want him ringing the house, to butt out, and he said, quite calmly, "All right, Bill, I understand. But there's something I want to tell you – share some good news.

Agree to meet me, and I won't bother you again." I didn't want to see him – I didn't believe what he said, because with Paul there's usually an agenda, something he's got up his sleeve, but I didn't know what else to do. So I said, reluctantly, "All right. Where and when?" And he said, "Why not now, Bill? Just look out of your front door, and you'll see me." He's always been one for drama – always watching those cloak-and-dagger films when he was a boy. Loved to dress up, even had a spell of wearing stage make-up. It's all to do with his, what do they call it? Narcissism, that's it. Self-dramatising. He was a great one for that.

'Anyway, I did what he said, and it was just like one of those old black-and-white films: there he was at the corner of the road – bear in mind it was probably after midnight – under the street lamp, long black coat, hat pulled down over his forehead, smoke from a cigarette winding up into the air, and that was all a pose because he never smoked.' Bill shook his head. 'Well, I went and talked to him. It was all I could do not to deck him, I can tell you – Paul has that effect on me, and normally I'm not an aggressive sort of man, as anyone will tell you who knows me. He makes my fists itch, frankly.

'He asked after me and my family, how's Lisa, how's Robbie, all innocent as if we were having a normal conversation instead of lurking under a street lamp around midnight with him in disguise, and I refused to answer him, so finally he got to the point. I could see he was excited, almost dancing with glee. His eyes were flashing and he talked fast, nineteen to the dozen. "I've had some good fortune, Bill," he said. "I've come into money." You should realise that Paul and money don't go together – he can't hold down a job for long and I don't know how he supported himself. If he stole, and that's not unlikely, he must have been very clever, because he's never been caught that I know of. He's always kept just the right side of the law. There were a few close shaves when he was a teenager, as I know all too well, but he managed not to have charges brought. He's clever, full of dodges, but things usually go wrong because he's overreached himself. If there's one thing Paul's never short of it's self-belief. It's all the rest of us who are idiots, according to him.' He looked at the Hasans, listening silently. 'Does all this mean anything to you?'

Abbie finished her cooling coffee. 'None of us know him that well,' she said. 'But what we do know fits in with what you're saying. So what was his story?'

'He told me he'd found work in an old people's home. A private place that probably costs the earth. The pay wasn't good but he didn't need much in the way of qualifications – it can be a gutty job at times and maybe they were desperate for staff. Also I guess it might have been useful to have a male staff member. Anyway, knowing Paul, he probably had a drawerful of dodgy CVs. Who knows? I wouldn't put anything past him. Maybe he was cosying up to the woman in charge.' He shook his head.

'That's by the by. He worked in this place for quite a long time, he told me, a long time for him, anyway – more than a year. And having an eye for the main chance, he latched onto an old lady called Ivy Gower. A wealthy old lady who'd obviously had some sound financial advice, because although she was in this place that cost an arm and a leg, she'd manged to ring-fence a good proportion of her assets. She was a widow, she and her husband had owned a chain of shops which he'd sold at a big profit, and he'd been a canny investor, so Ivy had quite a pile salted away. Paul charmed this dear old soul, but I told you he was clever – he soon realised Ivy was no fool, so he learned not to overdo it, and the two became special buddies. Obviously he had to look after the other residents too, but once he found out Ivy was wealthy (I dare say one of the other workers told him; some of these people love to gossip), he made a point of doing all he could to help Ivy, to hang out with her, to chat and sympathise and fetch and carry. Of course it wasn't genuine. Paul doesn't do genuine. He did it for what he might get out of it. But he still stuck at it, and that surprised me, I have to say.

'Anyway, cutting this saga short, one day Ivy told Paul she had ordered a taxi for the next day, which she knew was Paul's day off, and she told him to meet her in town at an address she gave him, which turned out to be her solicitor's. Normally the residents wouldn't go out without someone accompanying them, but Ivy was determined, and probably thought it'd be some kind of triumph to assert her independence. Obviously, I don't know her mind – I can only tell you what Paul told me. She'd made an appointment, telling nobody, and that afternoon she changed her will, leaving a substantial sum to Paul in gratitude for all his kindness. Enough, she said, for him to buy a small property so that he didn't have to live in his seedy flat any more (he'd given her the sob story of his poverty and the way he had to live on the pittance they paid him – one damp, poky room because the low rent was all he could afford, etc). It wasn't all she had – she wasn't soft in the head – but Ivy had no children. She'd had a daughter, I think, but she'd died young. The only family she had was a niece who'd emigrated to Australia, who kept in touch but rarely visited, for obvious reasons.

"'I'll do right by my niece," she said to Paul. "She's my family, my brother's child, and she'll get most of my estate. I'll leave her the stuff that's been in the family for years, jewellery and suchlike, as well. That's no use to you. Some of it is quite valuable, but mostly it's sentimental value only. I just wanted to say thank you to you, Paul, for what you've done for me. With the fees they charge us, it's criminal how they undervalue people like you. Caring people who put others first." And this is what Paul told me, that night under the street lamp. He laughed like the proverbial drain when he told me Ivy believed he lived for others! If it wasn't so awful I'd be laughing too. Everyone at the home knew, of course, that Ivy had cancer, poor soul. A few months later she died, and Paul eventually got his money. The people at the home were pretty outraged, but Paul didn't care. The will was legal. By the time I saw him he'd left the home, anyway.' Bill took a deep breath. 'Any chance of another cup, Mrs Hasan? All this talking is making me dry.'

'Of course. Anyone else?' Julie said. Abbie and Tariq shook their heads. 'Go on, Bill.'

'Mum, I'll do it,' Abbie said. She got up and filled the kettle. She leaned up against the worktop, looking at Bill, while she waited for it to boil.

'I had the feeling there was more to this story of his,' Bill said. 'There was something in his manner – he does a particular combination of sneaky and triumphant that's very Paul – and that's just how it turned out. He went all quiet and conspiratorial. He took hold of my coat-sleeve. "The money is great, Bill," he said. "And it's come at just the right time. Because after all these years, I've found him! Can you believe that, Bill? I've been looking for him for a long time: the man who ruined my life. I've found him, and I've worked out just how I'm going to get my own back. I'm going to be his neighbour, but he'll never know it's me. And you know what, Bill? I'm going to bring him down. He's going to feel just how I felt when he told those lies about me. It'll be so sweet, Bill, seeing him in despair – and letting him know just who's responsible. It's the best pleasure there is. Better than fast cars, better than alcohol or drugs or sex. Just you watch." And then, to my amazement, though nothing Paul does should surprise me, he pranced and pirouetted down the street, laughing his head off and singing out goodbye! How the neighbours didn't all wake up, I don't know. And that's the last time I saw him.'

Abbie put coffee into Bill's mug and added boiling water and a splash of milk. 'Hope that's not too strong.'

There was silence for a moment, and then Julie said, 'Who was he talking about, Bill? The man he wanted to get even with? What was this man supposed to have done?'

Abbie heard the front door bang and Daniel's voice shouting a greeting before he went upstairs for his post-football shower. His arrival made her think of Olly, and for a fleeting moment she felt that familiar tug of anxiety. She hadn't seen Olly in a while. Were they still an item? She put the thought of Olly firmly aside. He would have to wait a bit longer.

Before Bill had a chance to answer, Julie said, 'I have a horrible feeling I know what you're about to say, Bill.' She turned to Abbie, and Abbie saw how pale she had gone. 'Do you remember that evening when we invited Will – I mean Paul – to dinner?'

Abbie looked at her with narrow eyes. 'Yes, so?'

'Perhaps you weren't in the room.' She turned to Tariq. 'Do you remember, Riq? How David said he thought Will looked familiar? And Will, I mean Paul, told us a story about living abroad, going to school in – where was it? Pakistan? Because his father was a diplomat?'

'Ha!' Bill interrupted. 'His father, mine too, was a postman. He died of a heart attack, on his way home from the pub, a week before Christmas. Paul had just turned four at the time. He went to school right here in the UK, I can assure you. Of course all that was rubbish. He's brilliant at stories.'

'He said he was here to write a novel,' Tariq said, shaking his head. 'Had a laptop in his back bedroom, notebooks, the lot.'

'A novel? I doubt that very much,' Bill said grimly. 'He hasn't got the stamina for consistent effort. But you could say his whole life's a novel – pulp fiction. Anyway, after he'd left that night I thought long and hard about who he could have had it in for. Who could, in his view, have ruined his life? When did he think that had happened? I had to try and get inside his head, and it's not a comfortable place to be. I could only think it was when Paul was expelled from school the year before his A levels. I don't see how it ruined his life – he did his exams by correspondence, funded by me. But it was after that I chucked him out. Perhaps that's it. He inherited a bit of money from our mum's estate when he turned eighteen, and he could have used it for something useful, but no, he blew it – as far as I could find out, he spent most of it supplying drugs for a bunch of no-hopers who called themselves his friends. Some friends they were. But as to his expulsion from school, I remember at the time he laid the blame on a young teacher, in his first year at the school. I've no idea why. There was no evidence it was him that found Paul out and reported him, but Paul believed it and hated his guts. I thought I was getting to the bottom of it, but it took me a long time to remember the man's name. Not surprising, when it was over twenty years ago.'

Julie stared at him, her eyes wide and a little wild. 'David Calladine.'

Bill nodded. 'Yes! A friend of yours? I know he lives here. I know he's a Headmaster at a school in Walburn. I found that out. It's not difficult. A man like him has a public existence.'

'Oh, yes,' Julie said miserably. 'He's our friend. And it seems your brother has succeeded, Bill.'

'So what has Paul done this time?' Suddenly he gaped. 'Oh! Please don't tell me it's *his* wife – ?'

'His wife. My friend. Maggie Calladine. Not normally easily duped. And nobody knows where they are.'

There was silence for a moment. Then Bill said, 'If you did know where they were, what difference would it make? She's an adult, isn't she? Able to make up her own mind? I can't say the relationship will last, and I have to say I'm sorry for the woman getting mixed up with him, but it's her decision, surely?'

'Oh, yes, it's her decision,' Julie said. 'I don't know if it would make any difference, no. She's made her bed. I don't suppose he drugged her or tied her up and threatened her with a knife.'

'That wouldn't be his style, no,' Bill said gloomily. 'More a case of mind-games.'

'Hold on,' Abbie said. 'You haven't told us why you want to find him, Bill.'

'Ah. No, I haven't. I'll be brief, because my wife doesn't know I'm here. She thinks I'm playing golf. I've even got my clubs in the car.' He grimaced. 'I don't like deceiving her, and normally I wouldn't think of it. But if she knew what I was about she'd go mad. She'd certainly think *I'd* gone mad.' He took a deep breath.

'About a fortnight ago there was a knock on my door. I was alone in the house – it was a Saturday, and Lisa and Laura had gone into town to do some shopping. A middle-aged couple I didn't know stood on my doorstep. They introduced themselves as Sharon and Lenny Traynor, from Western Australia. My heart practically dropped out of my chest. I invited them in. As you must have guessed, Sharon Traynor was, is, Ivy Gower's niece. Their holiday in the UK had been planned for some time, and part of their plan was to visit relatives here. Sadly they weren't in time to see Aunt Ivy, of course. They'd received the inheritance without problems – it had helped to fund their trip – but they were concerned. Who was this unknown man Aunt Ivy had left so much money to? Was she in her right mind? Was the will legal? Could they, perhaps, contest it? They'd been to see the solicitor, and he'd assured them that there were no grounds for contesting the will; it was legal, he himself had drawn it up, and in his opinion and that of Mrs Gower's doctor, there was nothing amiss with her mental faculties.

'However, there were certain items that had been specifically bequeathed to Mrs Traynor, items that, as it happened, were still in the safe at the home where Mrs Gower had spent her last days. The solicitor as executor should have kept these items but there had been a delay in collecting them. No one was unduly concerned – they were presumably quite secure in the safe at Gable Grange. So the Australian couple went to the Grange to collect the box of jewellery, because that was what it was. However, when they opened it they discovered that there were pieces missing. They checked with the inventory, supposedly made by the manageress at the Grange, and indeed, valuable items that should have been there, weren't. They hesitated to blame the Grange staff. But the manageress, realising no doubt that she herself might be under suspicion, told the Traynors about Paul.

'The staff at the home had no love for Paul, as you can imagine. They envied him his good fortune, and they recalled how, before he left, he'd crowed about what he was going to do with the money

165

– buy up an old place and renovate it and become a man of property.

'The Traynors decided they wanted to talk to Paul, to see if he could throw any light on the missing things. The address the Grange had on file for Paul was mine, which was how the Traynors ended up at my house. Paul had, maybe still has, that horrible little flat, but he kept it quiet – it was his bolt-hole if things went wrong.' Bill paused for a moment, clearly wrestling with his thoughts. 'You'll probably think I'm stupid,' he said. 'Lisa certainly would if she knew. But I told you our dad died when Paul was a toddler, and I was a teenager. There are two sisters too, in between – married now with kids of their own. Our mother was left with the four of us and very little money. Dad wasn't just a drinker – he was a gambler too, and there were debts. Mum had to work hard to keep us together, fed and clothed. It wasn't easy.

'I saw myself as the man of the house, even though I was no more than fourteen when my dad died. I promised Mum I'd be responsible for Paul. And I did my best, though it turned out to be a heavier burden that anyone could have imagined. Mum died when Paul was twelve – cancer, but she was plain worn out. Before she died she made me promise again to look after Paul. Mum was no fool – she knew there was something wrong with her baby son, but she wouldn't let anyone ever say he was bad. Paul was different. Paul was difficult, yes, sometimes. She made excuses. He'd lost his father. I guess it must be hard for a mother to admit, even to herself, that her child is wicked. Or maybe sick. To be honest, I don't know. I've given up trying to understand.' He sighed deeply.

'Well, there I was, a young man, living in digs, working hard, trying to make my way in the world. And I was landed with a toxic brother. No exaggeration. I could make your hair stand on end with some of his capers. It was never proved, but I strongly suspect he set his mobile classroom on fire – at the age of eight.' Julie gasped, her mouth open, and Bill shook his head grimly. 'Oh, that's not the worst of it, I can assure you. Anyway, I did my best. I'd promised my mother I'd look after Paul, and I tried. Until he stalked and threatened and tormented and terrified a young girl at his school and got expelled for it. That was it – I'd give him till he was eighteen, and then I thought I'd served my time and my obligations were discharged.

'But when the Traynors came to my door that day, that sense of obligation came back. Rashly perhaps, I promised to try to find Paul and ask him about the jewellery. Privately I thought if he'd stolen the stuff, he'd probably already sold it. Anyway, he wasn't going to admit stealing it, not to the Traynors, at least. And some shred of family pride stopped me from saying to the Traynors, "Oh, yes, my brother's a rat, he'll almost certainly have pinched it. Sold it by now, I shouldn't wonder." He had every opportunity. He knew where old Ivy kept her stuff. He may even have helped with the inventory. I don't know.

'Anyway, the Traynors left, and when I had the chance, I went to Paul's flat, but there was no sign of him. Neighbours said he hadn't been there for some time. I thought hard. I recalled what he'd said to colleagues at the home about buying an old house. I remembered his threat to bring down David Calladine. I put two and two together. I did some research on the internet. And here I am.' He heaved a sigh, took off his glasses and cleaned them on his shirt sleeve. 'I've done what family honour demands, I think,' he said with a little sneer of black humour. 'I've done what I promised Sharon Traynor I'd do. I'll tell her I found him, and he has no idea what happened to her property, but he refused to meet her in person. Now all I want to do is forget Paul again. Go home for my Sunday lunch. Get on with my life. Stop deceiving my family. I'm truly sorry he's done such damage to your friends, but I can't do anything more about Paul. He's a grown man, not under my jurisdiction. He hasn't broken the law. It's out of my hands.'

'That's pretty much how I feel too,' Julie said softly. 'Maggie's burned her boats, well and truly. I know a bit about her life, and in some ways you can see why this has happened. But she's trodden all over years of friendship. I'm still feeling pretty bruised.'

'Paul leaves a trail of destruction wherever he goes,' Bill said. 'Sometimes it's like a bolt of lightning. Other times it's more of a slow burn, coming to a head after hours of planning. Or at least,' he added thoughtfully, 'I assume his methods are the same as before. It's been a long time since we had any contact – apart from what I told you about.

'Look, I really must go. I've taken up more of your time than I should.' He nodded in Abbie's direction as he got to his feet. 'Thank you for the coffee. I'll be on my way.' He held out his hand, and Julie and Tariq shook it. 'Goodbye.'

'I'll walk you to your car, Bill,' Abbie said.

They walked up the drive in silence. Bill unlocked the car and paused with his hand on the door handle. 'Something on your mind, Abbie?'

'Bill,' Abbie said. 'As you may have gathered, my mum's pretty carved up about what's happened. You heard her say Mrs Calladine's her friend. Yeah, well, she's only pretending she wants to wash her hands of her. One of these days she's going to want to see Maggie, find out if there's anything she can do to help. I know my mum. Right now she's really shocked. She isn't thinking straight. Her feelings are hurt. I don't know when, but one day she'll be kicking herself that she had the chance to find out where her friend went, and she let it slide. So please, give me the address of your brother's flat, if that's where you think the pair of them are holed up.'

'You realise, Abbie, they might not be there,' Bill White said gently. 'They might have gone to South America, or New Zealand, or … anywhere. I doubt it, because he's probably broke. But if as you say, he's selling the cottage, once he's got the money he could go anywhere.'

'All the more reason to know where they are now,' Abbie said.

Bill looked at her keenly. 'I hope you're not thinking of doing anything silly,' he said. 'Please, don't go sticking your neck out. I'd be horrified if you put yourself in Paul's sights. Just keep away from him, I beg you.'

'I'll be sensible.'

'Promise me, if I give you his address, you'll give it to your mother.'

'That's the idea.'

'All right. Perhaps something can be salvaged from this mess.' He found the notebook he had kept his brother's photo in, tore out a page and wrote on it. He handed it to Abbie. 'It's not too far. Just the other side of Moxhurst.'

'Right.'

He opened the car door, sat in the driver's seat and wound down the window. 'Something else bothering you?'

Abbie hesitated. 'Molly was his dog, did you know? You don't think we'd have to give her back, do you? He doesn't deserve her. He was cruel.'

Bill shook his head. 'He won't want her, Abbie,' he said. 'He did this before, I remember. Got a dog from a rescue centre on an impulse. Left it in my garage. I had to take it back, and they weren't impressed. I'd hazard a guess he did that with Molly, just before he came to Halstead. What do you think when some stranger turns up with a dog? Makes them seem more normal, more trustworthy, kinder – doesn't it? No, Molly would have been just a sort of prop for Paul, to allay any suspicions you might have had. She's a million times better off with you.'

'He went away and left her locked in the shed. She could have died.'

Bill nodded. 'Horrible as it is to say this, you have to realise my brother cares about no one and nothing but himself.'

'Poor Maggie.'

'Yes. It doesn't look too good for her, does it? Well, I'd better go. If I'm late back there'll be questions asked. Bye, Abbie. Nice to have met you, and your parents. All the best.'

'Yeah, you too,' Abbie murmured. 'Bye, Bill.'

She watched as the car rolled up the road, stopped at the top and turned right. Moments later it was out of sight. She stood for a moment, thinking hard. Then she looked at the scrap of paper in her hand and memorised the address. Flat 2a. Parker House. Presbytery Lane. Moxhurst.

She walked slowly down the drive and back into the kitchen.

'Mum, Dad? You OK?'

Julie gathered herself with an effort. 'Yes. That was a turn-up, wasn't it? That man finding us. You were right all along, Abbie. Should have listened to you. Too late now.' Abbie saw the tears glinting in her mother's eyes, and her father taking her hand and squeezing it.

'Well, Mum, here's something I got from Bill,' Abbie said. 'Maybe you don't want it now, but one day you might.' She handed Julie the scrap of paper. Julie read it, and looked up. 'This is Will's flat? That's where his brother thinks he is?'

'I guess so.'

Julie scowled. 'And why would I want this?'

'Because Mrs Calladine's your friend.'

'Well, she was. Perhaps not any more. Her choice, not mine. No, Abbie, put it in the bin. What's the point? I'd better start getting lunch ready.' She turned away and Abbie sighed. When Julie was upset, Tariq was the best person to smooth her feathers. 'OK, Mum. I'll come down in a minute and give you a hand.' She left the room, dropping the scrap of paper in the kitchen bin as she passed.

June 2010

Maggie sat at the open window, looking out but seeing nothing. Not that there was much to see: only the deepening evening, the street lights casting a sickly light. There were sounds, though: raised voices from across the car park, the sudden yowling of fighting cats, the clang of an overturned dustbin, and behind it all, relentless, the drumming of the traffic on the dual carriageway. Night or day, it never seemed to stop.

It has come to this.

Her hands were shaking, and she gripped them together tightly. Despite the warmth of the summer evening, she shivered with cold; but to close the window made a reeking prison of the flat. The air that came in at the window was hardly fresh, but compared to the stale foulness inside, it was a garden of roses. Somehow, claustrophobia increased her nausea.

She turned her head stiffly, like a much older woman, and stared with something like loathing and horror at the thing on the table. It was barely visible in the darkness, but she knew it was there, staring at her like an evil eye, her death sentence. She smiled to herself, a bitter little smile, and shuddered as the summer air wafted around her bare arms.

It seemed impossible that so much – everything – had changed, and with such bewildering speed. Time had ceased to have much meaning. She saw herself, as if through a distorting lens, looking out of her kitchen window early that morning – how many days ago was it? – not many, she knew – a week? less? more? – and seeing him, Will, putting things in the boot of his car, not just any things, she realised with a small shock, but all his belongings. She threw down the dishcloth and ran outside.

He looked up, and his frown was instantly replaced by that wide, welcoming smile. 'Hey.'

'You're leaving, aren't you?' she said, her voice low and urgent. 'Without me. You're leaving me behind.'

He shook his head. 'Of course I'm not, silly. Why would I do that? You're getting paranoid.' He glanced swiftly round, then stroked her face with his fingers. 'I'm taking some stuff over to the flat,' he said. 'I've got to clear the cottage, haven't I, to sell it.' He sounded so reasonable, and she so desperately wanted to believe him. 'The flat's a mess. It's worse than the last time I saw it – I think there must have been squatters in. Maggie, love, it's not fit to be seen, let alone lived in, especially for someone like you, used to nice things. I was going to clean it up a bit, make it half-decent. Then come back for you.'

She shook her head. 'No, I don't care what it's like. We can clean it up together. I'm coming with you, now. If we're going to do this, let's just do it, no more wavering. Wait for me, OK? I'll only be a few minutes. I'll put some things in a case, pick up my handbag. I should leave a note, I suppose. David hasn't gone to school yet; he'll see it when he comes downstairs. I'll follow you in my car. Please, Will.'

He seemed about to argue, but then shrugged and smiled and shook his head. 'Sure, if that's how you want to play it. Don't be long.'

Later, seeing the flat, her spirits had quailed for a moment. 'There's nothing to clean *with*, Will. Where's the bleach, the mop, all that stuff?'

'Sweetie, I told you,' he said mildly. 'I'm sure there've been squatters. It happens all the time round here. And I haven't been here for ages, have I?' He crossed the room, wrapped his arms around her, and looked down into her face. 'I've been in a little place called Halstead, in case you'd forgotten, having an amazing time with an extraordinary lady.' He kissed her eyes, her forehead, her neck, her mouth.

She wriggled in his arms, then relented. 'OK, OK. Let's go and buy the stuff, then. You weren't joking, were you? It's pretty disgusting.'

'I did warn you. But you wouldn't listen.' A wicked gleam sparked in his soft brown eyes and he pulled her closer. 'I'll get some cleaning things, and some food – later. Now we're going to start as we mean to go on. I don't think the bedroom's quite so bad.'

'What?' She tried to pull away.

'Don't tell me you don't want to, gorgeous. You always want to.'

Thinking about that morning, she shuddered. She had been so weak, so needy; it was pathetic. By the time they'd wriggled free of those soiled, damp sheets it was afternoon, and she had a thundering headache.

'Will, I haven't eaten for hours. You can go shopping by yourself. Just get something to eat, can you? And bottled water, and something to clean this place with. And some painkillers. I feel awful.'

He pulled on his shirt. 'You were supposed to feel better,' he said, sounding hurt.

She was lying on the bed, one arm in front of her eyes against the sun that blazed through the thin curtains. She reached out and took his hand.

'I did, of course I did, I always do,' she soothed. 'But that was before we went to sleep. I don't know why – I just woke up feeling grim. I'll probably be OK once we've eaten something.' She sat up. 'These sheets need washing. Do you have a washing machine here?'

He shook his head. 'No. We'll have to use the launderette down the road. But first things first – food, water, painkillers.' He hesitated. 'Bit of a snag, though, darling. Until the cottage is sold, I've got a bit of a cash flow problem. And my car's playing up. Didn't you notice it coughing when you were following me this morning?'

'You can use mine. Put some fuel in it while you're out. And use my credit card for now. There's cash in my purse too. Take what you need.' She got to her feet, and swayed, feeling a sudden wave of nausea. 'Oh, boy.'

Will came to her side, holding on to her arm, steadying her. 'Are you all right?' He sounded so concerned, and she leaned her head on his shoulder.

'Sorry,' she mumbled. 'I don't know what's the matter with me. But you're probably right – I need some nourishment. Especially after all this activity. Too much excitement.' She attempted a smile, but her eyes were watering.

'Sit down quietly and wait for me,' he said. 'I won't be long.'

But he was – even that first day, he was out for hours. By the time he came back, it was getting dark. She'd found a mug in one of the cupboards, and rinsed it out at the sink, which she'd had to clean first as best she could. Even the water coming out of the taps was an unsavoury brown. She ran it till it came clear, then drank several mugfuls. After a while she felt better, but unaccountably tired. She lay down again on the bed, rank as it was, and slept.

Will woke her when he came back. 'Sorry I've been so long,' he said. 'I had to take my car after all, and it wouldn't start when I came out of the shop.' He looked worried. 'Maggie, I'm sorry, but while we were asleep someone pinched two wheels off your car.'

'*What?*'

'I'm sorry,' he repeated, sitting on the edge of the bed. 'This is a terribly rough area. And your car's obviously so much better than anything else round here. The trouble is, my car's really unreliable. I need to get it fixed.'

'Well, for goodness' sake, *get* it fixed!' She sat up, feeling disorientated. 'I told you. Use my card for what we need. We need transport, surely?'

'OK.' He frowned. 'I don't like using your money. But I'll pay it back, just as soon as the cottage sale goes through.'

'Look, Will, we're in this together. Aren't we? The money doesn't matter. We have to get the things we need.' She got up. 'Did you get food?'

'Yes. Bread, ham, apples, milk.'

'Wonderful. A cup of tea will set me up.'

He bit his lip. 'We can't have tea.'

'Why not?'

'Because the electricity isn't connected.'

Her eyes widened. 'You're kidding me. You mean there's no power, no light?'

He shuffled his feet on the worn vinyl floor. 'Look, I didn't have time to sort it. I guess there was a bill I missed. Don't worry, I'll do it tomorrow.'

She groaned. 'Oh, Will. I wouldn't mind so much, if only I didn't feel so ill.'

But she felt better when she had eaten, and things seemed more cheerful. 'Did you get any cleaning stuff?'

'No, they didn't have what I wanted. We'll just have to go out tomorrow – you can get the kind you like. You can bear it one more night, can't you?' He'd looked worried for a moment then, as if he thought she might be angry. It was a look she found hard to resist, as if he was a small boy caught out in some misdemeanour.

'I guess I can.'

'I got you some paracetamol, though,' he said, handing her the packet. 'How are you feeling?'

'Much better,' she said. 'I'll be even happier when I can wash, and get this place smelling a bit fresher. We need to get my suitcase out of my car, before someone makes off with that as well. You do still have my keys, don't you?' He nodded, jangling them in his pocket. 'But tomorrow's another day – day two, Will! Shall we go back to bed?'

It was some time later, when the headache came back with a vengeance, that she discovered the medicine he had brought was two years out of date.

Things didn't improve; instead, they got markedly worse. The next day, and the day after that, and every day, it seemed, he left her alone in the flat with little in the way of food, and without light or power. She had no money, no transport, and her phone was in her car, to which he had the keys. No doubt its battery was dead anyway. Sometimes he returned only to go out again, often while she slept. Sometimes he left a note: 'Getting things sorted. Back soon.' But he rarely was.

Then one day he returned just as it was dusking outside. She had spent the day trying to clean the flat with cold water and a bit of towelling she found under the sink, punctuated by trips to the repulsive bathroom to vomit. She had barely eaten, but wanted nothing except water. The out-of-date painkillers helped for a while, even if only to knock her out. Whatever she tried to tell herself, that things must get better, that everything would be OK – somehow – there was no escaping her deepening misery. She dared not think about what she had left behind, or ask the looming question, *Oh, Lord, what have I done?*

Will came back that evening positively beaming and bouncing, flinging open the flat door, calling out to her, obviously barely noticing her ragged hair, her grimy dress, her washed-out face. He gave an excited twirl. 'What do you think?'

She saw, without comprehension, that he was wearing a new, and obviously expensive, black leather jacket.

'And,' he added triumphantly, pushing up the sleeve, 'I got this as well. Beautiful, isn't it? And at a knock-down price!' A chunky watch gleamed on his wrist.

'Are you telling me,' she said dully, 'that you have left me in this grotty hole for *days and hours on end*, with no power and light, with barely any food, feeling ill, while you have been buying yourself expensive presents – with my money? I don't understand.'

He looked crestfallen, then sulky. 'I told you I'd pay you back,' he said. 'And it *is* my birthday next week.' He tiptoed closer to where she stood, her arms wrapped around herself. 'Are you still feeling ill? You look terrible, it's true.'

'Yes, I don't feel great. But I might feel better if I could see you were making some effort to fix things up here.'

'But I am, darling! Of course I am! I've spoken to the electricity company. I've paid the outstanding bill. We'll be reconnected in no time. And I've left the car with a garage, to have a look and see what the problem is. As for food, I thought we could go out. But if you're feeling ill, I can get a takeaway.'

'Please don't bother on my account,' she said. 'I can't keep anything down, not even water.' Suddenly she sniffed. 'What's that smell?'

He grinned. 'What smell? The only smell around here is quite unpleasant, and it's coming from the bathroom.'

'No, there's a smell around you, kind of aromatic.' Light dawned suddenly. 'Will, have you been smoking weed?'

He burst into peals of laughter, grabbed her by the waist and twirled her round. 'There's no getting the better of you, is there, my love? Yes, I bumped into a very old friend while I was snooping around in the market, someone I used to know way back. He put me in the way of this jacket, actually – got me a good price.' He preened, glancing at his reflection in the spotty hallway mirror. 'Anyway, we had a chat, did a bit of catching up, and he asked me back to his place, and we had a little party! Just like old times!' He patted his pocket. 'I've got a little stash with me. Would you like some?'

She felt her head reel, and she sat down abruptly on the only armchair – a stained wreck with springs protruding. A puff of dust rose into the air, making her cough and gag. 'No, I wouldn't,' she said. She didn't trust herself to say any more.

He shrugged. 'Suit yourself. I'll go and get a takeaway for myself, then, if you don't want anything.'

'Wait,' she said, her voice icy. 'We need to talk. This can't go on.'

'What can't?'

'Living like this. Me in a slum, a prison, feeling like death, while you swan off for hours. How can I possibly believe you care for me at all, if that's how you treat me?'

He was all contrition, if only she could have believed it. 'I know, darling, I'm sorry, I've been very selfish. I'll do better, I promise.' He brightened. 'One thing, though – I've put the cottage on the market. If I get a buyer soon – and why shouldn't I? – I'll have money. We can go away.'

Something about this last comment sounded hollow in her ears, and in a moment all the doubt, all the suspicion that she had been holding at bay came creeping, trickling, flooding back until it was a roaring, inescapable cascade. 'No, that won't happen, will it?' she said. Her tone was quiet, but there was iron in it. 'You don't care, do you, Will? Not one bit. It's all a pretence to you.'

He gaped, but said nothing.

She held out her hand. 'I'll have my credit card back, I think. I'm not having any more of my money spent without my say-so.'

He took several steps back. 'You gave it to me,' he growled. The charm and gaiety were gone, and he looked almost feral, a cornered animal. 'You said I was to get what we needed.'

'Yes – what we needed, not what you fancied. I see now I was stupid. Give it back, Will.' She advanced on him, her hand outstretched.

He held up his hands. 'Now, sweetie, this is silly, you can't go out, not feeling ill, and with your car off the road; be sensible. You need me – you have to trust me.'

In some corner of her mind she acknowledged the truth of what he said. Like it or not, she did need him. But the anger was boiling in her, making her feel hot, and her voice rose out of control. 'That's just it, Will,' she hissed. 'I don't trust you. You give me no cause to. Now, give me my credit card back.'

He folded his arms, his eyes narrow. 'Or what? You'll knock me down and take it by force?'

'If you don't give me back what's mine, it's as good as stealing. I could involve the police.'

'Huh! How are you going to do that? Your phone's dead, for a start.' He sneered, but the mention of the police had unsettled him. 'And then what? What are you going to do with your card?'

'Stop you spending my money, at least.'

'Not so long ago you were calling it *our* money,' he said. He smiled suddenly, biting his lip. 'Look, Maggie, I was going to go to a travel agent tomorrow, make enquiries – '

She cut him off. 'No, you weren't. You're just using me, aren't you, Will? You couldn't care less what happens to me. My money's useful, and that's about it.' She stared at him. 'I'm right, aren't I? If I hadn't seen you packing up to leave, you'd just have disappeared without a word. Leaving me to wonder what it was all about.'

'You'll find out what it's all about,' he said. His voice was soft, but it held an undertone of menace. 'You'll find out, soon enough.'

She shivered. 'What's that supposed to mean?'

He made no answer. Instead he put his hands on her shoulders and turned her round, so that she was facing the mirror. 'Just look, Maggie,' he said, his smile an unpleasant lip-curl that just showed his teeth. 'Look in the mirror. Do you see that old, fat, ugly, stupid woman? You ask me if I care about her. How could I? Answer me that.'

Despite herself, Maggie felt a wave of shock. 'Why?' she wailed. 'Why are you doing this? Why have you changed?'

He leaned back against the wall, arms folded. 'I haven't,' he said calmly. 'You're right – I never wanted you to follow me. It's over and done, Maggie. It never really was much of anything, was it? Not for me. Once the cottage is sold, I'll disappear. With your credit card.' He smirked. 'Maybe I'll buy a nice new car with it. I saw one I liked today. Red, it was.'

'You can't do that!'

He bared his teeth. 'Watch me.'

Maggie stared at him open-mouthed. 'But what about me? I've thrown away my life for you! What am I supposed to do?'

He waved his hand as if to ward off an especially evil smell. 'Whatever you like. I haven't forced you into anything, remember. It was always your choice. I can't help it if you don't like what you've chosen.'

She was silent for a moment, digesting the unwelcome truth of his remark. One last card she had to play, and she had small hope of it. She spoke urgently, controlling her desire to shriek. 'Will, listen. This illness of mine. Don't you think it might be because I'm pregnant?'

He threw back his head and laughed. 'So what, my lovely? So what? Why should I care if you are? It's what you've always wanted, isn't it? Why aren't you happy?'

'Because it has to be yours, Will, don't you see that?'

He shook his head. 'Oh no, Maggie. Don't try and pull that one. I told you, I can't have kids.'

'You say that, but don't you remember? I told you how rare it is for mumps to cause sterility.'

He shrugged. 'So you tell me. I don't care about that either.' He came close to her, and spoke into her face, slowly, as if to an idiot. 'Open your ears and listen. Just understand this. I don't want you. I don't want your squalling brat. I don't plan to stick around. Got it?'

There was silence for several moments, punctuated only by his heavy breathing.

'What am I going to do?' she muttered, almost to herself. 'I haven't even got any money.'

He sneered. 'I'll leave you your taxi fare. Go home to hubby, why don't you?'

'How can I? Now?' she moaned. He said nothing, just looked at her with a little smile on his handsome face. 'I'd be better off dead.'

'Like I said, what do I care? I don't do guilt-trips, sweetheart. Just remember, it's always been your choice. You've brought all this on yourself.' He fished in his pocket, fetched out a handful of notes and coins, and threw them on the table among the leftovers. 'There you are – don't say I left you with nothing, OK? I'm going out now, but I'll have to be back from time to time. Don't be here when I get back, will you? One way or another – ' he grinned nastily – 'be gone. Know when you're not wanted for once.'

That night, alone in the darkness, Maggie faced the reality of Will's treachery and the even deeper yawning pit of her own unaccountable folly. She faced it steadily, despite the knowledge of all she had thrown away. So maybe her marriage needed some work, she thought, clenching her teeth to stop them chattering. But what about her work that she loved? The children who welcomed her every morning? Her clean and comfortable home, her brightly flowering garden? Her church family? Her friends? At the memory of what Julie had tried to say to her, she groaned softly. Finally, while she was facing up to her own failure, she steeled herself to face her God also: Him whom she had banished from her thoughts so deliberately and so thoroughly these last few months. She called on Him, tentatively and expecting nothing except just condemnation, but calling nevertheless out of her abject need. *Oh, Lord. Please help. I don't deserve anything. But I don't know what to do.*

It was little enough, as prayers go. She sighed, acknowledging her exhaustion, lay down heavily on the rank mattress, and slept.

In the morning she knew there was one thing that had to be done, before anything like a decision could be taken. She smoothed down her hair, washed her grubby face and hands in cold water, brushed down her soiled dress, and crept out of the flat. There was nobody about. Like a daytime ghost, she crossed the car park and the service road, and headed downhill. Half way down there was a small parade of shops, some shuttered and blank, others just opening up for the day. A man was sweeping the pavement outside his shop, and he nodded to her. Clearly her dishevelled appearance was no surprise to him.

She found what she was looking for on the far corner, and timidly went inside. The doorbell jangled, and a woman in a white overall looked up at Maggie over her glasses. 'Morning.'

Maggie muttered something barely audible and hid herself among the shelves. She found a rack of home pregnancy tests, and took the nearest. Feeling almost like a criminal, she handed it over to the assistant, along with a £10 note.

The assistant wrapped it. 'For yourself, is it?'

'Er, my daughter,' Maggie whispered.

'Make sure she reads the instructions,' the woman said as she handed Maggie her change.

Maggie nodded, retreating as quickly as she could. Outside the shop she stopped, breathing raggedly, feeling her heart pounding. Slowly she made her way back up the hill, across the road and the car park, and up the stairs to the flat, where she had left the door on the latch: she had no key. For a moment she paused: what if he were there? She pushed the door open silently. But there was no one.

It took her another few hours to gather her courage enough to take the test. In the end she went through the steps with a sense of leaden fatalism, and there it was: the narrow horizontal blue line, crossed by a strong, wide, incontrovertible vertical one. It seemed nothing could have been so positive.

What should have been the moment of sheer delight and hope that had eluded her for so many years was now little short of a death sentence. As the day wore on and she still sat, sometimes looking balefully at the test sitting on the table, mocking her, the noise of the thundering traffic came close to her ears and mind. All she needed, or so it seemed in that bleak moment, was the courage to step out into the road.

I thought things were getting difficult before. But now – it's gone off the scale. What am I supposed to do? Who can I talk to? Maybe it's just too big to deal with. Maybe Mum is right – I should just keep my distance, let whatever's going to happen just happen. Is it really my business anyway? I wondered if someone should tell Mr Calladine what Bill told us. But there's no way I can talk to him, and it doesn't look as if Mum will either.

Thing is, right now I'm more worried about Olly. I wouldn't really want to admit this to anyone, not even myself, but I do really like Olly. He's just a boy, but he's showing distinct signs of growing up. When I compare him with some of the stupid louts at school, he's practically heroic. (And extremely attractive.) Ha! What happened to bookish little stay-at-home Abbie? I have even been contemplating – well, how do I say this? The girls at school are always in little clusters, heads together, sniggering. Sometimes they're talking about relatively innocent things like what colour to paint their nails. But sometimes, and I know this even though they don't share these little chats with me, they're whispering about 'who they've done it with' and 'did you hear about Louise and that guy Tim' and how far you let a boy go if you're not actually going out, etc, etc.

They are literally obsessed with casting off their virginity the first possible chance they get, even if, and this baffles me, they don't really fancy the boy in question! It's all so weird – the girl who actually does it (and with most of them it's just empty bragging, I'm sure) gets a day in the sun, number one in the popularity stakes, loads of kudos. But within seconds all the others are talking about her behind her back, self-righteous and spiteful! How does that work? I'm glad not one of them is my friend. They're all cut out of the same mould as Zara Chesterfield. Or maybe there are one or two that are OK. But I haven't found them. Maybe, like me, they keep their heads down. The only grief I get is having no friends (except Olly; at least, I hope he is) and being sneered at and shut out for being weird.

But I'm worried I've given Olly the wrong idea. The last little while I've been a bit distant with him, just because of everything that's been happening. I'm scared if he gets to know me any better my weirdness will put him off. I know he likes head cases, but there are limits. The trouble is, I don't really know how much he likes me. He's hardly ever serious, and there are rather a lot of serious issues going on in my life these days. Maybe he'll think I'm boring and find someone else that's more fun — like that girl, what's her name, Paige or something, she's almost as tall as me, but MUCH more curvy with nice legs and long blonde hair. The thought of hearing her whispering one day about how she's 'done it with Olly Bradshaw' makes me want to howl and break something. Like her neck. I want to scream, 'Hands off, he's mine!' But is he?

And what do I do about my plan to … well, not to put too pernickety a point on it, have sex with Olly? (Not just yet, of course. When the time is right. But he could know my thoughts on the matter!) Does that make me like them? The difference is, I wouldn't be broadcasting it all around the common room. I'd just be wearing a smug expression.

Oh, but what's the point in all this, anyway? It won't come to anything. It'll all fizzle out. Maybe I'll find he's just as loud and stupid and arrogant as the rest of them and prefers gorgeous Paige to Abbie the lunatic. The reality is, tomorrow's Monday. Time to get some sleep.

June 2010

Abbie woke, restless and hot. She looked blearily at her clock: 4.25. Why was waking at this hour so deadening? And why had she awoken in the first place? She groped on the bedside table and picked up her phone. Its face glowed an eerie blue, signalling some message had arrived. Maybe it was the annoying little bleep that had woken her. She pushed her hair out of her eyes and thumbed the appropriate keys.

Hey, doll. You still breathing?

Olly. She grinned, embarrassing herself by the wash of sheer happiness that those five inane words could bring. She sent a reply.

Just. Lunch? Usual place.

She turned over in bed, wrapping her arms round her torso. There was no need for a reply, and none came. But all was well. Perhaps she could forget the troubles of the adult world and concentrate on age-appropriate things: homework, exams, university applications, learning to drive; and working out just how far to go with the good-looking devil who by some awesome chance just happened to be hers.

Two hours later she resurfaced, and sat bolt upright, gasping. She had a vanishing memory of her own voice shouting, 'No, no, no!' She put a hand to her face and found her cheeks were wet with inexplicable tears. *What was all that about?* Then she remembered, and shuddered.

In her dream – and it was a sleeping dream, not a seeing, no question about that – she had been with Maggie Calladine. Both of them were wearing long, heavy black clothes in many trailing layers, and everything they wore was soaked through. Their hair hung in saturated strands down their cold necks as they walked, Maggie gripping Abbie's hand with painful tightness, through a dark wasteland in which there was little to see except the dim but vaguely threatening outlines of buildings. Trees and hedges were lashed by a powerful wind, thunder crashed and lightning blinded their eyes as a cold rain, whipped by the wind, pounded their shoulders, making progress slow and strenuous. Abbie felt helpless and afraid, but Maggie had hold of her, pulling her along with desperate strength, until Abbie, feeling herself weaken under the weight of her wet clothes, cried out, 'Where are we going?' and Maggie stopped, and turned to face her, her eyes dark pits, her teeth bared in a terrifying grin, and whispered, 'Why, don't you see, little seer? It's the end of the world.'

Shivering, desperate not to return to the world of her dream, Abbie threw back the covers and sat on the edge of her bed, her elbows on her knees, her head bowed. *Well, so much for thinking I could walk away. Seems like this trouble belongs to all of us. If dreams come from a part of our brains we don't normally visit, or is just not accessible consciously, then I guess that's a message from me to me. And what's it saying? Abbie, get your skates on, Mrs Calladine is in dead trouble, and nobody's going to do anything about it. They're going to let that creep Will Chambers – or Paul White, or whatever his name really is – drag her down and throw her away. It's her world that's ending, and maybe taking ours down with it.* She shook her head, trying to dispel the clouds of sleep and confusion, and sighed deeply. *That bit of my brain – is it a wise bit, or a mad bit? – is telling me to do something.*

She threw on some comfortable trousers and socks and a hooded jacket and crept downstairs. The dog looked up at her from her basket in the kitchen, wagged her tail lazily and yawned. 'Fancy a *very* early stroll, Molly?' Abbie whispered. She took Molly's lead down from its hook, found a pair of grubby trainers and unlocked the back door. 'Come on then, and be quiet.' She clipped the lead to the dog's collar and they crept out into the pearly summer morning.

The sun was already clipping the tops of the tall oaks that grew in clumps round the green. Filled with sudden energy Abbie trotted along the deserted road, speeding up to a run as Molly caught up. She raced twice round the green before she was forced to stop, hands on knees, gulping lungfuls of air. She straightened up and ruffled the dog's head. 'Better get back before they discover us, old girl. They'll think we've gone bananas. But you don't care if I'm crackers, do you?' The dog looked up at her, eyes bright, tongue lolling, mouth stretched in an amiable canine grin. 'Come on. Time for some breakfast. I've got a tiny little glimmer of an idea. We'll start with Olly, and go from there.'

At the end of the morning, Abbie left the school grounds by the front gate. There was no sign of Olly. By their normal arrangement she left alone, walking head down past the clusters of other sixth formers allowed out for the lunch break, and strode up the road and into the small convenience store that formed part of a parade of shops, where she bought a packet of biscuits and two apples. Other students were crowding into the shop as she left, and one lad leaned in front of her. 'Hey, geek girl, where you going?' She ignored him, pushed open the door and turned right. At the top of the hill was a small, dusty park, frequented mainly by old men with scruffy dogs. She walked briskly across it and down a wooded incline to where an old brick bridge crossed a dried-up stream.

Olly was waiting for her under the bridge, hidden in the shadows. He had left the school by the playing field gate and come round the back of the grounds. Abbie simply wanted to avoid the jeering gossip; he, she suspected, quite liked the cloak-and-dagger aspect of their assignations. As she came up close, he pulled off his sunglasses, seized her body in a muscular grip and kissed her so she could barely breathe.

'Hey! Take it easy,' she gasped, shoving him away.

'See how much I missed you,' he growled, trying to be menacing. 'Count yourself lucky I don't fling you to the ground in a frenzy of lust.'

'Fool,' she said. 'Do you want an apple?'

'Oh, OK.'

For a while they sat on the dusty ground, amiably munching.

'Olly, I need to run something past you.'

He raised his eyebrows.

Ignoring his leering expression she said, 'Do you remember when we saw Mrs Calladine and that guy Will Chambers in the shopping centre in Moxhurst?'

'Yeah. The day you went spacey and saw an eagle and I decided to do a psychology project on crazy girls who see things that aren't there.'

'Shut up for a minute. There've been developments since then, and I have a really bad feeling about it.'

'I'm listening. Are those chocolate biscuits?'

'No. The chocolate gets disgustingly melty this weather. Have some, though.'

While Olly crunched his way voraciously through most of the packet, Abbie brought him up to date.

'I told you, didn't I, that I'd told my mum, and this time she believed me?'

'Yeah, and that's the last time I heard anything from you. I thought you'd died, or decided that Charlie bloke was a better bet than me.'

'Please,' Abbie said with a shudder. 'You are an idiot, but he is an ugly, bragging idiot. No contest.'

'Phew. What a relief. And how wonderful to know you think so highly of me. Thank you so very much.'

'Just zip it, OK? I'm trying to explain.'

'Right.'

'It all went a bit pear-shaped after that.' She told Olly about Julie's quarrel with Maggie, Will Chambers' disappearance, and David Calladine's accusations. 'No, honestly,' she said in response to Olly's gape of amazement, 'I'm not making this up! She'd left him to go with Will, and Mr C was accusing my mum of plotting!'

She glanced anxiously at Olly. 'Don't say anything about this to anybody, will you? They're in enough trouble as it is.'

'I won't say a word,' Olly said solemnly. 'But I might make notes. Could come in handy, all this stuff, for my future career.'

'As what? Writing for the tabloids?'

Olly gave her a withering glance. 'Tell me the rest, or we'll run out of time.'

'Do you have anything first period this afternoon?'

'No. You?'

'Me neither. We could skip registration.'

Olly whistled. 'What a rebel you are turning into, Miss Hasan. OK. Go on, then.'

'Well, as a result of all this I, we, have got the dog.'

'What, Molly? Chambers' dog?'

'Yep. He left her locked in the shed. She had no food and she'd drunk all her water. She's ours now.'

Olly swore under his breath. 'You were right about him all along. So what then?'

'Well, it all went quiet. Nobody seemed to want to do anything.'

Olly frowned and helped himself to another handful of biscuits. 'What was there to do? She'd decided to go off with her psycho lover, and that's that.'

'But I had a bad feeling about it. Like she was in danger.'

'What, you think he'd actually harm her? Like, physically?'

Abbie sighed. 'I don't know. But there's other kinds of danger, aren't there?'

'She's a grown-up lady, Abbie. Maybe she's acting like an idiot, but – '

'Yeah. That was my mum's attitude. She said, "Don't interfere." And I didn't want to. I wanted it all to go away. But I'm worried.' When Olly did not respond, she stumbled on. 'Anyway, then something really bizarre happened.' She told him about her meeting with Bill White, and how so much had become clear: who the man

189

they knew as Will Chambers really was, and why he was gunning for David Calladine.

Olly shook his head. 'Wow. So to get at Mr Calladine, he's run off with his missus. He must be dead chuffed with himself.'

'Probably.'

'Does anybody know where they've gone?'

Abbie shrugged. 'Not for certain. But Bill – that's the brother – reckons they'll have gone to this crummy flat Paul White rents, on the other side of Moxhurst. Bill gave me the address.'

Olly turned to face her, and grabbed her hand. His face was unusually serious. 'Abbie, please tell me you aren't thinking of going over there.'

Abbie avoided his gaze. 'I got the address for my mum. I thought she'd relent in the end. I thought she'd want to have another shot at persuading her friend to see sense.'

'You mustn't go there. If this guy's as nasty as you say, he could be dangerous.'

Abbie was silent for a moment, chewing her lip. 'I thought I just wanted nothing to do with all this,' she said, her voice low. 'Like it's not my business, and I wouldn't know how to deal with it anyway. But then, last night I had this awful dream about Mrs Calladine, and I just knew she's got to get away from him. Someone has to help her.'

'Abbie, you can't take risks because of a stupid dream!' Olly yelled. 'Please tell me you won't do anything by yourself.'

For several long stretched-out moments Abbie stared at the ground, thinking. Then she looked up at Olly's frowning face.

'I'll do a deal with you,' she said. 'I've just realised, like in the last two minutes, there's someone I have to talk to – that's if they'll let me in. I'll ask his advice, and I'll do what he says. OK? He's a wise person; we can trust him. I may not get to see him, though.'

'What are you talking about?' Olly said, scowling.

'Never mind. I'll tell you later.' She leaned forward and put her arms round his waist, under his jacket, feeling the warmth of his body through the thin cotton of his shirt. She looked up at him. 'How would you feel about bunking off school for a day?'

'What day?' he said guardedly.

'Tomorrow.'

He thought. 'OK.'

'It might not come to that. But if have to do something, I won't do it without you.' She smiled awkwardly. 'And thanks for being all manly and protective. My hero.'

'Now you're taking the mickey,' Olly said sternly.

'Not as much as you might think.'

He narrowed his eyes. 'You'd better explain yourself pretty soon,' he muttered. He pulled her closer. 'Because you're doing my head in with all this mystery. And my head was already swimming just looking at you.'

She grinned. 'You know what? When you pull a face like that, you look exactly like a gorilla.'

At twenty to four, Abbie found her brother at the bus stop. He was lounging against one wall of the shelter, alone, morosely chewing gum. 'Hey, bro. Where are all your mates?'

He shrugged. 'They live here, don't they? Walk home.'

'Oh. You OK?'

'Not bad.'

'Sure? You look like the cat ate your homework and threw up in your football boots.'

He grinned despite himself. 'We don't have a cat.'

'No, just as well, since we now have a dog. Who might appreciate you taking her down the woods.'

'Maybe. You getting the bus?'

'No, that's just it. I need you to cover for me. I'll be late home. Can you tell Mum I'll be in time for dinner? If she asks, I'm finishing some schoolwork.'

Dan frowned. 'Where are you really going?'

She shook her head. 'I can't tell you yet. Look, have you got any money?'

'I dunno. If I have, I want it back.'

'You'll get it back. Tonight. I just need some extra now.'

Dan foraged in his trouser pocket and extracted a battered wallet. He inspected its contents. 'Three eighty-five. That's it. My fortune.'

'I'll have it all.' Seeing his appalled expression she said, 'You don't need money, Daniel, you have your bus pass. What do you need money for between here and home? Paying off blackmailers?'

Reluctantly he put his wealth into her outstretched hand. 'Don't know why you have to be so sneaky,' he grumbled.

'I'll tell you when I can,' Abbie said. 'Thanks for the cash. See you later.' She crossed the road to the opposite bus stop, leaving her brother frowning and puzzled, still chewing his gum. Five minutes later her bus rumbled into view, and she jumped aboard. Grinning, she waved at his grumpy, slumped figure in the bus shelter, but she didn't get a wave back.

It was a long, slow, hot journey to the other side of Walburn. She took off her black jacket and undid the two top buttons of her shirt, until she noticed a spotty young man further down the bus eyeing her salaciously, when she hastily did them up again. She closed her eyes to blot out his leering face and hugged her bag closer to her chest. She thought of Olly, and felt a warm blush flood her face.

Thoughts of Olly, and of the summer holidays to come, with maybe taking – and passing! – her driving test, and borrowing the car, and going out somewhere with him, with everything that might entail, were like a pink fluffy cloud in her mind, sweet as candyfloss. But round the edges, demanding attention, were black threads staining the glow, creeping inwards, growing, enveloping her fantasy with their menace. She shifted in her seat and opened her eyes. *Business before pleasure. That's what Mum used to say when we were little. Get your chores done before you go out to play. Do your homework, then you can watch TV. But how nice it would be, for once, to have pleasure before and after pleasure! Not likely, Abbie. You're in the real world. And a poky, crummy hole it is at times.*

She looked out of the window. The sun was slowly creeping down the far side of the day. It was hot and dusty, the tarmac warm and sticky, the little businesses shuttered or devoid of custom, the vegetables in the greengrocers' racks limp and stale. There were few people about here in the outer suburbs: just the occasional mother wearily pushing a pram, and groups of unemployable youths laughing and smoking on benches. Then the bus turned into a long, leafy avenue, the trees on either side giving pleasant shade. Here the houses were much larger, some almost stately, with ranks of windows painted white, and well-tended flowerbeds: houses too big for the average family, and more than one now doing duty as a nursing home or a small hotel. Abbie got up, put her jacket on, and slung her bag over her shoulder. The bus ground to a halt, and the driver said, 'Here you are, love. St Oswin's.' He looked sympathetic. 'Visiting someone, are you?'

Abbie put on a suitably sad face. 'Yes. Thank you,' she said, years of training making politeness a default. She stepped onto the baking pavement and the bus creaked away with a crunching of gears.

She pushed open the door into a tiled hall, cool after the heat of the street. There was nobody about, and Abbie hesitated. She saw a large noticeboard on one wall, and moved closer to study it. *So many activities. I never knew dying was so much fun.*

Heels clacked crisply, approaching from a corridor on the other side. A short, stout middle-aged woman, smart in a floral suit and adorned with rows of glittering necklaces, stopped and said, 'Good afternoon. Can I help you?' Her voice was pleasant, cultivated, Abbie noticed. *Not from round here, then.*

'Hello. Yes, I was hoping to visit Reverend Westwood.' As she heard herself speak these words, sounding so calm and confident, a shiver of fright rippled through her body. What was she doing here, what was she thinking of?

'Ah. Are you a relative?' the woman asked, exuding the same brand of sympathy as the bus driver. 'He's very poorly, you know.'

'Yes, I know. I wasn't going to stay long. I'm not a relative, just a friend. He's our vicar at Halstead.'

'Of course, I see.' The woman positively beamed. *Why do people think it is so wonderful to meet a Christian that isn't at least fifty years old? Not that I am one.* 'Well, I'll take you up to his room. Mrs Westwood is there, you realise. She is very protective. She might not want to let you in.'

'I know Mrs Westwood,' Abbie said with a false smile. 'I'll take my chances.'

The woman smiled back. 'This way, then.'

Abbie followed her along the corridor from which she had just come and up a curving, elegant staircase with a polished wooden handrail. Watercolours in soothing muted shades, scenes of sunlit pools shaded by trees, or deer feeding tranquilly in untroubled meadows, adorned the pastel walls. At the top the woman turned right, her heels making no sound on the deep wine-coloured carpet. It was very quiet; through the open windows Abbie saw tall trees and heard the gentle sound of lazily buzzing insects. *Crikey. The anteroom of death. But so nice, so unthreatening, just like sleep. Who'd think that behind these doors is horror? Suffering, pain, open sores, amputations? But then again, maybe not. Maybe they're all doped to the eyeballs on morphine and kindness, waiting for the exit. Maybe it's just my warped imagination supplying the gruesomeness. Still, I hope when my turn comes it's sudden and quick, clobbered by a speeding lorry or something, here now, then gone. Blackout.*

'Here we are.' The woman stopped at a door and tapped gently. A moment later the door opened a few inches, and Abbie saw half a familiar, and formidable, face. 'Hilary, my love, a visitor for John.' She turned to Abbie. 'I'm sorry, young lady, what was your name?'

'Abbie Hasan. Hello, Mrs Westwood.'

The door opened wider, and all of Hilary Westwood appeared. She was smartly dressed as usual in a straight linen dress, accentuating her lean figure. Despite herself, Abbie was struck by the look of exhaustion and despair on her face.

'Oh, hello, Abbie. This is a surprise. You mother was here not long ago.'

'I know.' Abbie hesitated. 'I'm sorry to disturb you, Mrs Westwood. I know it's a terribly difficult time. But I have something I need to discuss with Mr Westwood.'

Hilary frowned. 'He's hardly in a state for discussion,' she snapped. 'He's gravely ill. Didn't you know?'

'Yes, of course,' Abbie murmured. 'I wouldn't dream of bothering you if it wasn't urgent. Mr Westwood has always been there for us, all of us. I know he's very ill, and I'm sorry, truly. But I think he might want to know what's happening.'

'I should think whatever it is is hardly important enough – ' Hilary Westwood stopped mid-sentence and turned her head inwards to the room. 'Coming, John.' She disappeared, and the woman who'd guided Abbie there smiled and shrugged. A moment later Hilary opened the door wide. 'He says you're to come in,' she said grudgingly. 'Please don't exhaust him.' She came out into the corridor and pulled the door to. 'He hasn't got long,' she said quietly. 'And our son is coming this evening. John needs to conserve his strength.' Abbie was dismayed to see tears in Hilary Westwood's eyes.

'I'll try. And thank you.'

The other woman took Hilary's elbow. 'Why don't you come downstairs, Hilary,' she said gently. 'I'll make you a cup of tea. You should have a break now and then. You've been at his side almost constantly, I know. I expect, um, Abbie will let us know when she's going.' She smiled brightly at Abbie. 'Won't you, dear?'

'Of course,' Abbie murmured.

The two women walked back down the corridor, and Abbie pushed the door open and put her head round it.

'Come in, come in, Abbie!' She was shocked by the strength of John Westwood's familiar voice. 'Don't lurk in the doorway, come here where I can see you.'

Abbie approached hesitantly. He was propped up in the bed, and he looked ghastly. His face was sunken and yellow, his white hair sparse with the scalp visibly pink beneath, and the hands that rested on the white sheet were fleshless claws. But oddly his blue eyes were bright and lively with intelligence.

'What a delightful surprise!' he said. 'You look like a tropical flower, my dear. Like a shower of rain in a dry desert. Do sit down.' Abbie sank into a chair that had been placed close to the bed. 'You mustn't mind my wife, bless her. She seems fierce, I know, but it's always in defence of me.' He smiled. 'I don't need defending, of course. And that fierceness hides a good heart. So, dear Abbie, what brings you to my sanitised deathbed? Hm?'

To her own surprise Abbie found herself moved by his good humour, his gaiety in the face of horror and decay, the familiarity of his voice that she had heard so often in church as a child, and she stammered, 'I'm really sorry you're ill.'

'Oh, well, as to that, don't you worry. Don't be sad. We all have to die, and I'm looking forward to being in a far better mode of existence.' He chuckled. 'Of course, it's no picnic being ill, but death doesn't bother me.' His face became serious. 'I imagine there's something going on in my little patch, is there? It must be something thorny to bring you all the way out here to see a dying old man. So tell me, before I fall asleep, which I might.'

'All right.' Abbie took a deep breath. 'You're right. There are bad things going on. I think someone you know is in danger. And nobody wants to do anything about it. I thought, if anybody could tell me what to do, it would be you.'

'I'm listening.'

Abbie gathered her thoughts, and started to talk. The more she talked, the faster the story poured out: the arrival of Will Chambers, his deceiving charm and helpfulness, his mowing of the churchyard and helping old ladies; the gradual rising of suspicion, his lies and deceits, then seeing Will and Maggie together, and finally his and Maggie's disappearance, and her own doubts borne out by the arrival of Bill.

'Wait a moment,' John Westwood said. 'There's something that isn't clear to me. Why you? And why me? I mean, what is your part in this? And why do you think I can help?'

Abbie swallowed. 'You remember four years ago, when I had a – a kind of vision of the Kashmir earthquake? I know my mother told you about it.' John Westwood nodded. 'Well, it happened again. After a dinner party my mum gave for Will Chambers, when he first came to Halstead. I saw a great swarm of locusts, like in the Bible. Eating everything up, leaving just desolation. And then, after that, I saw other things, always in connection with him. A bird of prey, like an eagle, with an open beak, and a hooded cobra, poised to strike. Very threatening, very frightening. I just knew, I don't know how, they were all about him. They *were* him.'

John Westwood's eyes were closed, and Abbie thought he had gone to sleep. She felt despair rise: if he could not help her, no one could. But he was not asleep. A moment later, his eyes snapped open. He stretched out his hand with painful effort, and grasped Abbie's wrist. His expression was sombre. 'You were right to come here,' he said. 'And I have no doubt who was leading and guiding you. Perhaps you are sceptical. Perhaps you don't believe in God as you used to. Well, that's no surprise, and it's a good thing.'

Abbie's heard jerked up. 'It is?'

'Of course. Some people never move on. They stay with the same simple, childlike faith they had when they were small. Nothing wrong with simple and childlike up to a point, or so some people think – but never examined, never appraised, as far as we know. And we don't know everything that goes in another person's mind, for sure. Others lose it and never get it back. But some people struggle and doubt, grow and change, and that's not always a painless process. I don't think I believed in anything much at your age either, nor for years after. But you're different, Abbie. You always have been.' He hesitated for a moment, then cleared his throat. 'When your mother came to see me,' he said softly, 'after that first time – the first time we knew about, anyway, when you saw the earthquake – I wondered, I really wondered about your peculiar gift. I asked myself if I should mention it to anyone. But in the end I didn't, because you were obviously going through the mill with all the medical and psychological tests, which must have been so worrying and wearisome for such a young person. I told myself that perhaps when you were older ... But then I became ill, and I never spoke of it. But you know, I always thought about you, and you were never far from my prayers. I guess you may not welcome the idea that you are different, but you might as well accept it and use your gifts for some good purpose – as you are trying to do now. And never doubt that what you have is a gift. It's in the use that such things are proved.'

'So what can I do?' Abbie whispered.

'Hm. You say your parents, and David, are inclined to let things lie?'

Abbie nodded. 'They seem, I don't know, immobilised somehow.'

John Westwood shook his head slowly. 'It's been a shock to them. To be so deceived, to have welcomed evil into their midst. And I'd guess there's been some failure of prayer. I'm in here, and my little flock have lost their way. That's a worry.' He frowned and thought for several long moments. His breathing was rough and laboured, and he winced in pain. 'The morphine's wearing off. Someone will be along in a moment to top me up. But I'll need to keep sharp. The body must take its turn. Let me think.' He fell silent again, his eyes closed, and Abbie watched him struggle and felt herself battling with him.

At last he said, 'I am anxious that you don't put yourself in danger. On the other hand, without doubt you've been led here, and you will have protection.' He took a steadying breath. 'Abbie, only God Himself can be our guide here, not our own inadequate wisdom. I don't know if this man you speak of is sick, or wicked in himself, or a carrier of evil, deceived in his turn. I want you to go home, and tonight, when you are alone, I want you to pray.' He saw her horrified expression. 'It doesn't matter if you think you have no faith,' he said gently. 'God is not proud. He will answer if you call on Him. Even if you say, "I don't know if You are even there. I don't know if You exist. But I know I need You to help me." Do it, Abbie. Nobody will know but you, and me, and God Himself. If you really want to help, pray. Then sleep. And in the morning, perhaps you will see the way ahead.' He smiled faintly. 'It seems to me that the very fact you chose to come here and see me is a kind of acknowledgement on your part.'

A tap came on the door, and a young nurse appeared. 'Time for your meds, John,' she said cheerfully, as if she was offering him a cold beer on a sweltering day.

'Not just yet,' John Westwood said. 'I'll have them later. Right now I need to keep sharp. Just until I send this young lady on her way.'

The nurse glanced at Abbie, then turned her attention back to John. 'Aren't you in pain?' she said dubiously.

'Just a bit. But it doesn't matter. And, Jenny dear – don't go running off and telling tales to Dr Miller. I'll take my poison – in half an hour. You can spare me that long.'

The nurse came close and looked at the sick old man with genuine tenderness.

'All right, rebel,' she said. 'I'll get you up in the bed a bit and sort out your pillows. Then I'll be back. Half an hour, no more. Otherwise you'll be asleep when your son comes.'

When she had gone, John Westwood turned to Abbie and spoke with renewed urgency. 'Pray for guidance, Abbie. And here on my fluffed-up pillows I'll do the same. I can't come with you – I would if I could! But I'll be with you in spirit, asking for God's protection on you. Because, my dear, you may not have understood this, but you were right in your instincts. This man represents spiritual danger, and Maggie Calladine is in the middle of it. He may never lay a violent hand on her, but he can do great damage nevertheless.'

'He's already done damage,' Abbie said bleakly. 'She and my mum were friends. Now they're not.'

'I pray these things can be mended. Will you do as I've said?'

Abbie nodded. 'I came here to look for help, so it would be stupid to reject it, wouldn't it? Whatever I believe, or don't believe. It's got to be worth a try.' She got up. 'I think I'd better go. Thank you for talking to me. I'm still scared, but in a different way. Not so helpless somehow. I hope – I hope someone can help you too.'

John Westwood smiled, and for a moment his hollowed-out face was transformed. 'I have plenty of help from kind people,' he said. 'And the best help of all from the Lord I love. I'll see His face, and it can't come soon enough. Thank you, dear girl, for coming to see me. You have made me feel better.'

'I don't know how,' Abbie said, her voice shaking slightly. 'I'll go now, and leave you in peace. I hope you have a good visit with your son.' She backed away, pausing in the doorway. 'Goodbye. Thank you.'

The old man lifted a feeble hand. 'Don't thank me, Abbie. Thank God. Don't forget what I said, now. Pray! Goodbye, dear child.'

On her way down the corridor, Abbie met Hilary Westwood coming back. The older woman walked stiffly, with a straight back, and her lips were a long thin line, as if she was holding something in, something so powerful that it would wreck everything in its path if she lowered her guard and let it out. Abbie surprised herself by the pity she felt. 'Thank you for letting me talk to him, Mrs Westwood,' she said.

'Hm. I hope you haven't worn him out.'

Abbie was at the top of the stairs when a harsh voice called her name. She turned to see Hilary Westwood standing in the corridor. She walked back a few steps towards her. 'He says he forgot something. He says, if you feel afraid, read Psalm 91. I suppose you do have a Bible, don't you?'

Well, she knows I'm a heathen. No fooling her. 'Yes, I have my Sunday school Bible. But my parents have several, anyway. Please thank him again for me. Goodbye, Mrs Westwood. I'll remember: Psalm 91.'

Well, that was the oddest night I can ever remember. I don't think I slept much, but when I did it was very deep, which meant that there were no dreams – or at least, none that have come back to haunt me. Which has got to be a good thing from my point of view. It's all very well saying all this stuff – seeing things, having insights – is a gift, but it's hard to live with. To me it feels more like a pain in the neck.

I did pray. Did I? Only because I couldn't think of anything else to do, and because I have a lot of time for Mr Westwood. At least he really lives out his faith, which is more than you can say for some. And he's wise, and kind, and very courageous. If I was in pain and all shrivelled up and shrunken from cancer and only had days to live, I'm sure I'd be a mess. Of course he believes he's going to better things; that must help. And he is quite old.

Anyway, long after everyone else was asleep, I lay on my bed and started what seemed to me to be Abbie talking to Abbie. But as I got into it, it seemed easier, and even if it was only me and me chatting away, at least it helped to clarify my thoughts. I fell asleep mid-sentence, and woke up feeling quite chilly. So it took a while to get back to sleep and in the meantime I did some more chatting. I asked God to show me what I should do, and I also asked Him to keep Mrs Calladine safe, because I feel certain she needs protection. My own voice was still the only one I could hear, though. Even just in my head.

The next time I woke up it was still dark. I got up and went to the toilet, and when I came back I had a really strong feeling that gave me gooseflesh. I couldn't even describe it. But I knew for certain I had to go and find her – Mrs Calladine. That's why I'd been given the address. And I was the only person, it seemed, that felt compelled to act – except poor Mr Westwood, and he can't get out of bed, let alone drive to Moxhurst. It's a shame I haven't passed my test yet. I knew I'd have to go on the bus, and my funds were running low, especially as I had to pay Dan back. *Anyway, I went back to bed knowing I'd find a way somehow* — it was weird, because I rarely feel that confident about anything.

But in the morning, when it was light and the house was waking up and people were moving about and getting ready for the day and everything was normal, then it hit me. What was I doing? What was I thinking of? Was I really planning to bunk off school, and get Olly to do the same? Up to now I'd always been a model pupil: hard-working, good results, good attendance, polite and obliging. *Practically perfect! So as not to be noticed more than anything.* No wonder the other kids can't stand me. Sometimes I can't stand myself. Well, that's changing a bit.

So I felt utterly terrified! I got dressed for school as usual, but I couldn't stomach breakfast. Mum looked at me in that way mothers do and asked me if I was feeling OK, and when I said I was she made me take some fruit in my bag. I knew I had to message Olly before he left his house, but I seemed turned to stone by sheer panic. How could I ever have thought I was up to this? It feels like I'm getting into deep water, and I won't be able to keep my feet on the ground. Plus, we're both going to be in trouble if we are found out.

I sat on my bed for a while battling with my thoughts. Then I remembered Psalm 91. I got my Bible down from the bookshelf — for the second time! — and some of it was like it was speaking directly to me. For example: 'You have made the LORD your defender, the Most High your protector, and so no disaster will strike you, no violence will come near your home.' And then, 'You will trample down lions and snakes, fierce lions and poisonous snakes.' It even said this: 'You will look and see how the wicked are punished.'

Well! Will Chambers is certainly wicked. And I'd had a seeing of him as a cobra. So maybe John Westwood was right. On an impulse I put the Bible in my school bag. Maybe there were other gems in there. I did have a moment of doubt: perhaps if Olly thought I was some kind of Bible-bashing fanatic he'd go right off me. But there were bigger things at stake; I'd have to take that risk. I sent him a hasty text: *Don't go to school. Wait for me at Walburn bus station, soon as. Bring money. Xx*

I deliberately loitered so that I'd miss the early bus. I thought if I caught the later one there'd be no one to notice that I didn't get off at the school gates. With

202

the end of term getting close and things other than schoolwork going on – end of term plays, sports, etc – the teachers aren't quite so vigilant, and maybe they won't clock that I've been late a few times recently.

On the bus, which I shared with people going into town or to work but not with any schoolkids, I loosened my hair and tried to look more like a young professional in her dark suit. No one took any notice, and that was the main thing. The bus trundled along, stopping far too often. Had Olly got my message? Would he be there?

I needn't have worried. As the bus pulled in to the bus station with a weary sigh, there he was, lounging on a bench, wearing those flashy shades as usual, his hair gelled and spiky, looking more like a lout than a schoolboy. When I got off the bus he got up and came over, and there was a big grin on his face. He put his arm through mine. 'So, doll,' he said in his fake gangster voice, 'what's the plan?'

I had to straighten him out. I told him if he thought this was some humorous little adventure, some escapade, he'd better wise up, or just back off and go to school. I was very stern, and he pretended to be hurt.

'I'm coming to protect you,' he said. 'I'm your knight in shining armour, remember?'

I relented, a bit. 'OK,' I said. 'But you have to do as I say.' And he sighed like a big drama queen and said, 'When don't I?' Which is rubbish.

Anyway, we had a bit of a wait for the Moxhurst bus, so we went to the café in the bus station and had a coffee and some doughnuts, because I was starving. Luckily Olly paid, so I had to admit it was a good thing he was coming along.

The bus took forever to get to Moxhurst. So we had plenty of time to chat and look at the scenery – bits of fields in between crummy old industrial parks and rundown housing estates, for the most part. For once it made me glad I lived in Halstead: usually I moan because it's so dead, but at least there are proper woods and farms and stuff. But then something happened which reminded me just how serious and scary our mission was. We were talking about Bill White, and I was filling Olly in with some of the details of what had happened on Sunday morning, when it hit me like a collapsing wall.

'Abbie! Hey!' Olly sounded uncharacteristically anxious. 'You're not having one of your visions, are you? You've gone white as a sheet. Please tell me you're not about to throw up.'

'No,' Abbie hissed. 'And keep your voice down! I'm not struck on the idea of the whole world knowing about, you know, my seeings. And I wasn't having one then. But I have just realised something, and you're right, it *is* making me feel sick, so maybe you'd better keep your nice new trainers out of the way.'

Olly shifted his feet sideways. 'I hope you're kidding,' he muttered. 'So what have you just realised?'

'We were just talking about Bill White showing me that old photo of his brother, weren't we? I didn't pick it up at the time, but it must have seeped into my brain at some level, because I've just this minute remembered where I've seen Will Chambers before. I told you I had the feeling he looked vaguely familiar, didn't I?'

'You said Mr Calladine thought the same.'

'Yes, and we know why, don't we? He taught Will, I mean Paul, and Paul thought Mr C was responsible for getting him expelled. But why would *I* have seen him?'

'Well, when did you?' Olly said with a puzzled frown.

Abbie swivelled in the bus seat to face him and spoke in low, urgent tones. 'It was when I was having all those tests. When I was seeing the psychologist. Four years ago. He was the guy I crashed into when I went flying out of the room in a fit of temper and sent all his files flying. He was a bit younger then, of course. And I'll tell you another thing – he was definitely blond.'

'Told you,' Olly said triumphantly. 'He dyes his hair.'

'And ...' Abbie said, screwing up her face as she tried to remember, 'if I'm not mistaken his eyes were blue. Bright and blue. Not brown.'

'That's no problem, is it?' Olly said. 'He could easily have been wearing coloured contacts these last few months.'

Abbie shivered. 'He went to some trouble to be someone else, didn't he? To deceive, cover his tracks, whatever. Which makes me remember what a devious rat he is and what a snakes' nest we might be getting into. I'm scared, Olly.'

'I wouldn't ever let him hurt you. That's why I'm here.'

'I know. But I don't imagine he'll be thinking of murder, or kidnap, or violence of any sort. I had the feeling he recognised me, didn't I? He'll try and use that knowledge somehow. He knows I can't stand him. So maybe he'll have it in for me as well as Mr Calladine. I reckon he'll be looking for a way to hurt both of us – but in a way he can't be done for. His brother said he's always managed to keep just on the right side of the law. Either that or he's never been caught.' She shuddered.

Olly put his arm round her shoulders and hugged her. 'Don't worry,' he said. 'It's broad daylight and I'm with you. What can he do to hurt you?'

Abbie sucked in her breath. 'I can't imagine. But what you just said sounds horribly like famous last words.'

'If it helps, I'll be right behind you, whatever you decide to do.' He frowned. 'What *are* you going to do?'

Abbie thought. 'First of all we have to find this place. Parker House, Presbytery Lane. It sounds quite a nice place, doesn't it? I bet it's anything but. Maybe we can ask at the bus station. And then – and then I'll decide.' She looked up at him, her face set. 'But one thing I already did decide,' she said quietly. 'You're not coming into that flat with me.'

Olly's eyebrows shot up and his jaw dropped. 'What!'

'You can be outside. With your phone on. We can arrange a time limit – I don't know, twenty minutes or something. Then if I don't come out, you can come in. But you have to see, Olly – Mrs Calladine knows me, but she doesn't know you. We can't tell what the situation is, and I don't want her freaking. If I can, I want to try to persuade her to go home. Maybe she still thinks Paul White is God's gift, and if she refuses to be helped, then I can't do anything more. But somehow I doubt it. He was already showing his true colours before he left Halstead. One way or another I have to find out, and I have to do it on my own – for her sake.'

Abbie had never seen Olly's face so bleak. 'If something bad happened to you, how would I ever explain it to your parents?' he muttered. 'Oh yeah, "Sorry, I went to keep Abbie from harm, but when it came to it I lounged on the street corner and let a madman chop her up with a fish knife." Some hero I am.'

Abbie smiled faintly. 'If a fish knife is all he's got, I think I'll be fine. Anyway, I'm pretty sure he won't try anything. Even if he's there, which he may not be. She is, though,' she added thoughtfully. 'I'm pretty sure of that. Where else would she go?' She looked at Olly. 'It's nice you're worried about my safety,' she said softly. 'Thanks.'

Olly sat back in the seat and folded his arms, scowling. 'I don't like it.'

'Look, what I didn't tell you is where I went yesterday, after school.' She hadn't meant to talk about this, but now it seemed she had to.

'Where?'

'I went to see our old vicar, Mr Westwood. He's dying of cancer in St Oswin's Hospice.'

'How can he help?' Olly said, baffled. 'If the poor bloke's dying? Wasn't he up to his eyes in morphine or something?'

'He did help, actually.' Abbie sighed. 'I wasn't going to mention this at all, because I was afraid you'd think I was a total freak, but he advised me to pray.'

Olly turned to her with a sudden movement and grabbed her by the shoulders. 'When will you get it into your thick skull,' he said through clenched teeth, 'that I *like* freaks? Why else would I be with you? When you're so stupid and ugly and boss-eyed and smell so rancid?'

Abbie collapsed against him, laughing till her eyes dripped. 'OK, I give in.'

Olly smirked. 'At last.' Then he sobered, and said, 'So, did you?'

'Did I what?'

'Pray.'

'Kind of. Anyway, I made my mind up. Or someone made it up for me. And Mr Westwood said he'd be praying for me too. So maybe I will be well protected and there's no need for you to be anxious.' She hesitated, then searched through her bag and found her Bible. She opened it at the marker she had put in earlier. 'He said to read this if I was scared. Psalm 91.' She passed the Bible to Olly, who gave her a strange look but bent his head and read.

'Do you believe all this stuff?' he said finally.

'I don't know if I do or not,' Abbie said. 'I mean, my parents do, and I know *about* it, Sunday school and all that. For me the jury's still out. But yeah, I'm thinking about it.' When he didn't answer, she added lightly, 'What about you?'

He shook his head. 'I don't know either. But if you think there's a couple of whopping great angels going into that flat with you, with their flaming swords or whatever, then I'll feel a lot happier.'

She pulled away and wiped her eyes with her hands. 'I don't want to make you even more conceited than you already are,' she said. 'But maybe you really are a bit of a hero.'

Olly leapt to his feet and flung his arms wide. 'Recognition at last!' he shouted, twirling round on the points of his toes.

Two old ladies at the front of the bus turned and stared as he collapsed into his seat.

'Come on, embarrassing boy,' Abbie said. 'We're here.'

When they enquired at the bus station's information desk, they found that they had passed within 100 yards of Presbytery Lane two bus stops before.

'We should have got off the bus opposite that boarded-up car dealership,' Olly said.

'What, the one with the flaking green paint in that frightfully upmarket area?'

'Spot on. We could wait for another bus back.'

'Or,' Abbie said firmly, 'we could walk. It won't take long. Come on – with all that football, you must be super-fit.'

Olly looked surprised. 'Oh, didn't you know? I only pretend to play football to impress girls.'

'Consider me duly impressed. You coming?'

They backtracked down the dusty wide road along which they had just come in the bus. It was a longer trudge than Abbie had anticipated, and they were deafened by the roar of unrelenting traffic. Presbytery Lane crossed this road in both directions.

'Up or down?' Olly wondered.

Abbie thought for a moment. 'Down, I reckon. That end looks sleazier.'

'Hm, marginally.'

They raced across the lethal road and arrived panting on a scabby grass verge planted with sick-looking saplings. At this end of Presbytery Lane, several unlovely blocks of flats, three storeys high, lined the road. They looked neglected, with peeling paint and cracked windows. One or two had made an effort: window boxes of red geraniums wilted in the rising heat. But for the most part, it was a scene of neglect. Abbie wrinkled her nose. 'I smell mouldering dustbins.'

'I think this is it,' Olly said. '"arker House. Someone's pinched the P.'

'Oh! Olly, look.' Abbie pointed to a small car park in front of the building. 'That's Mrs Calladine's car.'

They edged cautiously closer, as if fearing ambush, but there was nobody about.

Olly eyed the blue Peugeot, parked alongside several more battered vehicles. 'Someone's pinched both wheels on this side,' he said. 'No wonder it's leaning at a drunken angle.'

'I don't see Will Chambers' car.'

'What is it?'

'I don't know. Green. A bit wrecked-looking.'

Olly shook his head. 'Apart from your Mrs Calladine's disabled Peugeot, they all answer that description.' He looked at her with a worried frown. 'Abbie, I really don't like this – '

She laid a hand on his arm. 'I'll be OK. My phone's on and in my pocket. You stay here and keep watch. If I'm not back in half an hour, come after me.'

'Half an hour?' Olly protested. 'Anything could happen in that time.'

'I'll be sure to keep away from fish knives. Wish me luck.'

Olly shook his head. 'I hope that old bloke in the hospice is praying. You might need it.' He sat down on the dry verge of the car park where the grass had been rubbed away by countless careless wheels. 'Half an hour. Not a second more, OK? And ring me or text if you need me.'

'I will.' Gingerly Abbie pushed open the entrance door to Parker House and looked swiftly round. The doors on the ground floor, circling the stairwell, were all labelled 1. She started up the stairs. Here the smell of rubbish, old fat, sour milk and urine intensified. *Yuck. Who'd live here, if they could choose?* She came to a landing where once there had been some kind of vinyl flooring, now almost totally worn away, revealing stained concrete beneath. The doors were painted a uniform hard blue. Here the numbers were mostly missing, but she identified 2a by a process of elimination, remembering the layout of the flats on the floor below.

She closed her eyes for a moment, remembering John Westwood in his bed in the hospice, his body frail but his spirit still strong. *I hope you're praying now. I hope it works.* She took a deep breath and tapped on the door.

She waited, but there was no answer, and no one came. She wondered if perhaps there was no one there. Perhaps they had gone away; perhaps they had never come here. She tapped again, more loudly, and then again, as a last resort hammering with the heel of her hand. And then she heard, or thought she heard, a small sound like a cat growling. She banged on the door again, and the sound came back to her, recognisable this time as a human moan. She bent down and tried to look through the keyhole, but could see nothing but darkness. She put her mouth to the keyhole and called out. 'Mrs Calladine? Are you in there? Please, open the door! Don't be afraid – I want to help you.'

After what seemed an age she heard shuffling feet on the other side of the door, getting louder as they approached. A hoarse whisper, barely audible, sent shivers up her arms. 'Who is it?'

'It's me, Mrs Calladine – Abbie Hasan.'

'Abbie?' came a shocked voice. 'Wait.'

Abbie heard a chain rattle and the door slowly opened. Maggie Calladine stood in the shadow of the door, difficult to see in the darkness of the hallway. The smell from inside the flat was as bad as the staircase – unwashed bodies and dirty clothes, stale food, other odours which Abbie couldn't identify, the sharp stomach-clenching stink of vomit, and hanging in the air like a fog, the sickly smell of old marijuana smoke.

'You shouldn't be here, Abbie,' Maggie whispered. 'Please, go away. I'd never forgive myself if anything happened to you.'

'I'm not going anywhere,' Abbie said, more bravely than she felt. 'Are you alone?'

'For now.'

'Please let me in. I just want to talk to you.'

'He'll be back.' Maggie's voice shook.

'When?'

'I don't know. Maybe lunchtime. Maybe tomorrow, or next week. Maybe never.' Maggie began to moan quietly, and Abbie felt the hairs stand up on the back of her neck. She pushed the door, and Maggie stumbled backwards. 'No, Abbie!'

'Let me in. I'm not going away, so you might as well.'

The door swung wider, and Maggie scuttled away down a short passage, followed by Abbie. The stale smell worsened as she went deeper into the flat.

She found Maggie sitting crouched at a table which was covered in old newspapers, dirty plates and dishes, and bits of partly eaten bread. Maggie sat hunched, perched on the edge of her chair as if ready to bolt, her hands gripping the edge of the table. She was wearing a dress that Abbie recognised and knew to be lemon-yellow, trimmed in white. Now it was grey and grimy. Everything in the flat smelled; Maggie herself smelled unwashed, and her hair hung down in matted clumps.

'Abbie, why are you here? Is your mum somewhere nearby?' Maggie looked around, her eyes wild.

'No,' Abbie said. 'Mum doesn't know I'm here. She'd have wanted to stop me coming.'

'You shouldn't be here,' Maggie repeated. 'It's no place for you. It's a hell-hole.'

'I want you to come away with me, as soon as you can get ready.'

Maggie's eyes widened. 'I can't. You don't understand.'

'Why not?'

'He's got everything. My bank card, most of my money. There's no petrol in my car, and it's only got two wheels.'

'None of that matters. I can phone my mum, and she'll come straight over and get you.'

'But I was so horrible to her! She won't want to know me any more. No one will.'

Abbie shook her head vehemently. 'She's your friend. We all are. She'll be here like a shot.'

Maggie looked at Abbie with red-rimmed eyes. 'How can I go back?' she whispered. 'After all I've done?'

'You can sort all that out later. But you can't stay here – with him.'

To Abbie's dismay Maggie started to sob, a dry, cracked, desolate sound. She held her head in her hands. 'Oh, Abbie! I can't tell you what it's been like!' She scrabbled in her pocket, fetched out a wad of dirty tissues and scrubbed her face. 'He was all right at first. I realise now he never wanted me to follow him. He just wanted to get out. He'd done the damage. But then he must have figured out I'd be useful, so he switched the charm on again. And like a fool I fell for it. I knew – of course I did. But I didn't want to admit it, even to myself. I wanted the dream to go on. I was so stupid – I let him have my bank card – he said he wanted to fill my car up, in case we had to leave in a hurry. And then he wouldn't give it back. So I was stuck. And desperate. He was out most of the time, but when he came back he'd always have something new and expensive – a watch, a leather jacket, all bought with our money, mine and David's! And bit by bit the charm went out of the window, of course. He told me to get out, and he didn't care how. I couldn't blind myself to the truth then. No, I saw the real Will, and it wasn't pretty.'

'Oh!' Abbie said, covering her mouth with her hand. 'Of course, you don't know. His name's not really Will Chambers.'

Maggie gaped. 'What?'

'You'd already gone. We had a visit from his brother. His real name's Paul White.' She leaned forward. 'Mrs Calladine – listen. You need to know this. He came on purpose, to deceive and destroy. You're not the only one he cheated. Don't beat yourself up too much, please. He's the one to blame. You've been a victim of a very horrible plot.'

'What? But why?'

'Because he believed Mr Calladine was to blame for getting him expelled from school, and, I suppose, for every failure that followed. Do you remember that dinner party at our house? Where Mr Calladine said he thought Will looked familiar? It *was* him. Twenty years older, with dyed hair and brown contact lenses and a pack of lies about his past.'

Maggie looked bewildered. 'But David had nothing to do with that. I remember him talking about that boy. Paul, yes, of course! The boy harassed a young girl in his school. He was obsessed with her. Flattered her at first, but when she tried to back out he stalked her, tormented and threatened her. It was the girl herself who broke down and told her father, and he reported Paul to the school. I seem to remember David helped to support the girl, who was in his pastoral group. But he'd just started at that school – he had nothing to do with the decision to expel the boy.'

'Well,' Abbie said grimly, 'Paul believed it. He must have held on to that grudge for years.' She looked round the flat. 'Look, you can't stay here. It's foul.'

Maggie shrugged. 'Oh, yes. It was bad enough to start with, but he's been doing his utmost to drive me out. There's no food – I haven't eaten since yesterday morning. And then today, I realised he must have been here while I was asleep, because he'd even turned off the water, and padlocked the cupboard where the tap is. I can't wash. I have a bucket for a toilet. It's horrendous. But I feel so helpless. And that's just what he wants. He's using my money until he can sell the cottage. But meanwhile he'd be happy if he drove me to such despair that I went out and threw myself under a lorry.'

'Don't even think about it!' Abbie cried. 'Don't let him win! Look, you *do* have friends. But we may not have much time. I have a friend outside, and if I don't appear he'll come barging in. And Paul White might come back. Let me ring my mum.'

Maggie gripped Abbie's arm. 'You don't understand. I can't go back. It's not just the shame. My whole life's a wreck, and it's my own fault.' She paused, breathing hard. 'Will – Paul – doesn't want me. He never did. And David won't want me back, not now. Not just because I betrayed him. But because there'd be a shadow over us for the rest of our lives. I'm pregnant.'

Abbie stared at her in disbelief. 'But – '

Maggie laughed bitterly. 'Ironic, isn't it? It's what I've wanted for years. But not like this. Will denies it can possibly be his. But after all these years trying to have a child with David, who do you think's likely to be the baby's father?'

Abbie stared. She could think of nothing to say, and felt not only aghast but deeply embarrassed. These were secrets she would much

213

rather not have known. 'So you see, Abbie, I'm not awash with choices,' Maggie said dully. 'Under that lorry may well be the best place for me and my fatherless infant. I feel a pang for the lorry driver, that's all.'

'No,' Abbie said desperately. 'If you do that, you'll be saying he's won. Evil's won. You don't stand for that, I know you don't.'

Maggie opened her mouth to speak, but stopped and lifted her head, her eyes wide. They both heard feet pounding the stairs, then a key in the lock. 'It's him – !' She shrank back against the wall, trembling.

The man they had known as Will Chambers came swiftly down the passage. He stood in the middle of the room, hands on hips, grinning broadly. 'Well! How nice of you to call, Abbie! What a pleasure! How are you?'

Abbie bit her lip. 'I'm taking Mrs Calladine away with me.'

He threw back his head and laughed. 'Oh, I wish you would! She's an absolute bore. Trying to fob off her brat on me, and she smells pretty rough too. Go, take her – you're welcome to her.'

Abbie gasped, her fists clenched. 'You – '

'Abbie, don't!' Maggie pleaded. 'It's not worth it.'

The front door, left open by Will, banged loudly against the wall, and they all turned towards the sound. Olly stood in the doorway, red-faced and panting.

'Abbie, something really bad's happened. You need to see this.'

Abbie felt sweat break out on her face. 'What?' She went up to Olly and put a hand on his arm. He was waving his phone.

'I just had a text from my friend Jake,' he gabbled. 'It's all over the school. They're saying you posted on Facebook that Mr Calladine's been, what did he say, "behaving inappropriately" with some of the girls.'

Abbie said nothing for a long moment, chewing her lip. She turned and looked at Will. 'This is you, isn't it?' she said quietly. 'This is your revenge. It wasn't enough to steal his wife. Now you want to wreck his reputation and kill his friendship with my family.

You want to destroy him and take me down too. Because I saw through you.'

Will chuckled, his bright blue eyes alight with triumph. 'Sweet idea, wasn't it? Got you both in one go.'

'But it won't work,' Abbie said. 'I won't let it. In the end you'll be the loser. Because I guess you always are. You don't have any friends, do you? The only one who's stuck by you, at least some of the time, is your brother, Bill, and you hate him for it. We met Bill the other day, did you know that?' For a moment she saw uncertainty in Will's face, before the sneering mask closed over it again. 'He told us a few stories about you. Made everything clear. Whatever you think, you haven't won, Paul. Because all you know is self-love. You'll never have what we all have, do you understand that? You know it exists, but you can only look in from the outside. But you – you'll always be alone and loathed.' She turned to Olly and Maggie. 'Come on, let's go. I need some fresh air. Olly – help Mrs Calladine, can you?'

They found a wall some way down from the block of flats. Abbie sat with Maggie, her arm around her shoulders. Olly had gone in search of a shop.

'My stuff's still in there,' Maggie said dully. 'What there is of it. Most of it's still in the car. No idea if it's still there.'

'I'll look in a minute, 'Abbie said. 'The things you left in the flat – are any of them irreplaceable?'

'No. Only a few clothes. It hardly matters.'

'I'm going to ring Mum now, OK?'

Maggie began to cry, a low, keening wail. She brought out the same dirty tissues and wiped her face, but the tears went on flowing as if they would never stop. 'Why are you doing this, Abbie?' she said, her voice breaking. 'Why are you bothering with me?'

'Because – because what he did to you is wrong. What he's trying to do now is wrong. He's a destroyer, and we have to resist him. You and Mr Calladine are good people. Our friends. That's what friends do, isn't it?' She looked up. 'Here's Olly. He didn't take long.'

Olly ran up to them, waving a carrier bag. 'I got some water. And some wet wipes. I thought you might want to clean up a bit,' he said to Maggie, suddenly shy. 'And some sandwiches. I don't know how long Abbie's mum will be. You should eat and drink something.'

Maggie took the bag from him. 'Thank you, Olly. You're very kind. What about you two?'

'We're OK,' Abbie said. 'Olly, can you keep Mrs Calladine company for a moment? I'm going to ring Mum.'

She left them sitting on the wall, and saw Maggie drinking from the bottle of water that Olly had bought. She walked away from them but kept them in sight; somehow, while Paul White was anywhere in the vicinity, she felt Maggie still needed protection. When she was out of earshot she rang her home number. It rang and rang, and went to voicemail. Abbie frowned in frustration and tried again. This time, to her relief, Julie answered. She sounded breathless.

'Mum, it's me. Abbie.'

'Abbie? What are you doing? Why are you ringing me?'

'Mum, listen. I'm not in school.'

'Not – ? I don't understand.'

'Olly and I are in Moxhurst. We've got Mrs Calladine.'

'What?'

Abbie spoke fast and urgently. 'Mum, he made her like a prisoner. I mean, she could have physically walked out, but he fixed it so she couldn't. The flat was disgusting, and she had no food or water. He took her bank card and her money and he's been spending it. Her car's here, but it's got no fuel and someone's stolen two of the wheels. She's in a terrible state, Mum. She thinks no one will want anything to do with her now. She's, I don't know, demoralised, kind of *crushed*. Like she's lost all her self-respect. She was even talking about throwing herself under a lorry.'

'Oh, dear Lord!' Julie wailed. 'Where is she now?'

'Sitting on a wall with Olly. He got her something to eat and drink.'

'And you two cooked this up between you? Played truant?'

'Yes. I just couldn't get it out of my head that she was in danger.' She paused for a moment. 'I went to see Mr Westwood in the hospice.'

'You did what? When was this?'

'Yesterday. He told me to pray for guidance.'

There was a long silence, and for a moment Abbie thought they had been cut off. 'Mum?'

Julie sighed. 'I think you and I need to have a long talk,' she said. 'All right, I'll come and fetch her. And you and Olly.'

'Thanks, Mum,' Abbie said, feeling a wash of relief. 'She thought you wouldn't want to know her any more. I said you would.'

'My poor Maggie. I should have known,' Julie said. She sounded deeply upset. 'All right, Abbie. Tell me exactly where you are.'

Abbie explained as best she could and rang off. She walked back to Olly and Maggie.

'I think we need to move away from here,' Olly said, his voice low. 'He's up there, looking at us. See? Behind those blue curtains.'

Abbie looked up, and saw the curtains move. Paul White was a shadow in the room. She looked down at Maggie, sitting hunched on the wall, her eyes wide. She was trembling.

'Come on, Mrs Calladine,' Abbie said gently. 'Let's get away from here. Don't worry – he can't hurt you any more.' She took Maggie by the elbow and helped her stand. 'Mum's on her way. Do you want to look in your car to see if any of your things are there? Do you have the key?'

Maggie shook her head 'No. He took the car key as well. But I don't care about those things. Can we just get out of his sight? I can't bear him watching, laughing.'

'There's a little café down the same road as the shop,' Olly said. 'We'll go and get you a cup of tea while we wait for Abbie's mum. We can ring her again and tell her where we are.'

With Maggie between them they crossed the road, and walked down to the parade of shops. Most of them were closed but there was a greasy spoon still open, and they went in and bought three mugs of brown tea. While Maggie used the café's toilet Olly said, 'How did your mum react?'

'With astonishment,' Abbie said. 'But she soon realised it was an emergency. Mum's got her head screwed on. I'd better call her again and tell her we're here. She might have already left.' She rang Julie's mobile number, but it went to voicemail, and she left a message. 'She must be on her way.'

'This could be interesting,' Olly said thoughtfully. 'If I'd known I was going to meet my future mother-in-law, I'd have shined my shoes.'

Abbie gave him a look that would have shrivelled ripe fruit. 'This is no time to be frivolous,' she said sternly.

'Did you tell her about what he's done?' Olly asked. 'The Facebook thing?'

'No,' Abbie said. 'I thought I'd given her enough to digest. Anyway, I want her to focus on Mrs Calladine. Once we've got her away safely we can face the fallout.' She sighed heavily. 'You and I are in for a rough ride, Olly. Mr C is going to be beside himself with fury. Hope you're prepared.'

Maggie came back from the toilet. She had borrowed Abbie's hairbrush and managed to look a little less unkempt. She sat with them in silence and drank her tea.

Forty minutes and three more cups of tea later Abbie heard the sound of her mother's car pulling up outside the café. She pushed her chair back. 'Wait here for a minute.' She flew outside. Julie was just getting out of her car.

'Oh, Abbie! Are you all right?' She rushed up and gave Abbie a hug.

'I'm all right,' Abbie said, pulling free. 'But Mrs Calladine isn't. She really needs you now, Mum.'

'Leave Maggie to me,' Julie said. 'I'll look after her.'

'She'll need a bath and some clean clothes. She can have my room for now,' Abbie said. 'I'll sleep on the sofa. But Mum, you need to talk to her. I mean, properly. Get her to tell you everything. And tell her about what Bill White said to us. I've told her a bit, but she needs to know the sort of man Paul White is, what we've been dealing with. She thinks it's all her fault. I know she made a bad decision, but he's played her. He's taken advantage of her. She feels totally rotten.'

'And you and Olly need to get back to school,' Julie said, frowning. 'You're going to be in hot water. Whatever are you going to say?'

'We'll think of something,' Abbie said. 'Olly's good at improvising.'

She followed Julie into the café.

'Maggie,' Julie said. 'Oh, my dear, what a mare's nest!' She hurried to their table, sat beside her friend and put her arms round her. 'You're coming home with me.'

Maggie started to cry again. 'Julie, can you forgive me for the nasty things I said? I'm so sorry. I was out of my mind.'

'Don't give it another thought, my love. Come on. The car's outside.' She looked up and smiled. 'Hi, Olly. Nice to meet you. I hope you're not in too much trouble.'

'It doesn't matter,' Olly said, and Abbie was amused to see him blush.

They took Maggie out and put her in the front passenger seat next to Julie. Abbie and Olly got into the back. 'Mum, can you just drop us off at school?' Abbie said.

Julie turned round, clicking on her seat belt. 'Don't you want me to come in with you and explain?'

'No, thanks,' Abbie said hastily. 'I think we need to do that ourselves. And you need to get Mrs Calladine home as quickly as possible. As far away as we can from him. She needs to feel safe.'

Julie nodded. 'I'll want a full rundown this evening, though,' she said. 'And so will your dad. Chapter and verse. OK?'

'Hm. Yeah, OK.'

Julie started the engine. 'You all right, Maggie?' She looked over at her friend, and saw that Maggie was drifting into sleep.

By the time Julie approached the school it was almost lunchtime.

'Mum, on second thoughts, can you drop us off at the shop?' Abbie said. 'I don't know about Olly, but I'm practically dead from starvation. That thick tea was sustaining for a while, but ...'

Olly whispered, 'Bit of a problem. Your personal banker has run out of cash.'

'Oh, yeah, and Mum, can you let me have some money? I'll pay you back.'

Julie pulled up outside the shop. 'What with?' she asked, her eyebrows raised.

'A week of washing-up?'

Julie sighed and hunted through her handbag, found her purse and extracted a £5 note. 'Now I'm broke as well. Bread and dripping for the rest of the week.'

Abbie shouldered her bag and gave Julie's back a pat as she climbed out of the car. 'You always say that, but I don't think I've ever had bread and dripping in my entire life.'

Olly leaned in at Julie's open window. 'Nice to have met you, Mrs Hasan,' he said politely. He grinned. 'I'd eat bread and dripping with you any day.'

'In that case you'd better come for dinner,' Julie said. 'Friday?'

Olly's grin grew wider. 'Yeah, thanks.'

Julie restarted the engine and released the brake. 'Good luck with the inquisition, you two. Hope you don't get the thumbscrew.'

Abbie and Olly watched her drive away. 'I see now where you get your sadistic sense of humour from,' Olly said.

'Ha! You're a one to talk. Shall we get some supplies? Seems to be we're going to need all our strength.'

'Hm,' Olly said gloomily. 'That thumbscrew may be just the tip of the iceberg.'

They bought fruit and biscuits and water, and walked up the road and into the dusty park. 'We don't need to lurk under the bridge today,' Abbie said. 'There are no kids about. We can sit on a park bench.'

'The height of luxury,' Olly said, stretching his arms along the back of the bench and lifting his face to the sun.

'Shove up a bit, then.'

They munched in thoughtful silence for a while. Then Olly said, 'What do you think the old man's going to say? Are we in *really* bad trouble?'

Abbie shook her head. 'You don't get the ultimate penalty for bunking off for a morning,' she said reasonably.

'Maybe not,' Olly said. 'But you're supposed to have run a social media campaign trampling our dear Headmaster's reputation in the dirt.'

'A bit more serious, true,' Abbie said.

'So ... what, in your view, is *the ultimate penalty?*' Olly said. 'Scourging? The rack? Death?'

Abbie ignored him. 'I just have to get in first, don't I? Before he starts using me as a mop.'

'What?'

'Wiping the floor with me, dimwit.'

'Oh. Yeah.' He heaved a sigh. 'You ready? I'd quite like to get this over.'

They trudged back across the park and down the road. Students were spilling out of the school gates by now, and when they saw Abbie and Olly approach, there were gasps and whispers and one or two catcalls. They shouldered their way through the throng, staring ahead, faces set.

'Hey, geek girl.' It was the same youth who had accosted Abbie in the shop the day before. He planted himself squarely in front of her, legs apart, hands on hips. 'You and young Oliver here are in something very deep and very smelly, I hear.'

'Get lost, little boy,' Abbie said wearily. 'You are boring me.'

Olly grabbed her elbow and pulled her past the lad. 'Ignore him,' he muttered against a backdrop of hoots and jeers. 'He's a total waste of space.'

It was the same all down the corridors of the school: clumps of children whispering, pointing, giggling.

'Are they usually this nasty?' Olly said quietly.

'Some of them are OK, I guess. But they're doing the herd thing, aren't they? – laughing at us because they're glad it's not them in the firing line. We're like a couple of gladiators in ancient Rome – about to be chopped up for the entertainment of the plebs.'

'Nice image, if a little daunting,' Olly said. 'A few mixed metaphors there as well.'

'I find my metaphors are not the first thing on my mind right now.'

They arrived at the door of Abbie's form room.

'Do you want me to come in with you?' Olly said.

'No, you go to your room and I'll see you later. Or not.'

H grabbed her hand. 'Whatever happens, whatever they say, *I'm* proud of you.'

'Steady on, Olly.'

'I'm serious.'

A strident voice came from inside the room, making them start. Abbie felt her scalp prickle.

'Abigail Hasan? Come in, please. Is that Oliver Bradshaw with you? Yes, you too.'

Meekly they approached Abbie's form teacher's desk. Normally an even-tempered, if rather caustic, lady, today she was flushed and flustered.

'I hear you have been making a spectacle of yourselves,' she said. 'I have to say, I am astonished. Especially at you, Abbie. You've been such a blameless little mouse up to now. Just goes to show what hidden depths a person can hide.'

'Mrs Temple – ' Abbie began.

The teacher interrupted. 'Don't bother talking to me,' she said. 'The Head wants you in his study straight away. Now.'

'Right.'

They left the room. Olly still had hold of Abbie's hand, and seemed determined not to let it go. They crossed the hall, angled left up a sloping corridor and stopped outside a door marked Head Teacher.

'You ever been in here before?' Olly whispered. Abbie shook her head. 'I have. Believe it or not, I was a little bit wicked once.'

'Only once?'

'Yeah. He is quite … formidable, isn't he?'

'Nice enough normally,' Abbie said.

'Today's not normal. Go on, then.'

Abbie lifted her hand, hesitated, then knocked firmly. She heard David's voice. 'Come in.'

They opened the door, stepped inside and closed it behind them. David Calladine was standing behind his desk, in his usual crisp blue suit and dark tie, resting his hands on the lid of his laptop. He looked at Abbie and Olly with undisguised disgust.

For a moment there was a tense silence.

'So, you have decided to return,' David said heavily. 'Good of you. I hardly know what to say. Your behaviour has exceeded my wildest expectations of adolescent infamy. I had not realised you harboured such enmity towards me personally. Please tell me you are not going to pass off this … this *foulness* as some kind of prank.'

'Sir,' Abbie interrupted desperately. 'Please, I beg you, listen. *It wasn't me.*'

David frowned. 'What?'

'I didn't post that muck about you,' Abbie said. 'I'm surprised you could think I would, even for a moment. I thought you knew me better than that.'

'I thought the same,' David said. 'Until today.' His voice was harsh, but there was a note of uncertainty in it. 'Explain.'

'My profile has been hacked,' Abbie said. 'And I know who did it. I think you might know too. I promise I had nothing to do with this. It wouldn't have crossed my mind. I don't want to bring disgrace on you – why would I? None of it is remotely true.'

'Of course it isn't!' David snapped. 'But the fact is, every pupil, every member of staff, and many of the parents, have seen the allegations.' He sat down heavily. 'All right, both of you. Perhaps you'd better tell me what's going on.' He looked up and spoke more quietly. 'And if I have misjudged you, I apologise. If this is going to be a long story, you'd better sit down.' He waved them in the direction of two upright chairs.

Abbie carried hers closer to the desk, momentarily marvelling at her own brazenness. Olly stayed by the wall.

She leaned forward, and spoke softly but with growing intensity. 'Sir, the man we knew as Will Chambers did this. He admitted it. He wanted to get at you *and* me. But that's not his real name. He's really called Paul White.'

David nodded and heaved a deep sigh. 'I know. And that's a name that's come back to haunt me, more than twenty years on.'

Abbie frowned. 'You know? How?'

'It was your father, Abbie. He came round to see me the Sunday before last. He had a crumpled scrap of paper in his hand – he'd retrieved it from your kitchen bin. He'd told no one, apparently, not even your mother.'

'My dad?' Abbie said, stupefied.

'He said he thought I had a right to know the latest developments, and the address where White may have taken my wife. He said that Julie, who might have taken action, was angry and hurt and determined to let matters take whatever course they might.' He paused, gathering his thoughts. 'I didn't think of this at the time – I wasn't really thinking straight at all – but your father was a true friend that day. He told me some of what Bill White had told you. And of course I remembered what Paul White had been like as a boy. I should have had more insight long before this all blew up. But I didn't. I thanked Tariq, of course. But I also threw that paper in the bin. The reasons are too personal to rehearse here, and they don't concern you. But I believe you when you say you aren't responsible for this morning's revelations. Of course, it's untypical of you, and I'm sorry I thought anything different, even for a moment. But unfortunately it's all too typical of him. I had no idea he'd borne this grudge so long – a grudge that's wholly unfounded, by the way.' He looked up at the two young people. 'We do have an issue of an unauthorised morning's absence, however. Oliver!'

Olly looked up, a picture of guilt. 'Sir.'

'What is your part in this?'

'I, um, I just went along to watch out for Abbie. What she told me about this guy was worrying. I didn't think she should go anywhere near him alone.'

David stared at him long and hard. 'I quite agree,' he said at last. 'You can go.'

Olly gaped, but stood up, banging the chair against the wall. 'I can – ?'

'Yes. Just tell your form teacher there will be no repercussions. And you, Abbie. Go.'

Olly scuttled to the door, and paused, looking back at Abbie, his hand on the handle. Abbie rose from her chair, leaning forwards, fists clenched. 'Sir, please, there are things I have to tell you. You have to know.'

David also got up, his chair scraping against the floor. 'In the circumstances,' he said, his voice all cold steel, 'I cannot be in this room even for a moment with a pupil who has, as far as all the world knows, made a very serious allegation against me.'

'But –'

'Abbie,' Olly said urgently, *'come on.'*

'Mr Calladine, I have to tell you, it's important –'

David Calladine shook his head and spoke more gently. 'Abbie, if you really want to help, please leave my office now.'

Olly came back, took Abbie's hand and almost pulled her from the room. As they came out into the corridor, Abbie called desperately through the crack of the closing door. 'Sir, please! Mrs Calladine's at our house – Mum came to get her – she's been through hell – you need to talk to her!'

Abbie tipped her purse out into her hand. It didn't look good. She hoped her bus pass would be sufficient to take her on a journey that wasn't strictly to school and back. All she had was the meagre change from the £5 note Julie had given her to buy lunch, and that seemed a long time ago. Her stomach was protesting, but she couldn't risk buying anything, and she doubted that she could borrow any more from Dan. Besides, he, and Olly, had gone to football practice. She'd seen them both in shirts and shorts after the end of school.

Once more she waited at the bus stop on the far side of the road. When the bus rumbled to a halt she flashed her bus pass and got away with it. She wondered what awaited her at the other end. Was John Westwood even still alive? And if he was, would he be able to understand her message? Whatever the case, she felt she had to try. It seemed to her that even in his last extremity, he was concerned for his flock – even more now that he knew how disastrously they had been deceived. She had no doubt that he would have been praying all the while his heart was beating and a spark of understanding still glimmered in his brain.

Sitting in the half-empty bus, staring out of the window yet seeing little of the unlovely view, focused inward on her teeming thoughts, she considered the vast, mysterious universe of prayer. She had, reluctantly and feeling like a hypocrite, done what John Westwood had asked. She had experienced a powerful and urgent inclination to go to Moxhurst after Maggie. But were these two things causally related? How could she possibly know? It seemed to her a quite different world of reasoning than a scientific experiment or a problem in geometry. How could she enter this world, supposing that she wanted to? She shook her head and sighed. Not so very long ago all these things had seemed so simple. She believed what her parents said, without question, because she trusted them. And of course she did trust them still – but now she admitted the possibility that, like anyone, they could be in error. Honest error, sure. But if something's a mistake it's still one, however sincere the belief in it.

She was no further forward when the bus halted, engine still throbbing and wheezing, outside St Oswin's. She pushed open the heavy door and again found herself in the cool, tiled hallway. There was no one about. Dutifully she signed her name in the Visitors' Book and made her way back to the room where she had first visited the sick man. Taking a deep breath, she tapped lightly on the door.

After a moment, Hilary Westwood's face appeared as she opened the door a few inches. Abbie was greeted by a black frown.

'Oh, it's you, Abbie. I'm sorry, you can't see him.'

'How is he?' Abbie whispered.

Hilary compressed her lips. 'They say he won't last much longer.'

'I'm so very sorry,' Abbie said, and meant it. 'Do you think – '

'What?' Hilary said impatiently.

'Can he understand what's said to him?'

'Maybe. He's full of drugs, but they say hearing's the last sense to go, even if it seems the patient is barely there.'

'I don't want to keep you,' Abbie said. 'But would you please just give him a message from me?'

Hilary sighed. 'I'll try. But I can't guarantee he'll know what I'm talking about. What is it?'

'Could you please just say, "We got her back"? He'll know what I mean.'

Hilary nodded. 'I think I know too,' she said, 'and I'm pleased to hear it. He told me something about it, but it was all a bit garbled, so when I finally come home, perhaps you can tell me what's been going on. I feel as if I've been practically living in this place for weeks. Not that I begrudge it, of course not, but it's a bit like a nice, soft, kind, caring prison sentence.'

It was the longest speech Abbie had ever heard from Hilary Westwood. 'Nobody knows what's going to happen from now on,' she said softly, 'but at least she's in a safe place. And I thought he would want to know. I'll leave you in peace, Mrs Westwood. Goodbye.'

Hilary managed a smile, but there were tears in her eyes. 'Goodbye, Abbie. Thank you.'

A little after five o'clock, David's silver BMW slid to a halt on the Hasans' drive. Julie, preparing dinner in the kitchen, saw him get out and stretch his arms high above his head. He'd taken off his suit jacket and loosened his tie, and as Julie watched him through the window, unseen by him, she saw him run a hand distractedly through what remained of his hair. She busied herself with vegetables until she heard him tap hesitantly on the door.

'Yeah, come in if you're good-looking and rich,' she sang out.

David appeared, a stiff little smile on his face. 'That's me out then,' he said.

'Hello, David,' Julie said more soberly. 'Come along in and sit down. Would you like some tea? Or something stronger?'

'I'm tempted by a bit of Dutch courage,' David said wryly. 'But perhaps it's a bit early. Thank you, tea would be nice.' He lowered himself into a chair with a deep sigh and rubbed his eyes. 'You on your own?' he asked, looking round.

'Yes – Dan's at football, and Riq is supposed to be picking him up on his way back from work. Where Abbie is I don't know. She's got this boy in tow these days, and sometimes her movements are most mysterious.' She filled the kettle and switched it on.

David looked up at her and spoke cautiously. 'When did you last see Abbie?'

'Around lunchtime.'

'When you dropped her off at school after rescuing Maggie?'

'Oh! You know.'

'I gathered,' David said gently. 'I've had Abbie and Oliver in my office. I don't know the details, because I wouldn't let Abbie tell me. But I do know that Maggie's here. Thank you, Julie.'

'I hope she's not in too much trouble. Abbie, I mean.'

'No. I am thankful to her, to you all. But she gave me a shock this morning, or at least, I thought she had.'

Julie poured boiling water into two mugs. 'What shock?' she said, frowning.

'Didn't she tell you?' David shook his head. 'This morning I was made aware of a long, rambling post on a social media site – Abbie's own page – accusing me of inappropriate behaviour with girls at my school, specifying lewd remarks, extremely personal comments on their physical attributes, even that I had suggested trading favours in some way – all very distasteful as well as inflammatory. Not to mention career suicide.'

Julie's jaw dropped. 'I don't believe it!' she whispered. 'Abbie wouldn't – '

David raised a hand to stop her. 'No, she wouldn't. And didn't. At first I was so flummoxed, so angry, so shocked, I didn't think straight. You can probably understand, though I know it's no real defence, I haven't been thinking straight for the last few weeks. Sometimes I've felt I've barely been holding together at all.'

Julie passed him a mug of tea and sat down opposite him. 'Abbie never said anything about this when I collected them. Not a word. She just wanted to get Maggie out of that place, away from *him*.'

'Yes, that much I guessed. No, the young people are not in trouble, Julie.'

Julie was silent for a moment. 'Did she tell you she went to see John?'

David looked up, startled. 'No, that I didn't know. She was pretty desperate to tell me numerous things, but I cut her off. I couldn't be in my office alone with a pupil who'd apparently been accusing me of very serious wrongdoing. So there's a lot of details I don't know. Abbie just said, "Talk to your wife." And I will, of course.'

There was a long silence as both drank their tea, thinking their own thoughts.

'So ...' Julie frowned. 'How did that post appear on Abbie's page if she didn't put it there?'

'A hacker. Who do you think?'

'Oh, no, David – surely – '

'You knew from Bill White how his brother hated me, thinking I'd got him expelled all those years ago. He wasn't content with taking my wife. He thought it would be fun to wreck my reputation, my career, my whole life.'

'Hold on,' Julie said. 'I think I'm beginning to lose the plot. How do you know about Bill White?'

'Tariq told me.'

'*Riq* did? When?'

'After Bill White had left. He came round and gave me Paul White's address in Moxhurst. He said I had more right to know than anyone else.'

'This is so weird. He never said a word.'

'He probably would have eventually.'

Julie rubbed her face with her hands. 'My family seem to be getting very secretive these days. What's next? Is Dan going to come home and tell me he's married?' Her voice rose half an octave.

'I doubt that, since he's only fourteen,' David said with a slight smile.

'David – ' He raised his eyebrows. 'I feel we're skirting round the issue here, aren't we? What does any of this stuff matter? Have you come for Maggie? You have, haven't you?'

David's face flushed. 'Yes. If she wants to come home.'

'Of course she does!' Julie cried. 'But she thinks you'll never forgive her for what she's done.'

David's dark brows contracted. 'All she's done is fall foul of a smooth-talking, plausible liar. A charming snake with no conscience. Why? Because I drove her to it by my selfishness, my neglect, my cowardice. I'm the one who should be looking for forgiveness.'

Julie looked at him for a long moment, her eyes wide, unable to reply. Finally she said, 'It's her you should be saying these things to, not me.'

'And I will, if she'll let me.' His voice cracked and broke.

'Look, she's been asleep for hours. Wore herself out earlier, talking and crying. Perhaps I should go and get her up, so you can take her home. So you can talk in peace. You'll need to be very gentle – she's had a horrible time.'

'I know. I feel like a complete … Tariq gave me that address, and I threw it away. Too stiff-necked, too full of my own hurt to do anything. I could have saved her from days of torture. Instead of which I told myself she'd made a choice, that she obviously preferred him – younger, sexier, more charming, better-looking, etc. I was so self-righteous! I just left her to the mercy of that wicked man – who *has* no mercy. Tell me how I could have done that, Julie! What sort of a husband am I? Apart from a rubbish one. I feel so ashamed.'

'So does she.'

David shook his head. 'No, if anyone should be asking for forgiveness, it's me.' He looked up, and his face was bleak. 'If we get through this, I'll have learned something, at least. Something I thought I already knew. Something I forgot for too long – that next to my service of God, my wife should be my top priority.'

Julie rested her hand on his for a moment. 'You will get through it, of course you will. I have faith in both of you.' She got up, hesitated for a moment, then said, 'Why don't you go into the lounge – you'll have some privacy there. I'll go and get her and bring her down. Don't mind us – just take her home when you're ready.'

David nodded. 'Thank you, Julie,' he murmured. 'I appreciate everything you've done.' He stood up, steadying himself for a moment on the back of the chair. Then he left the room, closing the door quietly behind him.

Half an hour later Julie looked at the kitchen clock. She picked up her phone and keyed in Tariq's number. He answered almost immediately.

'Riq? Where are you?'

'Sitting in the van, waiting for Dan to come out of school.'

'Oh, good.'

'Why? Did you think I'd forget him?'

'No, it's not that. I'm just glad you're not driving, and that Dan's not with you. Listen, love, when you get home come in by the back door, and don't make an unholy racket.'

'Eh?'

'I've got David and Maggie here. In our lounge.'

'Oh.' There was a pause. 'Not sure I understand.'

'It's a long story. I'll tell you when you get in.'

'Is everything OK?'

'I don't know. I brought her down and made her go in and talk to him. There was quite a bit of crying at first, and not just her. But it's gone quiet now. Maybe I'll make them some tea. They might have gone by the time you get here. I hope so. They need to be in their own home, sorting things out.'

'Do you think they will?'

'Maybe. But there's a big problem. Maggie told me, but David didn't mention it, so I didn't either. I didn't want to blunder in and put my foot in it if he doesn't know. Maybe he does now, I don't know. But I'll tell you about that as well. And another thing, Riq – Abbie's not home. Where's she got to? It's late.'

'Oh, don't worry, sweetheart – she's with me.'

'With you? How come?'

'She was over the other side of Walburn. Bus pass only runs up to five o'clock, and she had hardly any money. Rang me as a last resort, and I picked her up.' He cleared his throat. 'From St Oswin's.'

Julie sucked in her breath. 'She's a dark horse, our daughter. We have a lot to talk about, I think. Including you keeping secrets from me.'

'Oh. Yeah, that.'

'It's OK, Riq. You did absolutely the right thing. Thank God you don't always do what I say I want.'

'Well, I'm glad I'm not going to get shot down,' Tariq said. 'Anyway, my darling, here's Dan. I'll see you later.'

Abbie and Daniel appeared twenty minutes later, leaving Tariq to unload the van. Dan threw his bag into the hall, shouted, 'Going for a shower, OK?' and vanished upstairs. Abbie hovered in the doorway, then came in to where her mother was washing saucepans at the sink, and gave her a hug. 'Are you annoyed with me?' she asked. 'I know I've done a few crazy things the last couple of days. I told Dad.'

Julie took down a towel and dried her hands.

'How did he react?'

Abbie shrugged, her expression sheepish. 'I don't think he knew what to say.'

Julie shook her head. 'It's worked out fine, so I can't really get too mad. But you took a risk. And,' she mock-scowled, 'I didn't realise you'd got so sneaky.'

'What was I supposed to do?' Abbie said. 'You'd have done your utmost to stop me.'

'I guess so.' Julie nodded soberly. 'How was John?' Her face was anxious as she looked at Abbie.

'I didn't see him today. Mrs Westwood was on guard, and he was too far gone to resist her. Yesterday he was in pain, but lucid and able to listen and talk. It seems he's not got long, Mum. Sadly. Well, sad for us – he didn't seem at all bothered.' She picked up her bag. 'I'll just shed this stuff upstairs and then I'll come and see if you need a hand. Oh, yes, I didn't see him, but I asked Mrs Westwood to give him a message – just to say we'd got Mrs Calladine back. I thought he would be glad to know that, if he could hear and understand with all the drugs they've given him.' She made for the hall door, then paused. 'How is Mrs Calladine?'

'Gone home with her husband, I'm glad to say. They were both in a bit of a state, but calm enough when they left.' She looked at the clock. 'They've not been gone long. Right, go and get ready because dinner will be on the table in ten minutes. Hurry your brother up too, can you, Abs?'

'Great,' Abbie said with feeling. 'I'm about to expire from hunger.' She went into the hall and a moment later Julie heard her skipping up the stairs, humming under her breath.

Tariq came in at the back door.

'She eats like a Shire horse and stays as skinny as a piece of string,' Julie said. 'Where does she put it?'

Tariq wiped his hands down the sides of his jeans. 'Hey.' He took hold of Julie and pulled her close. 'Am I forgiven for my sneaky ways?' he muttered, resting his chin on top of her head.

'I don't know. The jury has yet to reach a decision.' She pulled away, grinning, and looked up at him. Then her smile faded. 'David was thankful you took him that address, even if he didn't act on it.

He's kicking himself now, of course. Seems only Abbie realised what was going on. I'm still reeling a bit.'

'I know. Me too. Oh yeah, what was that problem you were going to tell me about? That you know, that Maggie knows, that David might or might not?'

'I'll fill you in later. When we're on our own. I don't know what the kids know – well, with Abbie there's no telling, but Dan certainly doesn't know anything. It all needs very delicate handling.'

Tariq raised his eyebrows. 'You're being very mysterious.'

'Can't be helped. Riq, go and wash. You're filthy, and I need to see to these veg.'

'Yes, ma'am.'

They were clearing away the plates when the phone rang. 'I'll get it,' Abbie said, and skittered into the hall, hair flying.

'What's she on?' growled her brother. 'Birdseed?'

A few minutes later she reappeared, her face now sombre. 'Mum, Dad, that was Mrs Westwood,' she said gently. 'I'm afraid he's gone. About half-past five, she said. Holding her hand and smiling.'

'Oh!' Julie put down a stack of plates and clutched Tariq's sleeve. Her eyes filled with tears. 'Oh, dear man.' She wiped her face with the dishcloth that happened to be in her hand. Tariq, his face grave, slid an arm round her shoulders. 'How was Hilary?'

'She seemed matter-of-fact. Weary more than anything,' Abbie said.

'Is she back at the vicarage?'

'Yes. Said she'd just got in.'

'I'll go round and see her later. Maybe I can help.' She glanced at Abbie, who was hovering in the doorway. 'Did she manage to give John your message?'

'Yes,' Abbie said. 'And apparently he opened his eyes a bit and muttered something. "1 Thessalonians 5, verses 19 and 20." She said they were the last words he spoke, and that you'd understand.

After that he kind of drifted off and after a while he just stopped breathing.'

Julie sat down abruptly at the kitchen table, still cluttered with dirty dishes. She held her head in her hands and wept. Tariq stood beside her, stroking her hair. 'I know we all knew he wasn't going to make it,' she whispered after a while. 'But oh boy, we're going to miss him.' She looked up at Abbie and managed a feeble smile. 'I'm glad he got your message, though, Abs. At least he died knowing that Maggie was safe.'

'So ... what does 1 Thessalonians have to say?' Abbie said, frowning.

'Hold on a minute.' Tariq went into the lounge and came back with a Bible. He found the place quickly. 'Here we are. "Do not restrain the Holy Spirit; do not despise inspired messages." And then it goes on, "Put all things to the test; keep what is good and avoid every kind of evil." What do you make of that?' He looked at Julie, and saw that she was staring wide-eyed at Abbie.

'Is that what you had, Abs? "Inspired messages?" Is he telling us we should have listened to you?'

Abbie, still standing in the doorway, shifted from one bare foot to the other. 'I don't know,' she mumbled. 'I thought my seeings were just ... something and nothing. Random flares. Until just recently. But, Mum, please,' she added earnestly, 'don't go thinking they make me anything special. I'm hoping they just go away, like Dad's did. It would be nice just to feel normal, like everyone else.'

'You might find there's no such thing, sweetie,' Julie said drily. 'And there's that other bit Dad read, don't forget – about shunning evil, and keeping the good. Simple on the surface, but not always easy to discern.'

'Whatever, Mum. I'm really sorry about Mr Westwood, though; he was a cool old man. I'm going to ring Olly. I'll stack the dishwasher in a minute.'

When she had gone, Julie and Tariq were quiet for several minutes.

'Well. All change, it seems,' Tariq said at last.

Julie heaved a deep sigh and got up. 'Let's get this lot tidied up, then I'll go and see Hilary.' She turned to him and lowered her voice. 'Look, Riq, I'll tell you what the problem is, so you can be mulling it over. We can't talk about it, not till we're on our own and there's no chance of being overheard. Maggie's pregnant.'

Tariq's eyes widened. *What?*

Julie nodded. 'When she suspected she was, she went to a chemist and bought a test. He, Paul White, had already gone. He knew she might be pregnant, but just didn't give a hoot – apart from refusing to believe it could possibly be his. Anyway, it was well and truly positive.'

'But ...' Tariq struggled. 'Who the heck's the father then?'

Julie's face was grim. 'That's just it, Riq. Nobody knows.'

Much later, lying in bed side by side, sleepless, Julie said, 'Thing is, it looks pretty damning, doesn't it? Obviously, now that she knows how she's been deceived and used, now that this temporary insanity, as she calls it, has passed, Maggie'd give anything for this baby to be David's. And it could be, of course it could. God can do anything, and I've been praying for this to happen – for years. But the evidence seems pretty stacked against it. I mean – she and David have been married seventeen years, and they have no kids. Paul White comes along and – well, you see the problem.' She turned on her side to look at him. 'What would you do, if you were in David's shoes? How much does biology matter?'

Tariq rubbed his eyes. 'Whoa, I don't know. Suddenly your wife's got what she's always wanted. That's great. But this baby could be not only the child of another man, but of a man who hated you and wanted to wreck your life. Could you put all that aside? You might want to, but I don't know if I could if I was him. It's a horrible situation.'

'Yeah.' Julie sighed. 'It's like a sick joke. I wonder what they'll decide.'

Julie had just opened her laptop the following morning when she heard a quiet tap at the kitchen door. To her surprise when she opened it Maggie was standing outside.

'Oh!' Julie said. 'I didn't expect to see you this early. Or at all, actually. I thought David would have taken the day off and you'd both be recovering.'

'Can I come in?'

'Of course. I'll get the kettle on.'

Maggie sat at the kitchen table and Julie made coffee. She gave a cup to her friend. 'This is weird,' she said slowly. 'It's like it's always been – us sitting here, or at yours, drinking coffee and chatting – but we both know it isn't. Everything is different.'

'I know,' Maggie said softly. 'But I wanted to tell you what's been happening. David *is* going to take today off, but he had to go into school early. There's going to be a special assembly, so he can talk to all the pupils together about this social media hacking thing. He was anxious that they should all know Abbie wasn't to blame. I guess he won't go into any detail about why he was targeted, but he said he wanted to take the opportunity to point out to the youngsters the dangers of sharing personal information on these sites.'

'How did he do it, Maggie?' Julie said. 'Will, I mean. Abbie wouldn't have given him her password.'

Maggie sighed. 'Who knows? He had so many schemes and scams going, and he was, is, pretty conversant with the internet. Did I tell you how he'd supported himself over the years? Online gambling. Only just recently he's had a lot of expenses and he'd been making losses. You know what? I think if he hadn't needed me for money, he'd have just left Halstead without a word. He tried to, except I saw him packing the car and insisted on going with him, fool that I was. He never wanted me, did he? It was all to get at David.'

'None of us saw him for what he was, Maggie,' Julie said. 'Except Abbie. Don't be too hard on yourself. Look, I know I was pretty unforgiving, and I'm sorry. David said he was only thinking of his own hurt feelings, and I guess I did the same.'

'David *was* partly to blame, Julie,' Maggie said. 'But not you. You just acted out of friendship and concern, and I rebuffed you. You had every right to be angry.'

'Well, we went through all this yesterday,' Julie said. 'As far as I'm concerned, if forgiveness is required, it's yours and it's behind us. I'm more worried about the future now. Do you know what you're going to do?'

Maggie brushed a tear from her cheek. She picked up her coffee cup with a shaky hand and took a gulp. 'It's not good, is it? We went round in circles a bit, David and I. Talked till very late. At least we're talking. I suppose that's something.' She took a deep breath. 'I said we should go for some kind of genetic test. I guess these things aren't always conclusive, but if it seemed likely that the baby was Will's – sorry, I can't think of him as Paul – I said I would have the pregnancy terminated.'

'Oh, Maggie – no! Not after all these years of waiting! That would be cruel.'

Maggie shook her head and ploughed on, her expression grim. 'Yes. But just think of the reality, Julie. David is human, not super-human. Think what trouble we would be storing up for ourselves. Just when I've come to realise – or, really, to remember – what a strong marriage we had, and how insanely stupid I was to think even for a moment of throwing it away – I'd be asking him to raise the child of a man who hated him and used me. How could he not think of that every time he looked at the baby, the child, the young man or woman that was supposed to be his own son or daughter? What sort of relationship could he hope for with him or her? And what effect would it have on him and me? No, I saw it all with horrible clarity, what a curse I'd be calling down on us both.'

Julie was silent for a moment, staring at her friend, chewing her lip. 'So,' she said at last, 'what was David's reaction?'

'He argued with me.' Maggie smiled sadly. 'At the moment he's relieved I've come to no obvious harm, that I've seen Will for what he is and come home, that we are on the way to forgiving one another and trying to put things right. He wants me to be happy, and this is what I've wanted for a long time. He wants to make up for his neglect and coldness to me over the last months, his lack of support, his unkindness. He's very repentant. He says the baby won't be Will's, or his – it'll be ours. And, of course, he doesn't believe in abortion, unless it's for a very compelling reason. Neither do I, but I think what we have here *is* a compelling reason. So, I'm afraid, my dear, we are no further forward. Not yet.' She finished her coffee. 'I have you to thank for something else, I think.'

'Really? What's that?'

'Apparently you suggested to David that he make up some story to cover my absence from work. I might have been out of a job as well as all the rest. So I'm sorry you had to lie, but thanks.'

'Have you spoken to your Head?'

'Mary? Yes, just now. She was very understanding. I'll have to make an appointment at the doctor's, of course, to get signed off. But it's so near the end of term ...'

Julie looked up suddenly, her eyes widening. 'Wait, Maggie ... I've just thought of something.' There was excitement in her voice.

'What?'

Julie leaned forward. 'It came to me just then, when you said about going to see the doctor. You haven't been yet? About the pregnancy?'

Maggie looked puzzled and shook her head. 'What, you mean taking a genetic test? No, there hasn't been time.'

'No, I'm not talking about that. Aren't you supposed to have a scan? Not just to see if everything's going OK, but to get an idea of the due date?'

'Well, yes, I suppose so, but I thought I'd only be consulting the doctor about a termination, if the genetic test indicated that the baby was Will's. That was the only urgency – not to leave it too late. What are you on about?'

'I just had a sort of ... revelation, and it made me go a bit hot and cold.' She blinked, exhaling. 'I just thought about that day I came to see you. You remember? It was a Saturday. The day I asked you, point blank, if you were having an affair. You behaved very strangely, not like yourself at all, cold, almost hostile. As if you disliked me, found me annoying and intrusive. You were so antagonistic about Abbie too.'

Maggie winced. 'Yes, I know. I was horrible. I suppose I knew at some level that you were right, but I had no intention of admitting to any guilt or any doubt. I was, I don't know, bewitched. No, that's a cop-out. I'm making it sound as if I wasn't responsible for my own actions, when of course I was.'

'Maybe. But what I just remembered was how you *looked*, Maggie. You didn't just act oddly, you actually looked different too. I didn't really think of it till this minute.'

Maggie frowned. 'Different how?'

Julie hesitated. 'It's hard to describe. But I've seen it with other pregnant women. Sometimes they have a sort of shininess, a kind of smooth plump look. It usually comes after the horrible period of being sick, or at least feeling nauseous – not just in the mornings – any time of day or night. Not always, though, if your experience is anything to go by. Some of them just look really well. You seemed like that to me. Your hair was glossy, your skin was clear, you looked especially healthy. I noticed it, but I didn't really think anything of it.'

'I don't understand,' Maggie said with a shake of her head. 'Maybe I was just feeling pleased with myself, because of all the flattery and adulation I was getting from Will. Not to mention all the sex. I wasn't even pregnant then.'

Julie grabbed Maggie's hand. 'But that's just it! *Perhaps you were!* And oh! Yes, I just thought of something else!' Her voice rose to breathless urgency. 'Do you remember the day you came round and told me about that peculiar episode when Will, Paul, went with you to bell-ringing practice? That was way back, I can't remember exactly when, but it was before you, um, before you and he were anything but chummy neighbours. You asked for black coffee, and you said milk made you feel queasy. Oh, Maggie, please, go and see the doctor, get yourself scanned! Find out how far along you are. Because that might just be the clearest evidence you could have that this baby actually *is* David's.'

Maggie stared at Julie, her mouth open. 'How likely is that?' she whispered. 'After all the years of fruitless trying?'

'You're forgetting something. I was praying all those years. Probably others were too. You were yourself, I know. It's possible, Maggie. It's worth a try. Better to find out, if you can, than – than what you are proposing to do.'

Maggie said nothing. There was a silence that seemed to Julie to last for hours, not minutes. At last Maggie murmured, 'If you're right, Julie ... oh, but how can I even think about it? How can I even let that hope into my mind, even for a second? How could it be possible? It would be like a reprieve, and I don't deserve it.'

'That's stupid talk,' Julie said crossly. 'Not one of us deserves anything, you know that. All the blessings we have are free. Look, Maggie,' she added determinedly, 'you've got to get a doctor's appointment. I'll come with you, if you like. We don't have to say anything to anyone, if that's what you'd prefer. Not even to David – well, especially not to David. Not yet. If it doesn't work out, if it's still inconclusive, if the dates don't tell us anything clearly, nobody will know but us, and you'll be back where you were with a terrible decision to make. But don't you think you need to find out? You won't be worse off, will you? And it might be better news than you've had for a long, long time.'

Maggie stared, her eyes seeming unfocused. Her hands were gripping the edge of the table as if she feared to fall. 'I can't let myself hope too much,' she said, her voice strained. 'But I'll call the surgery today. Maybe they can fit me in over the next few days.' She pushed herself to her feet. 'I'll go home now, Julie,' she said. 'You've got work to do, and I'm shattered. Anyway, David said he'd come home once the assembly is over. He's got to ring the Local Authority as well, and make an appointment to consult their legal department. It's a very serious business, you'll understand that, something that has to be contained. He's going to write to all the parents as well.' She smiled faintly. 'You'll get a letter, won't you? In fact, you'll probably get two. How silly.'

Julie laid her arm across her friend's shoulder and went with her to the door. 'You go and put your feet up, my love. You look worn out – no surprise.' A thought struck her and her face registered dismay. 'Oh, Maggie! I almost forgot – you probably don't know about John!'

Maggie shook her head and tears filled her eyes. 'He's gone, then. What else could it be? Oh, Julie. This is desperately sad.'

'I know. Did David tell you Abbie went to see him?'

'Yes. I have John as well as Abbie to thank for getting me free of Will.'

'She went to see him again, yesterday after school. She told me about the first visit, but I didn't know anything about the second till after the event. She didn't get to speak to him – he was too ill. Obviously he'd gone downhill very rapidly. But she left him a message, to say that you were safely home. Hilary told us, when she rang with the news that he'd died, that he seemed to understand. We can be thankful for that.'

Maggie looked at the floor. 'I'm thankful for a lot of things. Not least to your very resourceful daughter. Bless her! I'm going to think of a way to say thank you to Abbie. When the dust has settled.' She opened the door, letting in the warm breeze. 'Any idea when the funeral will be?'

'Well, I went to see Hilary yesterday evening,' Julie said, 'and she's all for having it as soon as possible. You know Hilary – practical and determined even in the midst of grief. She'll let us know, I dare say. Maggie, you will ring the doctor, won't you? I mean, today?'

'I'll do it as soon as I get indoors and take off my shoes. Good enough?'

Julie squeezed her arm. 'OK. And let me know. I'll take you to the surgery. That's if you'd like me to.'

Maggie gave her friend a hug. 'Thank you, dear Julie. What would I do without you?'

July 2010

The day of John Westwood's funeral fell on a warm, muggy Monday, the 12th of July, ten days before the end of term. Abbie was allowed to take time off school on the strict understanding that she would go back straight afterwards. David Calladine, perhaps surprisingly, offered to drive her and there was no reason to refuse, even though the thought of sitting in a car with him for twenty minutes filled her with faint alarm. With all that had gone on, with all that she knew and wished she didn't, what could they possibly talk about? And yet she felt it would be gauche and rude to sit in silence for the whole journey.

In the end it was David himself who started to talk, soon after leaving the church and getting into his car. 'What did you think of the funeral?' he asked.

Abbie shrugged. 'I don't really know. I've never been to one before. Was it fairly typical?'

David glanced at her, eyebrows raised and a faint smile on his sombre face. 'No, not at all,' he said. 'It was most unusual. I suppose there may have been funerals where the deceased person wrote his or her own eulogy, but I've never been to one. I certainly haven't heard of a clergyman preparing the message for his own funeral. But then again, John Westwood was no ordinary man. It was, I suppose, his last gift to the flock he cared for.'

'I didn't realise,' Abbie murmured. 'No wonder everyone gasped and started crying.' She thought for a moment. 'Except Mrs Westwood. She didn't cry. She just looked ... I don't know, a bit put out.'

David smiled as he swung smoothly onto the dual carriageway. 'Hilary would have wanted everything done with restraint,' he said.

'She wouldn't want a circus. John was more tolerant of emotional displays.' He indicated and moved off the slip road, gathering speed. Reluctant as she had been to travel with him, Abbie had to recognise how classy his car was, especially compared to her family's well-used saloon and the rattly van Tariq used for work. Since her driving test had been booked she found herself more tuned in to cars. *Not that I will be able to run one of my own for about twenty years.*

'So, what did you think of John's posthumous sermon?' David pursued.

'I think it might take me a while to process it,' Abbie said. She saw his eyebrows quirk upwards again and knew he recognised her prevarication for what it was.

David said no more until he pulled up in his space in the staff car park. Abbie opened the car door. 'Thanks for the lift,' she said politely.

'You're welcome,' he answered. He paused, and Abbie waited. 'Abbie, before you go, I just want you to know I'm thankful for everything you did for my wife.'

'That's OK. I'm glad it came out all right,' Abbie said. Then, feeling inexplicably bold, she added, 'I haven't congratulated you, have I, sir? Great news about your baby.'

David looked surprised, and amused. 'Thank you.'

'You're going to have a bit of a busy Christmas, I guess. With it, him, her, whatever it is, arriving on Boxing Day. Rather you than me.'

'I dare say we'll cope. And Abbie,' his smile faded and his face resumed its stern look. 'I don't want you taking any more days out of school. It may be almost the end of term, but this is an important year for you. Your record so far has been exemplary – don't mess it up.'

'I won't. My truanting days are over.' She got out of the car.

David looked at her and his expression changed. 'Before you go, I just want to make sure of something,' he said. 'The need for discretion – '

'Please don't worry,' Abbie said softly. 'Nobody in our family will ever breathe a word. And I'll vouch for Olly too. He understands. No one else knows, and no one will. Not from us.'

David nodded, clearly relieved. 'Thank you.'

Olly was waiting for her outside her form room. 'Hey! Can I take madam out for lunch?'

'Oh, yes, please! Where are we going?'

Olly took out his wallet and inspected its contents. 'Hm. The corner shop. And the park. Sorry, not the Ritz. However,' he brightened, 'that is all going to change.'

'What? How come?'

'I've got a job for the holidays.' He named a well-known fast-food outlet, situated in the Walburn shopping centre.

'How did you manage that?' Abbie said. 'You never said anything.'

'Let's get out of here,' Olly said. 'I need sustenance.'

Once in the park they found a bench tucked away out of sight of the road and shared their scrappy and not very healthy lunch. 'I applied online – found out they were recruiting,' Olly said. 'You could probably get a job there too if you wanted to. Might be handy for filling up the car. Once you've passed your test you can take me to all sorts of exotic locations.'

Abbie leaned against him and sighed. 'Thanks for the vote of confidence, but I have to pass first.'

He put his arm round her shoulders. 'You will. So, how was the funeral? And the journey here in our beloved Head's flash motor?' He frowned. 'Don't you think it's a bit strange him offering to bring you back? You know, what with everything ...' He tailed off.

'The journey was fine. And I think he wanted to make sure we realised we had to keep all of it a secret. I swore we'd never say a word. That means you have to keep quiet too.'

Olly looked pained. 'I'm not a blabbermouth. What do you think I'm going to do – sell his story to the papers? Though I guess,' he added thoughtfully, 'it would be an easier way of earning money than serving up burgers.'

'Olly!' Abbie said warningly. 'Don't joke.'

'Sorry. So was there lots of weeping and wailing?'

'Some weeping, no wailing. This is the C of E, remember. But there was an unusual feature. I know it was unusual because Mr Calladine told me it was. Mr Westwood wrote his own funeral sermon, and the visiting clergy chap delivered it. Except that he fumbled and flapped and got overcome, and Mrs Westwood took the paper off him and finished reading it herself. She's some woman.'

'Wow. What did it say? Bottom line.'

'Actually,' Abbie said, disengaging herself so she could look at him, 'it was weird. As if he knew all along what was going on in his little patch. But he couldn't have, could he? Until I went to the hospice and told him. It's just that it was so ... so spookily appropriate. There was quite a lot of stuff about enemies and spiritual forces. And he quoted a parable where a load of weeds came up in a field of wheat, and the owner said, "It was some enemy who did this." Like he knew about Will Chambers. But he can't have – it must have been a coincidence.'

'Maybe he just knew the sort of trouble people get into,' Olly said thoughtfully. 'Did he leave any instructions? On how to avoid spiritual attack?' He spoke lightly, but Abbie could tell he was genuinely interested. She supposed it represented a world totally unfamiliar to him until now.

'Prayer, of course. There were loads of examples out of the Bible about the need for prayer.'

'Well,' Olly said, stretching, 'much food for thought there. Meanwhile, what are we going to do for the next six weeks of freedom?'

'You'll be working, you said.'

'Not all the time. I'll do a certain number of shifts a week. I'll have free days, and a bit more cash than usual, I hope. A chance to hang out with my favourite nutter.'

'That reminds me,' Abbie said. 'There's something – two things, actually – I wanted to ask you.'

'If you want to know if I'm free for a night of unrestrained passion, I'll have to consult my diary. But in principle ...' he tried to look lecherous, but succeeded only in squinting.

'Down, Rover,' Abbie said sternly. 'I just wondered if, you know, at the very beginning, did you like me because you thought I was weird, or in spite of it? How did you come to the idea I was weird, anyway?'

Olly sucked in his breath dramatically. 'Ooh, word travels,' he said with relish. 'Even as far as distant Ketley College. No, silly,' he added, seeing her horrified expression, 'of course that's not true, but if I start telling the truth who knows where we'll end up? At the very least I'll look like an idiot.'

'That's already the case,' Abbie said. 'So you might as well come clean.'

'Thanks,' he muttered. 'No chance of getting big-headed with you around, I see. Well, yes, I did hear some things when I first came to this school. Not very nice things. And someone showed me a screenshot of a young girl in strange head gear.'

Abbie groaned. 'That was four years ago! Haven't they got anything better to think about?'

'Well, that got me interested. You know I like anything to do with abnormal psychology. But at first I didn't connect the gawky, miserable-looking thirteen-year-old with the very stunning girl whose brother I happened to be acquainted with on the footie field. Wow, that was a revelation. I thought to myself, "Oliver, old man, she's gorgeous, she's bright, and she's a head case. What more could you ask for?" It was better than winning the lottery.'

Abbie looked at him with narrow eyes. 'I don't know whether to kiss you or bash you.'

He grinned. 'Can I help you with that decision?'

'No. I can make my own mind up.'

'OK, so what was the other question? You'd better be quick – we have to get back.'

'Let's walk and talk, then.'

They threw their empty cartons and packets in a nearby bin and walked back down the road. Olly looked at her enquiringly.

'I told you, didn't I,' Abbie said, 'a bit anyway, about my dad and Kashmir and the earthquake that set all this thing off – my mum observing me going all spacey as you put it, and everything that came after that. I think I might have said something about how my dad came here from Kashmir and why he didn't go back.'

'Yeah. Changed his religion and moved in with your mum.'

'In a nutshell. But he did go back, once, and his dad hit the roof and disowned him. Did I tell you that bit?'

'Yeah. Sort of.'

'Well, I was thinking it might be cool to go there. Kashmir's supposed to be amazing. I thought I might get a job and save up and then travel out there before uni. See what it's like, and see if I can hook up with any of my Indian relations, if there are any left. I thought – well, I thought you might like to come too. That's assuming we're still speaking.'

Olly frowned and took her by the arm as they crossed the road. 'You know what,' he said, 'that sounds brilliant. I really want to travel, see a bit of the world. But this trip of yours … well, it seems to me that it shouldn't really be me that goes with you. Much as I might like to.'

'What?'

'I hope you realise how unselfish I'm being, because travelling in remote areas, sleeping under the stars, etc, far from civilisation, parents or policemen, would give me the ideal opportunity for having my evil way with you.'

'Olly, get to the point. I promised Mr Calladine I'd be the perfect pupil from now on, and it's minutes to registration.'

'It's obvious, isn't it? The person you should take with you is your dad.'

'Oh!'

'Well, isn't it?'

'I never thought of that.'

'You get on with your old man, don't you? I thought he was pretty OK when I came round to yours the other day.'

Abbie shook her head. 'Of course I do, but I don't know if he could afford to take the time off work. But – no, Olly, you're right! He *should* try and find out what happened to them all after the earthquake. He hardly ever says anything about it, but we all know he thinks about them a lot. He broods. Not knowing must be awful.' She stopped outside her form room, oblivious of jostling students shoving past. 'Come home with me tonight,' she said. 'You suggest it to him.'

A skinny blonde girl sidled past, arm in arm with her much fatter friend. 'Ooh, did you hear that?' She mimicked Abbie's voice. '"Come home with me tonight!" Your luck's in, Olly!'

Olly looked at the girl with disdain. 'Jealous are we, Maddie?' He turned back to Abbie. 'OK, I will. Let your mum know, though, because I'm hoping she'll feed me. See you after school.'

'Riq? You awake?'

Tariq groaned. 'I am now.'

'I've been thinking.'

'Honey, it's one in the morning. Can't it wait?'

'No, I want to tell you now. I think it's a great idea. What the kids came up with – you and Abbie going to Jammu.'

'Where are we going to get the money from?' Tariq mumbled. 'Flights are expensive.'

'I've got a bit salted away – from what Gran left me. It might be enough.'

'You were going to save that for something really important.'

Julie turned on her side to face him. '*This* is really important,' she said. '*You* are really important. It's high time you went there and found out what's going on. Don't you think it's rather wonderful that Abbie wants to go? If she wanted to travel she could have gone anywhere, and with anyone. No, Riq, she's doing this for you. You have to go. We'll find the money. And Dan and I and the dog will manage just fine. But – '

Tariq, now fully awake, turned to face her. 'But what?'

'But I don't think you should wait for next year. Anything could happen in a year. How old's your dad?'

Tariq thought. 'He was born in 1929. So he'd be eighty-one. And my mother'd be seventy-nine. They could be dead, even if they survived the earthquake.'

'Yes, they might be. But they might not. And you still have sisters, nephews and nieces, as far as you know. But that's just it, Riq. You don't know. And I think it's well and truly time you did. Don't wait for Abbie's gap year. Go now, this summer.'

Tariq stretched out his hand and stroked her cheek. 'Are you crazy?'

'Maybe. But I'm also right.'

Julie found her daughter kneeling on the sofa in the living room, staring out of the window at the rain. Water was pouring down the glass, obscuring the trees that were swaying in the stiff wind.

'Hey. This is not what I would expect someone to be doing on the first day of the summer holidays,' Julie said. She plumped down on the sofa next to Abbie. 'I'd be thinking she might be likelier to be sleeping. It's barely half-past nine.'

'Hm, well, sleep's good, but lying in bed trying and failing to sleep isn't so great.' Abbie slid down and sat next to her mother, leaning against her. Molly, who had been stretched out at the foot of the sofa, shifted with a faint grunt of protest.

'So, is something bothering you that sleep's so elusive?' Julie said as lightly as she could.

'Plenty of things are bothering me. You can take your pick: my exam results. My driving test. The trip to Jammu. Etc.'

Julie sighed. 'Your exam results are out of your control now, so you might as well just wait and see. Your driving test? Practice is all you can do. What's bothering you about the trip? Aren't you looking forward to it? It was your idea in the first place.'

Abbie wriggled, making herself more comfortable. 'Yes, I am looking forward to it, but there are aspects that are ... I don't know, unsettling. I mean – ' she turned to Julie suddenly, her face serious. 'Do you think it really is OK for the Calladines to contribute? I feel a bit, well, a bit embarrassed about that.'

Julie pursed her lips. 'Maggie was most insistent. She said if it wasn't for you things might have turned out very differently for her. She said to regard it as an early birthday present for you as well as a fortieth birthday present for your father, if that makes it easier. She and David have both been working for years with no children to drain the bank account, and they certainly have more than we do. I'd say accept it graciously, sweetheart. It's a present to us all in a way – perhaps most of all to your dad. An expression of friendship.'

'OK,' Abbie said slowly. 'If you think about it that way, maybe ... but also there are worrying aspects about going to Kashmir. Dad must be a bit anxious too – about what'll greet him when he gets there, who's alive, who's not, who wants to know him and who doesn't – that sort of thing.' Her brow creased, and she sighed. 'I suppose if the family aspect goes belly-up we'll just have to be tourists, won't we? He can show me the sights.'

Julie put her arm round Abbie's shoulders. 'I understand too,' she said gently, 'that your idea of travelling in your gap year has been a bit hijacked. Maybe you wanted to go with Olly, or another friend.'

Abbie pulled away, shaking her head. 'No, it's not that. If I want to take a gap year and travel, I still can. I can get a job, save up. Even if I apply to universities in the autumn, I don't have to accept places I'm offered. I can take a year out, work, travel, apply again knowing what A levels I've got. If Olly wants to come, great, but he may have other ideas. Things may be different then, anyway, with him and me. No, I'm happy Dad and I are going together. He'll be the best guide, and I feel safe with him. I'm just wondering, that's all, what we'll find when we get there. Maybe it won't all be happy ever after.'

Julie smiled. 'Don't worry about your dad. He's a realist, love. Probably thought all this out for himself long ago. You can ask him yourself. Maybe on that long flight! How long is it exactly, anyway?'

Abbie groaned. 'Seven hours and thirty-nine minutes. I looked it up. Actually,' she said, grinning, 'I have an idea how to pass the time. Dad may think he's going to have a nice long snooze, but I'm going to ask him how a nominal Muslim became a signed-up card-carrying Christian.'

Julie laughed. 'Good luck with that! He can't even remember what he had for breakfast, let alone what he was thinking twenty years ago.'

Abbie shook her head. 'We'll see. Anyway, don't *you* know? Didn't you talk to him about it when you first met?'

'I suppose, a bit. But don't forget his conversion predated meeting me. It had a lot to do with some good friends of his, a couple he met, students like us, who were very kind to him when he first came to London and was feeling a bit lost. What were their names? Sophie and … no, I've forgotten. Your dad will know.' She heaved herself up from the sofa. 'I've got some ironing to do. Come and talk to me while I do it.'

'OK.' Abbie followed her mother into the kitchen and sat down at the table. Molly followed at her own shambling pace and flopped down in her basket with a loud sigh.

Julie pulled the ironing board out of a tall cupboard and plugged in the iron. 'How did you get on at Olly's parents' barbecue? You didn't say much last night.'

'Oh, it was OK. Nice food, lots of people I didn't know, but that didn't matter. They have a big garden, and they'd put up a couple of gazebos in case it rained, but it didn't. The rain waited for today, luckily.'

'What are they like?'

'Olly's mum and dad? Yeah, they're OK. Nice enough to me, though we didn't talk much: they were busy with their other guests. His sister's a bit of a pain, though.'

'How old is she?'

'Eleven. Starting at our school in September. Hung around Olly and me asking us all sorts of questions. Some of them just a bit too personal. I thought she was rather a spoilt brat, quite honestly.' She paused, thinking. 'Olly doesn't seem like he belongs to his family sometimes – he's very different.'

Julie arranged one of Tariq's shirts on the ironing board. 'In what way?'

'Well, they seem quite … materialistic. Not just the nice house, the two smart cars, lots of people have those, I guess, but it's their attitude to their possessions. I heard Olly's parents talking to some friends and it was all about the price of this and the value of investments and who had what and what houses were worth and getting tradesmen to do a decent job – all that. I didn't like it much. Olly has an allowance, so he's always better off than me, but it's not a big deal for him, he always shares what he has and he's happy to work.'

Julie passed the iron thoughtfully up and down the shirt sleeve. 'Do you think you seem to belong to your family? Does Dan? I mean, in the eyes of other people.'

'I don't know what people think. And I suppose all children start doing things their own way as they grow up. But I'd say Dan and I are both recognisably yours and Dad's. Even though neither of us has your faith, I think we both have your values. Most of them, anyway.'

'That's good to hear, love. That gives me a nice warm glow.'

'Don't get too carried away, Mum,' Abbie said. 'I'll revert to snarling ungrateful teenager soon enough.'

'You haven't really been all that nasty for ages, actually,' Julie said.

'What about that time when you were dragging me to all those shrink appointments?' Abbie reminded her. 'I think I might have been just a *little* ratty.'

Julie shook out the finished shirt and draped it over the back of a kitchen chair. She grinned. 'Maybe.' She took another garment out of the laundry basket at her feet. 'Anything else on your mind that I should know about?'

'Mum, you don't miss much, do you?' Abbie said, her eyes wide. 'Well, if you really want to know, and if you haven't anything better to be doing, I wonder about the future a fair bit.'

'About Olly in particular?'

Abbie shrugged. 'It just seems to me that everything's changing. Not necessarily for the worse, but ... after this year, who knows where we'll be? And even this year, everyone's looking ahead. I'll tell you what it was – it was Mr Westwood's funeral that got me thinking, rather sad and dreary thoughts they were too.'

'Such as?'

Abbie sighed. 'Like what does life mean, and why does love matter? When death will end it all, for every living thing? It makes a bit of a mockery of everything, somehow.'

'Yes, it does,' Julie agreed, 'if you are sure that this life is all there is.'

'Some people say anything else is a cosy fiction.'

'Some people say a whole lot of things. You have to make your own mind up in the end.' Julie picked up the iron again.

'*They* say we live for a while and then it's oblivion.'

'But they don't *know*, do they?'

'But do *you* know?'

Julie inclined her head, setting the hot iron on its end. 'It rather depends what you mean by "know", doesn't it? If you're talking about proved in a human sense, then no, I don't. If you mean strongly believe because of your own experience, then yes. Well, for example, let me think … if someone said to you that your dad had cheated them in some way, something to do with work he'd done or money he was paid, what would you say?'

'I'd say there was no way he would cheat anyone knowingly. If there was a discrepancy it would be down to a misunderstanding, or a failure of communication.'

'What would give you that certainty?'

'Because I know him, of course. I know he would never do anything underhand.' She paused, frowning. 'You're saying you know God like you know Dad?'

'No, hardly. Not in the same way. But I do still know Him, God that is, by experience. I also believe He has all the knowledge a human being can never have, and none of the faults. So I trust Him. If He says He is coming back for us, I believe Him. And unlike all the people who say death is the end, He, Jesus, actually did come back. Bit of a clincher in my book, that.'

Abbie pondered for a long moment. 'Mr Westwood was a wise old man, I think. You thought so, didn't you?'

'Yes. Wise, lovable, perceptive, but humanly imperfect too.'

'Did I tell you what he said to me?'

'You said something about him urging you to pray.'

'Yes. Which is weird,' Abbie said, staring down at the table. 'Seeing as I don't even know if I believe in God, and he – Mr Westwood – knew that as well. Mum, did he think I have some kind of prophetic thing?'

Julie shook her head. 'I don't know. I don't know if even he knew himself what he thought, but he was certainly very interested in the ... the spiritual implications of your visions, if I can put it like that.'

'I looked them up,' Abbie said bleakly, 'the prophets in the Bible. Some of them, anyway. I don't want to be anything like them, Mum. They mostly had a horrible time. Like Jeremiah, for instance. He hated what he had to do, and people hated him for it. Chucked him down a well ... But he couldn't *not* do it, he said. What a bind to be in! And some of the others were mocked and spat on and tortured and killed! All I want is to be normal. I want these things to go away, like Dad said his did.'

'Yes ... "your message is like a fire burning deep within me." Poor old Jeremiah. He didn't much want to be a prophet, did he?' Julie looked at Abbie with a smile. 'But you did what you did from good motives, and God honoured that. It's what He does – brings good out of evil. Because look what happened: Will Chambers, or Paul White, whoever he was, tried to destroy the Calladines, but they are back together, stronger than they were before, with a miracle baby on the way. Not only that, we've all learned something: how things go wrong when God's people fail in prayer.'

Abbie laughed. 'Crikey, Mum, who needs a visiting preacher? You could preach the sermon any Sunday!'

'Oh, please! Do me a favour!' Julie grimaced. 'Spare the congregation, I should say.'

'Seriously, though,' Abbie said, 'you call Calladine junior a miracle, but are you really, *really* sure it's not a little cuckoo?'

'The dates add up, my love,' Julie said firmly. 'A Christmas baby. Seems to me God's had the last laugh.' She noted Abbie's pensive face, and said gently, 'Anything else weighing you down?'

'Not exactly,' Abbie said. 'Something I'm wondering about, that's all. You said something once about being innocent as doves but not wise as serpents, didn't you? And I've sometimes thought that Christians can be naïve. But you're not supposed to judge, are you? You're supposed to think the best of people, not be suspicious of them. You're supposed to forgive, and leave the final reckoning to God. Where does that leave you with Paul White? Do you forgive him? Does Mrs Calladine?'

'Well ...' Julie considered. 'I can't speak for Maggie, obviously. All I can truthfully say is I hope to eventually. Not that he's hurt me personally, but he hurt my friend. Sometimes that's harder to bear.' She paused. 'Actually, as we're on the subject, your dad and I had a long chat about him – Paul White. Very late last night.'

'Oh? Did you come to any conclusions?'

'Just the one,' Julie said, her voice low. 'Your dad was all for sweeping it under the carpet, letting it go, getting free of the mess. But I said we should at least pursue the debt. Paul White disappeared owing the business nearly £700. Work and materials your dad had provided in good faith. We can't afford to lose that money.'

'Also,' Abbie said, frowning, 'it just isn't right.'

Julie nodded. 'That's what I said too. It's one thing to forgive someone, but letting him get away with it? Not if I can help it. Maybe we can't achieve anything, but I'd like to do *something*. You never know, we might just save some other poor soul from being swindled.'

'What can you actually do, though?'

'I'm going to have a chat with Hugh Preston,' Julie said. 'He's a retired solicitor, isn't he? I'd have thought he can advise me, point me in the right direction – or even tell me not to bother because it isn't worth it. I hope not, though. I hate the idea of Paul White running off laughing with someone else's money. I hope I'm not being vengeful. It just offends my sense of justice.' She paused, thinking, and picked another garment from the laundry basket. The ironing was getting done, but very slowly. 'So what do *you* make of him, Abs? Sick? Mad? Or just plain bad?'

Abbie shook her head. 'According to Olly, who's studying these things, he probably has Antisocial Personality Disorder. But that's still going to vary from person to person, isn't it? Not all of them are like Paul White, though I guess there are common characteristics. I'd just like to know how you're supposed to behave if a person like that crosses your path. Maybe now we're more aware, more alert. But could you just cut them dead, even supposing you recognised the problem in time? Where's the compassion in that? I mean, can he actually help how he is? Was it kind of locked into his genes from the beginning? On the other hand, you don't want to be manipulated. Tricky, isn't it?'

'I'm pretty sure,' Julie said wryly, 'on the evidence we have, *he* isn't cudgelling his brains to search out the right thing to do. He doesn't care. All he wanted was the best outcome for himself; others didn't count. I wouldn't want to be like that, ever, and I wouldn't want you to be like that – without a conscience. But having a conscience makes you vulnerable. I don't know, love. Compassion balanced with caution, maybe. Happily we don't meet a Paul White every day.'

'I hope I never, ever meet another one,' Abbie said feelingly. 'I don't want to see another locust as long as I live.'

January 2011

This will be my last journal entry, I've decided. It was a kiddie thing anyway, and as tomorrow is my eighteenth birthday it seems appropriate to put 'The End' today. But when I thought about it I realised there was a lot of stuff that perhaps I needed to record – so much has happened over the last few months, and I have had so many thoughts which maybe I need to remember.

One big thing that's different – I actually have some friends! Apart from Olly, I mean. Friends who are girls, too, and that's a first, ever since Lucy went away. It was weird the way we met in the first place. When school started in September Mr Calladine asked me to do a presentation to the whole of Year 13 about the trip to Kashmir. I was a bit dubious at first but then I thought it would probably be OK as Dad and I took loads of photos. But when it came to preparing the talk part I realised how little I actually knew, apart from what I'd seen and what Dad told me. So I did some research, and after a while I got quite carried away with it. For the talk I only included cool stuff I thought would interest the other students, but I found out a load of information I didn't put in – geography, history, religion, politics, war, etc. I suppose it was while I was doing all this that I first got the idea of changing what I wanted to do next in my life.

Once I got over a horrible wave of stage fright the presentation went OK, and the next day I was getting lunch in the cafeteria and these two girls, Mel and Bea, came over and said how interesting it had been and how they wanted to go to Kashmir now! They'd been talking about travelling during their gap year and said now they would definitely include Kashmir because it's so beautiful and mountainous and dramatic, as well as culturally so different. We got talking and they asked me why I went and who with, and when I told them they were even more curious and asked me loads of questions. We've been friends ever since, and I'm finally having some fun! Unlike some of the other girls, they aren't catty or two-faced.

I don't see so much of Olly now. We're still friends, of course, but obviously with A levels coming up we are all working like slaves, plus he still has his job serving burgers and I found a job as well, just at weekends, in the shop attached to a filling station in Walburn. Not very exciting, but it's money. That and a bit of babysitting means I've been able to save: not much, but it adds up. Which I need, for life in general, for the travelling fund, and for sometimes putting petrol in the car. That's another thing that happened – not the first time, in August, but the second time – I passed my driving test! So now Mum's moaning I've always got the car.

I never did get to take Olly to exotic places, which is kind of sad, but you move on, I guess, and things change. As for my plan to have sex with him, I see that for what it was: a sort of lonely bravado. He had something to say about it, of course. He said ever so seriously that it was probably not a good idea, because since I am about to be eighteen and he doesn't have his birthday till April, I might get done for corrupting a minor! He always was an idiot. Now I don't feel so bad about the idea of separating when we leave school. We were always going to different universities anyway, and now I'm thinking of taking a year out. Looking back I see that my relationship with Olly kind of peaked with the rescue of Mrs Calladine (that's what she calls it, anyway). So you could say I feel generally more normal these days (whatever normal is!). And a bit more confident: I see that you can be different without being weird, and normal without being boring. But I haven't told my new friends about my seeings: that seems like a step too far.

I know more about Kashmir now – not a lot, and it's mostly superficial, but more than I did. The thing is, we almost didn't go at all. With everything that had been happening with the Calladines, and Will Chambers aka Paul White, and me and Olly, and poor Mr Westwood dying, and so on, not to mention us getting a dog, we were all a bit inward-looking for a while and even Dad, who likes to keep up with the news, didn't really cotton on to what was going on in Kashmir. It was only after we'd made plans to go – straight after his fortieth birthday on 3rd August – that he told us one day, looking very pensive, about the awful things going on there. Apparently there'd been political unrest ever since June, with young people protesting about Indian rule and getting arrested and even killed. Of course Mum panicked, thinking we were going to get caught up in it, but Dad said that there'd been trouble there ever since he could remember, and long before he was even born. It's mostly to do, as far as I can gather, with the Muslim majority in Kashmir objecting to what the Indian government decide. But Dad said, when he was about sixteen, he and his dad travelled to Srinagar to see a cricket match featuring a famous cricketer called Aftab Ahmed, playing for something called the Ranji Trophy, and this was at a time when there was a lot of rioting. I'm not surprised they went regardless: Dad's mad about cricket, so he was a bit disappointed when Dan preferred football. I suppose if there are always riots and protests and trouble generally in your country, you learn how to live with it. He also said to Mum that we would be safe just as long as the saints were praying for us. He means the people in their church, who don't seem that saintly to me.

So we booked our seats on a flight to Jammu, via Delhi. That's all we did — no accommodation, nothing else. Dad said he would sort that out when we got there. Perhaps he hoped someone in the family would take us in, I don't know. But then something else happened which caused an almighty uproar round the whole world. A pastor in America said he was going to mark the anniversary of 9/11 by burning 200 Qur'ans! How stupid is that? All the Muslims went ballistic, and who can blame them? There were protests all over Asia and the Middle East, and people were killed. Anyway, the Qur'an burning didn't happen, but I know Dad was worried. He thought it would increase anti-Christian feeling in Muslim countries — no surprise. But by then our plans were set, our tickets were bought, and after a bit of to-ing and fro-ing, of course we went.

Our flight was pretty early in the morning — nine something, so we were all up at a ridiculous hour. I say all, but of course that didn't include Dan. I went into his room to say goodbye and he just put an arm out of the pit he calls his bed and patted me vaguely and said, 'A'right, sis, have a good time, don't get murdered.' Brothers should definitely be abolished. But then we were about to go, me sitting in the back of the car, Mum just strapping herself in to the driver's seat, and Dad was putting some last thing into the boot, and Dan appeared in his PJs, looking unwashed and gross, with his hair sticking up in all directions, and he puts his arms round Dad's neck and hugged him, not saying a word.

Then he staggered back inside. Dad didn't say anything either. He just got into the car, smiling and shaking his head.

Mum drove us to the airport, and I don't know if they talked on the way, because I was asleep before we got onto the main road. When we got there, though, she was obviously upset and worried. I heard her mention Ephesians 6, whatever that meant, and something about armour. It's not that bad in Jammu, surely? But then later, on the plane, I asked Dad about it and he laughed and said it was stuff from the Bible (of course) and that the armour was spiritual and that I should look it up one day. I also heard Mum say, when they thought I was reading rather than listening, 'Don't let any harm come to her, Riq.' I thought it was him she was worried about, not me. Maybe it's both. But she was definitely crying when she said goodbye.

It was a long, long journey, all seven hours and thirty-nine minutes of it, some of it scarily bumpy, most of it deeply boring with nothing to look at but clouds outside and sweetly smiling cabin crew inside, offering snacks and drinks at punctual intervals. I read, and watched a couple of daft films, and occasionally dozed. Dad did a lot of sleeping. Once in a while I looked at him and for a moment I saw him as someone different: not just familiar everyday Dad, but a man approaching middle age, getting a bit grey above the ears, weighed down with past history and present responsibility, and probably not feeling up to it most of the time. I suppose I was seeing him as just another human being. He's my dad and I take him for granted, I guess, but on that flight, though we didn't talk a lot, there were moments when I loved him so much my heart felt squeezed and choked. Soppy, yeah, I know.

We had three hours to wait in Delhi, because there was a problem with the plane. I don't need to say anything here about what it was like, because all that stuff is in my presentation, but I thought I would die of the heat. As soon as the aircraft doors opened it hit us like a steamy blanket. After a while I got more tolerant of the temperature and humidity, but that day it was a shock.

We endured the long, weary wait and then at last we boarded the plane to Jammu. That was just a one-hour flight, but by the time we touched down, counting the delay and the time difference (four and a half hours), we'd been travelling all day and it was gone midnight local time and we were both exhausted. Dad had obviously been doing a bit of research before we left, unknown to me, because he'd found a little hotel in a quiet leafy street near the centre of the old part of the city, and we were taken there in a taxi that went at a crazy speed and honked its horn repeatedly. It was dark, so I didn't take much in. All I wanted was a shower and a drink of cold water, followed by a very long sleep, and that's what I got. The shower was a bit unreliable, but the rooms were clean. I told Dad I wasn't hungry, what with all the snacks on the plane, and he told me just to take it easy and unwind. In the morning he was going to check out some people and places, and I was to stay put till he got back. It was best, he thought, to do this initial exploration on his own. All I wanted to do was sleep, so it was OK with me.

It was midday before I surfaced, and I had another shower and went to find Dad. He wasn't in his room, and I was beginning to feel uneasy when I got a text from him. 'On way back, time for lunch?' He arrived fifteen minutes later, and despite his reassuring smiles I thought he looked awful: haggard, grey, tense. He took me by the elbow and we left the hotel. Instantly we were on a street thronged with humanity and eye-wateringly colourful. The noise was crazy and I couldn't even begin to describe the smells. But Dad found a little restaurant off the main street and in we went, and before long we had food that I definitely recognised. Luckily, I like curry.

There were few other customers, and while we ate he told me the result of his morning's expedition. Obviously the place had changed in the time he'd been away, but he managed to get his bearings and he went first to the house where his sister Aleesa had lived with her husband, Sayid, and her two children, and from where he'd escaped to the airport all those years ago. But he was told the family had moved.

He finally tracked them down to a big newish place in a respectable suburb. Sayid's business was clearly doing well. He knocked, and after a while the door was opened by a nice-looking young guy carrying a baby girl about eighteen months old. Dad gaped a bit, he said, like a stranded fish, and then he realised that this was his nephew Umar. The last time Dad had seen Umar he was a tiny boy no more than three or four years old, and now he had a child of his own. Umar, I guess, was even more astonished to find out who his visitor was: that apostate with three heads, wicked Uncle Tariq.

Umar welcomed him and asked him in, but Dad could tell he was uneasy. After a while of stilted conversation, in a mixture of Dad's clunky Urdu and Umar's interesting English, he understood that Sayid was expected home soon with his wife, and Sayid was not likely to be pleased to see Tariq, especially with all the furore over the guy that wanted to burn Qur'ans. I think it was then that Dad realised something was very amiss – when Umar referred to 'his wife' rather than 'my mother'. Apparently Umar then said, looking very upset, 'Oh! Uncle Tariq, I am so sorry to be carrier of ill news. My mother is no longer alive. My father, he got married again three years ago. We all live here – my wife, my child, all. I am so sorry.' It turned out that Dad's sister Aleesa had died of breast cancer around the time of the earthquake. No wonder there had been such a silence since then.

Poor Dad. He was obviously devastated, but there in the restaurant he controlled himself enough to go on with his story. Umar quickly filled him in with news of the rest of the family. None of them had died in the earthquake, although some people had lost property and suffered financially. Dad's parents were both still alive, but Grandpa Rashid had suffered a stroke about nine months before and was in a wheelchair. His speech was badly affected and it was difficult to know how much he still understood of what people said or what was going on around him. He and my grandmother still lived in the family home and were being looked after by some servants who'd been with the family since the year dot. Dad remembered them from his childhood. My grandmother was training to be a nurse before she got married so she felt able to boss everyone about, even the nurses who came in from time to time to see to her husband. Dad smiled and said, 'She was only training for about a year before she got married, and then she had Zaynab, and after that she never took it up again. Children kept coming at irregular intervals and interrupted her career. But I'm sure she didn't mind.'

I said, 'I'm so sorry about your sister, Dad. What a nasty shock. She was your favourite.' He said, 'Yes. It's very sad. But it answers a lot of questions.' His face then grew very bleak again. He told me that he was about to leave the house when Sayid came back, in a sleek new Mercedes, accompanied by a very glamorous, well-dressed woman wearing a dazzling amount of jewellery. Sayid himself was the image of the successful businessman in his beautiful suit and expensive watch, etc. He wasn't at all pleased to see his errant brother-in-law, of course, and his wife behaved as if Dad had just crawled in from the sewer. Sayid was extremely angry. 'How dare you turn up unannounced like this! What makes you think you can just walk back into this family as if nothing has happened? Do you imagine that just the passage of time would wipe out what you did? Your father felt disgraced, as did we all, for years afterwards. You might do well to keep a low profile: Christians – ' he spat the word out as if it burned his mouth – 'are not too popular around here right now.' And he demanded that Dad leave his house.

Umar saw Dad to the door, and they managed to have a few words of quiet talk. Umar told Dad that not everyone felt as strongly as Sayid, nor would they have expressed their views so rudely even if they did, and that he himself would try to help us. He offered to go to his grandparents' house and prepare his grandmother for our arrival, rather than us giving two old people a heart attack by just turning up on their doorstep. And Dad was able to explain that most Christians were appalled by the whole Qur'an-burning business.

'So there we are,' Dad said. 'If you're ready, I thought we'd go and see your grandparents this afternoon. If Umar has got word to my mother, then I can't leave her in suspense.' He paid the bill and we left the restaurant. 'How do you feel about seeing them?' I asked. He took a deep breath. 'I hope and pray my mother has forgiven me,' he said. 'As for my father – well, I don't know. We'll see.'

Umar had told him that many family members were at the other house, up in the hills near Srinagar. 'Not all of them,' Dad said, 'because obviously people have work to go to and businesses needing attention, and there are quite a few children now. Your cousins are all older than you and most of them are married. And your grandfather's too frail to travel. I don't know if we'll see any of them, eventually. I hope we do.'

I found that I hoped so too, because it occurred to me that here in this strange country was all the extended family I had. In England there was no one. Mum was an only child; she'd lost her parents when she was young and been brought up by her grandmother. This lady died when I was too small to remember her. So I was quite curious to meet the Indian cousins.

We went back to the hotel and got the lady at the reception desk to call us another taxi. Dad was still a bit too chicken to entrust our journey to a Matador. (That's what the buses are called.) It took about fifteen minutes of screeching round corners and our driver swearing at other vehicles, and then we came out of the craziness into a wide, rather quieter and dusty street on the edge of what looked like a more modern suburb. Trees grew, or rather wilted, on each side, and the pavement was cracked and rutted. We were dropped off at a green gate which squealed when Dad pushed it open, and beyond it there was a big, dry garden with little growing in it, and then a set of steps leading onto a roofed verandah and an open front door. To one side of the main house was another, smaller building with an orange-tiled roof. I wondered if this was a separate dwelling for the servants, or perhaps where the cooking was done. I had no real idea. Dad said quietly, 'Just hang around here by the gate for a while. It's going to be enough for my mother to deal with, seeing me after all this time. As far as I know, she doesn't even know you exist.'

He walked across the garden towards the steps, but before he got there a tiny woman appeared in the doorway. Seeing him she let out a high-pitched screech and hurtled towards the steps. I was afraid she was going to fall down them in her haste, but Dad arrived at the top first and she threw herself into his arms, flapping her hands and wailing. She was wearing traditional dress, with a sort of long, floaty scarf round her neck and over her head. Her hair was white and scraped back into a bun. A moment later she freed herself and stepped back, looking up at Dad, who seemed huge beside her. She was dabbing her face with the end of her scarf. Then she took him by the hand and began to pull him towards the door, still making quite a racket with what was to me incomprehensible squawking. They'd almost gone into the shadows of the interior when Dad stopped her. For a moment her caterwauling stopped and she turned and gazed across the garden straight at me.

Dad called, 'Abbie, come up.' I walked towards them, feeling very self-conscious, but despite her obvious excitement at seeing her son I wasn't prepared for my grandmother's reaction to me. For a moment she stood open-mouthed, clutching the ends of her scarf to her wizened old face. Then she let out the most ear-splitting scream I have ever heard, bizarrely loud from such a tiny frame, and she seemed to sway, but luckily Dad held her up and led her to a wicker chair on one side of the door. By this time the scarf was over her face and she was rocking to and fro and moaning.

I climbed the steps. 'What's the matter?' I whispered to Dad. 'What have I done?'

'Nothing,' he said. There were tears in his eyes. 'I think for a moment there she thought you were Zaynab.'

'What?'

My grandmother uncovered her face and looked up at us, and a flood of Urdu came pouring from her mouth.

Dad said, 'She says you are like Zaynab come back from the grave. She can see now that you are different, but it gave her a terrible shock. She thought she was losing her mind.'

My grandmother stretched out her little claw-like hand and I crossed to where she sat and took it, squatting down beside her. She studied my face intently, murmuring all the while, and then a smile broke out on her face and her expression was transformed.

I looked at my father. 'She hasn't forgotten you, and she hasn't forgotten Zaynab.'

'No, she hasn't.'

We went indoors, into a room that ran the width of the house. Here it was shady and a little cooler. A ceiling fan creaked slowly round. Another very old lady appeared with a tray of glasses and a jug which she put on a low table. This lady cackled with delight to see my dad, showing an almost toothless mouth. She kept patting and pawing him, almost as if she didn't believe he was real. He spoke to her hesitantly and she laughed aloud. She was still laughing when she scurried from the room. I guessed this was one of the old servants who'd been with the family for years.

Then there was a long, intense conversation between my grandmother and my dad, with a lot of hand-flapping and moaning on her part. I just sat there, looking from one to the other, sipping a pale green drink and understanding nothing. Once in a while Dad threw me an apologetic look. Then my grandmother got to her feet, said something sternly to my dad, and left the room.

'What's going on?' I hissed.

'Not much, really,' Dad said. 'She's just trying to take in what's happening. Don't forget she only knew I was here an hour or two ago, and she wasn't expecting you at all. How odd that she thought you were Zaynab – especially the way you're dressed.' Dad had suggested I look as modest as possible, so I was wearing some blue cotton trousers and a loose, long-sleeved purple top.

'Where's she gone?' I whispered.

Dad pursed his lips and took a deep breath. 'To talk to my father.' He looked worried. 'I was pretty sure she'd be pleased to see me. But I don't know about him. He could just as easily tell me to clear off – again.' He smiled rather painfully. 'At least we gave an old lady some joy, eh, Abs?'

We waited. Then I heard a squeaking, trundling sound, and an ancient man came in, bent almost double, pushing a wheelchair. An equally ancient man sat there: my grandfather Rashid.

He had been a tall man once, I guessed; now his frame had shrunk, but his back was still straight and he tried to hold his head high. His white hair was neatly brushed, and he carried his great beak of a nose before him proudly, like a ship's prow dividing the sea. The stroke had made him a bit lop-sided, and he clasped his bony hands together in front of him. But to my mind he didn't look at all doolally. His small black eyes were bright, and they were fixed on his son.

My grandmother flew back into the room, talking nineteen to the dozen, and stood beside my dad. Neither he nor my grandfather took any notice of her. Dad hesitated a bit, then he went forward, and to my astonishment he sank to his knees beside the wheelchair with his hands on the armrest and bowed his head. After a moment's pause my grandfather unclasped his hands, and I saw that they were shaking. Very slowly he stretched out one hand, obviously having great trouble controlling his movements. Finally, grunting a little with the effort, he rested his hand on my father's head. Not a word was spoken by either of them. But when at last my dad lifted his face, I saw tears on his cheeks, and when he found his voice it was husky and cracked. I didn't understand what he said, of course, except he called his father 'Baba'. The old man said nothing, but he nodded his head stiffly a few times. Was the errant son forgiven? Or was it just that a sick, fragile old man couldn't say what he wanted to say?

My grandmother said something then, quite loudly, and Dad stood up and beckoned me over. I stood in front of my grandfather's wheelchair and he looked up at me, craning his neck painfully. I squatted down so he could look at me without straining, and his eyes flew to his wife and back to me, and he gave that strange grunting sound again. My grandmother said something, and Dad said softly, 'She says he can see Zaynab in you too. She was tall like you, and she had green eyes – very unusual here. They are both remembering.'

That's what happened our first day in Jammu, the day my dad went home.

Of course, my grandmother insisted we move from the hotel to their house, and while we were collecting our things she had the ancient servants scurrying (or rather, hobbling) to get rooms aired and ready. We spent the next few days with them, but I saw little of my grandfather. He spent most of his time in his room. On the other hand, my grandmother barely let me, and Dad, out of her sight. I learned a little bit of Urdu in those days, including calling her 'Daadi', and Dad explained she would never have heard it before, because it is the name reserved for a paternal grandmother. Daadi, it turned out, spoke some English, so we managed to communicate quite well in a clunky sort of way. I soon found that my grandmother was funny, sharp-witted and lovable. Even if she had been none of these things, her sheer joy at having us with her would have melted stone.

We spent quite a few hours laughing over mispronunciations and misunderstandings. We pored over family photo albums, and I saw my dad as a baby and a small boy and a good-looking young man. There was one of him as he left Kashmir to come to London as a student, and I could see why Mum was smitten (not that I'd tell him that!). I saw photos of my aunts as children, cute in their matching dresses, and especially touching pictures of Aleesa, the aunt I had hoped to meet but now never would. There were no photos of Zaynab, or none that I was shown, and after that first day she wasn't mentioned, but I had my own plans about that. I was just waiting for the right moment, when I had got to know my grandmother better. When he wasn't with us, talking to his mother, answering her questions about Mum and Dan and his life in England, or interpreting for us, Dad was usually somewhere in the garden, searching for a signal so he could ring Mum. When I told Year 13 that Kashmir was only connected to a mobile network in 2003 they couldn't believe it. But I know now how backward that wonderful place is in many ways, and so much of that comes down to all the political upheavals, uprisings and military activity the people have had to suffer.

Anyway, this journal is supposed to be about my family, so I mustn't wander off the point!

My grandmother was keen for us to travel to the summer house in Srinagar, and she was on the phone a lot to family members who were already there, checking on the situation, because there were still protests going on in July with people taking to the streets and police and soldiers everywhere. Finally we did decide to go, but she was horrified when instead of flying my dad said we would go on the bus so that I could see more of the country – there's no rail station in Srinagar. Apparently the bus journey takes fourteen hours, but I was up for it. It was an amazing experience, but I've recorded all that elsewhere, so ...

Not everyone was in Srinagar, but I met my aunts and some of their families. Farida was tall and well-built, with her father's nose and a loud, commanding voice. Her husband, Uncle Abdullah, was a rather lazy man who obviously loved his food. I never saw him once contradict his formidable wife. Aunt Mahasin was built like Daadi, tiny and rounded like a brown robin, perky and twittering. Uncle Fawaz was not much taller, almost bald and sweetly smiling. Some of the aunts' grown-up children were there, mostly their daughters and daughters-in-law, and their small children. The sons were back home attending to work and business, but they flew up and joined us from time to time. I learned all their names and who was married to whom and which kids belonged to which parents, but I didn't get to know anyone well. My Urdu was next to nothing, their English was halting in the main, and those who did speak English were either not very interested in me, or slightly suspicious.

The men talked to my dad, and some of them got quite heated, but none as bad as Uncle Sayid. We didn't see him or his wife, and I wasn't disappointed. Daadi had shaken her head when he was mentioned and raised her eyes to Heaven. Since the death of his wife, her daughter, and his remarriage, he had drifted away from the family. But she still saw his children. My cousin Umar was there with his shy wife, Parveen, and their little girl, Kamilah, and they were kind and polite to me and Dad. I had been hoping to meet Umar's sister, my cousin Badia, but she was training to be a doctor in Delhi, so she was busy and a long way away. She was my youngest cousin, the nearest in age to me – though still five years older – and the only one who wasn't married.

Dad thought it would be a good idea to go and see some sights while we were in Srinagar, just as we had in Jammu. We saw plenty of places where the earthquake had caused destruction and nobody had started to rebuild, even though it was nearly five years ago. Dad said that there was worse damage in the more remote places and not enough money to fix things up. Of course there are still some beautiful places and amazing things to see in the area, and it gave us the chance to get away from the family for a few hours. But after a few days both of us went down with some horrible stomach bug, or it may have been something we ate. Anyway, we were both really ill. Luckily I had my own bathroom – the house in Srinagar is shabby but vast with loads of rooms – because I practically lived there. I have never felt so ill in all my life! I was never fat, but I must have lost a few more pounds those days that I was ill, and I don't think Dad was much better. The aunts fussed over us, and Aunt Farida made up foul potions she swore by, but I couldn't keep anything down, not even boiled water. It was miserable.

I woke one morning with a terrible headache, feeling a bit better but very sweaty and frazzled, and when I staggered to the bathroom I heard a commotion downstairs and looked over the stair rail to see a large, unfamiliar backpack in the hall. Then out of the kitchen area strode someone I didn't know. She looked up and saw me.

'Hello, little cousin,' she said in her accented English. 'I've been sent for. But I was coming anyway.' It was Badia, and she'd flown up from Delhi on a night flight. She bounded up the stairs, took me by the elbow and propelled me back to bed. Her nose wrinkled. 'You need a shower,' she said.

'I know,' I replied feebly. 'But Aunt Farida wouldn't let me.'

'Ha!' she snorted. 'Aunt Farida doesn't know everything. Well, it can wait.' She drew the sheet up around me and eyed me keenly. 'You look like death.'

'I feel like death,' I said. 'But I thought you weren't coming.'

'I didn't think I could get time off,' she said. 'But I managed to wangle it. I wanted to meet my wicked Uncle Tariq.'

I was going to protest, but then she grinned broadly. 'My mother told me about him. I know what happened all those years ago. But she never confessed to keeping in touch with him. I guess she knew my father would have gone mad. So she never told me about you. I had to come and see for myself, didn't I?'

Badia couldn't have been more different from the rest of the family. Clever and independent, she'd managed to persuade her father it would be OK to study in Delhi; he had a brother there and she lived with his family, so they could keep an eye on her. For one thing, she didn't wear anything like the rest of the women with their flowing, colourful dresses. She was dressed for hiking in jeans and a cotton shirt and walking boots, and she had (horror of horrors!) cut her hair! She'd told them it was necessary for her work on the wards. 'Not strictly true, but ...' she said with a wicked smile.

She still had two years of training before she would be a fully fledged doctor, and her leave was short, but once Dad and I were on the mend (she took over our care, banning Aunt Farida's mysterious medicines) she spent a lot of time with us, especially with me. Many good things came of that visit to Kashmir, but my friendship with my cousin Badia had to be one of the best. She was endlessly curious about our life in England and envious of my freedom. 'I will come there one day,' she vowed, 'or maybe to America. Not to stay for ever, just to work, and learn. But here – well. There are some good people working here, but the facilities are so limited. I might do research, if I can get the grants.' She was restless and ambitious and full of energy, always laughing and fooling around. I loved her.

We spent hours walking, away from the city, or just hanging out and chatting. She was especially interested in my love life! I told her about Olly, and she told me a long, involved and eye-wateringly salacious (is that the right word?) story about a lorry driver she was having an illicit affair with, but in the end it turned out to be a total fiction! 'Can you imagine,' she said with a grimace, 'my uncle and aunt ever letting me out of their sight long enough to find any man – let alone a lorry driver!' She burst out laughing. 'Even if work gave me any time off to do much except sleep. I dare say my father gave strict instructions – "Don't let Badia wreck her chances of a good marriage!" Which is the last thing I want. I expect you've heard them all, twittering away about my shocking avoidance of matrimony.'

'You're only twenty-two,' I said.

'My brother's only twenty-four, and he has an eighteen-month-old baby. Well, they can twitter. I shall resist.' And off she went again with peals of laughter.

Our time in Srinagar came to an end, and Dad and I went back to Jammu on the bus. Badia had long since gone back to Delhi to work, but not before she had extracted from me a solemn promise to return. 'Next year is Nani's eightieth birthday,' she said. 'You have to be here. It would make her so happy.'

Looking out of the bus window as day turned to night and the scenery disappeared into the shadows, I thought about my life and came to some conclusions about my future. I'd thought about university and had been leaning vaguely towards philosophy, but now there seemed to me stronger priorities. The gap year idea looked more and more attractive, now that I had a focus. Yes, I would come back to Kashmir. My grandparents, after all, could not last for ever. But I felt the need to travel on, to explore further. In the darkness I thought and dozed and my mind ranged over many possibilities which I promised myself to explore later. But first, back in Jammu, there were questions to be asked.

A few days before we were due to leave, with my grandmother already weepy at the prospect, I thought I'd better run it past Dad. At first he looked worried, then he thought about it and said, 'Maybe it's time we opened up that touchy subject. If anyone can get away with it, I guess you can.'

'Be on hand for translation duty,' I said. 'We might get into difficulties.'

Daadi and I were sitting on a swing seat in the garden, under one of the few trees leafy enough to give shade. She had hold of my hand and sighed from time to time.

'I wish you were not going,' she said for the umpteenth time. 'Who knows if I will see you again?'

'You know I have to go back,' I said. 'I have important exams coming up this year. You wouldn't want me to neglect my education, would you?'

'No, no, no. I would not. And my son wants to go, this I know. He misses his wife and his boy.'

'Anyway, dearest Daadi, I am coming back. I told you. Next year, for your birthday. I hope you are planning a big party.'

'Maybe,' she murmured. 'If I am still alive.'

'Please be sure to be alive,' I said. 'The party wouldn't be quite so jolly otherwise.' She chuckled despite herself and smacked my hand. 'But meanwhile,' I said seriously, 'there's something I want to ask you.'

'What is it? You want my best necklace?'

'No, not that. I don't want to make you sad. But I would like to see a photo of my Aunt Zaynab.' I heard her gasp, but ploughed on. 'When you first saw me, you thought I was her, didn't you? You do have photos, don't you?'

For a long time she didn't say anything. Then she sighed deeply. 'Yes, I have albums, of course. But I haven't looked at them for a very long time indeed.' She turned suddenly towards me, making the swing jolt and shudder. 'Very well, Poti. I will see if I can find an album. Wait here.'

She hurried into the house, holding up her skirts. Dad appeared and sat by me on the swing.

'Dad, what did she call me? Poti?'

'It just means son's daughter, Abs. That's all.'

We waited for what seemed ages. Finally she reappeared, carrying a dusty box. Dad moved along the swing to give her room and she sat down between us, blew the dust off and carefully took out an old album. 'There you are,' she said. Her voice wavered. 'My little Zaynab.' She looked at my dad. 'You haven't seen these either, have you?'

I opened the album. There she was: Zaynab as a cute chubby baby, frothy in lace; as a toddler, and as a solemn little girl with a big white bow in her hair, holding her baby sister. I remembered that for six years she was their only child. Zaynab through the years – nine, ten, twelve, perhaps. And as a teenager, very serious, tall and angular, with that haughty look of Grandpa Rashid. And there was, I had to admit, a bit of a resemblance to me. Then the photos came to an abrupt end. I closed the album and turned to my grandmother. She looked as if she was carved in stone.

'Thank you for letting me see,' I said quietly. 'I hope it hasn't upset you too much, Daadi. She was a beautiful daughter, and it was tragic you lost her so young.'

Daadi looked up at me, and her dark eyes were full of tears. 'I am glad we have got her out at last,' she said. 'She has been locked away too long. No one wants to talk. Sometimes I think maybe she never was. But here are the photographs. Maybe one day I can look and not be sad.'

I squeezed her hand. 'Why did she die, Daadi? Was she ill?' I was almost holding my breath as I waited for her to answer.

'Yes, she was ill,' my grandmother said. She didn't look at me; she simply stared into the distance, and her voice was so quiet that I had to strain to hear her. 'We did not know, your grandfather and I, what was the matter. She was always sad, always crying, in her room. She would not come out.' She looked at me then, frowning. 'We did not understand. She was a happy little girl, before. She had a good life. A good family, three sisters who loved her. I think maybe we did not help her enough. In the end we did understand, but I think it was too late.' She turned to my father. 'It is an illness, isn't it, Beta? I don't remember what it is in English.' She brushed the tears from her cheek with her little bent hand.

'I think we are talking about depression, Ammi,' my father said gently. 'And it is an illness, a very terrible illness because you can't see it and it's difficult to know what to do. It's not like a broken arm or a dose of measles. And anyone can get it, even people who have kind families and happy homes. It wasn't your fault.'

'Perhaps not,' she whispered.

I took a deep breath. 'Daadi, forgive me if this is too painful. Did Zaynab – did she take her own life?'

She clutched my hand convulsively. 'Oh, my dear! We never knew,' she said. 'It was strange. She seemed to be getting better. She went out for walks, always alone, but she seemed more, what's the word, more calm and settled. We hoped she was going to be well. One day she said she wanted to borrow the car, to go shopping in town. I was happy for her to go – I thought, good, she is going out and seeing people, she must be feeling better. She was gone a long time. I was getting worried. Then we had a phone call from the police. She had driven the car into the river, into the Tawi. We don't know if she did it on purpose or by accident. There were witnesses, but their stories were confused. Now, we will never know.'

My father groaned and put his arm round her shoulders, drawing her close. 'Oh, Ammi. That is a terrible, terrible story. Poor Zaynab. Poor you, poor Baba.'

They were both crying, and I didn't trust myself to speak. After a moment my grandmother wiped her eyes on a corner of her scarf. 'It is good to talk about her,' she said. 'She cannot come back, but we shouldn't forget her.' She looked at me. 'And here you are, my son's child, and you are so like her, Poti. Only you have a happier face.'

I hesitated. 'Daadi, there's something else I'd like to know, if you don't mind. I'm not sure I know how to explain it to you.' I turned to my father. 'Dad, can you ask her in Urdu? Did Zaynab have seeings like me?'

Dad pulled a face. 'Well, I can try,' he said. 'She'll remember how I saw things that weren't there, but I'm not sure my Urdu is up to it.' He scratched his chin, thinking, then launched into a hesitant stream of incomprehensible words. My grandmother frowned, obviously puzzled, then she threw her hands up in the air and replied, high-pitched and rapid. I looked from one to the other, wishing I could understand. My dad said something else, and to my surprise she began to laugh.

'I think you're OK,' he said finally to me when things had quietened down. 'She'd forgotten about my little quirks – they never amounted to much, anyway. No, Zaynab didn't have any experiences like that, not that anyone ever knew. The poor girl was just ill, and it sounds as if no one understood what was wrong so she had no treatment, no real help. What a terrible waste.'

I nodded. I was almost the same age as Zaynab when she died. The thought of being dead made me feel cold inside.

We said goodbye at the house. I said to my grandfather, 'Goodbye, Daada. I hope you feel better soon.' It was an empty hope really, but I think, despite his stiff, twisted face, he was trying to smile. My grandmother held on to me for a long time, moaning and crying. 'I will come back,' I said. 'I promise. For the party.'

I didn't see my dad take leave of Grandpa Rashid, but when he hugged his mother she said, 'Goodbye, Beta. I am so glad you came. But I don't think you will be coming back.' He just smiled and didn't contradict her, and I understood that by then all he wanted was to get home. He made his choice twenty years ago, and nothing had changed his mind. Yes, he'd been born here and spent the first eighteen years of his life here, but his home was where my mother was, without a doubt. I know it's a bit cheesy and cringe-making when applied to middle-aged people like your parents, but secretly I did wonder if I would ever have anything like that.

I thought about this on the flight home, and it struck me as strange. He was nodding off, so I tugged his sleeve, and said, 'Do you realise, Dad, we took this trip so you could go back to your roots and see your family. But it was actually me that found them, and I didn't even know I was looking.' He opened one eye, smiled, patted my hand, and went back to sleep. I never did ask him the story of how he was converted, but that can wait for another day.

Soon I have to draw this record to a close. It's far longer than I meant it to be, and I still haven't included everything. One thing I did do when we got home was to look up that reference to Ephesians 6. I shivered when I read these words: 'For we are not fighting against human beings but against the wicked spiritual forces in the heavenly world, the rulers, authorities, and cosmic powers of this dark age.' It reminded me of John Westwood's funeral sermon, and it made me think about Paul White. I wondered again if he was ill, or crazy, or an agent of evil, or something else altogether. I hoped he was not, even at that moment, deceiving some other too-trusting people. But I wondered what would become of him, and for a moment I felt a pang of pity, because in the end, for all his plotting and getting the better of people, he was the loser, because his life had no love in it. I read on, and it got better: 'So put on God's armor now! Then when the evil day comes, you will be able to resist the enemy's attacks; and after fighting to the end, you will still hold your ground.'

I still don't know what I believe, but I'm thinking about it. That will have to do!

I almost forgot! How could I forget such an earth-shaking event? What reminded me was Mum shouting up the stairs, 'Abbie, have you seen the time? You're going to be late!'

I can't afford to be late, not tonight. I'm supposed to be babysitting, and they'll be as jumpy as only, it seems, new parents can be. It's the first time she's been out, and it's only to some school function, so they won't be gone long, but it's a very big deal indeed. I refer, of course, to the young prince himself, born on 15th December – Thomas Edward Calladine, not even a month old yet, and I have the heavy responsibility of looking after him for a few hours. It'll probably take half an hour to give me all the necessary instructions!

When I first saw this unparalleled baby I whispered to Mum, 'He may be only days old, but he's got a whole lot more hair than his dad.' She pretended to box my ears, but I figure it's fine to cheek your headmaster when he's acting all bowled over by fatherhood. And I'm not really as cynical as I sound. I hope I've got years and years yet of travelling and studying new stuff (maybe even learning a new language – Arabic!) and meeting interesting people before I even let the idea of doing anything permanent like having kids enter my mind. But seeing Mr Calladine with Thomas, and remembering Dad with Grandpa Rashid, and the whole sad story of Zaynab, has brought it home to me that we have to try our utmost to get things right with the people we love, because in the end they're the best treasure we have on earth.